the ISLANDERS

VOL. 2:

NINA WON'T TELL *and* BEN'S IN LOVE

KATHERINE APPLEGATE *and* **MICHAEL GRANT**

PREVIOUSLY PUBLISHED AS THE **MAKING OUT** SERIES

HARPER TEEN
An Imprint of HarperCollins Publishers

HarperTeen is an imprint of HarperCollins Publishers.

Grateful acknowledgment is made for the use of extended quotations from *In the Electric Mist With Confederate Dead*, by James Lee Burke. Reprinted by permission of Hyperion, Copyright © 1993 James Lee Burke

Originally published by HarperPaperbacks as *Boyfriends Girlfriends*

ISBN 978-0-06-234078-8

Typography by Ellice M. Lee
❖
15 16 17 18 19   PC/RRDH   10 9 8 7 6 5 4 3 2 1
First Edition

NINA WON'T TELL

PART ONE

Zoey Passmore

Who do I think is sexy? That's easy. I mean, Lucas, obviously. I almost slept with him, so I guess that tells you something.

Of course, the circumstances were pretty unusual. His dad was going to kick him out of the house and ship him off to Texas, which, in case geography isn't your best subject, is a long way from Maine. Anyway, we were at that point where you think, Oh my God, am I actually going to do this? Then Claire showed up and straightened everything out with Lucas's dad and well, the moment was past.

I'm grateful to Claire for her timing. Definitely. At least I think I am.

I'm pretty sure that Lucas isn't.

Still, I have to be honest and say yes, I think Lucas is sexy. Very sexy. Of course, so is Liam Hemsworth, and I'm not going to sleep with him anytime soon, either.

Claire Geiger

Hmm. That's a more complicated question than it sounds. There are lots of guys who are definitely very good-looking who I don't

3

find sexy. Liam Hemsworth comes to mind. Or Dylan O'Brien and Jesse Williams. I mean, pretty, yes. But sexy? On the other hand, there's someone like Zayn Malik. Not handsome, but kind of sexy.

Ideally, you want a guy who combines both. Lucas was both. He was my boyfriend a long time ago. Benjamin was both, too. He was my boyfriend until very recently. Jake? Hmm. Jake. He's different. Not as cute as Benjamin, not as obviously sexy as Lucas.

Still, I'm strangely attracted to him. Maybe because he's decided to blow me off. Maybe because he doesn't want anything to do with me. Maybe I just like a challenge. Maybe that's what I think is sexy.

Aisha Gray

You hear some people talk about chemistry. Like there's some automatic, out-of-control thing involving pheromones and hormones that just happens between two people. Blame it all on the 'mones. But I think that's too easy. That's all just an excuse for people who don't want to take responsibility for their own feelings.

Personally I think what's sexy is a guy who shares your interests and who treats you with respect. He has to be smart and have a good sense of humor. And be ambitious.

All of which describes Christopher. Which is why it was sensible and reasonable for me to finally go out with him even though I didn't want to at first. See, I already knew he would treat me with respect and that he had a sense of humor and was smart and ambitious. What I had to find out was if he shared my same interests.

Sure enough, as we rode the ferry home from our first date, we discovered we had a shared interest in making out. We shared this interest to the point where other passengers were covering their kids' eyes. I'd have been embarrassed except that I knew I could just blame it all on the 'mones.

Nina Geiger

Sexy? I'll tell you who's sexy. Cam from Modern Family. Yeah, the pudgy guy. Oh, yes. I'd love to have a poster of him wearing nothing but briefs and a smile. Hey, hey, bay-beee.

Okay, I wasn't being serious about that. I don't think that guy is sexy. No. No, it's Paul Shaffer who gets me hot.

Still kidding.

You want the truth? The truth is, look, I don't think that way. I don't think of guys as being sexy.

Now, girls . . .

Sorry. Okay, I'll be totally honest. Totally honest I really, really like Benjamin. We went out on one date. As least I think it was a date. He thinks I was his chauffeur for the evening. I'm surprised he didn't try to give me a tip at the end of the night.

I guess this means he doesn't think of me as exactly sexy, either. Which is fine. I don't care about that stuff; not that I'm a prude or anything. Really. It's just that what I feel for Benjamin is more spiritual. I think more in terms of us being, I don't know, like together in a kind of, you know . . . I'm not explaining this well, am I? Never mind. Next question.

ONE

THE WHISTLE SHRIEKED, OBLITERATING EVERY other sound. The ferry strained and vibrated and churned the dark water to a cheerier blue-green. It pulled back from the dock, turning clumsily away from the already failing sun, and pointed its blunt nose across the cold, oily chop toward the island.

Nina Geiger pulled the red-and-white pack of Lucky Strikes from her purse, extracted one cigarette, and popped it in the corner of her mouth. She drew deeply on it and exhaled contentedly.

The young man on the bench behind her leaned forward over her shoulder. "Do you need a light?" A yellow plastic lighter was in his hand.

"No thanks, I don't smoke," Nina said, speaking around the cigarette. She turned to Zoey Passmore, a willowy blonde seated beside her. "The guy's trying to kill me," Nina said with mock outrage.

Zoey refused to look up from her book. Nina bent forward

and looked past Zoey to Aisha Gray. "What's with Zoey?"

"Studying," Aisha said with a shrug. Her eyes were closed and her head tilted back to savor the cool breeze on her face. Her mass of black curls floated and bounced like something alive.

"She doesn't need to study," Nina said to Aisha.

"Yes, *she* does," Zoey muttered.

"I'm the one who needs to study," Nina said. "Algebra. It's only the third week of school and I'm already four weeks behind."

"Who do you have for algebra?" Aisha asked, cracking open one eye.

"Ms. Lehr."

"You don't have to study for Ms. Lehr's class," Aisha said.

"Maybe *you* don't have to study for algebra, but trust me," Nina said, "I do. You can't b.s. algebra. History you can b.s. English is the ultimate b.s. subject. But not math. Math is either right or wrong."

"Aisha's right," Zoey said, still studying the book open on her lap. "I had her last year. You can't get less than a *B*-plus in Ms. Lehr's class."

"Watch me," Nina said.

Zoey looked up at last, turning amused blue eyes on her friend. "You're not listening, Nina. Ms. Lehr is all into

8

self-esteem. Everything is self-esteem. She took some seminar or something where they taught her that students have to have self-esteem, and you can't have self-esteem when you're flunking algebra, right? So she gives everyone a good grade."

"No way."

Aisha held up her hand as if taking an oath. "True fact."

Nina laughed. "You're saying I can blow every test—"

"And you'll get a *B*-plus," Zoey said. "If you want an A-plus, you have to work a little harder."

Nina thought it over for a moment. "Wait a minute. How about if I tell Ms. Lehr that my self-esteem will be crushed unless I get an *A*?"

Zoey and Aisha exchanged a look.

"Damn," Aisha said.

"Never thought of that," Zoey admitted.

The ferry was up to top speed now, heading across the harbor with its cargo of high school students, homeward-bound shoppers loaded with bags, and early commuters hunched over folded newspapers. The trip to Chatham Island took twenty-five minutes.

Nina saw her sister, Claire, come up from the lower deck. She appeared first as a head of glossy, long black hair rising from the stairwell, then step by step revealed the body that had half the guys at Weymouth High quivering. *Okay, three quarters of the guys,* Nina corrected herself.

Claire glanced at Nina, then looked away, searching the deck uncertainly for a place to sit. Nina felt a momentary twinge of sympathy but suppressed it. Claire could take care of herself.

Jake McRoyan was leaning against the forward railing, looking thoughtful and distant, his big football player's shoulders hunched forward. Zoey's brother, Benjamin, was toward the back with his earphones on, staring sightlessly ahead through his Ray Bans and taking an occasional bite from a Snickers bar.

Poor Claire, Nina thought, without too much pity. Trying to find a safe, neutral place to sit, somewhere between her two ex-boyfriends and her sister.

Zoey nudged Nina in the side. She too had caught sight of Claire. "Come on," Zoey said. "It won't kill you to be nice to your sister."

Nina made a face. Zoey was a hopelessly nice person. But then, Zoey had spent her life growing up with kind, considerate, decent Benjamin as her only sibling, while Nina had grown up under the ruthless tyranny of Perfect Claire. Ice Princess. Holder of the Record for Early Breast Development. Claire the Zit-proof. Claire of the perfect taste in clothing who had never once worn anything to school that caused large numbers of people to wince and turn away. Claire who must have sold her soul to the devil because she certainly didn't have one that Nina had ever—

"Come on, Nina," Zoey said in a chiding voice that Nina hated.

Nina growled at Zoey. Then she called out, "Oh, Clai-aire."

Claire came over, looking reserved as always and a little skeptical. "Yes?"

"Would you like to join us?" Nina said, using her fingers to squeeze her mouth into a happy smile.

Claire rolled her eyes. "It's come to this. You're actually feeling sorry for me."

"No, we're not," Zoey said quickly.

"Yes, we are," Nina told her sister. "No one's ever seen you looking pathetic and lost and boyfriendless before."

Claire sat down beside Nina. "So, of course, you're enjoying it," she said dryly.

"No, we're not," Zoey said sincerely.

Aisha made a so-so gesture with her hand.

"You bet we're enjoying it," Nina said. "At least I was."

"How are things between you and Jake?" Zoey asked. "I mean, we haven't really talked since . . . since that night."

Claire shrugged, her eyes uncharacteristically troubled. "I told him everything. He told me to get out."

Aisha and Zoey stared at her expectantly.

"That's it," Claire said.

"You know, you're quite a storyteller," Nina said. "You really made the moment come alive."

"I went to his room. He was asleep, so I knocked louder. He eventually woke up, and I told him the truth," Claire said simply. "I said, 'Hi, Jake, you know how for the last two years you blamed Lucas for crashing the car the night your brother was killed? Well, guess what? It's all come back to me now, and it turns out *I'm* the one who was driving. I ran the car into that tree. Surprise!' " She shook her head. The lightness in her voice had turned to bitterness. "Then he told me he never wanted to speak to me again." She paused, her eyes studying her hands. "Does that make the moment come alive for you?"

Nina lowered her gaze. "Sorry."

"Yeah, so am I," Claire said sharply. "Sorry about what happened two years ago, sorry I didn't remember, sorry Lucas suffered. Where is he, by the way? I could grovel for him a little."

"He's at his parole officer's. He still has to go until you guys get all the legal stuff cleared up," Zoey said.

"Excellent," Claire said. "Another thing for me to be sorry about."

"Well," Nina said, for lack of anything better to say.

"You know, we're all still your friends," Zoey said, reaching across Nina to put her hand on Claire's arm.

"Really," Aisha joined in. "What happened two years ago is ancient history. And just because it took you a week longer than it should have to decide to do the right thing, that's not going to turn us against you. It's not like we ever thought you were Joan of Arc."

"We know how hard it was for you," Zoey said. "And I know Lucas is cool with it."

To Nina's amazement, her sister actually looked touched. Claire nodded mutely and looked away. For a moment Nina was afraid Claire might actually cry. It was an unnerving possibility.

"So. All forgiven, all forgotten," Nina said cheerily. "I guess there's nothing left now but the big group hug."

Claire gave her sister a dubious look.

"Anyway, we're all friends, right?" Zoey asked hopefully. "I mean, you know, island solidarity and all."

"I am glad you guys don't hate me," Claire admitted.

"I never hated you," Aisha said. "By the time I found out what was going on, it was all over."

"I still can't stand you, Claire," Nina said helpfully.

Claire smiled her rare, wintry smile. "We're sisters, Nina. We're not supposed to get along. Although Dad will probably want us to try, for a while at least."

"What do you mean?" Nina asked. "He knows better."

"You know. While Aunt Elizabeth and Uncle Mark are here."

Nina felt her heart thud. The unlit cigarette fell from her mouth and rolled across the gray-painted steel deck. "What are you talking about?" she demanded.

"Didn't Dad tell you? They're doing the leaf-peeping thing through Vermont and New Hampshire, then they're coming to stay with us for a week. What is the matter with you, are you choking?"

Nina realized her hand was clutching at the collar of her shirt. She forced herself to release her grip. "I better pick up that cig," Nina said in a low voice. She bent over to retrieve the cigarette, but her fingers were trembling. She took a deep breath and sat back up.

"Are you okay?" Claire asked.

"Fine," Nina said with forced cheerfulness. "Fine."

"So," Nina's father said, smiling at Claire down the length of the elegantly set dinner table, "how come we never seem to see Benjamin over here for dinner anymore?"

Nina snickered and looked down at her plate. Claire shot her a dirty look.

"Benjamin and I have sort of gone our separate ways," Claire said.

"Well. I guess I'm always the last to know," Mr. Geiger said, grinning ruefully. Then he looked more serious. "This isn't because of . . . that whole thing, is it?"

That whole thing. Nina turned the phrase over in her mind. That's what the car accident and Wade McRoyan's death, Claire's memory blackout, Lucas's false imprisonment, and Mr. Geiger's attempt to cover up the truth was going to be called. *That whole thing.* Nicely succinct.

"No, Dad," Claire said, sipping at her soup. "It just, uh . . . sort of happened."

"Yeah," said Nina, "it turns out Benjamin's been drunk continuously for the last couple of years. He finally sobered up, realized he'd been going out with Claire this whole time, and broke up with her immediately."

"Too bad," Mr. Geiger said, sparing Nina no more than a distracted glance. "I always liked Ben. I admire the way he's been able to deal with being blind. Never any whining or self-pity. Half the time you forget he can't see."

"I know, Dad," Claire said impatiently. "He's the son you never had."

"I'm just saying he's a hell of a young man," Mr. Geiger persisted.

"What do you think of Jake McRoyan?" Nina asked brightly, seizing the opportunity. Claire sent her a look that would freeze lava.

Mr. Geiger shrugged. "Good kid, I guess. Stays out of trouble, from what I hear. His father's a sensible businessman, does a good job running the marina. Why, are you seeing him?"

"No, not me," Nina said.

"Nina's only sixteen," Claire said sweetly. "She's not really interested in guys yet, even though every other junior in the school is."

The barb struck home, but Nina tried to laugh it off.

Janelle, the family's housekeeper, came in and traded the soup bowls for plates of codfish and red potatoes.

"Claire said Aunt Elizabeth is maybe coming for a visit," Nina said suddenly, struggling to control the faint quaver in her voice.

Her father nodded as he chewed. "They're not positive, but it looks like it. Which reminds me—Janelle?"

Janelle stopped at the door and turned. "Yes?"

"You'd better air out the two spare bedrooms and get them ready for the weekend, just in case."

"Ayuh," Janelle said. She was the only person Nina had ever known who actually used the classic Maine response.

"Both bedrooms?" Claire asked.

Mr. Geiger looked embarrassed. "Sometimes when people get older, they decide it's easier to sleep in separate bedrooms. If they do come, you two will have to use my bathroom, God help me, and leave them the other bathroom."

"Better give Aunt Elizabeth the front bedroom," Nina suggested. "You know, it has the view of the lighthouse and all."

Mr. Geiger shook his head. "My sister is the early riser of those two, and the back bedroom gets the early morning light. Besides, if I don't give your uncle Mark the good room, he'll think I'm mistreating him. He's got it into his head that I don't like him. He's defensive because I've always made more money than he does."

"So what?" Nina persisted. "Who cares what he thinks? I like Aunt E. better anyway. She should have the better room. After all, she's a blood relation."

"Who cares what room they stay in?" Claire asked, wrinkling her forehead in annoyance. "What's the difference to you?"

"I'm just trying to be fair," Nina said sullenly. She finished the rest of her meal and pushed away the plate. "I think I'll pass on dessert. I have a raft of homework to do."

Nina left the dining room and climbed the stairs to the second story. The back bedroom was just to her left. Nina opened the door and looked inside. It was nicely decorated, like all of the Geiger house, but had the sterile feel of a guest room, with no personal touches or sign that it had been occupied.

She closed the door and slowly, carefully paced off the distance from that door, around the open stairwell, down the hall to her own bedroom. Sixteen paces, maybe even seventeen.

Then Nina crossed over to the other spare bedroom and looked inside. It was a nicer room, no question about it, with two tall windows looking out over the northernmost point of the island and the little lighthouse on its rocky islet.

She turned and paced off the distance back to her own door. Eight paces in a nice straight line.

That was the difference: seventeen paces, past her father's bedroom door, around the stairwell, past what should be Aunt E.'s room. Or if Uncle Mark got the front bedroom, it would mean just eight steps, in a nice straight line, passing nothing.

Nina ducked into her bedroom and stared for a while at the doorknob. It was the old-fashioned kind, made of clear glass, with a keyhole beneath that had been painted over dozens of times in the two-hundred-year history of the house. She had never seen a key. In all likelihood the key had been lost a century earlier.

She closed the door. He wasn't going to come. Her father had said it was only a possibility. Fine. She was going to assume the best: he wasn't really coming. He and Aunt Elizabeth would call up and say they just couldn't make it. That's the way it would be. That's the way it had to be.

TWO

CLAIRE LEFT THE HOUSE RIGHT after dinner. She had homework to do, but she was too preoccupied by other things to concentrate.

The other things were really just one thing. One thing named Jake.

She walked along Lighthouse Road, enjoying the nice swell that was sending dramatic plumes of spray surging up and raining down noisily on the tumbled rocks of the north shore. The passing beam from the lighthouse turned a cloud of spray to silver dust before sweeping on through the dark.

Claire was disappointed in the weather. A huge high-pressure system seemed parked over New England, and it was clear as far as the eye could see. Claire liked weather, especially the extremes Maine could conjure up in fall and winter. Well, the storms would start soon enough.

She followed Lighthouse as it curved and headed south, past the island's only tiny gas station, past the small hardware store, past the commercial dock and the bright, empty ferry landing.

She hadn't really decided on her goal. She harbored some vague hope that she might run into Jake, and having accidentally, casually, run into him, that she might find a way to get him to talk. Talking was the necessary first step.

She spotted Zoey and Aisha sitting out in front of the Passmores' restaurant, sipping sodas and looking bored.

Claire hesitated. They'd all kissed and made up that morning, but still, where Zoey was, Lucas couldn't be far away. And she still wasn't ready to make small talk with Lucas Cabral.

Claire cut discreetly up Exchange Street through the candy stores and souvenir shops that catered to the summertime tourist trade. Many were already closed down for the winter, their glass fronts shuttered, doors barred, upper-story windows dark.

Getting around Zoey and Aisha without being seen would take her several blocks out of her way—assuming, as she had just admitted to herself, that her goal was Jake's house.

Was that her goal? What could she possibly do? Just walk up, knock on his door, and pretend nothing had happened? What could she say? Sorry?

The detour through town eventually brought her to Dock Street. It curved along Town Beach, a placid, underused strand of sand, crushed shell, and washed-up seaweed. In the harbor sailboats were moored, ghosts in the dark. She reached the intersection and hesitated. She could either follow the road along toward Jake's house or turn right to go out onto the breakwater. Claire stood and considered, her gaze drawn by the slowly flashing beacon that marked the end of the breakwater.

She heard his steps on the sand and gravel only after it was too late to think what she should say. She turned and saw him just as he, raising his eyes from the ground, spotted her. He was carrying a canvas bag slung over his shoulder and a can of Budweiser in his free hand.

"Huh" was all he said.

"Hi, Jake," Claire said.

He looked as if he was trying to summon up something harsh to say, but the effort went nowhere. He just shrugged and said, "Yeah, hi, Claire."

"Jake . . . I thought maybe we could talk," Claire said. It was the most clichéd thing in the world to say, but she didn't know how else to put it.

"Maybe you need to talk. I need to drink beer."

"You're just going to walk down the road drinking beer?" Claire asked, trying not to sound too much like his mother.

"Better than driving down the road drinking beer, as you should know, Claire." He laughed shortly at his joke. "Actually, I'm going to go sit at the end of the breakwater and drink beer."

Claire shot a look down the long, concrete expanse of the breakwater. The surf that had been giving the north shore a good pounding was even more forceful as it slammed against the breakwater. It was nothing that would have been dangerous to Jake . . . if he were sober.

"I wonder if I could come with you," Claire asked. "We wouldn't really have to talk."

Jake cocked a sarcastic eye at her. "I don't know, Claire," he said. "You might *accidentally* knock me into the water. My father would be pissed. There would be no one left to carry on the proud McRoyan name."

Claire bowed her head. "I deserve that, I guess."

"No, you deserve to spend a couple of years at Youth Authority," Jake said coldly. "But that's what Lucas got. Wade got dead . . ." His voice quivered a little, but he regained control by redoubling the venom in his tone. "Lucas got jail. And Claire—the one actually driving the car—Claire got to walk away unhurt, untouched. Just a little bruise on the head, just enough so that she could claim her memory was screwed up. Lucky Claire."

He brushed past her, heading down the short connecting road to the breakwater.

"Jake," she called after him.

He marched on, seemingly oblivious.

"Jake," she cried, "don't you realize how much I care for you?"

He stopped and hung his head, as if in deep thought. Claire held her breath. Then Jake drained his can of beer, tossed it in the general direction of a trash barrel, pulled a new beer from his canvas bag, and popped it open.

"Jake, the surf is up," Claire warned. "Let me come with you."

"Go screw yourself, Claire," Jake said. He walked on, and Claire watched him. He was still moving confidently. He wasn't drunk yet. But judging by the bulk of his bag, she could tell he would be, sooner or later. And even strong, powerful swimmers like Jake could be battered to death if they fell between the irresistible force of the sea and the immovable breakwater.

Let alone when they were drunk.

She waited till he had reached the end of the breakwater and flopped down on the wet concrete, a dark, hunched creature lit only by the dim glow from the lights of town and the intermittent flash of the green warning beacon.

Claire walked halfway down the breakwater toward him, stopping well out of earshot. She sat down on a dry patch of concrete and checked her watch.

Great. So much for getting her homework done tonight. She had to spend her evening baby-sitting a guy who hated her.

Why? Claire asked herself mockingly. Why was she doing this? Like Aisha said, she wasn't Joan of Arc.

Because she didn't want anything to happen to him.

And why did she care what happened to Jake? Because she felt guilty? Because she felt she owed him?

Because she'd started to love him?

All of the above?

Jake started on his third beer and Claire lay back, looking up at the clear, star-strewn sky, and wished for a storm, or some other clear, easy answer.

"This table wobbles," Aisha complained. "You should tell your parents."

Zoey used her paper napkin to mop up the Pepsi that Aisha had spilled. "It's not the table," she explained. "It's the brick sidewalk. The bricks are uneven."

"Oh," Aisha said, looking under the table.

"Besides, you're complaining? The soda's free since you're such a good friend of the owners' daughter."

They were sitting on the sidewalk outside Passmores' at one of the restaurant's three small outdoor tables. The other two tables were empty. It was a slow night for business, and her dad and mom had both gone home for a couple of hours, leaving Christopher Shupe to deal with the kitchen and Zoey to watch the dining room and bar. Their only patrons at the moment were a man and woman who were such regulars they could pour their own beers and keep track of what they owed. From inside the restaurant came the sound of CNN on TV.

"Who's complaining?" Aisha asked. "I always like to save fifty cents."

"Fifty cents?" Zoey echoed. "In what universe? We charge a buck and a quarter for sodas. A dollar seventy-five during tourist season."

"Then I guess I'm extra grateful," Aisha said.

"Well, what have we here?"

Zoey looked up to see Christopher emerge from the doorway, wearing a white chef's jacket and stained apron over shorts.

"All the beauty and class and charm that Chatham Island has to offer," he said. "Oh, and you're here, too, Aisha."

Aisha fished an ice cube out of her drink and tossed it at him. He sidestepped easily and bent over to plant a light kiss on her lips.

"Where's Lucas?" Christopher asked.

"The ferry's not in yet," Zoey said.

"Oh, man," Christopher groaned. "Are you telling me it's not seven yet? This night is dragging. I've done all the prep I can do; I changed the oil in the fryer and mopped out the walk-in. If biz doesn't pick up, your dad will have to cut back my hours."

"It's always slow in the fall," Zoey said reassuringly. "When the cold weather sets in, we'll get more business because people don't want to drag over to the mainland."

"Christopher hasn't done the Maine winter experience yet," Aisha said, grinning at Zoey.

"Oh, that's right. You may want to get some long pants," Zoey said. "It gets slightly chilly." She saw the bright running lights of the ferry coming around the breakwater, twinkling through the masts of the sailboats anchored in the harbor. "Here it comes," she said. She strained, hoping for an early glimpse of Lucas. But he didn't appear until several minutes later, after the ferry had docked.

He came sauntering across the bright square, heading straight up the street toward his house, unaware that Zoey was waiting for him.

"You want me to get him for you?" Christopher asked.

"Would you mind?" Zoey asked. "I would, but I'm not supposed to leave the immediate vicinity of the cash register."

Christopher ran off and quickly caught up with Lucas. They came back at a leisurely walk.

Christopher was the taller and heavier of the two, by an inch and a few pounds. He moved with a bouncy, restless energy, like an overgrown puppy who couldn't wait to chase something. He always seemed to be checking out everyone and everything around him, like a serious shopper sizing things up in a hurry, analyzing, pricing, wondering how much he could carry. It was easy for Zoey to see why Aisha liked him—boundless self-confidence, intelligence, a sense of humor.

Lucas moved with more economy, conserving his energy. His interest in the world around him was more selective. His eyes roamed, considered, dismissed, and went on to the next thing. Yet there was always the sense that he was on guard, only pretending to be relaxed. He often seemed serious, as if he were distracted by important things that only he knew about. His smile, when it appeared, was a slow, rueful thing that made him seem, at least to Zoey's eyes, utterly irresistible.

"All the looks and style and manly muscle on Chatham Island," Aisha said as soon as Christopher and Lucas were within earshot. "Oh, and I see you're back, too, Christopher."

Christopher laughed and wagged his finger at her.

"Hey, Zoey, guess what?" Lucas said. "I'm free. My parole officer said it was obvious the conviction would be expunged, so he doesn't want me wasting his time anymore."

"That's great," Zoey said happily as she jumped up and threw her arms around Lucas.

"Expunged." Christopher tried out the word. "Excellent word. I'll have to use it sometime. Expunge me."

Lucas kissed Zoey's lips, sending a thrill through her that hadn't diminished at all in the weeks they had been together. After a few seconds she pulled away, jerking her head meaningfully toward Aisha and Christopher.

"You want us to cover our eyes?" Aisha suggested.

"I think they make a cute couple," Christopher said sarcastically. "They're both so sweet."

"Chew me, Christopher," Lucas said mildly. He closed his eyes and kissed Zoey again.

"You know," Aisha said thoughtfully, "you two do make such a nice-looking couple. And with homecoming and all, well, I think you'd be a cinch for homecoming king and queen. It would have such a nice symbolic thing going. I mean, Lucas *has* come home. All you need is like a dozen votes to nominate you."

"I don't think I'd be a contender," Zoey said, pulling away from Lucas. "Remember when I ran for student council and came in fourth behind Captain America?"

"You beat Thor," Aisha pointed out encouragingly.

"I'll have to remember to put that on all my college applications," Zoey said, laughing. "Anyway, I'm not one of those people who enjoy repeated humiliation."

"Oh, come on," Aisha said. "Cartoon morons aren't even eligible for homecoming queen, so you have a pretty good chance."

"Excuse me," Lucas said firmly. "But I'm not going to be king or queen of anything."

"You're just being modest," Christopher teased. "You know you want the job. The power, the glory."

"Uh-huh," Lucas said. "Check the weather forecast. The day they announce that hell has frozen over, I'll be glad to run for homecoming king."

In Zoey's room Lucas leaned into the dormered window and checked the quote wall where Zoey stuck bits of wisdom on yellow Post-it notes.

"Anything new and deep?" he asked lightly.

Zoey smiled a little self-consciously. Jake had never shown much interest in her quotes when he was her boyfriend. And her friends just dismissed it as a harmless quirk of character.

Lucas scanned the latest Post-it.

The world is a comedy to those who think;
a tragedy to those who feel.

He stood back. "And which are you?"

Zoey ran her hand through her hair and shrugged. "That's what I've been trying to figure out."

Lucas put his arms around her waist and pulled her to him. He kissed her lightly. "Did you feel that or think about it?" he asked.

"That?" Zoey asked. "That I thought about."

Lucas kissed her again, more deeply, till she closed her eyes and wrapped her arms around his neck and held him closer still.

"That I felt," she said in a husky voice.

"So it was a tragic kiss?"

"At least it wasn't a comic kiss," she pointed out.

He looked at her skeptically. "What would a comic kiss be?"

She drew him down to her again, pressed her lips to his, and made a sudden loud, razzing noise.

Lucas jumped back, laughing and rubbing his mouth.

"That would be a comic kiss," Zoey said. She let Lucas pull her onto her bed, and they lay back on her comforter side by side.

"That's the kind of dumb joke I'd expect from Nina," Lucas said. "You know, if she liked guys."

Zoey rolled onto her side. "What do you mean by that? Nina likes guys."

Lucas shrugged. "You know. I just meant Nina doesn't go out much. Even back before I went away, she wasn't into guys."

"Well, she's not gay or anything," Zoey said defensively, "if that's what you're thinking. Not that it would matter if she were. At least, it wouldn't matter to me. Besides, back then she was just fourteen. Lots of girls don't date when they're fourteen."

"Has she dated since then?"

Zoey sat up on the edge of the bed. "Once or twice, maybe," she said, feeling uncomfortable.

"She's a very pretty girl," Lucas said. "Not that I've ever looked at her in that way. I mean, when she took Benjamin to the concert down in Portland and she was all dressed up, I was surprised."

"I don't think Nina thinks she's attractive," Zoey said. "She's always going on about how Claire used up the family's quota of breasts and good looks. I think Nina just has an inferiority complex about her sister."

"I'll bet tons of guys would go out with Nina if she would give them a chance. But you know how she is. She's a ball-buster."

"A ball-buster?" Zoey repeated the phrase distastefully. "What exactly is that supposed to mean?"

"Nothing," Lucas said innocently. "Just, you know, any guy who might ever want to ask her out would be afraid she'd shoot him down."

"She probably would," Zoey admitted. Nina's total lack of a love life was a topic Zoey had always instinctively avoided. Aisha had asked her about it once and gotten quickly chopped off. "I don't like prying into other people's private lives," Zoey said.

"You are her best friend," Lucas said. "Doesn't she pry into yours?"

Zoey found herself grinning.

"What?" Lucas asked.

"Nothing," Zoey said, but her grin spread. "Okay, you're right. She does pry. She asked about you versus Jake."

Lucas sat up, looking wary. "What do you mean, me versus Jake?"

"She asked, you know, private stuff."

"Like what?"

"Oh . . . you know," Zoey teased.

"No, I don't know," Lucas said, suddenly very serious in a way that made Zoey laugh. "Like what?"

"Like—you know, about how you kissed compared to how Jake kissed."

"How can you compare things like that?"

"That's what Nina was asking."

Lucas gave her a dirty look. "Are you going to tell me what she asked you?"

"It was a private conversation," Zoey said.

"It was about me," Lucas said almost desperately. "You can't just go around discussing me with all your friends, talking about . . . all that stuff."

"Why not? You were just trying to get me to talk about Nina."

"That's different," Lucas said dismissively. "What did you tell her?"

"Them. What did I tell them," Zoey clarified. "Aisha was there, too."

"Oh, great."

"Really, most of it was too embarrassing to repeat. You know, stuff like when we make out, do you, you know . . . and what do you do then, and what do I do, and so on. And then we were talking about . . . well, never mind."

"Uh-huh. You know, guys talk about things, too," Lucas warned.

"I'm sure you do," Zoey said indifferently.

Lucas lunged suddenly and grabbed her around the waist. He threw her down on the bed and began tickling her ribs.

Zoey squealed and tried to squirm away, but Lucas was too strong.

"Did you say I was the best?" Lucas demanded.

Zoey gasped for breath. "You're going to make me pee."

"It's your bed. Did you tell them all I was the best?" he asked again, renewing his assault.

"Yes, yes, yes!" Zoey screamed.

He stopped tickling her instantly. "All right, then," he said. His face was just inches from hers. "And what did you tell them you liked the most?"

"I can't remember," Zoey said. "Let's go over it all and I'll try to remember."

Nina

I was different when I was eleven than I am now. People who know me now probably wouldn't even recognize eleven-year-old me.

My big concern back then was would I ever get my period. Zoey already had, of course, since she's a year older, and she was going around acting like she was a WOMAN. You know the kind of thing I mean—she'd stare off into space and sigh, and when I'd ask her what she was sighing about she'd just smile and say, "Oh, Nina, you're too young to understand." And Claire had started around age three; so . . .

But while I was worrying about becoming a woman, my mother was dying. It hurts to this day to think how preoccupied I was with myself while she was suffering. And I know I'll never, ever be able to think about her without wanting to cry, and feeling all over again how her death tore a hole in me that will never heal.

That's why my dad decided to send me away to stay with my aunt Elizabeth and uncle Mark. Dad said it would be good for me, change of scenery and so on. I guess it's true that my mom and I were especially close, just the way Claire and my dad are close. Not that Claire wasn't a wreck, too. I hope I never see my sister that upset again. It's especially terrible when these cool, unemotional, in-control-type people start to lose it.

Anyway. I was gone for two months.

Soon after I came back, I had my first period. I thought it was punishment for what had happened while I was at my aunt and uncle's house. Other times I thought it was punishment because I had somehow failed to save my mother. All I knew was that it was punishment, because I was sure I deserved punishment.

Like I said, I was different when I came back home from my aunt and uncle's house. It was like the real me never did come back. I started having dreams, often the same dreams over and over again. Some are so familiar now that I have them numbered. Dream number three, dream number four, and so on. Not pleasant dreams, but the sorts of dreams that after you wake up seem to echo through the rest of the day.

I miss my mother every day.

And I miss me, the way I was before.

THREE

EVERY MORNING BENJAMIN PASSMORE AND the rest of the high-school-age kids from Chatham Island caught the seven-forty ferry. It arrived in Weymouth at five after eight, allowing exactly twenty-five minutes for the walk from the dock, uphill along Mainsail Drive, to the school. More than enough time.

It was a distance of about a quarter mile and involved crossing eight separate streets. Benjamin had each of the distances measured out in strides. So many from the corner of Groton to Independence, so many more to cross the street, then another number from Independence to Commerce. All in all, Benjamin had memorized more than thirty blocks since losing his sight years ago, allowing him to move confidently within all of North Harbor, Chatham Island's only town, and parts of Weymouth. Some areas he knew so well that keeping count consciously was no longer necessary. They had become as familiar as his own home. In other areas he could keep his count almost subconsciously.

But on this morning there was a complication. Benjamin heard the high-pitched warning horns of heavy equipment backing up.

"Damn," he cursed softly. He was at the corner of Mainsail and Independence. Judging by the rumble of diesel engines and the oily smell of exhaust, he figured the equipment was probably just across the street.

Benjamin concentrated and could hear a familiar voice coming up the street behind him. Aisha. Then, as expected, he heard Zoey's voice.

He disliked relying on his little sister, but there were times when he had no choice.

When he could hear that Zoey was close enough, he smiled in her general direction and shrugged. "I think it's exactly twenty-two paces into an earthmover."

"Yeah, it looks like a water pipe broke or something," Zoey said. "It's a mess. I don't think this would be a good idea for you. Pipes and mud everywhere."

"Probably not," Benjamin agreed.

"You guys go on ahead," Zoey said. "I'll detour with Benjamin."

"I'll take him," Nina's voice said. A tractor roared, and Benjamin could now smell a whiff of natural gas.

"Hi, Nina," Benjamin said. "I didn't hear you."

"I know. Unusual, huh?" Nina said. "Come on with me. Go ahead, Zoey. You know I'm never in a hurry to get to school. We'll take the scenic route."

Benjamin put out his left arm and felt Nina insert her elbow. She had led him before and knew the routine. "Later," Benjamin said in the direction of the others.

Nina led him left, down Independence, through the busy, bustling early morning commuter crush of Weymouth. "You didn't have to do this," Benjamin said. "Zoey usually gets stuck."

"I know you don't like to ask your sister," Nina said.

Benjamin smiled. "You do, huh? How do you know that? Is that what Zoey thinks?"

"Nope. I just know," Nina said. "You always get a certain way when you have to ask her for help. Embarrassed or something."

Benjamin felt uncomfortable. "I'm not embarrassed," he said in a tone that was grouchier than he'd intended. He softened it a bit. "It's just that I don't want Zoey spending her life as my guide. She needs to live her own life."

"I know," Nina said.

"Oh, you know that too?" Benjamin said.

"Sure. We have known each other forever, Benjamin."

"Mmm. I just didn't realize you were observing me," Benjamin said. "It makes me nervous."

"You like being mysterious," Nina said.

"What is this? Nina Freud time? I should have had Zoey take me."

"Coming to a corner. Sixth Street. We have to cross here. Execute right turn."

"Okay."

"Light's red."

"I know. I can hear the traffic moving past. The cars over there"—he pointed to his left—"are waiting for the light to change. I could probably have done this on my own. It's just three sides of a square, right? Then we hook back up with Mainsail."

Nina sighed. "It's a good thing I don't wait around for you to be grateful. It would be such a long wait."

Benjamin grinned. "Sorry, kid. I am grateful."

"Come on. Curb. Can I ask you a favor?"

"How can I say no? You could just spin me around and leave me to wander through traffic."

"I don't like it very much when you call me kid. Curb, step up."

Benjamin stepped onto the curb, caught a seam of the sidewalk, and stumbled forward a bit before regaining his balance. "Hey, that was exciting." He walked along, swinging his cane in a short arc to the right but relying on his contact with Nina for truer guidance. "Why don't you like me to call you kid? I've always called you kid."

"Because I'm not a kid," Nina said a little heatedly.

"Oh. All right, if you say so. It's just that the only picture I still have of you in my mind was when I was twelve, so you were, what, nine or ten? You were a kid then. I have this image of you with your hair cut short, with barrettes. And I think you had braces."

"That's how you think of me? Braces on my teeth and really bad hair? Jeez, what a sad thought," Nina said. "But you've missed most of my later zit phase, so I guess it isn't all bad."

"I have no idea what you look like now," Benjamin admitted. "I have no idea how anyone's looks may have changed in the last seven years." He laughed to lighten the mood. "It used to be strange when I was going out with your sister. The Claire I was making out with looked about ten in my mind. Slightly bizarre at times."

"Fortunately for you, by the time Claire was ten she already looked like she was twenty," Nina muttered.

"Anyway," Benjamin said, fighting off a wave of sadness at the mention of Claire. They had broken up only a short while ago. He hadn't even begun to get over her. He wasn't sure he wanted to start.

"Anyway," Nina said, "I stopped being a kid years ago."

"Yeah? What exactly is the cutoff age for not being a kid anymore?"

"Eleven," Nina said.

Benjamin thought he detected a trace of bitterness in her tone. "Eleven? Why eleven?"

"Good question," Nina said.

Yes, she was definitely sounding angry, or resentful . . . something. "Well, I won't call you kid anymore. But it's hard for me not to see you in my mind as a kid with braces."

"I got rid of the braces."

"Yeah, I kind of assumed that."

"Turn here. Come on, we have a green light, curb, step down. Yes, I have very straight teeth now. I can eat corn on the cob very neatly."

"I'll be sure to update my mental picture. Braces out, teeth in."

"Step up. Let's blow off school and go do something fun," Nina said suddenly.

Benjamin laughed. "Right, Nina. Dragging me around by the elbow; that would be major fun for you."

"I think it would be."

"You're a sweet kid," Benjamin said.

"I'm not a kid," Nina said.

• • •

"Good morning, students. These are the morning announce-ments."

Zoey glanced up at the intercom box, then over at Aisha, two aisles away. Aisha was talking to another girl, so Zoey returned her gaze to her book. It was a paperback historical romance novel of the kind she hoped someday to write. The actual book was about two inches thick, with a lurid cover depicting the heroine, spilling her plump breasts out of her décolleté dress and clutching a nearly naked man with long blond hair. But since the entire book was too big to hide easily, Zoey had torn out a thirty-page section and concealed it inside her biology textbook.

". . . I would appreciate any information on the person or persons who caused the third-floor boys' bathroom toilets to overflow . . ." Mr. Hardcastle, the principal, droned on.

Zoey heard a noise beside her and saw Claire scuttling forward from her own desk to sit in a vacant desk behind Zoey. Zoey clapped her biology text closed.

"Too late, Zoey," Claire whispered over her shoulder. "I know you're reading one of your bodice-rippers."

"I am not," Zoey lied automatically.

"You are such a lousy liar," Claire said disgustedly. "You really shouldn't try it unless you're willing to practice a little more."

". . . On another topic, we have reexamined school policy and taken the matter up with the school board, and it remains the official policy of this school that no student may smoke cigarettes on school grounds. And this does, I repeat *does* apply to cigarettes whether or not they are lit. I hope this will put an end to . . ."

Zoey grinned. It looked as if Nina had lost another round. She heard Claire sigh.

"Is it possible to divorce your sister?" Claire muttered.

"Nina's an original," Zoey said. "You should be proud of her."

"She's just odd, Zoey. And you should be ashamed, reading crappy books like that. What would Ms. Rafanelli think if she knew you read that stuff? It would probably disappoint her. Disappoint her terribly, given the high opinion she has of you. Probably break her heart, thinking of her star pupil poisoning her mind with stories of virgins being despoiled by knights or whatever. I only hope she never discovers the truth."

Zoey turned slightly to look over her shoulder. Claire was looking carefully innocent, a sure sign she was up to something. "Oh," Zoey said as the realization dawned on her. "You're blackmailing me."

"Duh," Claire said.

"What do you want?"

"I want to look over your notes on the English assignment. I didn't get to the reading."

"You didn't get your homework done and now you want to borrow mine?" Zoey looked at Claire incredulously. "Why do you care? It would take a lot more than that to mess up your *A*."

Claire looked uncomfortable. "Okay, look, you're right. But Jake didn't do his homework, either. And he's shaky in that class."

"You want me to give you my homework so you can give it to Jake?"

"I know. It almost sounds kinky somehow, doesn't it?"

Zoey turned back toward the front of the class. She could just imagine why both Claire and Jake hadn't gotten their work done. Not that it was any of her concern now. After all, she and Jake were finished, so what did she care if Claire and Jake spent the evening groping?

Or whatever it was they were doing.

The possibility made her frown. She doubted Claire was doing *it* with Jake, but again, that wasn't her business. She glanced back over her shoulder. "So I should give you my homework because you and Jake were too busy doing . . . *whatever*?"

"We weren't doing *whatever*," Claire said. "The truth is, I was watching him get faced on beer at the end of the breakwater and trying to figure out if I was strong enough to drag him back out of the water if he fell in."

Zoey raised a skeptical eye. "Jake doesn't drink."

"Things change," Claire said. "I think he's really pretty messed up over all that's happened. It was probably just a one-time deal. He'll get over it. You know Jake."

"I *do* know Jake, which is why I'm having such a hard time picturing this scene."

"Okay," Claire said. "If you don't believe that, then we were making passionate love till dawn. It was magic. He made a woman of me."

Zoey grumbled under her breath and dug in her three-ring binder for the homework. She pulled it out and handed it over her shoulder. "Just have it back to me before class."

"No problem."

"You weren't, were you?" Zoey asked.

"We weren't?" Claire echoed coyly.

"You weren't," Zoey reassured herself.

". . . and nominations for homecoming king and queen must be made by the end of this school day. Once again, please do not submit the names of fictional individuals, musical performers, animals, cartoon characters, or the deceased."

FOUR

HALFWAY UP THE BLEACHERS, CLAIRE set the can of diet Coke on the plank in front of her and dropped her books beside her. Discreetly she began wiggling out of her pantyhose. If the weather was going to insist on being boringly sunny, she might as well get a little late-season tan.

She balled up her pantyhose and stuck them in her purse. Then she leaned back, stretched out her legs, hiked the hem of her skirt a few inches, and kicked off her shoes.

On the grass-and-mud field, the football team was going through a set of stretching exercises. They were dressed in bulky uniforms, with their helmets on the ground beside them. Jake seemed to be moving with the elaborate care of a person with a bad hangover.

He might not have noticed yet that she was there, Claire knew, but he would sooner or later.

He'd said little when she'd caught him in the hallway between classes and handed him a hastily transcribed version of

Zoey's notes. But he must have read them because later, in class, he'd correctly answered the teacher's question. And he hadn't seemed overly panicked by the snap quiz that had followed.

Claire saw him lie back on the grass and rub his eyes with the heels of his hands. Claire had been seriously drunk exactly once in her life—on the night she drove into a tree. Since then, alcohol had held no attraction for her. And as far as she knew, Jake had never been into booze, either. His sudden interest had come immediately after the dredging up of all the events surrounding his brother's death.

"Hey, Claire."

It was Aisha, climbing the bleachers nimbly with her long legs, almost making a dance of it.

"Hi, Aisha. What are you doing here?"

Aisha flopped down beside her. "Same as you—acting like a dumb female throwback who wastes her time watching guys strut around and act macho."

Claire smiled despite herself. She searched the field, then, in a far corner, spotted Christopher, who helped coach the ragtag intramural soccer team. "You can barely see him from here."

Aisha nodded. "I don't want him to think I'm here just to watch him."

"Oh."

"He has plenty of ego already."

"Then why be here at all?" Claire asked reasonably.

"Because he works about twenty different jobs, so if I don't see him while he's working, I don't see him at all," Aisha said, suddenly vehement.

"That's what happens when you go out with guys who are out of school, I guess," Claire said, not really very interested. Jake had just glanced over at her, hesitated, then looked away.

"Are you two together again, or still, or whatever the right word is?" Aisha asked, looking at Jake as he put on his helmet and formed up with the rest of the team.

"Me and Jake?"

"No, you and Zac Efron. Of course, you and Jake."

Claire shrugged. She disliked being asked about her private life. Especially the parts of her private life she didn't entirely understand herself. "I'm not exactly sure."

"I just assumed since you're here watching him practice. . ."

Claire shifted uncomfortably. "I'm getting my legs tan."

For a while Aisha didn't say anything, and at last Claire turned around to see what she was doing. It turned out she was staring at Claire with a speculative, thoughtful expression. "What?" Claire demanded.

"Nothing," Aisha said defensively. "I was just thinking this is kind of an unusual situation for you."

Claire was determined not to ask Aisha to explain what she

meant, but her resolve gave way to annoyance. "All right, spit it out, Aisha."

"I'm just saying that as long as I've known you, it's been guys chasing after you, looking at you all lovesick. Not the other way around."

"Don't ever use a term like *lovesick* to refer to me," Claire said frostily.

"How about *unrequited,* as in unrequited love?" Aisha asked.

"Are you trying to annoy me? Because you're doing it pretty well." She settled a hard glare on Aisha.

"You shouldn't worry about what I have to say," Aisha said, unabashed. "You have bigger things to worry about."

"Like what?"

"Like here comes Jake." Aisha batted her eyelashes dramatically.

Claire snapped her gaze back and saw Jake trotting across the field toward her. Her hand went instinctively to her hair, swooping it back over her shoulders.

"I will back off to a discreet distance," Aisha said. "But not *too* discreet." She moved up several rows and a dozen feet to the left.

"What are you doing here?" Jake demanded as he came within shouting range. He took off his helmet and gave her a cold look.

"It's a sunny afternoon," Claire said. "I'm getting some sun."

Jake pointed his index finger at her. "I don't want you here. The guys on the team are getting the wrong idea."

"What wrong idea is that, Jake?"

"Look, Claire, it's over. You and me? Over. You think I can just go on with you now that I know the truth?"

Claire considered the question seriously. "I think you can do whatever you want to, Jake."

"Why don't you go pick on some other guy?" He waved his arm back toward the team. "There are two dozen guys who would gladly go out with you. Lars over there would sell his mother to Vladimir Putin for a chance with you. Or else go back to Benjamin, not that I would wish that on Benjamin because he's a good guy. Just forget about me, all right?"

"No," Claire said.

He bounded up the bleachers to stand over her, his big body blotting out the sun. "What is it? You think you have to take care of me, compensate because you killed my brother?"

"I didn't kill Wade," Claire said softly. "We were all drunk. Any one of us could have been driving. If I hadn't gotten behind the wheel, Wade would have. Then who would you blame?"

Jake didn't explode the way she expected. Instead he just laughed cruelly. "That's not what you said when everyone thought Lucas had been driving. You said he deserved to go to Youth Authority for two years. And when he got out, you said he should be kicked off the island."

Claire cringed under his attack. She drew in her legs and hunched over, avoiding his gaze. "I know. I was wrong."

Jake laughed out loud. "That's what is so great about you, Claire. You can just instantly change what you believe so that no matter what, you're always somehow in the right. So long as you get what you want."

"I've just learned a few things, Jake. Maybe I'm smarter than I was."

"Very convenient."

"So I'm a hypocrite. Call me what you want. I'm in love with you."

Jake took a step back in surprise. "In love with me?" He paused for a moment to compose his face into incredulity. "That's a nice touch."

She met his eyes. "It's true."

For a second he wavered. His expression softened. But then he steeled himself. "Even if it is, I don't care."

"Yes, you do," Claire said.

"I don't need you to watch over me when I want to get drunk, Claire, and I don't need you covering for me when I don't do my homework. And I just plain don't need you," Jake said. He turned and walked away across the field.

"Yes, you do," Claire said again, this time to his retreating back.

Nina found the box in the storage room, a waterproof gray plastic tub with an airtight fitted top. She carried it up the stairs to her room and set it on the end of her bed.

She made sure her door was closed, then located a cigarette and popped it in the corner of her mouth. The top of the box came off easily and she peered down at the massive jumble of photographs. These were all the shots that hadn't made it into one of the family's two big leather-bound photo albums. Those pictures had all been carefully chosen, but none showed what Nina wanted to see.

She took a big handful of photos and spread them out on her bed, some color, some very old grainy black-and-whites with scalloped edges. Some weren't photographs at all, really, but postcards from people she knew vaguely, from places she'd never been.

Most of the pictures were of people she did know. She found several of her mother and father at the Grand Canyon, so young they almost looked like a pair of very uncool teenagers. Nina sifted through the photos, making a small pile of pictures of her mother, ranging in age from childhood to just before she died.

It was strange, but the more she looked at the pictures, the less they reminded her of her own faded memories of her mother, and the more they reminded her of . . . someone else. Someone she couldn't quite place.

In pictures of her father alone, he always seemed very serious. In his army uniform, standing with his hands clasped behind his back, his creases like knife edges, his lieutenant's bars just so. Or in a business suit, or even later, wearing a white shirt and slacks, his casual look. It always looked like the photo was being taken against his will. Only when he was in a picture with Nina's mother did he smile and appear to be having fun. There was one shot in particular that caught Nina's eye, showing both her parents, separated by two little girls apparently punching each other out on the floor. Neither was looking down at the kids, but there was an expression between the two of them, both cocking their eyes at each other, identical looks of love mixed with amusement and maybe a little pride in the two brats at their feet.

Nina set that picture aside.

But she still hadn't seen what she was looking for. She dug out another pile, more shots of Claire, looking as solemn as their father, even as a tiny child—serious, thoughtful, aloof.

"Haven't changed, have you?" Nina said, smiling wryly at Claire. *Did you stand out in the yard staring up at the clouds even then? Did you manage to look down on everyone around you when you were just two feet tall? I'll bet you did.*

Then, from the pile in Nina's hand, one picture fell out. A skinny, gray-eyed girl with braces on her teeth, wearing a dress that revealed long, knobby legs, one with a Band-Aid on the knee. She was twisting a hank of hair around one finger. Nina turned the picture over. A note in ink said *Nina. 11th b'day.*

She leaned back on her pillows, holding the picture before her with both hands.

"So. This is what Benjamin thinks I look like." Nina smiled ruefully. "You ain't exactly Karlie Kloss, kid," she told her image.

Eleventh birthday. Just two months before her mother died. Had her mother been there that day? Or had she been in the hospital? Nina couldn't remember.

She focused on the eyes in the picture. They were cocky, challenging eyes. "You think you own the planet, don't you?" she whispered.

If only that little girl had known what lay ahead. It would be only months until her mother died. Only a little while longer than that till she would be sent away to stay with her aunt and uncle.

For her own good.

"If only you knew, little Nina," she whispered.

She got up and walked over to the full-length mirror on the back of her closet door. She faced it and held the picture up beside her face.

Nina looked at her own present reflection and the small reflection of her past.

"You lost the braces," she said. "Filled out a little, which you never thought you'd do. The legs aren't quite as much like toothpicks, but now you have to shave them."

She realized the unlit cigarette was still dangling from her lips. "And you picked up one or two bad habits since then. Of course, you got rid of the Barbie dolls, so I guess it evens out."

She gazed into the eyes of five years ago. And back to the eyes in her mirror. Still challenging, still a little cocky, she noted, smiling wryly. She hadn't changed so much since then.

Then the smile faded and disappeared. "Only right now you look a little sad, Nina," she said.

She tucked the picture into her nightstand drawer. She would take it out and look at it the next time she had one of those dreams.

Nina

Here's the dream I call dream number two.

First of all, you have to get that dream feel, if you know what I mean. Where cause and effect aren't quite as clear as they are in real life. Where things can be sudden or very, very slow. Where you know things without knowing how you know.

It's always very gloomy in this dream. Like watching an old black-and-white movie on TV and turning the brightness knob way down. I see myself as if I'm some other person in the room. I see myself younger, at least at first, and my mom is squatting down, fussing with my clothes, trying to straighten this ridiculous bow on the front of a ridiculous dress, wiping my face clean, telling me to smile and stand up straight.

And while she's doing this, the little girl is tugging at her clothes, undoing all the straightening. She's playing with her hair, leaving it tangled and wild. And she's whining something about not wanting to get all dressed up. I don't want to, she says in a little boohoo voice.

Then the little girl is older, but still wearing the ridiculous dress with the ridiculous bow. She advancing uncertainly across a darkened room, toward a corner where all that she can see are two intense, staring eyes. She's afraid, but she can't stop because the eyes are telling her to come closer. Come here. Come here and give me some sugar.

And then, once more, the girl—the girl that is me—is somewhere else. She's lying in bed. And it's like maybe she's wet the bed because the sheets are warm and damp. She feels guilty; what if someone finds out? She plays with the ridiculous bow and pulls the covers over her head. The bow is magic. It can make her invisible.

And then I wake up. I feel guilty and ashamed. I also feel some lingering sense of undefinable pleasure, and that's the worst feeling of all.

And then the feelings fade. After a while I fall back to sleep and dream no more dreams.

FIVE

"OH, NO," ZOEY SAID, PUSHING her way back through the crowd. "Oh, no. He's going to freak."

She backed away from the list that had been posted on the bulletin board near the principal's office. Other kids took her place, crowding in to read the names on the list. Zoey glanced apprehensively down the hallway, but in the early preclass crowd it was impossible to spot Lucas. The halls were jammed with loudly gossiping, shouting, teasing, worrying kids, grouped in twos and threes and fours around open lockers, milling in and out of rest rooms, jostling around the water fountain. The stairwells were slow-moving conveyor belts of humanity, going up and down, stopping, screaming, a moving picture painted with strokes of hair and patterned spandex, dull books and bright plastic, objects thrown and caught and dropped. The walls were hung with posters, exhortations to various teams taped to pale blue cinder-block walls.

From somewhere in the tight-packed mass Lucas emerged.

Not the person Zoey wanted to see at that particular moment.

"Hey, Zo," he called. He grinned. "You're an island of calm beauty in a sea of noisy mediocrity."

She smiled uncertainly. "You're poetic this morning."

"Why wouldn't I be? I heard they're killing last period to hold an assembly. No French today. *Pas de français, chérie.*"

Zoey glanced nervously toward the list. "Uh-huh. Do you happen to know what the assembly is for?"

Lucas shrugged. "Probably the usual." He counted on his fingers. "It's either one, an antidrug lecture, which I don't need, or two, an anti-booze lecture, which I also don't need, or three, an anti-sex lecture, which you give me every couple of days." He grinned to show he was just teasing. "Or else it's some student-government-pep-spirit-we're-better-than-everyone-else-so-let's-cheer-some-crowd-of-jock-dorks kind of thing."

"Partly it's a pep rally," Zoey agreed. "It's also to introduce the candidates for homecoming king and queen."

"That would fall into the category of cheering some crowd of dorks," Lucas said.

Zoey winced.

"Oh, hell, I'm sorry, Zoey," Lucas said quickly, coming to give her a hug. "Of course if you're up for it, that's totally different. You could never be a dork. I shouldn't have said that. There's nothing wrong with being more into the school thing than I am. I hope you win. Really. That is it, isn't it? I mean, you're one of the candidates, right?"

"Yes, actually I am," Zoey said. "But you know, it's not like people nominate themselves. And anyway, to be on the list you have to have received a dozen votes."

"See? At least a dozen people realize how great you are. Hell, I'm sorry I didn't think of it or I would have been the thirteenth."

"Lucas . . ."

"What?"

"I'm not the only one on that list."

"Well, sure, there are other aspiring homecoming queens."

"And kings."

"Now, I'm sorry, but those guys *are* dorks," Lucas said. "It's one thing for a girl. But a guy? Homecoming king? Why not just tattoo *dork* on your forehead and get it over with?"

"There are five guys on the list," Zoey said.

"Five poor dumb—"

"You're number three," Zoey said in a rush.

Lucas stared at her strangely. "No, I'm not."

"Yes, you are."

"Homecoming king. Me."

Zoey nodded.

"No."

60

"Yes."

"I'm going to kill Aisha. She did this. She was the one talking about what a great idea it would be. Where is she?" He spun around and searched the crowd.

"It took a dozen votes," Zoey pointed out.

"Twelve people said to themselves, Gee, I know, I'll nominate Lucas Cabral. He'd love it. Oh, yeah, Lucas has always wanted to be crowned King of the Dweebs, Lord of Losers."

"It's supposed to be an honor," Zoey told him.

"Not for *me*," Lucas cried. "I'm not one of *them*. I'm one of the outsiders, the rebels, the misfits. God, don't these people understand anything? You know what my old cellmates would say if they found out I was running for homecoming king? This is the kind of thing people like Jake do."

"He's on the list, too," Zoey said. "And why is it okay for me to do it, and that's cool, but it's totally different if it's you?"

Lucas looked confused. "Why is it different?" he repeated, playing for time.

"That's right, why is it different?"

"Um, because you're a girl?" he asked tentatively.

"Ha!" She pointed an accusing finger at him.

"Wrong answer. Um, look, I'm me and you're you. You are the type of person who should be homecoming queen. I'm the kind of person who should be homecoming barbarian."

The bell rang shrilly, blanking out the murmur of background noise. When it stopped, a collective groan went up from hundreds of mouths.

"I have to get to class," Zoey said frostily.

"Are you mad at me? You are, aren't you?"

"I'm not mad. I'm just a little hurt."

"Oh, that's worse," Lucas said.

"I'll try to get over it."

Lucas grabbed her hand as she started to walk away and pulled her to him. He tried to kiss her, but she was feeling resentful.

"Why should I kiss you?" she asked.

He shrugged. "Because you like it?"

Zoey gave him a dirty look. Then she kissed him lightly on the lips. "I'm still a little hurt," she said.

"Yeah, but *I* feel better!" he yelled after her.

"Go, Warriors, go, go. Go, Warriors, go!" Zoey shouted.

"Go, Warriors, go, go. Go, Warriors, go!" Aisha said a little less enthusiastically.

"Blah blahblah, blah blah. Blah blahblah, blah," Nina said.

Claire read a book.

"I knew he was going to do this," Zoey fumed. She half stood in the bleachers and searched the densely packed rows of kids. The pep rally was well under way in the big, aging, and somewhat aromatic gym, and Lucas was nowhere to be seen. "He's bailed, the coward. He's hoping they'll get him for skipping last period and make him ineligible."

"I wish I'd thought of skipping this whole thing," Nina said glumly. "Here we go again."

"We'll hit 'em again, we'll hit 'em again, we'll hit 'em one more time!" Zoey and Aisha cried on cue.

"We'll castrate them using blunt knives," Nina cried, causing several people nearby to turn and glare. "We'll gouge out their eyes and swallow them like oysters!"

Claire glanced up from her book, gave her sister a pained look, and shook her head slightly.

"Beat Camden, beat Camden, beat Camden," the chant began, becoming rhythmic and mesmerizing.

Nina jumped up, clenching her fists. "I vow total destruction on everyone from Camden. Kill the Camdenites! Slaughter them like pigs! They are the epitome of evil and must be wiped from the face of the earth! Forget football; we'll bomb the bastards! We'll make slaves of their children and whores of their women! Their men will be turned into beasts of burden!"

"Hi, Nina. That is you, isn't it?"

Zoey turned and saw her brother four rows back, looking amusedly in Nina's general direction. Nina seemed to blush.

"Hi, Benjamin!" Nina yelled up to him.

"I don't think you're taking this very seriously," Benjamin said in mock disapproval.

"I'm just trying to get into the whole fascist-barbarian-fundamentalist school-spirit thing," Nina explained.

A swell of noise blocked out Benjamin's next response. Zoey pulled Nina back down to her seat.

"Am I embarrassing you, Mom?" Nina asked Zoey.

"No, but they're getting to the nominations now," Zoey said, checking once more for any sign of Lucas. She bit her lip in vexation. The jerk. Didn't it occur to him that at least a dozen people had shown some affection for him by voting for him? Didn't it occur to him that this was the student body's way of acknowledging that he wasn't the criminal creep they had thought he was?

"Lucas thinks I set this whole thing up, doesn't he?" Aisha asked.

"He'll get over it," Zoey grumbled.

"Make sure you tell him I didn't," Aisha said.

"I'll tell him, if I ever talk to the weasel again," Zoey said.

"Ah, true love," Nina remarked.

"With my luck Jake will win for king and I'll win for queen and then—" Zoey bit off the rest of her complaint as she saw Claire's head come up suddenly.

"Ooh, that got her attention," Nina said gleefully. "The king and queen do have to dance, right? Slow dance? And isn't there a big ceremonial kiss?"

"There is no ceremonial kiss," Claire said.

"Really?" Nina professed shock. "Then I guess the part where the royal couple retire to the couch in the teachers' lounge and try to make a little prince or princess . . . I guess that's not true, either."

Claire made her cool, superior smile. "The king and queen have an officially platonic relationship. You'd know all about that, wouldn't you, Nina? No kissing, no romance?"

Zoey and Aisha both swiveled their heads toward Nina, waiting for her next shot, but it didn't come. Instead Nina just made a face.

That was mean of Claire, Zoey thought. Nina's feelings had really been hurt. Although Nina had certainly been asking for it.

Nina yanked open her purse, pulled out a cigarette, and stuck it defiantly in the corner of her mouth.

"As you know, next week will be homecoming." Mr. Hardcastle had stepped up to the microphone. Cheers greeted his announcement. "And that means we have to choose a homecoming king and queen to officiate."

"Mr. Hardcastle for queen!" a voice yelled out.

"Good one," Nina said approvingly. "Wish I'd thought of it."

"We have a list of five candidates for each position . . ."

"He's not here," Zoey said. "He's not going to show up."

"As I read off the names, will the individuals please come down so we can all get a look at you . . ."

"Don't trip," Aisha whispered. "It makes a bad impression."

"Tad Crowley . . ."

"Isn't that the guy you made out with at that party?" Aisha asked. "You know, back when you and Jake were having a fight or something?"

"I didn't make out with him," Zoey said. "I just kissed him once."

". . . Louise Kronenberger."

"K-burger?" Nina said. "No way. You'll kick her butt, Zoey."

"The only votes she'll get are from guys she's slept with." Aisha smirked.

"So she'll be pretty big competition," Nina said.

". . . Jake McRoyan . . ."

Claire stood up and gave a completely uncharacteristic yell of support, joined by many others.

"Now I can die," Nina said, staring at her sister. "I've seen everything. The things people will do for romance."

"In your case, nothing," Claire shot back.

Jake was making his way, threading through the crowded

stands to trot out onto the shiny gym floor and shake hands with Tad Crowley.

". . . Kay Appleton . . ."

"Oh, not her," Aisha said.

"You don't like Kay?" Zoey asked.

"She's such a phony. She always comes off like Miss Sweetness and Light. But she can turn instantly into this total barracuda."

". . . Lucas Cabral . . ."

Zoey stretched up to look. The only movement in the stands was Kay, making her way down to the floor.

". . . Lucas Cabral?" the principal repeated. "Is he out today? Well, we'll skip over him for now. On to our next candidate for queen . . . Zoey Passmore."

Zoey rose to her feet, still annoyed at Lucas but trying to force an appropriate smile.

"Zoey Passmore?" Aisha said in a disbelieving tone. "Who nominated her?"

"Really, she's such a witch," Nina said.

SIX

NINA LOOKED BLEAKLY ACROSS THE top deck of the ferry. As far as the passengers of her own age were concerned, it was divided up into impenetrable territories. In one zone Zoey and Lucas, arguing in Zoey's usual discreet, quiet, restrained way. Some distance away, in zone two, Aisha and Christopher were standing close to each other, murmuring and occasionally kissing.

Then, in zone three, there was Claire. Nina didn't have to make any special effort to avoid Claire. That was second nature to both of them.

Claire had begun by standing beside Jake at the forward rail, but Jake had pointedly moved away, taking a seat. Claire had pointedly followed him and now sat several feet from him on the same bench. They weren't speaking. Claire was reading and Jake was scowling, but it looked like a moral victory for Claire.

Only Benjamin sat alone. And only Nina stood alone.

Any other time, Nina would have felt no great hesitation

about taking a seat beside him. They were friends, after all. But somehow the geography of the deck on this day would make it seem like she was being obvious. It was all boyfriends and girlfriends, even if Claire and Jake were in some type of limbo, and even if Zoey and Lucas were fighting.

Still, it was girls with the guys they liked. That was the arrangement, boyfriends and girlfriends, like it was in so much of life. And if she just went on over and plopped down beside Benjamin, wouldn't that make it look like she was trying to act like his girlfriend?

Claire had already teased her once about being in love with Benjamin. It had probably just been teasing. Certainly Claire couldn't know how true it was.

So it is true? Nina asked herself. Was it love she felt for Benjamin? Why should she? He obviously would never see her as anything but a friend.

She liked him, yes. But did she feel *that* way about him?

She stole a closer look at him, sitting there with earphones on, probably listening to some music she wouldn't even recognize, let alone enjoy. His eyes perpetually hidden behind the darkest-possible sunglasses.

She'd only seen his eyes a few times since he'd lost his sight. They were dark brown, and looked normal except that they never focused. They were always pointed just a little bit wrong.

Benjamin could fake it better with his shades on. Then you didn't notice that no matter how hard he tried to look like he was gazing right into your eyes, he was really staring at nothing at all.

"Would I like you if you could see?" she whispered, unaware until she heard the words that she was speaking aloud.

She looked at his mouth. Did she want to kiss him?

Well, did she? That's what guys and girls did. It's what Lucas was doing to Zoey, trying to get her to lighten up. It's what Aisha and Christopher were doing.

She tried to picture it—Benjamin leaning close, his mouth moving toward hers.

The only time a guy had seriously tried to kiss her and touch her she had practically hurled.

Nina realized she was wringing her hands, twisting her fingers together. She put her hands at her sides and leaned back casually against the railing. She was fine. She was cool. Who cared what people thought of her, anyway?

Could you be in love with someone and *not* want them to at least kiss you? Was that possible? Because that was how she felt.

She could imagine telling Benjamin she loved him. She could even imagine him, somehow, feeling the same about her. But the thought of him looking at her with that look Nina had so often seen guys aim at her sister, at her best friend. . . That look made her sick. That was the truth: it just made her feel sick and brought memories flooding up out of the hidden parts of her mind. Of course, Benjamin couldn't look at her that way, or any way. He couldn't stare at her. He couldn't even kiss her unless she wanted him to. And he couldn't touch her . . . He couldn't touch her unless she invited him to.

Zoey pouted, her chin raised loftily, gazing with feigned unconcern toward the island. If Lucas wanted to be a jerk, okay. He could be a jerk. If he wanted to act like he was too good to be involved in the lowly activities of the school, fine, then he was too good. She wasn't going to try to talk him into it anymore.

If he wanted to hurt the feelings of the people who had nominated him and basically slap them each in the face, it wasn't Zoey's problem.

Then she caught sight of Nina, standing alone by the railing. Maybe Nina's approach was better overall. Here Zoey was, unhappy because of a guy, and Claire was unhappy because of a guy. Aisha looked happy enough, but that was just one out of three, not very good odds.

Not that Nina seemed very happy at the moment, either. Something was bothering her. All day long she had been too shrill, too strange. Too *Nina*.

Lucas shifted on the bench beside her, drawing Zoey's

attention back to him.

The jerk. What was worse was that he was acting like he just assumed he'd *win* homecoming king. Not exactly a sure thing when one of the other guys running was Jake. Jake had lots of friends in school. He was a very popular guy.

In fact, he was the best bet to win. Then, if Zoey won herself, she would be in the awkward position of reigning with her former boyfriend.

She wondered how Lucas would feel about that.

A slow smile spread on Zoey's face. Had Lucas even thought of that possibility?

She sighed. "I've decided you're right, Lucas. If you don't want to be involved, I respect that."

"You do?" he asked suspiciously.

"Absolutely," she said. "It won't be so bad. First of all, I probably won't win. Second of all, even if I do, Jake will probably win for the guys and it will be like old times, me and him together. Me and Jake. Together."

Lucas looked at her impassively. "Nice try."

Aisha savored the feel of his lips on hers. Okay, she had been dumb to fight it so long. She was prepared to admit it, she had been dumb. She'd been attracted to Christopher right from the start, that was the truth. And she'd only resisted because she

72

didn't want him to take her for granted. She'd wanted to make the point that they weren't doomed by fate to be together just because they were both black and living on a lily-white island in one of the country's whitest states. She had been standing up for the principle that fate didn't decide things, *she* decided things.

Big deal. Principle.

She smiled at him, and he smiled back. He murmured something sweet and she said something back.

Then they kissed again.

I wonder if he knows how I feel about him now? I wonder if he's smirking inside, thinking "I knew all along she couldn't resist me"? He's enough of an egomaniac to believe that.

Who cares? So he was right. Good for him. I'm glad.

Am I falling in love?

No. That's not what it is. It's too soon for that. Love takes forever to develop, as two people get to know each other and respect each other, share the same interests.

This is just . . .

He kissed her again.

. . . really nice.

She opened her eyes as they kissed and, to her surprise, realized his eyes were open, too. He was looking away.

She pulled back and turned to follow the direction of his gaze. There was Benjamin, sitting a distance away. And beyond him, an attractive woman who commuted on to Allworthy Island. She was twentysomething and had hiked up her skirt to be able to rub a sore foot.

Aisha cocked a dubious eyebrow at Christopher.

He looked back at her innocently. "I was wondering what Benjamin was listening to."

"You weren't looking at that woman?"

"What woman?"

Claire stared down at the pages of her book without reading any of the words. Her whole attention was on Jake, sitting a short distance away. He was staring out at the water, staring without moving or shifting his gaze, staring just so that he could avoid looking at her.

This was pathetic. She was making a fool of herself. In her entire life she had never thrown herself at any guy. She'd never had to; they had always thrown themselves at her.

Which was the way things ought to be.

Why was she doing this?

She stole a glance at Jake. Yes, yes, he was good-looking. But her boyfriends had always been good-looking. And she never would have acted this way over Lucas, back when she was going out with him, or over Benjamin, either.

Screw him. If he didn't want her anymore, to hell with him.

She could take a hint. She'd never had to take a hint before, but she wasn't blind. Jake wasn't even being subtle. He'd told her to take a hike. Get lost

No one had ever told her to get lost before. It was infuriating. The way it worked was that *she* dropped guys, not the other way around.

That's why she was so intent on getting Jake back, she told herself. She wasn't going to let him have the final word. No. She'd win him back and then *she* could dump *him*.

That was it. It was just a matter of pride. Pride mixed with a little guilt.

Either that or she really had fallen for him, really was in love the way she'd told him she was.

In which case, she was just being pathetic.

Nina was crammed onto the stairs that led down from the upper deck to the gangway, with Zoey and Lucas behind her and Benjamin behind them. Zoey and Lucas seemed to have reached a level of polite truce.

For some reason, the line wasn't moving. "Oh, man, don't hold me up at the end of a long day of school," Nina muttered.

"They're getting the living dead off first," Lucas said in a low voice. "There was a crowd of them below."

"Lucas, we call them elderly, not living dead," Zoey said.

"Whatever they are, they're pissing me off," Nina said.

"Why are you in such a hurry?" Zoey asked.

"Did someone die down there?" Aisha's voice filtered down from above.

"No, but someone's going to if I don't get off this stairwell!" Nina yelled. A businesswoman turned to look at her. "PMS," Nina explained.

"I thought you didn't believe in PMS as an excuse," Zoey said. "You never let me get away with it."

"I don't believe in it when it's you," Nina said. "Only when it's me."

"That sounds fair."

"Later I'm going to get a high-powered rifle, climb up on the roof, and shoot passersby while babbling about some conspiracy."

"Before you do that, do you think you can read to me for an hour or so?" Benjamin asked.

The line began to move down the stairs at last. "Sure, Benjamin," Nina said. "Just let me check in at home and change into something more comfortable than this full-length, diamond-studded, Marchesa dress I'm wearing." Nina looked down at her oversized shorts and baggy, layered top.

"Hey, don't try to fool me," Benjamin chided. "I know those aren't real diamonds."

Nina got off the boat and headed toward her house. Claire was heading to the same destination, of course, but half a block behind. It would never have occurred to either girl to walk together.

She stepped inside the large, well-decorated entryway and peeked to the right, into her father's dark, book-lined study. He wasn't there.

"Anyone home?" she yelled without much interest. There was no answer. It was Janelle's day off and her father would either have to wait for the next ferry home or catch the water taxi.

Nina slung her island bag with its load of books onto the antique oak dressing stand and headed straight down the hall to the kitchen. Lunch at school had involved dead cow, which she did not eat. So she was hungry now for some dead peanut.

She noticed the answering machine on the counter blinking twice. Two messages.

"Food first," she said. In the refrigerator she found raspberry preserves. With bread and peanut butter she made herself a sandwich and was just taking a first bite when she heard Claire come in the front door.

"Anyone home?" Claire asked.

"Me."

"Besides you."

"Just me and my sandwich," Nina said, taking a second bite.

"Have you checked the machine yet?"

"Go for it," Nina mumbled through a sticky lump of Jif.

Claire pushed the play button. What came on was the truncated, last few seconds of a machine-produced message.

". . . so we hope you will take advantage of this special opportunity to consider switching to AT&T. Don't forget: switching is free. Thank you."

After an electronic beep, the second message began.

"Hi, is anyone home? If anyone is home, please pick up. All right, I guess no one's home . . ."

"That would explain why we have the machine on," Nina muttered.

". . . Anyway, Burke, if this is your machine, this is Elizabeth calling. I just wanted to let you know that Mark and I will be coming in Sunday, probably late morning if the traffic isn't too bad. We look forward to seeing you and the girls. Bye-bye."

"Are you trying to mangle that sandwich?" Claire asked, staring at Nina disapprovingly.

Nina looked at the mess in her hand. She had crushed the sandwich, and now jelly and peanut butter were oozing through her fingers. She threw it into the trash and began washing her hands in the sink.

"Are you okay?" Claire asked.

"Fine," Nina said.

Claire sighed. "Great. Relatives. Well, there's no way to get out of it."

"Don't you like them?" Nina asked suddenly.

Claire shrugged. "They're relatives. Which means they think they have the right to ask me a lot of dumb, personal questions and tell a lot of boring stories."

"No, I mean, do you dislike them especially? Aunt Elizabeth and Uncle . . ."

". . . Mark." Claire supplied the name. "They've always seemed okay. I mean, Aunt E. is like Dad in a bad dress and with no sense of humor. And Uncle Mark is just boring. But at least they don't have kids."

"Why?" Nina asked while her mind whirled.

"Why what?"

"Why don't they have kids?" Nina pressed, as if it had become the most important question in the world.

"How would I know?" Claire said, giving her a frustrated look. "Maybe they don't like kids, or maybe one of them has some physical problem. Or maybe they're still waiting."

"They're too old."

"Aunt E.'s only forty, I think. It's still possible."

"I have to go," Nina said. "I have to read to Benjamin."

"Tell him hello," Claire said, sounding a tiny bit wistful.

"Yeah," Nina said. "I have to go right now." She ran from the house and didn't stop till she reached the circle. There she slumped against the cold marble war monument and labored to catch her breath. Her heart was pounding.

He was coming. She couldn't tell herself any longer that it had all been a false alarm.

She couldn't read to Benjamin, not now. He would know from her voice that something was wrong. He would ask her, or else he would tell Zoey to ask her, and Zoey would want to know.

But Zoey could never know. No one could.

He had told her that so many times, and she accepted it—no one would ever believe her.

Nina

Ah, yes, dream number three. Dream number three is one I've had several times. It's extremely embarrassing the way dreams are sometimes. Extremely strange. I guess all I can say is, hey, it's just a dream.

This dream starts out like two. My mom is dressing me in a cute little dress with a ridiculous bow on the front. Only this time I'm getting dressed for a party, a grown-up party; you know, where I'm the official cute kid. It's not much of a party from my point of view. It mostly involves staring up at massively tall adults, so tall that their heads aren't even clearly visible. They just seem to disappear in the mist.

Did I mention it's kind of foggy in this dream? It is. And dark again, like a grainy old picture. And all the adults are tall, like redwoods or something, going up and up until they seem to converge.

And I'm feeling weird, like I'm drunk. A drunk eleven-year-old in a bad dress. Everything kind of veering like the old Batman reruns, where things were always at an angle.

Anyway, in the dream I get tired, so tired I almost can't walk anymore. And then I see the chair.

I climb up on the chair, which is really tall, so tall it's like climbing a mountain, only suddenly there I am, sitting, and I'm dangling my legs over the edge of the seat, way above the ground.

Which is when the embarrassing part comes in.

I suddenly realize all the tall redwood people are staring at me with these ax-murderer, blood-hungry-vampire eyes. Staring and staring, and I squirm, being understandably uneasy.

And then I realize I can feel the seat under my behind.

And then I realize I'm not wearing my dumb dress after all. I'm naked and starting to cry like a little baby.

And I never should have tried to go to the adult party, and I should have known better, and I knew I would be punished severely because it's my fault I'm there. My fault for being stupid.

When I wake up, I feel like throwing up.

And I don't think I don't understand this dream, and the others, because I do. I know what it all means, although I wish I didn't. I know the cause. I know. I know the dreams and the reality.

I just don't know how to make either of them go away.

SEVEN

"IT'S NEW. IT'S CALLED POLYNESIAN Surprise," Nina said, dragging her fork through the slimy mess on her lunch tray the next day. "I think it involves pork. And either bean sprouts or white worms. I'm betting worms."

"Thanks for making me sick," Aisha said.

"Based on your vast and superior knowledge as seniors, are Polynesians more likely to cook with sprouts or worms?" Nina asked Zoey and Aisha.

"Why don't you just bring your lunch if you're going to complain about it every day?" Claire asked, taking the remaining vacant seat.

"Tradition," Nina said promptly. "I like complaining about the food." She managed a tight smile, though her sister's voice was like fingernails on a chalkboard to her.

"What is it with guys?" Zoey asked, suddenly changing the subject. "I mean, would it really kill Lucas to go along with this whole homecoming thing?"

"Why do you go out with guys if you're just going to complain about them every day?" Nina asked, mimicking Claire.

"They're like food, my child," Aisha said in a low, husky voice, tossing her hair and closing her eyes to slits in a parody of worldly wisdom. "A necessary evil."

Claire shot Nina a mocking look. "Some people manage to do without. Sort of a starvation diet."

"And some people gorge on anything they can get," Nina shot back, more angrily than she'd intended.

"One point each," Aisha said. "A draw."

"I think all guys are at least partly jerks," Zoey said.

"Oh, it's worse than that," Aisha said. "All guys are *mostly* jerks."

"Trouble in paradise?" Nina asked Aisha, glad to divert attention from herself. Her leg was bouncing up and down under the table and she couldn't stop it. She felt wired and edgy. She hadn't slept well last night.

"No, not trouble," Aisha said. "Everything is great between Christopher and I."

"Me," Zoey said.

"Me what?" Aisha asked.

"Between Christopher and *me*"

"No way," Aisha argued.

"Yes. It's me."

"Who gives a rat's ass, Zoey?" Nina demanded. "Either way, things are fine, right?"

"Um, hi."

All four girls turned to look up at a tall, somewhat frightened-looking guy.

"Hi, John," Zoey said.

"Um, hi, Zoey. Hi, Claire. Hi, Aisha." He winced and made a face, almost as if he were in pain. "Hi, Nina."

Nina made a mechanical half-smile. John Blount sat a desk away in her English class. "What's up, John? We were just this second having a fascinating discussion of grammar."

"Um . . . could I, uh . . . talk to you?"

"Sure, I still allow the little people to speak directly to me on occasion," Nina said.

"Like, over there?" John pointed.

Nina made a groaning noise deep in her throat. This had all the signs of something embarrassing. And this was not the day for it. "Nobody touch my Polynesian Surprise." She got up and followed John a few feet away, hoping against hope that he just wanted to borrow her homework or something.

"There's like a football game tonight," John said, digging his hands deep into his pockets.

"Thank you for letting me in on that, John."

He laughed, then blushed. "Do you want to, like, go with me?"

Nina cringed, for herself and for him. She hated saying no, not that it came up all that often. "Actually, um, John, I wasn't going to go to the game."

"That's all right," he said quickly. "We could do something else."

"It's nice of you to offer, but I don't think so," Nina said, beginning to feel the electric edge of panic.

"Oh."

"Look, it was sweet of you to ask, all right?"

"So you're saying you don't want to go out with me?"

"I guess that sums it up," Nina said.

John's face instantly turned angry. "You think because your dad is rich I'm not cool enough for you?" he demanded, his voice rising. "Or is it because Zoey's your *real* boyfriend?"

He turned and walked away. Nina watched him go for a second, extremely reluctant to have to face her friends, who had, without any doubt, heard John's parting shot.

She drew a deep, steadying breath and turned back to them, sliding heavily into her seat. She covered her eyes with one hand. "What was it we were saying about guys being jerks?"

"I used to think he was a nice guy," Zoey said angrily.

"He is a nice guy," Nina said flatly. The edginess and panic were gone now, replaced by disgust for the way she had handled things. "He just thought I was trying to embarrass him, I guess."

"Hey, if he wants to ask you out, he's got to accept the possibility the answer will be no," Aisha said.

"Or the absolute certainty," Claire said.

Nina dug her fork viciously into the Polynesian Surprise. "Look, can we just drop it? John's cool; it was my fault."

"It was not your fault," Aisha said, outraged. "Tell her, Zoey."

"He had no right to dump on you," Zoey agreed.

"I could have said yes and then he wouldn't have said that, all right? So it's my fault, too," Nina said. She twisted the fork and bit her lip. She felt like pounding something. Screw the principal she wanted a cigarette. She began digging in her purse.

"I can't believe I'm hearing this prefeminist *blame the woman* b.s. from you, Nina," Aisha said. "What are you going to tell me next? That it was your fault because you lured him on with your short skirt?"

"I'm not wearing a skirt," Nina muttered, still looking for her cigarettes.

"That's just an example of the kind of crap you're saying," Aisha ranted, waving her hand dismissively. "Hamster Boy there had no reason to say that. Or drag Zoey into it."

"Sorry," Nina told Zoey.

"You're hopeless," Aisha said. "She's hopeless. It's a good thing you *don't* date, Nina. I mean, God, you'd be thinking it was your fault if you didn't want to do the old in-out on the first date. You have the right to say no without some guy calling you names."

"Damn it, can we just drop this!" Nina's sudden explosion silenced everyone within twenty feet.

"Get a grip, Nina," Claire said quietly.

Nina was on her feet. Her chair fell over backward, clattering noisily. *"You* get a damned grip, Claire. It's nobody's business, all right? I don't tell any of you what to do, so just leave me alone. It's not . . . It's my problem. Okay?"

"Okay, Nina," Zoey said, in the kind of cautious voice people use to talk to lunatics and vicious dogs. "Come on, we didn't mean to upset you."

"I'm not upset," Nina said, suddenly feeling empty and deflated. "I'm. . ." She raised her hands helplessly. "I'll see you guys on the ferry."

She turned and walked away, fighting the tears until she could find some private place to let them fall.

EIGHT

CLAIRE HAD BROUGHT A CHANGE of clothing to wear to the football game that night. Extracurricular activities were always difficult for island kids, given the inflexible ferry schedule. Games started at six thirty, which meant she would have had to take the four o' clock home, arriving at four twenty-five, run to her house, shower, change, then run back and catch the five ten returning to the mainland. Rather than getting forty-five rushed minutes on the island, she usually brought extra clothes over with her for dates and games and changed in the girls' locker room.

When she entered the locker room, she heard laughing voices—Zoey and Aisha, also changing. Zoey was drying her hair and yelling over the noise.

"You mean Jake told her to go away?" Zoey said. "You actually heard this?"

"Cross my heart!" Aisha yelled back. "At practice on Wednesday."

Claire faded behind a bank of lockers and waited.

Zoey turned off the hair dryer. "Excuse me? *Wednesday?* And you're telling me on Friday? Friday afternoon? Sometimes I despair for you, Eesh. You'll never make a great gossip. Nina would have told me within eight seconds."

"It didn't occur to me. I do have my own life to lead."

"And she's still going after him," Zoey said, marveling. "That has to be a first for Claire. Normally, all she has to do with a guy is look at him and he's ready to rip zipper."

"Well, I haven't known her as long as you have."

"Take my word for it. When she was in sixth grade, she had tenth-grade guys after her."

"Huh. Let me smell that perfume. I don't see why guys would be all that crazy over her. That's nice. Let me use some."

"Hmm, let's see. She has a perfect body, great hair, a beautiful face. She's very smart and manages to have that whole air-of-mystery thing going—you know, dark, mysterious eyes, the way she walks and all."

"Plus, she's kind of a bitch," Aisha added with a laugh. "Christopher says that's why he likes me."

"She's not really," Zoey said, sounding thoughtful. "Claire just lives in her own world. She's very . . . I don't know the right word—"

"Superior? Arrogant? Snotty? Condescending? Don't do your eyebrows that way. Watch me—like this, it's easier."

Claire smiled wryly. It was always useful to hear how other people saw you.

". . . ow, damn, that hurt."

"But it works better," Aisha said.

Claire crept back to the locker room door. She opened it noisily and let it slam shut. Instantly Zoey and Aisha fell silent.

"Hi," Claire said.

"Claire," Aisha said, "we were just talking about you."

"Good things, I hope," Claire said mildly.

"Why, are there *bad* things?"

"Have you seen Nina?" Zoey asked Claire.

"She went back home," Claire said.

"Huh," Zoey said. "I thought she was thinking of coming to the game for a change."

Claire raised an eyebrow. "After that scene at lunch, I don't think so."

"That shouldn't upset her," Zoey said unconvincingly. "No one noticed. Besides, people expect Nina to do surprising things. She shouldn't be embarrassed."

"Yes, she should," Claire said. "Not that I want to be snotty or condescending, but I think she needs to learn to deal with members of the opposite sex."

She was pleased to see Aisha and Zoey exchange an uneasy look.

"Maybe she doesn't like guys," Aisha suggested.

"Eesh!" Zoey chided.

"Look, it wouldn't bother me," Aisha said. "I'm open-minded. I'm just saying maybe Nina's gay."

"She's not gay," Claire said. "She's just weird."

"Are you sure?" Aisha pressed. "You two aren't the closest sisters on earth. Maybe it's possible she's keeping it a secret from you, too."

"I know plenty of other girls who don't date," Zoey said.

"Don't get defensive, Zo," Aisha said, laughing. "Even if she is a lesbian, it doesn't mean she has the hots for you. Although . . . you two are pretty close."

"You know, you sound like a guy, Aisha," Claire said. "Every time you tell a guy no—no to anything—the first brilliant theory they come up with is that you're gay. It never, ever occurs to the guy that maybe he's just a toad."

"Not every guy is a toad," Aisha said. "But Nina always says no. Has she ever had a relationship that lasted more than one date? Has she ever mentioned being interested in a guy?"

"Look, Nina's just Nina, all right?" Zoey said hotly. "She has the right to be however she wants."

"She's not gay," Claire said. "So you two can rest easy. I think there is a guy she's interested in."

Claire was gratified by the way both Zoey and Aisha stared at her, jaws open.

"Who?" Aisha asked.

"She would have told me," Zoey said.

Claire smiled. "Look, I've told you all I can without indulging in gossip. You wouldn't want me to gossip about my own sister behind her back, would you?"

"Why doesn't she go out with this guy, then?" Aisha asked.

Claire shrugged. "It's all one-way. I don't think he even knows she's alive."

"Poor Nina," Zoey said thoughtfully.

"Oh, well," Claire said lightly. "I guess unrequited love happens to everyone sooner or later." She turned on the water and began splashing her face. "Even to girls with perfect bodies and that whole air-of-mystery thing."

"Of course she heard us talking about her; she was toying with us," Aisha grumbled. "You think *air of mystery* is just a phrase that happened to pop into her mind? Now she thinks I think she's arrogant."

"She thinks I think she's very smart and has a perfect body. She'll think I'm jealous of her," Zoey complained.

They emerged from the gym, and Aisha glanced at her

watch. "We have time to kill. You want to go downtown?"

"We could get my folks' real car and drive out to the mall," Zoey suggested.

"Do you have the keys?"

"Sure. I can take the car anytime, as long as I'm sure my parents are staying on the island. I'll give my mom a quick call, then we hit the garage and get in a couple hours of shoppage."

Fifteen minutes later they were on the road toward the mall. "Do you think Claire was telling the truth about Nina?" Aisha asked. She didn't want to press the issue too much because she knew Zoey was sensitive about it.

"Who knows with Claire?" Zoey said.

"Nina would have told you if she was hot for some guy," Aisha said.

"Nina can't keep secrets," Zoey agreed. "But by the same token, she could never keep secret about being gay if she were. Personally, I think Nina's just . . . original."

Aisha nodded, unconvinced, as they cruised the mall parking lot.

"Is that a space?" Zoey asked.

"No, handicapped."

"How about—"

"Motorcycle."

"There," Zoey said, quickly pulling into an open space.

"Hey, isn't that Christopher?"

Aisha followed the direction Zoey was pointing. Just visible through several parked cars was Christopher, passing out of sight. Aisha opened the door quickly and stood up, ready to yell to him. But then she stopped herself.

Zoey climbed out, too. "There he is," she said, "see?"

"Yes, I see," Aisha said. She met Zoey's puzzled stare. "I also see that girl he's following." She had a blond ponytail that fell straight down her back to the middle of a behind that hung half out of a pair of Daisy Dukes.

"They're just walking in the same direction," Zoey said.

"And now?" Christopher had drawn even with the girl and was smiling. The girl smiled back and said something that made Christopher laugh.

"Now he's just saying hi," Zoey said.

"Uh-huh. Come on. But let's stay back."

"You want to follow him?" Zoey sounded shocked. "You want to spy on him?"

"No way. But we did come here to go to the mall, and if we just happen to all be walking in the same direction—"

"So we're not spying?"

"No."

"But we should be careful not to let him see us?" Zoey asked.

"You're very quick, Zoey, anyone ever tell you that?" Aisha set off, edging along the lines of parked cars, watching as Christopher opened the glass door of the mall entrance and held it open for the girl.

Christopher and the girl disappeared from view inside. Aisha, with Zoey alongside, entered a minute behind him. Christopher and the girl were standing just a few dozen paces inside. Aisha grabbed Zoey's arm and pulled her behind a pod of telephones.

She peeked cautiously around the side. The quality of Christopher's smile had changed, becoming subtler. Worse yet, the girl was playing with her hair, pulling the ludicrously long ponytail forward as if displaying it for Christopher.

Aisha slid back behind the phones. "Did you see that?" she asked Zoey.

"I wasn't looking," Zoey whispered.

"She's playing with her hair and smiling," Aisha said.

Zoey winced. "That scrote."

Zoey peeked cautiously around the side. "She's gone now," she whispered. "Christopher's over at the ATM getting some money out."

"You're sure she's gone?" Aisha asked.

"I didn't see her."

"Check again," Aisha said.

"Okay." Zoey leaned out again. "Now they're both gone."

"He's probably gone after her," Aisha said bitterly.

"I'm sure it wasn't anything. Maybe he knows her from somewhere. Besides, she left first, right? So it couldn't have been anything."

Aisha narrowed her eyes. "Uh-huh."

"Look, Eesh, you can't get jealous every time Christopher talks to a member of the opposite sex."

"They were grinning like baboons and she was playing with her hair," Aisha snapped. "I'm not blind."

"Maybe she just has a habit of playing with her hair."

"And maybe *he* just has a habit of trying to pick up on girls at the mall." She bit her lip, trying without much success to relax and stop the spiral of irrational anger that was building inside her.

"Did you guys ever say it was supposed to be a steady thing?" Zoey asked.

The question took Aisha by surprise. "We never said much of anything," she admitted. "But, I mean, I assumed . . ."

"Talk to him about it at the game tonight," Zoey suggested. "Straighten it out. Maybe all he needs is for you to ask him flat out whether you guys are going to make it monogamous. Talk before you get all upset, okay?"

"I'll talk," Aisha said, "but I'll go ahead and start getting upset just in case."

NINE

CLAIRE FINISHED GETTING DRESSED FOR the evening, emerged from
the gym, and walked toward Portside Weymouth, wandering
through the quaint shops that were so much like a somewhat
larger, better-stocked version of North Harbor. She bought a
pair of silver earrings at one shop and almost bought a sweater at
another before deciding against it. Then, glancing at her watch,
she decided to find something to eat. It was either eat now or
wait and be forced to consume the hot dogs the team booster
club sold at the game.

She walked through the cool, busy, cobblestoned streets and
aimed for Big Mikey's, a slightly disreputable but cheap diner
that was an after-school hangout for Weymouth High kids.

Big Mikey himself was behind the counter, looking dissatisfied and a little dangerous. Claire sat down on an empty stool
at the neon-trimmed counter. "Hi, Big."

"Ah, the banker's daughter," he replied, managing a half-
smile. "What'll you have?"

"Foie gras?"

"Sorry. Just ran out of foie gras."

"Okay, then I'll have a chicken breast sandwich and a salad," Claire said.

"Uh-huh," Big Mikey muttered. He glanced meaningfully toward the comer of the room.

Claire looked toward the corner but saw nothing of any particular interest.

"In the last booth," he said out of the corner of his mouth.

Claire looked again. From her angle, she couldn't see a thing. She held up her hands helplessly. "What? Is there something I'm supposed to be seeing?"

"Jake and some other kid."

Claire was surprised—both that Jake was there and that someone like Big Mikey would know that she cared. "So what?" she asked, acting nonchalant.

"The two of them ordered tall Cokes. Which they've been drinking for an hour now."

"So what, she repeated," Claire said impatiently.

"So the Cokes never get empty, but a little paper bag keeps appearing from under the table."

It took Claire a moment to figure out what the man was telling her. When she understood, she was shocked. "Are you telling me Jake's drinking? He has a game tonight."

"Yeah, and I have a twenty-dollar bet I'm going to lose if the star running back is faced on cheap rum. And it is cheap rum; I can smell it from here. Not to mention that my business could be pretty well screwed if some cop wanders in here and decides I'm letting underage kids drink."

Claire cursed under her breath.

"Exactly," Big Mikey agreed. He shook his head. "You'd think after what happened to his brother . . ." He let his words trail off, looking down in embarrassment. "Sorry. I wasn't thinking."

"Neither is he," Claire said. "Damn. You want me to get him out of here, I guess?"

"I was just getting ready to do it myself," Big Mikey said. "But I think it might go a little more peacefully if you do it."

Claire cursed again, this time silently. Damn it, what did Jake think he was doing, getting drunk a few hours before the game? Come to think of it, what did he think he was doing getting drunk, period?

She drew in several deep, steadying breaths.

"I'll buy your dinner if you can do it without any dishes getting broken."

Claire climbed off the stool and walked over to the booth. The second guy was Dave Voorhies. He and Jake were hunched morosely over two Cokes that were suspiciously light in color. "Hi, Jake. Dave."

Jake looked up quickly. His eyes were a little blurred, but he focused. Good, he probably wasn't too far gone.

"Well, damn, if it isn't Killer Claire," Jake said in a rowdy voice.

Claire forced herself not to react. It wouldn't help things for her to get emotional. "Jake, I was thinking maybe it might be time to head up to the school. You know, the game tonight?"

"I know the game, Claire, Claire, Killer Claire."

His voice was slurred. He might be drunker than she had realized. She forced a cool smile. "You know, you're supposed to be *in* the game."

Jake slapped his forehead in mock surprise. "No!"

"Yes," Claire countered.

"You know," Jake said, leaning forward to stare at Dave, "I really, really liked her, you know?"

"I can understand that," Dave said with a leer in her direction.

"Don't do that," Jake said sharply.

"I didn't do nothing."

"I saw that look," Jake said. "I was telling you something. See"—he grabbed Dave's arm—"she . . . see, I really liked her, only, you know what she did? And then, how can I?" He sat back. "How?"

He is drunk, Claire realized. Major drunk. Two hours before game time. "Jake, stop being a hole. You could get kicked off the team if you show up drunk for a game."

He looked up at her with moist, defiant eyes. But she could see the light of reason beginning to dawn just a little. "I'm not drunk."

"Sure you are, dude," Dave pointed out helpfully. "We're both drunk."

"I am?" Jake acted as if it was a pleasantly surprising bit of news.

"Your coach will dump you," Claire said. "This is your senior year; you don't want to get dropped from the team."

"What the hell do you care?"

Claire sighed. "I care, okay?"

"You don't give a damn about me," Jake said flatly. "You just feel guilty."

"You're wrong, Jake," Claire said in a steady voice, trying to shut out Dave's blinking, unfocused stare. "I do care. I'm here trying to help you because I care. If you don't want to believe that, fine. But what I want to do right now is get you sobered up and ready for the game."

He shook his head sadly. Then he lifted his head and stared

at her. "You are very, very, very beautiful."

"So I've heard," Claire said dryly.

"I have to go and get ready for the game," Jake said with sudden, drunken decisiveness.

"Let's go." Claire took his arm and guided him up out of the booth. He wavered and almost sat back down. But at last he was standing, weaving back and forth a little.

"Hot shower, then cold shower," Big Mikey said, still behind the counter. "And fill him with fluids; that will help him to get rid of the alcohol and keep from dehydrating."

"Come on, Jake," Claire said, leading, him toward the door. "That's it. Yes, it's best if you put one foot in front of the other."

Claire walked Jake up the hill to the school. The sun was just beginning to turn the sky pink in the west, throwing the Gothic-looking brick face of the school building into ominous shadow.

He walked sullenly beside her, wavering a little less, sweating profusely as the alcohol worked its way through his system. Just by the side of the building he tore free and made a dash for the bushes. Claire looked away and tried not to hear the disgusting retching sounds that seemed to go on and on.

At last he emerged, pale and shaken. "Must have been something I ate," he said weakly.

"Yeah," Claire said. She took his arm again and propelled

him toward the gym, taking the back way to avoid any kids who might be hanging around out front. Only a small, startled-looking group of juniors was in the back, passing a joint among themselves. Claire ignored them, and she and Jake reached the rear doors of the gym.

"Girls' shower," Claire said. "Some of your team might already be in the boys' shower. Girls' locker room will be empty."

"Too bad," Jake joked feebly.

They skulked around the edge of the bright basketball floor and entered the girls' locker room. The only girls who tended to use the showers after-hours were island kids and, as Claire knew, they were all accounted for. The lights were off, so she turned them on, reassured that the room was in fact empty.

Claire guided Jake to the shower, turned the water on full and hot, and tested it. "Get undressed and get under."

Jake gave her a bleary rendition of a rakish look. "Are you trying to take advantage of me?"

"Jake, right now you are a thoroughly disgusting creature," Claire said. "You're sweating like a pig and you reek of vomit. Just get undressed and get under the shower." She turned away and went to her locker. She dug out a towel and a bar of soap and set them on the bench. Then she pulled out a small blue bottle of Listerine.

She crossed over to Zoey's locker. Out of the corner of her eye she caught a glimpse of Jake under the shower. She fought down the impulse to satisfy her curiosity and concentrated on remembering Zoey's birthday instead. She tried the numbers out on the combination lock, and it opened easily. In Zoey's locker she rummaged until she found a tiny bottle of Murine and the vitamins Zoey popped every day before gym class. She dumped two of these and the Murine on her towel.

"Jake, I'm going to bring you some stuff," Claire warned. "Turn away."

He gave no sign of having heard her, but as she approached he was leaning headfirst against the tile wall, looking like he might fall over. "Here," she said, keeping her eyes fixed on his. "Take these with some shower water."

He held out a hand and swallowed the vitamins obediently.

"Soap. It's Camay. Sorry, I don't have anything more manly. There's a towel and some mouthwash and some Murine over by the sinks. Drink all the water you can hold. I'll wait outside and make sure no one else comes in."

Jake nodded mutely.

Claire turned and walked outside into the gym. She leaned against the wall and realized she was perspiring herself. She let out a long, shaky sigh.

Well, at least she hadn't stared or broken out in giggles. All in all, she had handled her first close encounter with a completely naked guy pretty well. Like a professional nurse.

Although certain images were now pretty well burned on her brain.

After fifteen minutes, the locker room door opened. Jake came out, dressed again in his same clothes, looking pale but alive. His eyes were downcast.

"Did you drink plenty of water?" Claire asked him.

"Gallons."

"Good. Alcohol dehydrates your body."

"What time is it?" he asked.

"It's five fifteen."

"I have to suit up in forty-five minutes," he said anxiously.

"You should eat if you think you can keep it down," Claire said.

Jake nodded passively.

"Probably not Big Mikey's," Claire said. "Come on."

They walked a few blocks in silence, ending up at a little diner, where Claire ordered Jake poached eggs, toast, large quantities of juice and coffee, and an Alka-Seltzer to help him keep it all down. As he ate, he seemed to revive. Color came back to his cheeks. His movements became more crisp and efficient. His eyes focused clearly.

"You want anything else?" Claire asked.

He shook his head. "I think I can make it now. I'm still woozy and I won't be a hundred percent, but I won't fall on my face. At least I don't think I will."

"I thought falling on your face was the whole point of football."

Jake didn't smile. Instead he looked down at his coffee. "Coach would have cut me if I'd shown up like I was," he said. "I . . . I have to say thanks. I mean, thanks. Thanks."

"No problem," Claire said, feeling a sudden welling of emotion.

"I, uh. . . Look, I don't know what's going to happen with us, all right? But anyway, you saved my ass."

Claire allowed herself an impish smile. "It is a really nice ass."

Jake groaned, but with some of his old good nature. "Please don't remind me. Ever."

"Jake." She paused. "Jake, why were you drinking?"

He shrugged. "Dave had a bottle."

"You didn't used to drink," Claire said, as gently as she could.

"It's been a bad week. It's been a bad couple of weeks."

Claire reached across the table and took his hand. He gave her fingers a light squeeze, then bit his lip as if he regretted it. "I have to go," he said. "I need major warm-up. I have to try and sweat out the rest of this stuff."

"I'll see you at the game," Claire said.

"I'll be the one falling on my face." He stood up and dug crumpled dollars out of his jeans to pay the check.

"I'll be the one cheering while you do," Claire said.

TEN

"HERE HE COMES," AISHA MUTTERED out of the side of her mouth.

Zoey was next to her in the crowded, rowdy bleachers with Lucas. Twilight had followed sunset, and the stadium lights bathed the field in unreal, bluish brilliance, turning red uniforms black and casting impenetrable shadows that completely concealed the faces of the players within their helmets.

"I don't see him!" Zoey yelled over a sudden roar of excitement. "Oh, wait, now I see him. He's looking for you."

"Are you sure about that?" Aisha asked. She plastered a phony smile of welcome on her face and waved her hand back and forth. "Christopher! Here he comes, the snake."

"Give him a chance," Zoey advised.

"Is something going on?" Lucas asked.

"No," Zoey said. "Nothing that would interest someone like yourself who is so far above all this day-to-day school stuff that occupies smaller minds like mine and Aisha's."

Lucas sighed, shook his head glumly, and returned his

attention to the game.

Christopher came winding his way through the seated kids and parents and townspeople, all either talking, cheering, or eating. He gave Aisha a big smile. She searched it for signs of falseness.

"Hi, Christopher," Zoey said.

"Hey," Lucas said, lifting one hand in a sort of greeting.

Christopher gave Aisha a quick kiss. "What's the score?" he asked Lucas.

"Nothing to nothing," Lucas said. "But our nothing looks a little better."

Aisha scooted over to make room for Christopher beside her. "So, what have you been doing all afternoon?" she asked brightly.

Christopher shrugged. "Stuff. Picked up my paycheck for the paper deliveries. I'm rich enough to buy you a dog, if you want. You can even get chili."

"No thanks," Aisha said. "Did you do anything after you picked up your check?"

"Yes, yes, no, no, no, look out!" Christopher yelled. Down on the field, Jake got the ball and ran five yards before being tackled.

"That had to hurt," Lucas said sympathetically.

"So you just picked up your check," Aisha persisted.

"Hm–hm. Bought some socks. That was pretty much the high point."

"Really? Socks?" Aisha asked, sounding terribly interested.

"They're going to the blitz," Christopher said.

"Uh," Lucas agreed.

"So where did you buy these socks?" Aisha asked.

A roar from the Camden fans across the field elicited a response from the local faithful.

"What?" Christopher shouted.

"I said, where did you buy the damned socks!" Aisha yelled.

Christopher looked at her skeptically. "Why?"

"Because I'm just curious. Zoey and I are both curious about where you bought your socks because we both would like to know where a good sock store is," Aisha said.

"Yeah," Zoey agreed unconvincingly. "Socks. We love socks. I probably have, oh, twenty pairs. All different colors and stuff."

"I bought them at that place downtown. You know, that place with the neon sign in the window shaped like a wave?"

"Spinners?" Aisha asked, beginning to seethe.

"Yeah, that's it."

"You should have tried the mall," Aisha said. "They have lots of great sock stores there. Cheaper than Spinners."

Christopher shrugged. "The mall's miles out there. I didn't

want to go all that way just to save fifty cents on a pair of socks."

There it was, Aisha realized. He had lied. A flat-out lie. She felt Zoey's hand surreptitiously squeeze her arm in solidarity.

She had seen him coming on to another girl. And then he had lied about it. Which meant there could have been lots of other flirtations with lots of other girls. And he was probably prepared to lie about them, too.

Or maybe it was nothing. Maybe he knew the girl from somewhere and was just saying hi. Maybe he forgot he was at the mall.

That's right, Aisha, she thought, *you can come up with some kind of bogus explanation if you try hard enough.*

"So, what did *you* do today?" Christopher asked her. "I hope it was something as exciting as buying socks."

"No," Aisha muttered. "I guess you had more fun than I did."

On the field Jake caught the ball and ran for a touchdown. The Weymouth High fans went nuts. Aisha was the only one left sitting. She sat through the next two quarters, but at the half, with Weymouth High well in the lead, they all headed for the rest rooms and the munchie stands.

Zoey and Lucas peeled off, still sniping at each other about homecoming royalty. Christopher took Aisha's hand and drew her under the darkened seats. Overhead there was the clatter of footsteps on the boards.

"I haven't had a chance to kiss you all day," he said, taking her in his arms.

She forced a smile. "And you were thinking about me all day?"

"Every minute," he said. "Every second."

"I'm sure there were a few minutes here and there when you might have thought about something else."

He held up his hand as if taking an oath. "On my Boy Scout honor."

"Were you a Boy Scout?"

"Nope." He grinned and lowered his mouth toward hers. She gave him a grudging kiss.

It would have been easy to make him admit the truth. She and Zoey had both seen him. And the fact that he lied about being in the mall just proved that he was hiding something. The girl with the long blond ponytail? Some other girl he had met later? She could drag the truth out of him right now. Was he seeing other girls? Was he going to go on seeing other girls?

"We can do better than that," he said in a lower voice. He tilted back her head with his hand, and she let him. He pressed his lips to hers, and she let him. And when he opened his mouth, so did she.

She could force the truth from him. But what if she didn't

like the answer? What if for him she was just one among many? How could she stand hearing that, when for her he had so quickly become the only one?

The front of the Geiger home had a balcony. The door to the balcony was halfway between Nina's room and the room her uncle would soon be staying in. Nina seldom went out on the balcony. Even just two stories up, it excited her fear of heights. But she went out on it now, keeping a nervous eye on the white-painted crosshatched railing. By looking west, she could see the water through the trees in the front yard, and beyond the water, the lights of Weymouth. A brilliant white point, like a star fallen to earth, marked the school's stadium where Zoey and Claire and Aisha would be.

She walked to the end of the balcony nearest her own bedroom and pressed up against the railing there to check if she could see inside her bedroom.

The view was clear. She could see most of her bed, the far closet door, her dresser. She went back into the house and lowered the blinds in her room. Then she went back out onto the balcony and checked. This time nothing was visible but the tiniest sliver of escaping light. At least that worked. With her blinds drawn, she would be able to hide.

She got off the balcony and closed the door behind her.

Then she went to her bed and spilled out the contents of an Ace Hardware bag. She had a brass sliding lock with screws in a shrink-wrapped plastic card and a Phillips screwdriver. She carefully read the directions on the back of the lock, then tore it open. The screws spilled out and she had to hunt for them through the folds of her quilt.

Once they were gathered up, she went to her door again and knelt to get a close look at the painted wood molding. She placed the lock where she thought it should go, and with her other hand tried to place the little eye. The two halves of the lock didn't match up. At least not perfectly.

Nina stared at the door in frustration. The problem seemed to be that the molding stuck out from the door. She placed the main part of the lock against the door this time and the eye against the molding. Still no good. She would have to damage the molding.

Too bad she'd never taken any shop classes. The use of tools wasn't her strong point.

She trotted downstairs to the kitchen and dug in the kitchen drawer for something useful. Then her gaze settled on a knife. It was a very sharp, serrated knife with a short blade, no more than three inches long. She stuck this carefully in her back pocket and ran back upstairs.

She went at the molding, using the serrated knife to chop

and gouge out a section long enough for the eye and deep enough to lie flush with the door. It took nearly twenty minutes before she had the lock in place, screwed down with its brass screws.

She closed the door and tried the lock several times. It stuck a little, but with some effort she could slide the bolt into the eye and make it work.

It wouldn't stop someone determined to get in. But it would slow someone down and force them to make noise. She nodded in grim satisfaction. He wouldn't want to make noise, not here in *her* house.

Nina scooped up the splinters and sawdust she'd generated and dropped them in the trash. Then she picked up the knife, intending to take it downstairs.

But with the black plastic handle in her palm, she hesitated. With unwilling eyes she stared down at its wicked blade. Would she ever use it? Would she ever really use it?

Would she have used it before, years ago, if she'd thought of it then?

Probably not. She wasn't that kind of person.

She sat down on the edge of her bed, still holding the knife. She pulled open her nightstand drawer and took out the picture of herself back then. A part of her mind told her that she wasn't acting rationally, that this was all unnecessary. No one would be stupid enough to try to . . . to reach her here, in her own house, with her father asleep just down the hall.

Nina laughed, a short, bitter sound as she looked at the picture of a more innocent, unafraid girl. It wasn't about being rational anymore. Reason had been lost forever, after that first time. "You were so dumb, you didn't even know what was going on," she told the photograph.

The first time had been so innocent. Just a request to sit on her uncle's lap in the family room of his house. And then, just innocent questions. Did she like Uncle Mark? Of course, she'd replied. Did she like him a lot? Sure, she liked him. That was good, because her uncle really liked her, too.

He thought she was a very pretty young lady. Someday the boys would go crazy for her, someday they would be all over her. No, not likely, she'd answered. Why not? She'd shrugged.

Claire was prettier, Nina had told him.

Yes, he'd said, but Claire wasn't as nice as Nina. Nina was nice, wasn't she? She wanted to be nice to people who cared about her and thought she was pretty. Didn't she?

That's good, he'd said. Give your uncle a little kiss. You can do better than that. Give your uncle a real kiss. Like this. Did she like that? Did she?

Nina realized her hands were shaking. She had dropped the knife on the floor.

Yes, she had answered, tucking down her chin and feeling almost sick.

Did she like that?

Yes. She'd said yes. And from that moment of weakness all else had followed. That *yes* had made it her fault as much as his, her sin. That's what he had said, all those many evenings when he'd sat across the family room, ignoring his wife who ignored him in return, and focused his blazing, relentless eyes on her. All those nights . . . All those nights when she'd lived the reality that would later become her nightmares.

ELEVEN

CHRISTOPHER WAITED UNTIL THEY WERE all on board the homeward-bound ferry before he pulled Lucas aside on a pretext.

"Okay, what's the deal?" Christopher demanded.

"What do you mean?" Lucas stared at him blankly.

"I mean the way Aisha and Zoey have been treating me all night," Christopher said, glancing across the darkened deck to see that Aisha and Zoey were still well out of range.

Lucas shrugged. "Zoey's been ragging me since yesterday about this dumb nomination thing. That's probably what you're picking up on. Has nothing to do with you, man."

"No, that's not it. I've been going for lip and getting cheek all night from Aisha. She's pissed and I don't know why."

"You could ask her," Lucas pointed out.

"I don't think so," Christopher said. He hunched his shoulders. "Zoey tell you where she went this afternoon?"

"I think she did," Lucas said, scrunching his forehead pensively. "I mean, I guess she did, but I don't—"

"Did she go to the mall?"

"Actually, yeah. At least in last period she said she and Eesh and maybe Nina were going to head out to the mall. I remember now because she wanted to know if I wanted to go with them."

"Damn," Christopher said, slamming his hand back against the rail and instantly regretting it when a jolt of pain shot up his arm.

"Like I'd want to go shopping," Lucas said, laughing at the thought. "I think she was just being polite. I don't think she really wanted me along. Unless maybe it would give her more time to make snide remarks about—" He fell silent, looking sideways at Christopher. "What's the matter?"

"I have a bad feeling Aisha saw something she wasn't supposed to see," Christopher said in a low voice.

Lucas leaned closer. "Yeah? What?"

Christopher hesitated. Was Lucas the kind of guy who told his girlfriend everything? Lots of guys were that way, and whatever he told Zoey would go straight back to Aisha. Then he grinned wryly. Hell, Lucas had done time. He probably knew how to keep a secret. "There was this babe—"

"Uh-oh," Lucas commented, glancing over his shoulder guiltily.

Christopher couldn't help but grin. "Blond hair down to

her ass," he said. "I mean, major babe. Major, major stuff."

"Oh. You think Aisha caught you looking?"

"I was looking, all right."

Lucas shook his head. "Girls never understand that we *have* to look. We *have* to. It doesn't mean we're going to do anything about it. And the thing is, girls look, too; they're just quicker. They're subtle; just a glance and boom—they've memorized everything down to whether the guy has clean fingernails. Guys, it takes longer. We have to give it a good five- or six-second look."

"See, you're right about that," Christopher said, nodding his agreement.

"And then the girl gives the guy a hard time even though she's just doing the same exact thing, only faster."

"Well, this girl definitely took more than a five-or six-second look," Christopher said.

Lucas grinned wolfishly. "Uh-huh."

"I got her phone number."

The grin on Lucas's face evaporated. "You did what?"

"I got her phone number. I told her I'd call her sometime."

"That's going a long way past looking," Lucas said.

Was it just Christopher's imagination or was Lucas looking disapproving? More likely jealous. "She was into it; what was I supposed to do? Just walk on past and go buy my socks?"

Lucas made a *don't-ask-me* face.

"Give me a break," Christopher said. "Are you telling me you wouldn't have done the same thing?"

"I might have wanted to," Lucas admitted.

"Right."

"But. . . Wait, it's not my business how you and Aisha work things out."

"Look, I'm into Aisha; she's incredible. But you know, I'm not ready to let her nail my feet to the floor. I'm a man. A man is an animal who is made to roam. It's unnatural for a man to limit himself to one female."

"How about one female at a time?" Lucas said dryly.

"Are you telling me you're not going to try and get a little extra on the side? You're going to be totally, one hundred percent faithful to Zoey?"

"That's the plan," Lucas said.

Christopher looked at him in amazement. "The world is full of women, Lucas. Maybe you were in jail too long to remember, but they come in all types and varieties. Tall ones, short ones, small, medium, large and extra large, blond, brunette, redhead, black, white, Asian. I mean, it's like you're saying here you are—you're what, eighteen?—and you're never going to eat anything but the same old meal every day and never try something different?"

"How about if it's my favorite meal?"

"How would you know for sure?"

"I know," Lucas said with a smug little smile that annoyed Christopher unreasonably.

"I guess we're different people," Christopher said, giving Lucas a deprecating look.

"I guess so," Lucas agreed. "I understand what you're saying, though. I do. The only thing is, does Aisha understand all this? I mean, shouldn't you be up front if you're not ready to make some big commitment?"

"She understands," Christopher said uncertainly.

"Then why is she upset?"

"I don't know," Christopher said in sudden frustration. "Look, I never said I was in love with her or anything. She never said she was in love with me, either. If that was how it was I might say, okay, I have to completely ignore other girls. Right?"

"Don't ask me, man," Lucas said. "I deal with things my way; you do whatever you want. I'm no example for anyone to follow. I'm only saying you have to try not to hurt Aisha, because she's not someone you just dump on."

"I'm not going to hurt her," Christopher said, trying to sound confident. "I'll work up something very romantic for Aisha. She'll forget all about it."

He stuck his hand in his pocket and felt the torn slip of paper where he had written the blond girl's number. Her name was Angela. If he called her and went out with her, he'd have to be very careful, because Lucas was right—he didn't want to hurt Aisha.

Nina

Dream number one is the worst.

Dream number one has no pictures and no story. It only has feelings. It only has pain and guilt and shame. Dream number one makes my skin crawl. It makes me feel like I'm choking, like I can't breathe, can't breathe, can't breathe, can't breathe no matter how I try I can't breathe, till I feel I may pass out or die, till my lungs are empty like flattened paper bags and my throat is convulsing and still I can't breathe.

Waking up is just as bad because I remember it so vividly, like it just happened, just then. Like he might still be there in the dark. I'm shaking. My insides are quivering. I feel like my entire body has been rubbed with sandpaper so that I'm tender, raw, even the sheets burn me.

The rest of the day after I have this dream I feel that way. On edge. Raw.

My friends just think of it as one of my occasional bitchy moods. They chalk it up to PMS. I tell them I've had too much coffee. All day long I feel like I have to gulp air, like I have to fill my lungs to bursting on every breath.

I know what this dream means, too. But it's not something I can talk about. Ever. Talking would only make it real, and I try very hard to convince myself that it is no longer anything but a dream.

TWELVE

ZOEY WAS OPENING THE GATE to the Geigers' front yard when a movement high up caught her eye. She shielded her eyes from the morning sun and gazed up at the widow's walk, high atop the third story of the house. Claire was up there, wrapped in a heavy, sky-blue silk robe. Her long black hair rustled in the cool breeze and she was sipping a mug of something hot enough to steam.

"Claire!" she yelled up.

"What on earth are you doing already dressed and running around this early on a Saturday morning?" Claire asked, looking down from her Olympian height.

"I came to see if Nina—and you—wanted to do anything today."

"Like what?"

"I have to get our car washed, and I'm supposed to pick up a package over at the main post office. Then I'm free to do whatever."

"What would whatever be?"

Zoey realized her neck was cricked from looking up. "Shop. Go for a drive somewhere."

"It sounds fascinating," Claire said, grinning at her own sarcasm. "But I think I'll pass. Go ahead and come in. Don't knock; Janelle is baking and it would just make her cranky to answer the door." She gave a little wave and backed out of sight.

Zoey climbed the porch stairs and opened the heavy front door. She was pretty sure Nina would still be asleep, so, feeling playful, she headed upstairs, intending to give Nina a nice, rude awakening.

She grabbed the handle of Nina's bedroom door, prepared to burst in screaming her head off and watch Nina flounder around. But the door resisted. She rattled the doorknob and gave it a push. It still wouldn't open.

"NO, NO, NO!"

The cry through the door was bloodcurdling. Nina's voice, only transformed into something inhuman.

"Nina, it's me, Zoey!" Zoey cried, pressing her ear to the door and rattling the handle again. "It's me, Zoey—are you all right?"

She heard a deep, profound sigh and a few low, muttered curses that sounded more relieved than angry. After a few seconds Zoey heard a metallic scraping through the door. It opened on a rumpled, annoyed-looking Nina, hair sticking out in every direction, the waffle pattern of a blanket pressed into her left cheek. But Nina's eyes didn't match the rest of the look. They were wide, alert, like she had been scared.

"Are you aware that it's morning?" Nina asked gruffly.

"I came by to see if you wanted to do anything today." Zoey peered closely at her friend. "Are you okay?"

"The next ferry's not for two hours," Nina pointed out. "I could have slept for those two hours." She backed away from the door and flopped backward on her bed.

Zoey followed her into the room. "I know. That's how long it usually takes to get you going on a Saturday A.M." She ran her fingers over the lock on the door. "What's this for?"

"It's a vain attempt to keep people from waking me up too early," Nina said hatefully.

"Ha-ha. No, seriously."

Nina sat up and gave a little shrug. "What are we doing today?"

"Washing my parents' car?" Zoey said. "And then I thought maybe we'd drive down to Portland. Experience a different mall for a change. Also I was going to hit the Braille bookstore there for Benjamin."

"Is Benjamin coming?" Nina asked.

"No. Just us girls. I asked Claire, but she wasn't into it. I tried Aisha, but she has to do some stuff for her mom. Get some rooms ready."

Nina stood up, suddenly interested. "Hey, how much does Mrs. Gray charge for those rooms?"

"Lots, I think," Zoey said. "They're very nice. Aisha said they may be in one of those magazines that do inns and bed-and-breakfasts."

"Like hundreds of bucks, I wonder?"

"Why, you want to get away from it all for a night?" Zoey joked.

But Nina didn't smile. "Maybe."

"You're serious. You want to rent a room at the Grays' inn for a night?"

"Maybe several nights," Nina said seriously. Then she smiled. "We have some relatives coming to visit."

"Oh."

"My aunt and her husband."

"You don't like them?"

"What is there to like?"

Zoey's attention was drawn back to the clumsily installed lock on Nina's door. What was going on with Nina? She'd been off for days, it now seemed to Zoey. More angry, more edgy than she usually was. Greater than usual annoyance with her sister, the scene in the lunchroom. Nothing big, really, nothing you could put your finger on. "Hey, were you having a nightmare when I knocked?"

The look on Nina's face was telling. Her eyes narrowed, her face fell. Then, with what looked like a deliberate act of will, she reconstructed her usual cocky, ironic expression. "Yeah," she said. "I had this terrible dream someone was waking me up too early. I'll go take a quick shower," she added before Zoey could interrupt. She grabbed a few items of clothing from her closet and dresser and at least one from a pile on the floor and disappeared in the direction of the bathroom.

Zoey sat on the bed and looked up quizzically at Ed Sheeran on a wall poster. "Is she all right?" she asked Ed. "Of course, you're just the guy to ask."

She glanced at her watch and looked around for something to read to pass the time. She slid open the drawer of Nina's nightstand and froze.

A small but wicked-looking knife lay on top of an aging picture of a ten- or twelve-year-old girl.

A nightmare? A lock? A knife? A semi-serious question about staying at Aisha's?

Zoey pulled out the photo and checked the back. "Nina, eleventh birthday," she read. She replaced it under the knife, feeling deeply troubled.

Suddenly it was as if she could sense something terrible in

this familiar room. Something was the matter with Nina. It seemed impossible, but for some reason Nina, fearless, in-your-face Nina, was very afraid.

By early afternoon Zoey had picked up the package at the post office and run the car through the car wash, deftly putting off the flirtatious guy who vacuumed the interior, and made the drive down to Portland. Portland was not especially exciting, being basically just a larger Weymouth, which was in turn just a larger North Harbor. But it had a bookstore with a few shelves of books in Braille. And in any event, it wasn't quite the same old places and faces as home.

"*Master and Commander,*" Nina read the printed title. "Sounds like something Benjamin might like. It's about ships and war."

"Grab it," Zoey said. "What do you think about *Winter's Tale?*"

"Never heard of it," Nina said. "What's it about?"

Zoey pulled out the huge volume and read the blurb. "Mmm, a magic flying horse and a girl with tuberculosis."

Nina laughed. "Benjamin doesn't like magic."

Zoey made a face. "Now, how would you know whether Benjamin likes magic?"

"I do read to him," Nina said.

"And you think he likes ships and war but not magic horses and wasting diseases?"

"He totally prefers war to illness," Nina said confidently. "He's a guy, you know. Ships, planes, guns, wars, adventure, spies, detectives. No magic horses or girls with tuberculosis. Now, *I* might read a book about a magic horse with tuberculosis, but it's not a guy book."

"Suddenly you're the big expert on guys?" Zoey said, teasing innocently. But she saw Nina's jaw clench up. "Nina, I was just teasing," Zoey said placatingly.

"I know," Nina said, paying close attention to the books and refusing eye contact.

They paid for two books, using Zoey's mother's Visa card, and walked in strained silence back to the spot where the car was parked. "Love that clean car smell," Zoey said on opening the door.

Nina nodded distractedly.

Zoey shook her head and started the engine. They drove to the freeway and took the ramp heading back north. Zoey made several more attempts to engage Nina in conversation but gave up after the fifth or sixth uninterested grunt. She reached for the radio and turned it on loud.

Nina clicked it off.

Zoey turned on her, ready to lash out angrily at Nina's

sullen mood. But Nina was staring grimly straight ahead, and Zoey subsided.

"Look," Nina said at last, "I'm not a lesbian, all right?"

"I didn't say you were," Zoey said. "Not that it would matter to me."

"Well, I'm not," Nina said. She turned the radio back on and dug a cigarette out of her purse.

This time Zoey turned the radio down. "Listen, Nina, we're best friends, aren't we?"

"That depends on whether you're getting ready to bug me," Nina said through clenched teeth. She was twisting her fingers together and biting the end of the unlit cigarette.

"Why did you put a lock on your door?"

"I just felt like it."

Now Nina had begun to rock, just slightly, forward and back, like a person impatient to get away.

"You have a knife in your nightstand."

"What the hell were you doing in my nightstand?" Nina shouted, horrified.

"Nina, something is scaring you."

"*You're* scaring me, Zo, going through my stuff."

"What's going on?"

"Will you shut up and just drive?" Nina snapped viciously.

Zoey recoiled. She had known Nina nearly all her life and

had seen every mood she had. This was not part of any normal mood. Nina's anger had always been weary, or ironic. This was fresh and violently intense.

They drove in silence for a while longer, Nina still twisting her fingers together, still nearly bouncing up and down in her seat. Zoey went over every clue in her mind—the lock, the nightmarish cry, the knife, the photo of Nina five years earlier.

Five years? That was when Nina's mother had died. Was it about that somehow?

Ahead she saw the off-ramp for a rest area. She veered onto it.

"What are we doing?" Nina demanded.

Zoey didn't answer. She slowed and pulled the car into a parking space and turned off the engine. She turned sideways in her seat. "Nina, you are my best friend in the world. I think you—"

"Leave me alone! Leave me alone! Goddamn it, you think you know everything? Just stay out of it!" Nina was shouting, a deafening noise in the enclosed car.

"I can't stay out of it!" Zoey yelled back, fueled by fear and frustration.

Nina's face suddenly twisted, like some huge wrenching sob was working its way through her features. Her eyes were wide, helpless. "Look," she said, mastering herself with difficulty. "I know you're trying to be nice." Nina seemed to be gasping for breath, pausing to suck in several deep, straining lungfuls of air. "Just . . . just leave it alone. There's nothing you can do."

Zoey took Nina's hand. Nina shook it off. "If you are my friend, Zoey, drop it," Nina pleaded.

Zoey hesitated. This wasn't even Nina. Not as she had ever known Nina to be. This was someone new. Someone deformed by terror. A thrill of fear tingled up Zoey's spine.

Zoey bit her lip and reached out, deliberately taking Nina's hand again. Again Nina shook it off. Zoey could see tears welling up in Nina's eyes. Nina flung open the door and ran.

Zoey ran after her, across the grass, past the brick rest rooms and the glass-covered maps of Maine, and on to the edge of the woods. There Nina collapsed, coming to a stop by a picnic table.

Zoey approached quietly, like she would a frightened deer.

Nina laughed, a sad, faint sob. "I can't exactly walk home from here, can I?"

Zoey sat down beside her, and for a third time took her friend's hand. This time Nina didn't resist.

Nina sighed shakily. "I told you my aunt and uncle were coming, right?"

"You mentioned it."

Nina nodded. "Yeah. Well, you remember back when my mom . . . back . . ."

"When your mom died?" Zoey finished softly.

Nina nodded mutely. "Yeah. Well, remember my dad said I should go stay with my aunt and uncle for a while?"

"I never understood that," Zoey said regretfully.

"I was real close to my mom," Nina said in a voice drenched in sadness. "He . . . my dad . . . he thought I needed to get away. Stay with my aunt and uncle. Change of scene and all."

Zoey said nothing. Facts were coming together slowly in her mind, coalescing to form the rough outlines of a picture.

"This has to be a secret," Nina said, her tone now more solid, almost devoid of emotion, flat. "I mean, you have to swear. It doesn't matter if you don't believe me, because I know you won't. But you can't tell anyone."

Zoey felt trapped. She had the awful feeling that what Nina was preparing to tell her should never be kept secret. But she had to honor Nina's wishes, too. "I'll never tell anyone."

"You swear."

"Yes. I swear. And I will believe you."

Nina nodded slowly for a long time. When at last she spoke, it was in a voice Zoey had never heard.

"I was at my aunt and uncle's house for two months. I was eleven. My uncle, he started off just kissing me. Then it was more."

Zoey felt her heart stop.

"Almost every night, for two months . . . He would come into my room. Into my . . . into my bed."

THIRTEEN

JAKE PULLED THE WHITE FACE mask down and pinched it over his nose. He lifted the heavy sander and pulled the trigger. It whined furiously, then changed to a lower, harsher pitch as he pressed the spinning belt against the wooden hull of the boat towering above him. Sawdust flew and collected on the plastic lenses of his safety goggles. It gave off a sour, burning smell.

After a while he stopped, lowered the sander, and ran his hand over the surface, feeling the smoothness. That would just about do it, he decided. He'd finish up with a finer-grade sandpaper by hand, and the repair would be ready for the coats of sealer and paint.

He set down the sander and wiped the sweat from his brow with the back of his hand. His father paid him eight dollars an hour to work for him in the marina, which was good money, but his dad always got his money's worth.

Jake glanced longingly at the water, sparkling cool, just a few feet away from the dry dock. He bent over and rummaged his watch from the pocket of his discarded shirt. Good enough. He had put in five solid hours, an hour more than he had promised, and the job had gone well.

He unlaced his heavy work boots and pulled off his socks. He was wearing raggedy cutoffs, which wouldn't be harmed by a little salt water. He walked to the end of the first pier and looked around. A scattering of people lying out on Town Beach to his left. The ferry halfway back to Weymouth.

He took a deep breath and dove in. He opened his eyes under the water and looked up at the gently rocking hulls of the boats tied to the pier. With several kicks he was out in deeper water and coming up for air.

The water was cold as always but invigorating, not numbing. He looked around, deciding which direction to go. The swell was gentle out beyond the breakwater, and somehow the confines of the harbor just didn't seem wide enough. He'd swim up around to the north point, maybe take a rest at the lighthouse. On the way he could check out the sailboat from Bar Harbor that had stopped on its way down the coast to Newport.

He swam hard, enjoying the feeling of his muscles burning while his skin cooled and the sweat and sawdust were washed away. He paused when he reached the beautiful fifty-four footer, rolling at anchor in the middle of the harbor. A look told him the owner and crew were probably ashore—the dinghy was gone. He hailed it anyway, yelling, "Hey, anyone aboard?" No answer.

Too bad; he'd have liked to look around inside. She had an opulent yet professional look about her. He took several deep breaths, then dived under, thinking to get a look at the keel. But something hanging underwater from the anchor line caught his eye. He swam over to it and smiled. Three six-packs of Killian's Red, hanging in a net bag to keep cool.

He started to swim away, intending to head on toward the point, but something stopped him. He looked back at the beer. *They'd never know,* he thought.

But just behind that thought came the angry denial. No way. He didn't steal.

Although it would certainly save money over what he'd have to pay Dave Voorhies for the use of his fake ID. He turned and kicked toward the bag. It would be no problem, and no one would ever know.

His lungs began to burn and he broke the surface, looking around guiltily. No, this was dumb. First of all, he didn't need any more beer. What he needed was to get himself in shape physically and get his concentration back. Beer wouldn't help either of those goals.

He began swimming north at full speed, stretching his muscles, and as his head came up for each breath he checked his progress against the shoreline.

Start stealing beer and you'll end up no better than Lucas, he warned himself. *No better than Lucas?* he repeated ironically. *You need to update your thinking there, Jake. You don't have much reason to look down on Lucas anymore. It's Claire who is the guilty one. Claire.*

Claire, who you can't stop thinking of. Claire, who had gotten away with everything, the only one unhurt. The untouchable, unreachable Claire.

He began inscribing an arc on the surface of the water, now breasting the heavier chop of the more open sea, fighting the current that resisted his advance. The lighthouse on its tiny island of tumbled rock came into view, a squat white-and-black structure.

He had to swim around the islet to reach the tiny sand-and-pebble landing. He drew himself up, fighting the heavy gravitational pull of the water, and threw himself back on a tuft of sea grass. A hundred yards across the water stood the row of restored homes that had once belonged to the whaling captains who operated out of Chatham Island. It was the quaint sort of picture that appealed to tourists. But it was one particular home that drew Jake's eye.

He realized he was disappointed not to see her up on her widow's walk. Still, she could be inside, right up there beneath the sloping roof, behind those twin dormers.

Claire.

Claire, who said she loved him.

The only way he had of making her pay was to be cold, make her feel at least some tiny bit of rejection for once in her charmed life. She wanted to gain total absolution from him for the damage she had done. At least he could deny her that. He could use that one small area of vulnerability to hurt her. He owed Wade that much. He owed it to his dead brother to at the very least not forgive the girl who had killed him.

That was the very, very least he had to do.

A motorboat roared past, halfway to land, bouncing and sending up a high wake. Someone onboard gave a wave and a faint yell. He waved back compliantly, having no idea who they might be.

Again he checked the still-empty widow's walk.

Wade would have ridiculed him for being a wuss. He could imagine Wade's words, hear his contemptuous voice—Man, Jake, you pathetic little wimp. You're so whipped by this babe you'd sell out your own brother. You were ready to try to make Lucas Cabral pay, but now that it's Claire, oh, that's totally different.

It couldn't be different. He had to be true to the memory of Wade. He was sure of that.

A flutter of movement on the widow's walk. His heart leapt. Claire!

But then the movement resolved itself into white wings, and the sea gull flew away.

Aisha knocked on the front door of Christopher's building precisely at six o'clock that evening. It was a huge, rambling, and somewhat rundown Victorian rooming house that fronted the landward side of the island.

When after several minutes no one answered, she cautiously opened the door and went inside. She'd been to Christopher's apartment only once, but she remembered he was on the third floor.

"Hello?" she called out to the gloomy foyer. Somewhere a radio was playing country music, but that didn't sound like Christopher. "Okay," she said. "Let's just hope none of the members of the Addams Family are home right now."

She climbed the stairs and easily found Christopher's door. He had the room on the top floor of an octagonal tower. Not huge, but very distinctive and with amazing views of the beach. She knocked. "Christopher?"

The door opened and there he stood, dressed in a suit coat and tie. Also in black shorts, a T-shirt, and white Nikes. The coffee table was decorated with a candle stuck in an empty bottle of Dr Pepper. The radio was playing softly.

"Welcome," Christopher said very formally, "to my humble abode."

Aisha gave him a skeptical look but went inside. "Candlelight?"

"I'm fixing you a gourmet dinner," he said, taking her hand and leading her to a pile of pillows stacked together before the table. "Paella."

"Pa-what?"

"Paella. Chicken, sausage, clams, shrimp, and calamari on saffron rice. Very Spanish."

"Oh, that's right. I don't know why I should be surprised. You do cook for a living. At least part of your living."

"I can make anything that's on the menu at Passmores'," Christopher said, heading toward the minuscule kitchen—really just a glorified hot plate with a tiny sink and ancient refrigerator. "In fact, this would cost you seventeen ninety-five down at work. Plus tax and tip."

Aisha laughed. "I like your outfit. I would have dressed up more if I'd realized this was such a formal date."

"Oh, this old thing?"

"Very distinguished. I like the tie and T-shirt look."

"You want some wine with dinner?" he asked. He reached

into the refrigerator and came up with a bottle of 7-Up. "We have white and"—he produced a Dr Pepper—"brown."

"I think white wine with seafood," Aisha said. She took the drink and watched as he lifted the lid from a casserole, letting a cloud of fragrant steam escape.

"There are appetizers over on the buffet table."

Aisha looked around the room and spotted a plate of food on his nightstand. "The buffet table? What do you call the bed? Never mind," she added quickly. She lifted a stuffed mushroom cap from the plate and popped it into her mouth. "Hey, this is delicious."

"Six ninety-five, plus tax and tip," he said over his shoulder.

She took a swallow of her soda and eyed his back contentedly. Tall, dark, handsome. Hardworking and ambitious. Smart, funny, sexy, and he could cook paella and mushrooms stuffed with crab. What exactly had she been thinking when she'd tried to get rid of him? He was like a textbook example of the perfect guy. If you looked *Mr. Right* up in a dictionary, they'd have a picture of Christopher Shupe.

It wasn't like she was just falling victim to hormones or some stupid crush based on the fact that he had a nice body. This was a perfectly sensible thing. It was logical. He was a great guy, no matter how critical you wanted to be.

As long as you overlooked the fact that he had a weak

memory when it came to where he bought socks.

"Okay," Christopher said, quickly filling a couple of plates and tossing on a garnish, "sit."

She sat on the pillows and crossed her legs. Christopher put a steaming plate of food down before her, and one for himself. He sat down and raised his soda. "A toast. To Aisha, which means 'life.'"

"And Christopher," she said.

"Which means?" he prompted.

Aisha smiled. It seemed like a long time ago that he had told her that the day would come when *Christopher* would mean "boyfriend." She had told him there was no way, but even then, his confidence had half convinced her. "To Christopher," she said, clinking her bottle against his. "Which, to my surprise, really does mean boyfriend."

"Okay, now eat. Don't let my great food get cold."

She dived in. "Hey. This really is fantastic."

"Maybe I should blow off college and go to the Culinary Institute instead," he suggested. "Everyone who graduates from there has like five solid job offers waiting when he comes out."

"You could do both. An MBA and a cooking degree? Could be deadly if you want to run a restaurant."

"You know something?" he said, narrowing his eyes shrewdly. "That's not a bad idea. I can see a whole nationwide chain, hundreds of restaurants Shupe's International House of Paella."

"That way you could use your business degree to figure out what to charge."

The telephone rang.

Christopher rolled his eyes. "Don't people realize I'm trying to seduce a woman here?"

"Oh, is *that* what you're trying to do?"

"Remember before, when I mentioned the tip?" He gave her an exaggerated leer and got up to get the telephone on the third ring. "Shupe's International House of Paella," he answered. He listened for a second and immediately his voice dropped. Not quite a whisper, just a low pitch intended to make it hard for Aisha to overhear his conversation. With the music from the radio, she could make out very little.

But she could hear the tone of his voice.

He came back after a minute. "I took it off the hook so we won't be disturbed again."

"Anyone I know?" Aisha asked nonchalantly.

He shook his head dismissively. "An old guy I do some landscaping for. He wanted to know if I could put in some rose-bushes for him. This time of year? Rosebushes?"

Aisha smiled for his benefit. *You are such a liar, Christopher. Such a quick, professional liar. Was it the girl with the long blond ponytail? Or some other girl? Because it certainly wasn't an old man you were using that voice on.*

"You work too much," she said.

"I know," he said, reaching to take her hand. "Too little time for what's important. Like being with you."

The amazing thing was, he still seemed totally sincere, Aisha noted. And the worst thing was that her insides still quivered helplessly at the touch of his hand on hers. It was terrible how much she wanted him, even now, even knowing.

Right guy or wrong guy. It was too late for her to push him away.

She used to laugh at Zoey for being a hopeless romantic.

Now it turns out I'm just as dumb as Zoey, after all, Aisha thought sadly.

FOURTEEN

BENJAMIN FINGERED THE TITLES OF the books Zoey had brought him and set them down on a ledge inside his oak rolltop desk. The desk had tons of cubbyholes of different sizes and shapes, which made it perfect for Benjamin, who could find things only by remembering exactly where he had left them. It also had wood of a wonderful texture that was a pleasure to run his hands over.

He heard a tapping sound, fingers on glass. Left window, he decided, orienting himself by the desk and aiming his sunglasses in that direction. The tapping came again, followed by a voice he recognized as belonging to Lucas.

"Ben, it's me, man."

Benjamin pondered for a moment why Lucas would come tapping at his window and speaking in a loud whisper, but really, the reason was somewhat obvious—it could only have to do with Zoey.

He felt for the window latch, opened it, and raised the

window. A whiff of cool breeze met his face.

"Is there some good reason why you don't just go to the front door?" Benjamin asked.

"Your sister," Lucas said, sounding exasperated. "Is she really pissed at me or what?"

"You think I'm dumb enough to get in the middle of you and Zoey having a lovers' quarrel? Do I look that stupid?"

"You don't have to get in the middle," Lucas said quickly. "It's just that we were supposed to go out tonight and she called a few minutes ago and said she wanted to cancel because she wasn't feeling well."

"Uh-huh."

"So is she really not feeling well, or is she blowing me off over this dumb-ass homecoming crap? I mean, that would be very petty, in my opinion. But she may have found out what I've been doing."

"What *have* you been doing?" Benjamin asked, against his better judgment.

"I've just been making a few calls. You know, kids from school, telling them not to vote for me or anything."

Benjamin laughed, delighted. "Only you, Lucas."

"I think maybe Zoey found out and that's why she won't go out tonight."

Benjamin shrugged. "All I can tell you is she went shopping

down in Portland with Nina and when she came back, she was very quiet. She sounded like she might not be feeling well."

"Really?"

"I only know what I hear."

"Huh. Well, maybe it's one of those female things."

"Maybe. Or else she hates your guts," Benjamin added helpfully. "Maybe she's found another guy. Could be up in her room with him right now."

"Thanks a lot," Lucas said sarcastically. "I'm giving you the finger, by the way."

Benjamin grinned and shut the window. Lucas was a relief, after Zoey going out with straight-arrow Jake for so long. He could get along with Lucas. Lucas had an edge of larceny in his soul.

How on earth was *Claire* ever going to have a relationship with Jake? The question popped into his mind, bringing with it a renewed dose of the sadness he'd carried with him ever since Claire and he had broken up.

He tried to push the thought aside. He couldn't spend his life crying over Claire. He sighed and thought about his sister instead. Was Zoey sick? Or was she really just giving Lucas a hard time?

He opened the door and climbed the stairs to Zoey's room. "Hey, Zo. You in there?"

"Yeah."

She sounded dispirited, depressed maybe. Or else like he had just woken her up from a nap. "Can I talk to you for a second? Can I come in?"

"Sure."

He went in and stopped after two steps, waiting for her to speak so he could locate her.

"What do you want?" Zoey asked, not rude but distracted. She was on her bed.

"I just had a visit from Lucas. He wanted to know if you were sick or something."

"I'm not sick," Zoey said.

But not exactly happy, either, Benjamin noted. "Are you okay?"

"Uh-huh."

"Uh-huh," Benjamin echoed disparagingly.

"Look, it's just something, all right?"

He shrugged. "Whatever you say." He started to leave, but she spoke again, sounding distant and strange.

"Can I ask your advice on something?"

Benjamin winced involuntarily. "My advice?"

"It's kind of a philosophical question, you know," Zoey said.

"You sure I'm the right person to ask?"

"I don't know who else to ask," Zoey said flatly.

Benjamin located the chair by her dormer desk and sat down. "Okay, shoot."

Zoey was silent for a while. "Which is better—keeping your promise to a friend, or breaking the promise if you think your friend needs help?" she finally asked.

Benjamin ran his hand through his hair. "Is that all you're going to tell me?"

"It's all I *can* tell you."

"Hmm. Let's see, is it a matter of life or death?"

"I don't think so, but it's close."

"Really," Benjamin said, suddenly feeling a premonition of some unhappiness. Zoey wasn't being Zoey. This was as grim as he had ever heard her. Who was the friend? Lucas? He hadn't seemed worried. Nina? When had Nina ever worried about anything serious? "If this friend is able to make his or her own decisions, then I guess you have to let them," Benjamin said uncertainly. "I guess that means if they want you to keep a secret, you have to keep a secret. Unless it's a crime or something," he added as an afterthought.

"Unless it's a crime," Zoey repeated thoughtfully.

"Jeez, I don't know, Zoey. I'm not a philosopher."

"I know."

"Can you at least tell me who we're talking about?" Benjamin asked.

"I haven't decided that yet," Zoey said. "I haven't decided what to do."

"You'll figure out the right answer," Benjamin said reassuringly. He got up to leave. When he was halfway out the door, Zoey spoke again.

"There are some real creeps in the world, aren't there?"

Her venom surprised Benjamin. "Are there?" he asked.

"Thanks for talking to me," Zoey said.

Benjamin heard her close the door behind him.

"Go away."

"It's me," Claire said.

"I know, that's why I said go away."

"I'm on a mission from Dad," Claire said, trying to remain patient. She heard a metallic scrape and the door opened suddenly.

"What?"

Claire stared at her sister. Nina's eyes were vacant and red-rimmed, as if she'd been crying. "What's the matter with you?"

"Nothing's the matter with me," Nina said shortly. Then she relented. "I tried to smoke a cigarette again, and it made my eyes puff up, all right?"

Claire shook her head. "Someday you'll have to explain to me why you would go out of your way to try and become addicted to something every sane person is trying to drop."

"I'm not a sane person," Nina said. "What do you want, anyway?"

"I'm delivering a message. Daddy wants to be sure certain people have their rooms clean for tomorrow."

"My room is clean," Nina snapped.

Claire pushed her way into the room. She looked around, nodding with satisfaction. "Pretty clean by your standards, I'll admit. Although some people think clothing should be in the closet, not on the floor. And some people even believe that sheets should be changed more than once a month."

"Claire, why don't you go jump off your stupid widow's walk and do me and the rest of the world a favor?"

"Look, Nina, I don't give a damn; I'm just delivering the message. You can start a fire in the middle of your floor and roast marshmallows for all I care."

She turned and marched to the door, shaking her head. Nina seemed to be in a fairly rotten mood, which just exacerbated Claire's own fairly rotten mood. To top it off, their father was also in a fairly rotten mood, brought on by the fact that his Sunday off and several subsequent days were going to be ruined by visiting relatives. Their branch of the Geiger family was not big on backslapping, trading old stories, and forced friendliness. It just brought out the crankiness in them.

Some, apparently, more than others.

"Home alone on a Saturday night, Claire?" Nina took a parting shot.

Claire pressed her lips in a steely smile and turned back to Nina. "Home alone *every* Saturday night, Nina?"

"I've decided to become a nun; what's your excuse?"

"Guys are afraid I have insanity running in my family," Claire said. "And those who have met you are sure of it."

Nina stared at her, presumably readying her return volley. "Who's getting what room?" she asked.

Claire was taken aback. It was a sudden shift of topic, like Nina had just changed the channel without warning. "What?"

"Aunt E. in the back bedroom?" Nina asked, her eyes unfocused, staring into middle space.

"Yes. Are you . . . Are you okay?"

Nina nodded, still staring. "When will they be here?"

"Tomorrow, late morning, around eleven, so you should consider getting out of bed sometime before then."

"Yeah," Nina said.

Claire started to leave a second time. But even by Nina's standards, she was behaving strangely. "Dad's doing the barbecue cookout thing. He said we can invite people." No response, just blank staring and a sort of continuous nodding. "I think Dad just wants people around so he'll have an excuse not to have to talk to Uncle Mark."

Nina looked up sharply. "He doesn't like Uncle Mark?"

"I guess Uncle Mark always gets defensive because we have money."

"He does?"

"That's what Dad says. I wouldn't know. I don't think I've seen him since we were little."

"Did you ever stay at their house?" Nina asked, her eyes boring into Claire.

Claire shifted uncomfortably. All joking aside, maybe Nina really was becoming a little unbalanced. "No, I never stayed with them. You did, though, right?"

"Uh-huh."

Claire was losing patience with this weird conversation. Was Nina on drugs or just being strange? "Well, then you'll all have plenty to talk about. Now, um, if you don't mind, I have to return to planet Earth."

"Bye, Claire," Nina said, sounding strangely sad and distant.

The door closed and again Claire heard a metallic scrape.

FIFTEEN

NINA WATCHED *SATURDAY NIGHT LIVE* on the TV in her room until it went off at one. Then she spent the next two hours switching back and forth between MTV, Home Shopping, and reruns on Nick at Night. Nick was doing a *Brady Bunch* marathon.

At three she made an effort to go to sleep, but gave up almost immediately. As soon as the comforting light of the TV screen went off, the walls seemed to close in around her. She switched the TV back on, but nothing held her interest. It had all become just disconnected sounds, shadows marching from left to right, right to left without purpose.

She had known for years this day would come. She had known that she was not really done with the man who had introduced her to shame. He was family, after all. Family. Sooner or later he would reappear, stepping out of her memories and nightmares into her real life again.

She gulped for air, straining for each breath as the memories flowed through her again. There had been pain, yes, but the pain was the easier part. Far worse had been the fact that at times there had been a sickening sort of pleasure, like being tickled and tickled while you screamed and pleaded and the person tickling you wouldn't stop. And afterward he would cry softly and say he was sorry. He was weak, he said, he knew it. But it was her fault, too. It wasn't his fault that she was so sweet and pretty. He couldn't help how he felt. How she made him feel.

And she could never, ever tell anyone, because if she did, no one would believe her. Who would believe a little girl over a grown man? He would tell everyone she was making it up, and people would call her a liar and say she was disgusting and sick. No one would believe her. Ever.

Except . . .

Nina sat up in her bed and pulled her blankets close. Except that she had told someone. Zoey.

And Zoey *had* believed her.

Had Zoey just been pretending to believe? Did she secretly think Nina was crazy or making it all up? She tried to remember everything Zoey had said as they sat by the picnic table, bothered by flies and the smell of garbage spilling out of the cans. Had she been just pretending?

No. Zoey had never lied to her.

Zoey *had* believed her.

No one would ever believe her, but Zoey had.

She jumped up and began dressing with hurried, clumsy fingers. There was one place she could go, and one person she could talk to.

It took ten minutes to dress, creep down the stairs, and emerge into a foggy night of silent streets and dark windows. She walked along Lighthouse, listening to the surf on the rocks and the impatient rustle of the trees that lined the street. She turned down Camden, past closed shops and colorful window displays that were all shades of gray, her steps loud on brick sidewalks and cobblestoned streets.

Zoey's house was as dark as everything else. No porch light, no glimmer of illumination escaped through drawn curtains and shades.

Nina knelt by the low landing of the front door and ran her fingers slowly over dirt and twigs and rocks, searching. It took several tries before she felt the right rock and picked it up. In the bottom of the rock was a sliding panel that concealed the Passmores' extra key. Nina had seen Zoey resort to it on several occasions.

Feeling frightened, but so much less frightened than she had in her own home, Nina used the key to open the front door. She closed it gently behind her, wincing at the click of the tumblers as she locked it again.

Up the stairs and she was at Zoey's door.

Now the only problem is keeping Zoey from screaming, Nina realized with some return of her usual good humor. *She'll wake up and see me and either think I'm a burglar or that I really am gay.*

She opened Zoey's door stealthily and stepped into the room. The only sound was Zoey's heavy breathing. Nina crept forward and stood by the bed.

She touched Zoey's shoulder.

"Unh," Zoey murmured.

"Wake up," Nina said. "It's me, Lucas. I have to have you."

It took several seconds, but Zoey's eyes opened at last. She blinked, squinted, blinked again.

"It's me, Nina."

"Nina?" A voice blurry with sleep and incomprehension.

"Yeah. I'm afraid so. It's three forty. In the morning. Or night."

"Nina?" More coherent this time.

Zoey's next question would be what the hell was she doing creeping into her bedroom in the middle of the night. Only Zoey didn't ask the question. She sat up and flicked on the dim, yellow bulb of her nightstand light. She was wearing a Boston Bruins jersey, twisted about twice around her body.

"I couldn't sleep," Nina admitted, "so I thought I'd make sure you couldn't sleep, either. Sorry."

"Don't be sorry. You're my best friend," Zoey said.

For some reason that simple statement brought tears to Nina's eyes. She tried to toss off some clever line, but the excitement of being out in the night alone had worn off, leaving nothing now but despondency and profound exhaustion.

Zoey leaned toward her and put her arms around Nina's shoulders and hugged her close.

Nina let her head fall onto her friend's shoulder, unable to speak. Unable to offer an explanation that Zoey had not even asked for.

"Take off your shoes," Zoey said. And Nina kicked them off.

Zoey lay back against the pillows and rested Nina's head in the crook of her arm. Nina felt tears running freely, wetting the sleeve of Zoey's jersey. And she felt a tidal wave of weariness sweep over her, paralyzing her limbs, numbing her mind and at last obliterating her consciousness.

An hour later, Zoey gently disentangled herself from Nina and got up from the bed. She needed to think, and she was ravenous. Nina seemed in no danger of waking up. She was in a sleep so deep she might have been in a coma, not even fluttering an eyelid as Zoey left the room.

Zoey padded down the stairs and went into the dark

kitchen. Even before she turned on the light, she knew someone was there. And she knew who.

She flicked on the harsh fluorescent light. Benjamin sat there, a Braille book open before him on the table, a bag of Doritos nearby.

"Zoey?" he asked.

"Yes."

"Is Nina with you?"

"No. She's asleep upstairs. How did you know?"

He shrugged. "I heard someone sneaking in. I figured it was Lucas, actually, having the somewhat sleazy imagination I do, but I wanted to be sure it was okay, so I stood outside your door for a while until I heard you say Nina's name."

Zoey opened the refrigerator door and stared in at the assortment of leftovers, milk, soda, lunch meats, and defrosting chicken. She opened the freezer and lifted the Ben & Jerry's Chunky Monkey. It was at least half full. Good for a start.

She grabbed a spoon from the drawer and sat down at the table across from Benjamin.

"I have the feeling that Nina was the person you were asking all those hypothetical questions about earlier," Benjamin said as Zoey took her first bite.

"I don't think you'd believe me if I denied it," Zoey said.

"No. She's obviously in trouble. Enough trouble to bring

her here in the middle of the night. And enough trouble to shake you up badly enough to say 'there are some real creeps in the world.' A very un-Zoey-like thing to say."

"Look, I don't think you want to get involved, Benjamin. It's not your problem. She's *my* best friend."

To Zoey's surprise, Benjamin looked angry. "She's my friend, too," he said. "I care what happens to Nina."

Zoey took another bite, but the ice cream seemed to have lost any flavor. She stared blankly at the toaster for a few minutes, going over all that Nina had told her. Then she snapped back, refocusing on her brother. Nina was carrying a huge load of fear and shame. Even secondhand, even just the part she had shared with Zoey felt crushing.

The decision to tell Benjamin happened before she was consciously aware of it. She simply began talking. "She has an aunt and uncle coming for a visit. They're arriving tomorrow, and this is the aunt and uncle she stayed with right after her mom died."

Now Zoey hesitated. Nina had sworn her to secrecy. Zoey had given her word. If Nina knew she was telling Benjamin, she would probably be humiliated beyond belief. But this had become Zoey's problem now as well as Nina's. It was too big for Zoey to be sure that her word to Nina was the most important thing.

Benjamin was waiting patiently, unmoving. It brought a smile to Zoey's face. So typically Benjamin. The smile evaporated as she made the final decision. "Her uncle molested her. Repeatedly."

Benjamin said nothing, just hung his head.

"I think she's afraid he'll try it again."

He remained silent, shaking his head almost imperceptibly. When he spoke, it was only to mutter a few unusual obscenities. Then he seemed to refocus on the problem at hand. "She's older now—she could tell her father."

"I think it's more complicated than that," Zoey said. "The bad thing is that she feels like she's to blame as much as he is."

"How the hell would *she* be to blame? She was an eleven-year-old girl. He was an adult."

"It's how she feels," Zoey said helplessly.

"It may be, but she has to realize that's just not the way it is. She was eleven, for God's sake. You can't vote when you're eleven, you can't drink, you can't drive. You can't play the lottery or go on half the rides at Disney World. She was just a kid. When you're eleven, your only responsibilities are doing your homework and feeding your dog. You don't decide whether or not to have sex."

"Maybe you should tell Nina that," Zoey said.

"Someone should," Benjamin said heatedly. "All the right is

on Nina's side. All the wrong is on her creep of an uncle's side. All of it. A hundred percent. Goddamnit, she ought to put that son of a bitch in jail."

"Could she?" Zoey asked. It hadn't occurred to her that would be an option.

"I don't know," Benjamin admitted. "I guess it depends on whether too much time has passed, things like that. I don't know. I don't know if that's what she'd want to do. But it is what should be done. He shouldn't get away with it."

"I don't think she wants to tell anyone."

Benjamin nodded. "Yeah, I can imagine."

"She's worried what people would think."

Benjamin smiled crookedly. "I didn't think Nina ever worried about what people would think of her."

"This is pretty major. She doesn't want people staring at her and whispering and saying there goes the girl who was molested by her uncle. Nina doesn't mind people thinking she's strange; she just doesn't want them feeling sorry for her."

"Tell me about it," Benjamin said dryly.

"I don't know what I should do," Zoey confessed. "I think someone needs to tell Mr. Geiger about this. And I think Nina should talk to a shrink or a counselor or someone who knows about this kind of stuff."

"And you're wondering if you should be the one who tells?"

"I don't know. What if Nina won't?"

"It would be better if she told," Benjamin said. "I mean, better for her, rather than you or me or someone else doing it. If she decides to tell, it will be like she decided to fight back, you know? Does this guy have kids?"

"No." Zoey shook her head. The same thought had occurred to her. "But there are always other ways for this kind of person."

"Maybe we should ask Mom and Dad," Benjamin suggested.

"I can't do that. I promised Nina. She said she had to have at least one person in the world she could trust."

Benjamin nodded in reluctant agreement. "Well, she has two."

Zoey got up and put the lid back on the half-melted ice cream. "I still don't know what to do."

"Sorry," Benjamin said dispiritedly. "You know, I used to get so pissed at people for feeling sorry for me, for saying poor Benjamin. But now all I can keep thinking is poor Nina."

Zoey smiled sadly at her brother, sitting there with his blank brown eyes filled with tears, staring into the fluorescent glare. "No one says poor Benjamin anymore."

A flicker of a smile. "Damn right," he said.

"I better go back up."

"Yeah. Good luck."

She began to leave but stopped, with her hand on the light switch. "Benjamin?"

"What?"

"I'm very glad I have you as my big brother."

"Don't go all sentimental on me, Zoey."

"Sorry," she said. "Must be the lack of sleep."

"Yeah. Good night. And . . . and I love you, too, Zo."

Claire

I don't know why Nina and I ended up having the kind of relationship we do. You see these families—sisters, brothers, brother-sister combinations of various types—and some are like the Brady Bunch or the Partridge Family, all gooey and close-knit. Others are more your basic Cain and Abel thing.

I guess Nina and I are somewhere in between. We won't be forming a bond and going on the road, but at the same time we aren't likely to kill each other.

I haven't really ever thought about it that much, but on those occasions when I do, I wonder if it all goes back to our mom having died. It seems like it was around then that we started sniping at each other a little more.

More likely, though, we are the people we are, and that's all there is to it. Nina is more involved with other people than I am. She's more provocative in some ways. Obviously she's more popular than I'll ever be, at least with other girls. And God knows she's funnier.

When I look at the future, I see Nina maybe doing comedy, blowing away the audience on Letterman. Or else writing funny plays in New York, still with an unlit cigarette hanging out of her mouth. Maybe by then she'll have graduated to cigars.

I see myself alone, studying climatological data in some lonely station in Antarctica, learning to create the computer model that will finally be able to predict weather all over the planet. That would make me happy.

We're different people. I know that doesn't necessarily mean we have to be ragging on each other constantly. But that's the way it's worked out. And it's too late now for either of us to change, or to want to change.

SIXTEEN

NINA WOKE TO A STIFF neck and cold toes. It took a moment or two for her to understand where she was, or to remember why Zoey was sleeping beside her. Clear, morning sunlight spilled around the edges of the curtains on Zoey's side window, threatening to banish the last of night from the room.

She sat up on her elbow and searched for Zoey's clock. Nine fifty. Late for Zoey to be asleep, early for Nina's normal weekend schedule. Poor Zoey. It must not have been a very good night's sleep for her.

Nina lay back down on the pillow. She didn't want to get up. If she got up, she would have to leave, and it was so safe here, so far from everything that awaited her at home. Maybe that was the answer. Maybe she could just stay here until her uncle was gone. Zoey would let her. Zoey was her friend, thank God . . . if there was a God. Zoey had believed her because that's what friends, really close friends, were required to do.

But her uncle's prediction still held true for everyone else.

Claire would never believe her. Claire would accuse her of having made it all up to get attention. And her father . . . like he would tell his sister her husband was a pervert? Not likely.

She heard the pattern of Zoey's breathing change. She was awake.

"Morning," Nina said.

"Mmm. Yeah," Zoey mumbled. She shook her head to clear away the sleep and sat up. "How are you doing?"

"My neck is stuck and my leg is asleep," Nina said. "Can't you get a bigger bed?"

"Sorry, I wasn't expecting guests."

"And your pillows are too soft."

"Oh, it's late," Zoey said, peering at her clock.

"I slept like a rock," Nina confessed.

"Good."

"Yeah. Thanks," Nina said a little sheepishly. "I just hope this never gets out around school. They'd all be *sure* I was gay."

"Look at it as a slumber party," Zoey said. "That's Lucas's line. He keeps saying, 'It wouldn't be like we were sleeping together, Zoey, it would just be a slumber party.' "

Nina nodded, only half listening. "I guess I should get going."

"You don't have to go, Nina," Zoey said. "There's no reason why you can't stay. We'll buy you a toothbrush. You can borrow my clothes."

Nina nearly choked up. She'd been certain Zoey would make the offer. "That's sweet of you, Zo . . ."

"You could read to Benjamin all day long," Zoey proposed, "you know, to earn your rent."

Nina smiled ruefully. "Just what Benjamin would like, another girl around the house using up the hot water and getting in the way."

"He'd like it if you stayed," Zoey said, sounding a little uncomfortable. "Look, I have to tell you something that might make you mad."

"Nothing you could say would make me mad. I owe you big time."

"I, uh, couldn't get back to sleep last night, and when I went downstairs to get some munchies, Benjamin was up. He'd heard you come in."

"Oh, God, you didn't tell him, did you? Oh, God."

"Look, Benjamin is—"

"Oh, you did. You told him." Nina leaned over and held her head in both hands. She wanted to crawl under the bed and disappear. She would never be able to face him again. "He'll think I'm nuts," she moaned. "He's going to think I'm so disgusting now."

Zoey put her hand on Nina's shoulder. "He's not going to think any of that, Nina—you're wrong."

"How could he not?" Nina asked desperately. "I go around saying my uncle and I did all those things together. Oh, God." She gasped for air.

"You didn't do all those things *together*," Zoey said sharply. "He did them to you. *To* you. That's what Benjamin said. He said you were just a kid. You probably couldn't even ride half the rides at Disney World."

"What?" Nina demanded, unable to make sense of what Zoey was saying.

"Look, you were a little kid. You didn't *decide* anything. But you know what? Even if you *had*, Nina. Even if it had all been your idea, and you'd wanted to do it, that still wouldn't change the fact that he was an adult and it was his responsibility."

"I didn't want to," Nina said, blazing suddenly.

"I know you didn't," Zoey said.

"I didn't, but he made me."

"You couldn't stop him. He was older and bigger and stronger. There was nothing you could have done."

Nina hesitated. Nothing she could have done? Of course she could have done . . . something. Something. She could have said no.

But she had said no. Hundreds of times. And she'd cried, and begged.

"There was nothing you could have done, Nina," Zoey

174

repeated. "None of it was your fault."

Nina tried to believe it, but somewhere deep in her mind a voice still said, No, Nina, it *was* your fault. Of course it was your fault. How could it not be? You could have done . . . something.

Yet now there was this new idea, just floating along on the edge of her mind, insubstantial still. Maybe it wasn't her fault. Maybe she couldn't have done anything.

Uncle Mark had said it was her fault. And he'd said that no one would ever believe her.

Only now, Zoey believed her. And so did Benjamin.

"My dad is having a barbecue for them," Nina said. "He said I should invite whoever I wanted."

"You know I'll come if you want," Zoey said. "So will Benjamin."

"If you guys were there, I wouldn't be so . . ." Nina's words were choked off by a fresh wave of emotion.

"Sounds like fun," Zoey said, so gamely that Nina had to laugh through her tears.

"Oh, yeah. Loads of fun."

The island's only grocery store was small, indifferently stocked, and notoriously overpriced. But the alternative was to take a ferry ride to Weymouth, travel by car to the Shop and Save, travel back by car, park, carry a week's groceries from the parking garage onto the ferry, and ride the ferry home. People went through all that to stock up on Cheerios and canned goods and beer, but if you wanted something frozen, or anything in a hurry, the Chatham Island Market was the only choice.

Claire pushed a cart through the aisles, having already picked up the Sunday *New York Times* her father liked to read, a pound of butter for the corn on the cob, and the cider vinegar that was so important to her father's homemade barbecue sauce.

That, along with one or two other items, completed the official list as Janelle and her father had written it. Now she was looking for anything new or interesting, anything she might want for herself. After all, if she was going to be forced to run down to the grocery store first thing on a Sunday morning, she deserved some sort of reward.

Nina, apparently operating from some sixth sense, had managed to be gone when the chore came up. Very unlike her to be up and about so early on a weekend.

Claire headed toward the front of the store, resigning herself to the fact that nothing else really seemed worth buying. She stopped suddenly as she saw Jake come into the store, heading right to the register where his own family's Sunday *Boston Globe* was on reserve. He was dressed for church. Claire glanced at her watch. She didn't attend church herself, but she was pretty sure the service started in fifteen minutes, meaning Jake had plenty of time. She quickly dropped a big sack of charcoal into the cart and beelined for the register.

"Jake. Hi."

"Oh, hi," he said, seeming a little flustered.

She made a point of straining to lift the charcoal from the basket to the checkout counter. After a fractional hesitation, Jake grabbed the sack and hefted it for her.

"My dad's throwing a barbecue this afternoon," Claire said, pointing to the charcoal as evidence. "We have some relatives coming in. Forgot the charcoal, and now I have to drag that all the way home." She felt a little ridiculous, pulling the old helpless female routine, but then, Jake seemed to be causing her to do all sorts of dumb things she wouldn't normally do.

"Yeah, your dad should have come to get it."

Claire shrugged. "I don't think he thought about how heavy it is. Especially with the rest of this stuff."

Jake wrinkled his forehead in a pained expression. "If you're going straight home, I guess I could carry it for you. I mean, I've got ten minutes to spare before the service."

"That would be great," Claire said gratefully. Poor Jake, she reflected, trapped by his own politeness. Although, to be honest, he owed her.

She paid and took the bag containing the food and the newspaper while Jake lifted the charcoal onto his shoulder.

"You know, my dad wanted us to invite some more people to this thing," Claire said.

"Uh-huh."

"It's swordfish and steaks and corn on the cob," she said.

"Sounds good," he said noncommittally.

"I don't suppose you'd come," she half asked.

He shrugged. "I don't know."

"If you want to, I'd like you to. Just as a friend. I promise I won't go around telling people you're my boyfriend or anything if you don't want."

He shifted the bag to his other shoulder. "I don't know what to do," he admitted bleakly.

"About the barbecue?" she asked, deliberately obtuse.

"About you," he said bluntly.

"Oh."

"I think about you a lot."

"Good things?"

"Not always," he said harshly. Then in a softer tone, "Some-times."

"I'm glad. About the sometimes."

"You'll laugh, but I was actually going to ask my minister about it."

"About me?" Claire said, vaguely threatened by the notion

of being discussed with a minister. Was she a moral dilemma now? A sin?

Jake laughed shortly. "He's basically cool for an old guy. And I can't really talk to my dad or mom about things like this."

"You could talk to me," Claire offered.

"You're the problem."

"Oh. That's right. I forgot."

He relented a little. "You're not the *only* problem, all right? You're just one problem."

They had reached the front door of the house. Jake slung the sack down onto the porch steps. Claire brushed charcoal dust from his shoulders.

Both realized at the same moment that they were close, their faces only inches apart.

Claire stopped brushing. He was looking at her with eyes full of doubt and something else. She moved closer, ready if he wanted to make a move, but not wanting to repulse him by being too direct.

"I want to," he whispered.

"Then do," Claire said.

He shook his head. "I don't know. I don't know what's right."

"What's *right*?" she repeated wryly.

"I should hate you," he said.

"But you don't."

He looked down at the ground. "No." He turned and began to walk away, slumped as if he were still carrying the heavy sack.

"Come by this afternoon," she called after him. "It's just food. It's not a commitment."

He turned, walking slowly backward. "Steaks, you said?"

"New York strip."

"Let me think about it."

"I'll save you one. Medium rare?"

He started to answer, but at that moment the church's bells began to peal from the direction of the circle. He gave a wave and took off at a run.

SEVENTEEN

NINA PASSED THROUGH THE CROWD milling around outside the church on her way home from Zoey's. The church did double-duty for Catholics and Protestants, with the Catholics getting the use of the historic building from eight to ten and the Protestants from ten on.

Lucas was just on his way out, along with his mother. Jake and his family and Aisha and her family were heading in. Aisha gave Nina a wave and a helpless shrug as her little brother pushed her toward the door.

Nina walked on, feeling the state that comes after tired. She was moving automatically, like a machine. Her mind was clear, racing at a frantic pace, processing the same information over and over and getting nowhere. What should she do? The question came up again and again and led only back in a circle to itself once more.

She needed a week of sleep. She needed to be far away. She needed to scream at the top of her lungs and shatter anything she could lay her hands on.

Someone had dropped a sack of charcoal on the front steps, and for a moment Nina stared at it as if it might be an omen. But the charcoal held no magic answers.

She went up to her room and sat on her cold bed. It seemed like a lifetime since she had lain in it before running in near panic to Zoey.

She looked at the clock. Ten minutes after ten. The next ferry had already left Weymouth and would be here in fifteen minutes. Fifteen minutes. If her uncle was on that ferry, he would reach the island in fifteen minutes. Two more to disembark. Five more to walk up to the house.

Or would her father go down and meet them?

Nina jumped up and went back out into the hall. "Claire. Are you up there?" she yelled up the stairs.

"Yes. Where have you been? I got stuck going to the store and it was your turn."

"Where's Dad?"

"Down at the ferry meeting Aunt E."

Nina went back into her room. He would be here in a very few minutes. And there was no way she could avoid seeing him again. Saying hello. Even a hug.

She sat down on her bed. If before her mind had been in hyperdrive, it now seemed paralyzed. It was as if she were caught moving in slow motion while the minutes flew past. Now the ferry would be docking, on time as always. Now they would be getting off, calling out to Nina's father. Big hugs for his sister, a handshake for Uncle Mark. How was your trip and oh, it's so beautiful here.

They weren't going to have to drag her from her room unwillingly. She wasn't going to take this like a little kid afraid of the first day of school.

She got up and headed down the stairs, feeling with each step like she was on her way to witness a tragedy she had no power to stop.

She was sitting in the living room when she heard laughing voices coming across the front yard. Closer, closer. The door opened. Her aunt was the first in, then her father, dropping luggage. Uncle Mark stepped in last.

He was shorter than her father, with a doughy complexion and slumping shoulders. But he had beautiful blue eyes that seemed out of place in a man otherwise so ordinary looking.

"Well, here's Nina now," her father announced as if they'd just been discussing her.

Aunt Elizabeth came forward and gave her a hug, making all the usual noises about how she'd grown, how she remembered Nina as a little girl and here she was practically a woman.

Nina felt her aunt release her. She stood there between living room and foyer, not feeling the floor under her feet, aware only of her heart pounding at twice its normal speed.

"Nina probably doesn't even remember me, it's been so long," her uncle said.

No hint of guilt in his voice. No shadow of doubt on his face.

She braced herself for him to touch her, but after advancing a few steps, he withdrew, dropping his arms to his sides. Now he searched her face with quick, darting eyes.

Fear!

In a flash of insight, Nina saw it revealed before he tucked it safely away.

He was afraid.

"We sure enjoyed having her stay with us, even though the circumstances were so unfortunate," her uncle said to her father.

"I was always grateful you were able to do it," her father said. Then he clapped his hands. "Nina, go tell Claire they're here. Or would you two like to go freshen up?"

"No, no," Aunt Elizabeth said. "We want to see you and the girls."

"I'll get Claire," Nina said. She climbed the stairs, still feeling a jumble of emotions. Part of her wondered if it had all been some hallucination on her part. How could her uncle stand there so calmly, knowing what he had done? Had that really been fear she'd seen in his innocent blue eyes? Or had he just picked up on her own tension?

She paused at the top landing. She had weathered the first encounter. But she was no nearer knowing what, if anything, she should do.

It was almost impossible to look at that dull, bland little man and see him as the man who had abused her so long ago. He had been a figure of nightmares for so long. Was this really the same person?

"So, how are your grades, Claire? This is your last year of high school, isn't it?"

Claire nodded. "My grades are fine. With any luck at all I'll be accepted to MIT next year."

Claire looked past her aunt's head and glared at Nina on the far side of the backyard. Nina was sitting by herself on one of the patio chairs, sipping a soda and by pointing her chair away from the others making it clear that she was not going to be involved in any way.

Typical Nina, Claire thought angrily. She had two modes for this kind of social occasion. She was either off in her own world or else driving everyone nuts with deliberately idiotic discussions. Frankly, right now Claire could have used the second Nina. Her aunt had been pestering her for the better part of an hour about guys, about school, about the island, about her plans, then back to guys. Meanwhile Uncle Mark seemed to have permanently attached himself to Mr. Geiger, nursing a bottle of beer and commenting on her father's handling of the grill.

"A climatologist? You mean like a weatherman on TV?"

"No, it's a little more involved than that," Claire said patiently.

Janelle bustled in and out of the house, screen door slamming, shuttling casserole dishes and napkins and pitchers of lemonade out to the table that had been set up in the middle of the yard. It was covered in a blue plaid tablecloth and set with plastic forks so there would be less cleanup.

Three of her father's employees from work, a man and two women, sat awkwardly by themselves, looking self-conscious about being at the boss's house. The neighbors, the Lafollettes, were due to come over any moment.

"Antarctica? Can't you study the weather somewhere nicer?"

"That's sort of the point. You study weather where there's lots of weather to study."

Suddenly Claire saw Nina jump up out of her chair. She trotted over to meet Zoey, who was coming around the side of the house, leading Benjamin.

Claire's stomach lurched. Oh, great. Perfect Nina touch,

inviting the guy Claire had just recently broken up with. Wonderful. Now, if Jake showed up, as she hoped he would, the scene would be complete—the guy she had dumped but who still, probably, liked her, and the guy who had dumped her, who she definitely still liked.

Where was Lucas? He would make the crowning touch.

"MIT? Isn't that a boys'—"

"Excuse me, Aunt Elizabeth," Claire said, interrupting the latest question. "I have to go and play hostess for a moment."

Claire got up, feeling no relief as she traded one awkward situation for another. "Hi, Zoey, Benjamin."

"Claire," Benjamin said with his usual smug mockery, "I'll bet you're thrilled to see me here."

"Daddy will be glad," Claire said. "You know you're his favorite choice for son-in-law. Or son, for that matter."

Claire grabbed her sister's arm and pulled Nina aside. "Nice move. Do you realize I've invited Jake?" she demanded in a whisper. "Me and Benjamin and Jake and Zoey?"

"Whatever," Nina said distractedly.

Claire sighed. "Do you always have to be a pain in the ass, Nina?"

Nina stared at her disconcertingly. Her eyes darted toward where their father and Uncle Mark were standing over the coals. Nina looked as if she were going to say something, but instead she just walked away quite suddenly, as if Claire didn't matter.

Benjamin was on Zoey's arm, since he wasn't familiar with the backyard. Aunt Elizabeth was introducing herself to them, peering closely at Benjamin's shades.

Benjamin was pulling one of his patented routines, Claire observed, trying unsuccessfully to keep herself from smiling. He was standing directly in front of her aunt, reaching to shake hands but deliberately aiming his hand far off to the side. When Aunt Elizabeth sidestepped to grab it he instantly turned in the other direction, forcing her to jump back.

"Are you a friend of Claire's, or of Nina's?" Aunt Elizabeth asked him, still staring at his sunglasses like she was trying to look around them.

"I'm the family chauffeur," Benjamin said with a perfectly straight face.

"Oh, I . . . Oh."

Benjamin smiled.

"Oh, it's *a joke*," Aunt Elizabeth said, looking relieved. "I get it."

The back door of the house swung open and slammed back on its springs as Janelle reappeared, carrying a covered tray of rolls. Immediately behind her came Jake, carrying two flats of beer.

Claire smiled and went over to intercept him. "You came,"

she said with quiet satisfaction.

He shrugged with the heavy burden. "My dad said if I was coming, I should contribute some beer. He gave me a couple cases."

"You didn't have to," Claire said.

"Where should I put it?" Jake asked, still refusing to smile or give any sign that he was anything more than a casual guest.

"There's a big chest full of ice over there." She pointed.

"I'll go ice them down, then," Jake said.

He shifted his arms beneath his burden and Claire noticed something. The two cardboard flats held only six six-packs, not the eight that would make two cases.

Probably Jake had just misspoken. Probably it never had been two cases. Either that, or Jake had stashed two six-packs away for himself. In which case that might have been the only reason he'd come at all.

EIGHTEEN

A PLATTER OF CORN, PASSING down the table, chased by a dish of soft butter. A piece of swordfish on her plate, smelling of hickory smoke. Zoey's voice, quietly telling Benjamin the layout of his plate—steak, already cut, at six o'clock, beans at two o'clock, lemonade just up from his right hand. One of the people from her father's office trying to make conversation with Jake on the subject of the football team. A fork dropping onto the grass and old Mr. Lafollette bending over to pick it up because his wife's arthritis is too bad. A sudden burst of brittle laughter from Aunt Elizabeth.

Nina stares down at her plate, filled with food. She is starving and nauseous at the same time. She picks at the fish and takes a bite, chewing it as if it is rubber.

Conversation rises and falls around her, swelling to near enthusiasm, then ebbing, giving way to slurping and chewing sounds before picking up again.

She steals glances from under a lowered brow. Jake, acting

as though no one will notice his Styrofoam cup is filled with beer and not lemonade. The three people from her father's job, falling into what is probably a very familiar ritual of talking among themselves about work, no longer so put off that the boss is sitting nearby. Claire, looking up at the sky as if she is praying for rain. She probably is. Her father, playing the role of genial host, trying to involve as many people as possible in the conversation, modestly accepting compliments for his skill with the coals.

Zoey is looking thoughtful, or perhaps just tired. And she is stealing looks down the table at Uncle Mark. Probably wondering whether this bland, ordinary-looking, middle-aged man in a short-sleeved plaid cotton shirt and silver-rimmed glasses could possibly be the man Nina had described. It's almost possible to see the doubt on Zoey's face, to read the thoughts—is Nina making it all up? Is it all some product of her overactive imagination? After all, this man looks so normal, and everyone knows Nina is not quite . . . quite.

Zoey looks at her. For a moment their eyes meet, and Nina is sure she reads guilt there. Guilt, because in her heart Zoey has begun to doubt.

Nina looks back down at her plate and drags her fork through the rapidly cooling beans. It's one thing to believe Nina's story in the abstract. It's another thing entirely to be sitting at the table with the man Nina has described as a child molester, a man who now seems so boringly ordinary.

She can't blame Zoey. She can't. After all, if the situation were reversed and it was Zoey pointing the finger at a man who looked like the soul of innocence, would Nina believe unquestioningly?

His voice rises against a general lull. Even the voice is unthreatening. Not exactly Freddy Kreuger. Just a man a little intimidated by his brother-in-law's home, making self-deprecating references to the way the noise of the jets from the airport makes it hard for him to cook out in his own, much smaller backyard.

"It is *so* quiet here," Aunt Elizabeth says admiringly. "You must sleep so well at night, Burke."

"Not everyone can live on an island," Uncle Mark says, grinning to show he isn't envious. "Riding that ferry back and forth every day must be a pain in the ass. Living your life according to a schedule."

"It can be inconvenient," Mr. Geiger allows.

Of course, Nina's father rarely takes the ferry. He can afford to use the water taxi, but that would seem like boasting.

"Although with bankers' hours . . ." Uncle Mark says. "I mean, what is it, Burke, about a five-hour workday?" He laughs to show he's just kidding. Just ribbing his brother-in-law.

Nina's father turns it into a bigger joke. "Hell, Mark, I don't even work that much. I just leave the tellers to run the place. Isn't that right, Ellen?" he calls down the table to his head teller.

A plate of rolls appears, and Nina must pass it on. When she listens again, her uncle is saying in a low voice that the young blind boy certainly does handle himself well. "You almost wouldn't guess, the way he can clean his plate," Mark says.

Nina feels a stiffening in her muscles. She is outraged. She wants to yell, *Don't you dare condescend to Benjamin! He's ten times the human being you'll ever be.*

But Benjamin, as usual, has a better way. Without acknowledging he has heard anything, he lifts his next forkful of fish and deliberately sticks it in his chin. He frowns and tries again, sticking it in his forehead.

Zoey, Claire, and Jake all stifle the urge to laugh, refusing to look at each other for fear they will lose control. Even Nina smiles at the memory they all share—the day Benjamin spent ten full minutes in the lunchroom trying to eat a spoonful of Jell-O. At first kids had thought it was for real. Then, one by one, they had caught on. People had laughed till they cried and fell out of their chairs.

Now her uncle Mark is staring. He has caught on immediately to Benjamin's little game and his cheeks are flushed with anger. He's being made fun of by a blind kid.

There! There, if Zoey would only look, she would see the true face of the man who hides behind pretty blue eyes and smudged glasses. Oh, he doesn't like being made fun of. No. Uncle Mark has no sense of humor about himself.

Benjamin takes a second bite, pops it effortlessly into his mouth. Uncle Mark looks away, smoothing over his fury, releasing it in another direction, telling Aunt Elizabeth in too loud a voice that she has a piece of food caught in her teeth.

Nina nods, feeling better. No need to be so afraid of a man who can be humiliated by Benjamin. Benjamin isn't afraid. She looks at Benjamin, inscrutable behind his shades. He's not a big, powerful guy like Jake. He's vulnerable to any sighted person who wants to walk up and take a punch at him. He should be afraid, always. Only he isn't.

She can survive this, she decides. She will keep her distance during the day and keep her door locked at night. In a few days it will be over and the monster will be gone again. He won't visit again soon, and in a couple of years she'll be gone from this house, at college, at work, in her own life where she will decide who has access. Then she will be done with him forever.

The conversation drops into another lull, this time deeper, more expectant. Nina listens. Her aunt is talking in a full, fruity voice, loaded with happy anticipation.

". . . never had children. It wasn't that we didn't want to. It was *me*," she adds quickly at a look from her husband. "I mean, *I* wasn't able."

"I was worried it might be me," Mark interjects, just in case anyone has missed the point, "but we got tested and it turned out I was fine."

"Anyway, we think now is the time to think about taking the big step. And we've been talking to an adoption agency . . ."

Nina feels her heart trip.

". . . and they have a little girl for us. She's not quite two years . . ."

Congratulations. Excellent news. This deserves a toast.

Nina sees Zoey, looking uncertain, worried. She sees Benjamin's lips pressed into a thin line. Nina feels dizzy, floating. She feels as if she might be fainting. Only she is still hearing the words. Her uncle's words now.

"I've always wanted a little girl of my own, ever since we had Nina stay with us all those years ago."

Nina's hand goes to her throat, her heart is banging in her chest, her breath coming in gasps.

No! No, no, no, no. He can't. He cant. He won't.

Before she realizes what she's doing, Nina stands up.

"Oh, my God," Zoey whispered under her breath.

Nina began to speak, but it was a low, hoarse whisper,

indistinguishable above the babble of happy voices. She cleared her throat. Claire had stopped to look at her disapprovingly, obviously expecting some joke.

"I don't think you're going to adopt anyone," Nina said softly, tears coursing down her cheeks.

Several of the people closest to her fell silent, looking at her uncertainly. The silence spread down the table.

"Did you have something to say, Nina?" her father asked in a patient tone.

". . . yes."

In a flash Zoey saw it—the blood drained from Mark's face. His eyes went wide, then narrowed. He stared daggers at Nina.

Zoey could see Nina falter, but then she recovered herself. "I said, I don't think you're going to adopt anyone. Ever."

Her father winced good-naturedly. "Nina, I don't think this is the time for playing games. If you want to say congratulations . . ."

"I don't think they let child molesters adopt," Nina said. "At least, not in most states," she added, stiffly ironic.

"Nina, that's enough," her father rapped angrily.

"He likes little girls," Nina said through gritted teeth.

"Goddamnit, Nina that's more than enough!" her father shouted, his face darkening. "What is the matter with you?"

Mark was frozen in place, his face an unreadable, rigid mask.

"Nina, I don't think this is going to get a big laugh," Claire said.

Nina wavered. Zoey could see her flinch before her father's anger and her sister's scorn. Zoey wanted to say something, come to her defense, but what could she say? All she knew was what Nina had told her.

"Daddy," Nina said in a different, pleading voice. "It's true. It's true. When I stayed with them . . . he . . ." She looked wildly around the table. "He . . . did things to me. At night he would come into my room and—" She was sobbing now.

"How long do I have to sit here and listen to this, Burke?" Mark snapped, suddenly alive again as he saw Nina weaken. "If you can't control your children—"

"Nina, leave this table at once," Mr. Geiger said in a menacing growl. "This is too much, even for you."

"But I'm telling the truth," Nina said in a whisper.

"No," her uncle said in a flat, utterly convincing voice. "You are not telling the truth."

For an eternity, thirteen people seemed to sit like statues, poised on the edge but unable to move one way or the other.

Then there was a new voice.

"Nina doesn't lie," Claire said.

"She *is* lying," Mark said. "Or else she thinks this is funny."

Claire shook her head. She stared coldly at her uncle. "No. I know Nina. This isn't a joke."

Mr. Geiger hesitated now, looking with new suspicion at his brother-in-law.

"Surely, Burke . . ." Aunt Elizabeth began.

Claire looked directly at her father. "I believe Nina."

Suddenly Zoey was speaking. "She told me a couple of days ago, Mr. Geiger. She spent last night at my house because she was afraid to face him. I believe her, too."

"This is absurd and offensive," Mark said. "I've always known you didn't like me much, Burke, but I didn't think you'd let this sort of thing go on. I've been slandered in front of all these people. If this isn't stopped instantly, well, brother-in-law or not, I'll sue your butt."

"Mark . . . Burke . . ." Elizabeth pleaded.

"Shut up, Elizabeth," Mark snapped.

"Mr. G.," Benjamin said, "you have a choice here. You believe him, or you believe your daughter."

"Burke, you know better," Elizabeth reasoned. "Do you think for one moment I would allow something like that to go on in my house? Do you?"

Mr. Geiger smiled sadly. He took his sister's hand gently. "Yes, sweetie. I'm afraid you would." He didn't look at Mark. "I can have you charged here in Maine, Mark, or you can catch the next ferry off the island and I'll have you charged back in Minnesota. Your choice. The next ferry leaves in thirty minutes."

Mr. Geiger stood up, walked around the table, and put his arms around his younger daughter.

NINETEEN

NINA KNOCKED AT THE DOOR to Claire's room. When there was no answer, she opened the door cautiously and went inside. "Claire? You in here?"

No answer, but when Nina looked up, she could see that the square hatchway that opened onto the widow's walk was open. She went over to the ladder and looked up at the patch of dark, star-strewn sky. "Claire?"

Claire's face appeared in the square, her long dark hair hanging down. "Oh, hi."

"Can I come up?" Nina asked.

"I can come down if you'd like," Claire said.

"No." Nina climbed the ladder till her head poked up through the hatchway into the cool night air. She leaned back against the opening, feet propped on a ladder rung. She had never gone out onto the widow's walk. The height made her nervous, and anyway, it was Claire's private turf. "It got colder."

"Yeah, there's a cold front moving in," Claire said, standing tall and looking off toward the mainland. "It's moving pretty fast, so we might get some nice storms. See, a cold front moves like a wedge beneath . . ." She stopped herself. "Sorry. I don't guess you want a lecture on weather tonight."

Nina shrugged. "I know you like a good storm."

"These probably won't last very long. Short but violent, if we get lucky." Claire sat down by the edge of the hatch. "You okay?"

"I had a talk with Dad."

Claire waited patiently for her to go on.

"Lots of apologies and remorse and all," Nina said.

"Yeah, well, I owe you some of those myself," Claire said, looking away.

"No, you don't."

"I should have . . . I don't know, I should have known, somehow."

"I didn't tell you," Nina said. "I didn't tell anyone."

Claire bit her lip. "I never exactly made it easy for you to talk to me."

Nina smiled. "Claire, it's not easy for anyone to talk to you. You're kind of a difficult person. Unlike me, Ms. Normal."

A fresher breeze lifted Claire's hair and rustled the top branches of the trees. Overhead the stars were obliterated by an advancing wave of cloud. "Definite storm," Claire said contentedly. "It'll be along soon now. I have to come down and get my poncho."

Nina descended the ladder, with Claire right behind her. Claire grabbed the yellow rubber poncho from the hook on the back of her closet door and slipped it on.

"You look like the aftermath of a terrible accident involving a school bus," Nina commented.

Claire went toward the ladder, then stopped and turned back. "Look, Nina. I know we haven't ever been—"

"The Bobbsey twins?" Nina supplied.

"But you know, I am your sister. You could always tell me anything. I wouldn't laugh at you or give you a hard time."

Nina grinned. "Sure you would."

Claire made her rare, wintry smile. "Okay, but only at first."

Nina looked at her sister, lush dark hair under a crumpled plastic hat and draped over the shoulders of a bright yellow slicker. She was preparing to go up and sit in the middle of a thunderstorm. *And you're supposed to be the* normal *Geiger sister*, Nina thought.

A flash of lightning lit up the square in the ceiling. "You don't want to miss your storm," Nina said.

"It will be over soon, you know, if you want to talk or anything."

"I guess I'm going to start seeing your old shrink," Nina said. "She did such a fine job of turning you into a model citizen."

"Probably a good idea," Claire allowed. "Make up some good dreams for her. She loves a good, symbolic dream."

"Yeah, I can manage that," Nina said dryly. "Look, um . . . thanks, all right?"

"For what?"

"Things were on edge there, this afternoon. You backed me up."

Claire made a no-big-deal face. "I just said what I know. I just said you don't lie, not about the important things. Fortunately, no one asked me what I thought about the way you dress, or act, or your idiotic habit of sucking on unlit cigarettes."

"Idiotic," Nina echoed. "From the girl who's going to go sit in the rain." Nina hesitated, feeling an unfamiliar urge. "Jeez, I hate to do this. It's such a cliché." She held out her arms.

"Well, if we have to." Claire put her arms around Nina, and they hugged each other for a long time.

"When do we stop?" Nina asked.

"It's up to you," Claire said. "You're the one who started this."

"I'm thinking this is plenty long."

"On the count of three," Claire said.

"Three," Nina said.

They stepped back from each other, both looking awkward and embarrassed. Lightning flashed again, and Nina could see Claire counting off the distance, "One one thousand, two one thousand, three one thousand—"

The thunderclap rattled the windows.

"Don't get hit by lightning," Nina said.

"I've taken the appropriate safety measures."

"Yeah, you're a real model of common sense," Nina said sarcastically. "I hope I can grow up to be just like you."

"I'm still betting you never grow up," Claire grumbled as she climbed the ladder.

Nina

Over time, I've added a new dream. Number four. It incorporates many of the same images from the other dreams. In it I'm still a little girl wearing a dress with a ridiculously large bow on the front. And I'm still feeling myself drawn across an open floor toward a man with burning, terrible eyes.

And in the dream I'm still afraid. I don't know when that will go away. I know it will someday, but I don't know when.

Only now there's something new. I feel someone else in the dream with me. And I know, as you sometimes just know things in dreams, that this other person is on my side.

When I wake up, I wonder who this other person is. Zoey? Benjamin? Then I realize it's both of them, somehow. Them, and a little of my father, and a lot of my big sister, Claire.

They can't protect me from the man with burning eyes, or from the fear, but because they are there I no longer feel the shame.

TWENTY

"HOW CAN YOU BLAME ME?" Lucas demanded for the hundredth time. "I did my best to *lose*. I called everyone I know. I called people I didn't know. No one could have tried harder to lose than I did."

He was trailing just a few steps behind Zoey, who was marching down the street from school to the homeward-bound ferry Monday afternoon. Nina marched beside Zoey and Aisha in solidarity, although frankly, Nina could see Lucas's point. It wasn't really his fault he had been voted homecoming king. It was funny, but it wasn't his fault.

"If I could find a way to quit without offending everyone in the entire student body, I would," he said.

"You and Louise Kronenberger." Zoey snarled the name. "You and dial-a-slut."

"It's not my fault I won, and it's not my fault you came in . . . that you didn't win."

"Third," Zoey said. "I believe what you were going to say

is that I came in third. Not even runner-up, while you, Mr. I'm-Too-Good-for-All-This-Juvenile-Stuff, Mr. Tough Guy, Mr. Way Too Cool, you win. *You* win." She threw up her hands.

Nina looked over her shoulder at Lucas. "You thoughtless bastard," she said, mimicking Zoey's tone.

"It's just a dumb contest," Lucas said. "You yourself said you lost student council last year to Thor."

Zoey spun around. "I did not lose to Thor. I *beat* Thor, I'll have you know, by eight votes."

"Yeah, she lost to Captain America, you insensitive jerk," Aisha said, giving Nina a wink that avoided Zoey's notice.

"K-berger," Zoey said. "She's slept with every guy in school already."

"Well, she hasn't slept with me yet," Lucas grumbled. He winced, and sucked air in through his teeth. "I mean—"

"Too late, Lucas," Nina advised, shaking her head sadly. "Now you're really in trouble."

"Tell him he can do whatever he wants with the homecoming queen," Zoey said to Nina. "Tell him he's the homecoming king, after all."

"She says if you so much as look at Louise Kronenberger, you're a dead man," Nina interpreted.

"Tell him I'm sure I'll find *someone* who's willing to take me to the homecoming game and dance, since my alleged boyfriend will be busy," Zoey said.

"I'll take this one," Aisha said. "Lucas, Zoey plans to find a really great-looking, possibly rich, probably older date who will make you feel absolutely insecure, so that your whole night will be ruined thinking that she may be off making out with him."

Lucas reached out both hands and grabbed Nina and Aisha by their shoulders. He pulled both girls to a halt. Zoey went marching on obliviously. "You two stay out of this," Lucas said.

He broke into a trot and went after Zoey.

"He's so forceful and manly," Aisha said mockingly.

"Twenty seconds to major lip lock," Nina predicted.

"He's not that fast, and Zoey will mess with him for at least another minute," Aisha said.

Nina held her arm up so that both could see her watch.

"She's stopped," Nina said.

"Come on, Zoey," Aisha muttered.

"Boom," Nina announced. "Twenty-four seconds."

"Damn."

"By the way, Eesh, it *was* you who started the move to nominate Lucas, wasn't it?" Nina asked.

"Of course. Just don't ever tell Lucas or Zoey. I thought they'd both win."

"That was very romantic of you," Nina said as they resumed their walk. "I didn't think that was your style."

"It won't be again," Aisha said. "You see how well this worked out."

"Down, forty-two, hut, HUT."

The ball snapped and Jake sprang forward. One step, sharp left turn, see the ball in the quarterback's hand, grab, tuck, right turn, there's a hole!

He ran. Two yards, three yards, first down and nothing in his way—

Something like a truck hit him from out of nowhere and he went flying. He hit the grass on his back, gasping for air, but still holding the ball. He was staring up at the clear blue sky when the grinning face of his teammate appeared above him, hand outstretched.

"Didn't hurt you, did I?" Mark Simpson asked.

"Didn't hurt *me*," Jake said, grinning ruefully. "But if you hit the running back from Bath like that next week, we might just win our homecoming game for once."

Mark slapped him on the back. "Hey, your girl is over there again."

"What girl?" Jake asked.

"What girl?" Mark echoed, not convinced. "I think you know what girl. But look, man, if you don't want her . . ."

"She's too smart to go out with a lousy lineman," Jake said.

"That's it for today, ladies!" the coach yelled out. "Hit the showers. And, uh, McRoyan?"

"Yeah, coach?" Jake answered.

"Keep *both* your eyes open and you don't get hit so often."

Jake gave a genial raised finger to the rest of the team, which laughed appreciatively at his expense.

He began to trot back to the gym, but he lagged behind as if some invisible power were pulling him backward. He stopped and watched the rest of the team run on ahead. He turned. Claire was still there, sitting on the bleachers.

He looked at her, a lonely, exquisitely beautiful figure. She drew him like the gravity of a black hole might draw a passing comet. What did she want with him? Was it all just guilt, or was there really something more?

And did it matter? Despite all his vows to himself and to the memory of Wade, he had allowed her to help him when he needed help. He had gone to that disastrous barbecue the day before. And he wanted to go to her now.

They were looking at each other across a hundred feet of grass and too many memories. If he ran to her now, it would all be over. He would have betrayed Wade at last.

He began to walk, pulling off his helmet as he went. She came down from the bleachers, graceful, perfect. He took her in his arms. Her lips opened to him.

Wade had always said he was weak. Maybe Wade was right.

But he wasn't as weak as Claire thought he was.

He pushed her away. Not roughly, gently. Then he walked away and didn't look back.

Nina wandered around the familiar deck of the ferry, enjoying the cool crisp air of Claire's cold front. The storms had swept through and left the world washed and newly perfumed. A pair of harbor seals was playing in the wake of the boat, diving and reappearing, staring in bemusement at the humans who were smiling down at them.

She sat down next to Benjamin. He had earphones on, some faint music escaping in wisps. For a while she looked at him. He was just a few feet away but unaware of her presence. *Pretty much as usual*, she thought ruefully. *Pretty much the way it's always been.*

She reached over and raised one earphone. "What are you listening to?"

"Music," Benjamin said. He switched off the music on his cell phone and pulled down the earphones so that they hung around his neck.

"Don't ask me," Nina warned.

"Don't ask you what?"

"Don't ask me how I'm doing. Zoey's asked me how I'm

doing. Jake asked me. Aisha asked me. Lucas. Tad Crowley. Two teachers and a cafeteria worker. The entire world is very concerned with how I'm doing."

"News travels fast," Benjamin said. "They're just trying to be nice."

"I know. It's getting on my nerves big time. I feel like I'm walking around with a neon sign on my head that says *victim*. I'm not weird, strange, out-there Nina anymore. Now I'm poor Nina."

Benjamin nodded. "Tell me about it."

"I'm supposed to start seeing the all-purpose shrink. I hear you're not allowed to graduate anymore unless you've had at least one major psychological problem requiring professional help."

"It's very fashionable," Benjamin agreed. "Have you considered going on *Oprah* and turning your private life into entertainment for half the country?"

"I want to do *Dr. Phil*. It's much sleazier. But actually, you know, I happen to be acquainted with someone who is the world's best expert at getting people to treat you like you're normal."

Benjamin grinned. "It's all an act."

"It doesn't look like an act," Nina said sincerely. "I've never seen you feel sorry for yourself, never once."

"Well, you want to catch me sometime in the middle of the night. Around three or four when I wake up and I can't get back to sleep. I lie there just making lists of all the jobs I'll never be able to have, and all the great places and things I'll never see. I imagine the day when I'll be walking down the street and some guys will come up and realize how helpless I really am and beat the crap out of me."

"I didn't know you did that," Nina said sadly.

"I've had a pretty good share of bitterness. Try having a dream sometime where you can see, see everything perfectly and then . . . wake up, and see nothing." He forced a wry smile. "God, now I'm even depressing myself."

"Well, we're sitting in the Depressed Losers section," Nina said.

"Are we? Damn. I meant to sit in the Giddy Optimists section."

"How could you know? You're blind," Nina pointed out.

Benjamin nodded. "You'll do okay, Nina. People will get past it. Soon you'll just be weird, strange, out-there Nina again. In the meantime, screw it. You can't let the pity get to you."

"I know you never did," Nina said.

Benjamin sighed, then smiled. "I did my best to make pity impossible."

"The Jell-O," Nina said, chuckling. "Classic. You made me

blow milk through my nose. Or how about the girls' locker room when the cheerleaders were all in there?"

Benjamin laughed. "Yes, I'm the happy blind guy," he said with just a trace of irony. "I always figure, hell, if people are going to feel sorry for you, you have to surprise them. They think they know what you are and how you must feel. So I always try to keep them guessing. Do the thing no one expects you to do—like make fun of the way you can't eat very gracefully, or make people think you've somehow found a way to turn things to your advantage. There are guys who still think somehow, they don't know how, but *somehow* I got a look at all the cheerleaders naked."

"People admire you," Nina said sincerely. "No one's said poor Benjamin in a long time."

"I don't think anyone exactly admires me," Benjamin scoffed.

"I do," Nina said before she could think about it and stop herself. "I think you're an amazing person."

Benjamin actually seemed to be blushing. For once he was at a loss for words. "Oh, it's . . . don't . . ."

"And you know what else?" Nina said with sudden recklessness.

"What?"

Now a lump rose in her throat, threatening to choke her.

"Well . . ." she began lamely, swallowing hard. "I . . . I kind of . . . you know, I like you." She ended in a mutter and immediately buried her face in her hands. She peeked through her fingers. Benjamin's brow was wrinkled.

"Really?"

Nina took a deep breath. "Look, it's no big deal. It's just that I happen to think you're a cool guy and all."

"So, it's not like you're—"

"Yes!" Nina said, exploding. "Yes, that's exactly what it's like, Benjamin. You know, you're not just blind, you're dense. If you could see, you'd still be blind. I don't know why I do like you, because you are the biggest dolt on earth sometimes."

"So . . . So, you want to go out?"

"Duh."

"How about homecoming? I don't have a date."

"Okay, I'll go out with you, but it's not going to be like when we went to that concert in Portland and you acted like I was your chauffeur for the evening."

Benjamin smiled impishly. "No one would expect to see you and me at the dance together."

"I always figure, hell, if people are going to feel sorry for you, you have to surprise them," Nina quoted his words back to him.

"You know, dancing with a blind guy can be dangerous."

"That's okay," Nina said. "When you touch me, I'll probably get hysterical."

"Then it's a date." '

"Yes," Nina said. "It's a date."

TWENTY-ONE

AISHA SAID GOOD-BYE TO ZOEY and Lucas at Zoey's house and started the climb uphill to her home. She had just reached the first big turn when she changed her mind. If she went home right away, her mother would probably draft her into some cleanup or fix-up chore, which, on top of her homework, would pretty well kill the night.

And it was Monday. On Monday nights Passmores' closed now, which meant Christopher wouldn't be cooking.

She took the turn that led back to Leeward Drive. Maybe Christopher would be home, maybe not. But she'd rather spend time with him than go straight home. Their date Saturday had been the most romantic evening of her life. And it had been followed by Sunday, when they had gone swimming together down at the pond. Far from making her feel that she had seen enough of him for a while, their time together seemed to have had the opposite effect.

Too bad he wasn't still in school. Too bad he worked so

much. She had to get an hour of him here and a few hours there. "It's official, girl," she told herself. "You've got it big time."

Maybe she should tell Christopher how she felt now. She never had, and he'd never asked her. At least, neither of them had spoken the dreaded *L*-word.

It would probably scare him to death, Aisha thought. He'd probably think she was crazy.

But on the other hand, he might feel the same way himself.

Aisha savored that possibility, turning it over in her mind. If she said it first, maybe he would say it, too.

Although it would be better still if he said it first. That way she wouldn't face the possibility that he would just look at her with his mouth gaping and stammer.

She walked along the road, energized by the coolness of the late afternoon. The beach to her right was half-devoured by high tide, and the sun was already dropping precipitously toward the horizon. The days shortened early in Maine. Soon it would be dark as night by five.

She reached the ramshackle Victorian and, now familiar with the routine, went on inside and up the stairs, humming with anticipation.

Maybe she would tell him, and maybe she wouldn't. Maybe she would wait for him to be the first. It was a dumb game, but then, she had abandoned all pretense to being sensible where

Christopher was concerned.

She knocked on his door. There was a sound inside, and her heart leapt happily. He was home.

Aisha straightened her hair with a quick swipe of her hand just as the door opened.

He stood there in shorts and no shirt, and Aisha decided right then and there—she loved him. She should tell him and to hell with games.

"Hi," she said, smiling.

"Aisha," he said in a low whisper.

She stood on her toes to kiss him, but he pulled back. Over his shoulder Aisha saw a movement.

She searched his eyes, which had gone opaque and evasive.

"This isn't a good time," Christopher said. "I didn't know you were coming over."

Again the flash of movement, and now Aisha could see more clearly as the girl with impossibly long blond hair rolled off Christopher's bed and stood up.

BEN'S IN LOVE

PART TWO

Zoey Passmore

Yes, I can describe my boyfriend.

First of all, his name is Lucas Cabral. I guess he's a little taller than average, but not basketball-playing tall. Just tall enough that when we're standing up and he kisses me, I have to tilt my head back a little.

He has blond hair that tends to fall down over his eyes sometimes, which is too bad because he has these great eyes that make you get sort of wobbly when he looks at you. I mean, that's what happens to me, anyway. I don't suppose his eyes have much effect at all on some people. Other guys, for example.

His body? Well, he's thin, which does not mean he doesn't have muscles; he does. They're just not those bunched-up, bulky, weight-lifting muscles like my previous boyfriend, Jake, had.

He has long legs, so he probably looks great in shorts or a bathing suit. I'm guessing, though, because I've never actually seen him in either. He's your basic Levis kind of guy.

I have imagined him in something other than Levis, though, like . . . Never mind.

What else? Okay, he has nice shoulders. And very nice hands, very gentle. Also, not that I have a lot of guys to compare him with, but I think he has really, really great lips.

Really.

And that's all I can say. At this time.

Except one more thing: When he holds me in his arms or kisses me, I have this feeling that we're a perfect fit. Do you know what I mean? Like we were designed especially to go together. Now, that's really all I can say.

Aisha Gray

Nude Descending a Staircase

It's a famous abstract painting of a woman coming down the stairs, except the artist has painted it so that it's all about motion, not about one still picture.

That's Christopher Shupe. Not nude, obviously, but always in motion. Always on his way somewhere. Sometimes he's a sort of blur, appearing, disappearing, back and forth, hello, good-bye, gotta run.

As to his actual body, it's mostly legs. And when I say legs I mean all the way up to his lower back, if you see what I'm saying. Long, very muscular, very tight, on-the-move legs. If Bugs Bunny were African-American (and come to think of it, are you sure he's not?), he could play the role of Christopher in a movie.

Although Christopher is much more handsome than Bugs Bunny. In fact, the smallest touch from Christopher makes me start to rethink all the wise things my mother told me about not getting too involved with guys too soon.

And he kisses all the way down to your soul.

When he can stay in one place long enough.

Claire Geiger

I've had three major boyfriends in my life, so I do have some basis for comparison. First was Lucas. Yes, Zoey's Lucas. This was a long time ago, of course, but even then Lucas had this great sensual-yet-dangerous thing going. Picture Harry Styles, only nicer, and without the tattoos.

Then there was Benjamin. Benjamin isn't someone you can describe in terms of his body. Benjamin is all about intelligence and wit, although he's also major cute. It's just that you don't think of Benjamin as cute. He's too complicated to be cute.

My current boyfriend (he would not agree that's what he is, by the way) is Jake McRoyan. Yes, Zoey's former boyfriend. What can I say? As they say at Disneyland, it's a small world after all.

Jake is a person you can describe in physical terms. First of all, he's large. He's a football player and looks it. He's six two and very muscular. Not "where's-his-neck?" muscular, just very solid, very hard. Chiseled out of marble that's warm to the touch. Very fun to look at, very fun to be close to.

He has dark, somewhat wiry hair, full lips, and gentle gray eyes that give away the fact that under the intimidating outer armor there's a very sweet guy. Nowhere in his face—or in his heart—will you find guile, or malice, or selfishness. He's the prototype of the nice guy, the loyal, duty-bond guy.

Which is why he would deny that he's my boyfriend at all.

Nina Geiger

This question is a little premature, actually. There's a chance that Benjamin Passmore will eventually become my official boyfriend. Or I'll become his official girlfriend. Or perhaps a mutual, simultaneous agreement that we are each other's boyfriend and/or girlfriend. Maybe we can get the UN to negotiate the details.

Anyway, what's he look like? It's sort of an ironic question since Benjamin's the only guy around who doesn't care much about looks. Yours, mine, his own; he couldn't care less.

He sounds enlightened, you say? Yes, he is. Also blind. Hasn't seen a thing in like seven years. He still thinks I look like a little toothpick girl with braces and no boobs. When in fact I am often mistaken for leggy supermodel Karlie Kloss.

Right.

Okay. Benjamin. Hmm. In a way everything about him is medium. Medium height, medium weight, medium-length medium-brown hair. Only when you put it all together, and especially when you add in that voice, and that sense of humor, and that whole very cool I'm-in-control thing, he's not medium anything.

I've never really had a boyfriend, but if it works out with Benjamin, it will be like I started right at the top.

ONE

"THIS ISN'T WHAT YOU THINK," Christopher said.

"Not what I think. You mean that's not a very pretty girl sitting on the end of your bed?" Aisha Gray demanded. She was standing in the open doorway of his small rented room, trembling somewhere between anger and the hope that maybe, somehow, by some stretch of the imagination, it really *wasn't* what she thought. "Hello in there, by the way. My name's Aisha."

The girl inside waved back, looking embarrassed and uncomfortable. "Angela Schwegel. Uh, nice to meet you."

"She's . . . she's a friend, is all," Christopher said, pointing to the girl, his voice unusually shrill. "We were just talking."

Angela stood up, looking annoyed. She retrieved her purse and walked toward them.

Aisha waited rigidly, trying to suppress the sense of humiliation and the growing realization that the feelings already eating away at her insides were only going to get worse. She felt like she was in free fall, weightless, knowing she would inevitably hit bottom.

"Christopher, you said you didn't have a girlfriend," Angela muttered.

Christopher's eyes went wide, but then he tried to work up a semblance of anger. "Hey, no one ever said I couldn't see whoever I want," he said to Aisha. "Not that it was like that. Not that I'm really *seeing* Angela." Without a break, he shifted his attention to Angela. "I mean, we're not, Angela, not really. More like we were getting acquainted. Right?"

Aisha glanced at Angela. Better to know the truth, no matter how devastating. "Is that true, Angela?"

The girl hesitated only a moment. "Actually, no. We were making out. I met him at the mall a couple days ago—"

"I know," Aisha interrupted. "I was there."

"You were there?" Christopher demanded in a convincing portrayal of outrage. "You were *spying* on me?"

"He seemed like a nice guy, charming and ambitious and all," Angela said regretfully. "I like guys who have goals, you know? Most guys don't."

Aisha nodded mutely. *Yes. I was one goal. This pretty blond girl was another. Christopher has many goals.*

"Anyway. I'm out of here," Angela said, giving Christopher a disappointed shrug. She pushed past him, using the back of her hand. "I don't like guys who screw around behind their girlfriend's back, Christopher. Sorry," she said to Aisha. "I had a boyfriend like this once. My advice is lose him."

"Wait!" Christopher yelled after Angela.

"I love your hair, by the way," Aisha told the girl, for no particular reason except that none of this was Angela's fault. Aisha couldn't blame her for falling for Christopher's act. He could be very convincing. He'd convinced her, hadn't he?

Angela stopped halfway down the steps and scooped the long blond ponytail over her shoulder. It fell to the middle of her behind. "Thanks, but I'm thinking of cutting it. It attracts all the wrong kinds of guys." She disappeared down the stairs, a clatter of sandals, and a moment later Aisha heard the front door of the rooming house close.

They were alone, face to face. If he would only apologize, explain that he would never deceive her again. If only he would give her some way to forgive him.

Aisha did not want to have to walk away alone.

"Now look what you did!" Christopher exploded. "I was going to . . . to do her parents' lawn. That's the only reason I was even . . . because, see, her parents have this big house with a huge garden and lawn and shrubs, and I was going to make a bid on, you know, on . . ." He seemed to run out of steam.

Aisha felt something collapse inside her. The first heat of

anger was gone from her now, replaced by growing sadness that seemed to rise around her like a flood. "You know, Christopher, as lame as that lie is, there's a part of me that wants to believe it. Which is really pathetic."

"Look, Eesh, you know—" He reached to take her by the arms, but she drew back.

"No more b.s., all right? Just no more lies."

"Fine, you want to do this?" His anger was back, blazing in his eyes. "I never said I was going to be faithful to you, Aisha. I never said that, all right? Do we agree on that?"

"You never said you weren't, either."

"Okay, so I never promised you anything. So I have nothing to be ashamed of here. How could I know you were thinking it was *that* way? For all I know, *you've* been seeing other guys."

Aisha felt weary. They were just going through the motions now, saying things that would not affect the final outcome. Trading futile arguments that were all beside the point. "If you have nothing to be ashamed of, then why did you lie to me about going to the mall where you met that girl? And why did you just now try to lie your way out of this?"

"I didn't want to rub your face in it," Christopher said smoothly. "I mean, okay, maybe I go out with someone else; that doesn't mean I want to make a big thing out of it. It doesn't mean I don't want to be with you."

"Nice try," Aisha said flatly.

He reached for her again, and this time he was too quick. Or maybe she didn't really want to avoid his touch. Maybe she wanted Christopher to draw her to him. Maybe she wanted to feel the hardness of his chest, the muscles of his thighs against hers.

"I don't want this to mess up what we have," Christopher said. "I don't think you do, either." He bent over to kiss her. His lips were just millimeters from hers when she twisted her face away. With the palms of her hands she shoved at his chest, breaking his grip. She wasn't going to cry. At least she could salvage that much dignity.

"You lied to me, Christopher. You've been trying to get me into bed, you were trying to get that girl into bed. Probably others, too." Aisha bit her lip to keep the tears at bay for a while longer. "I'm not some number. I don't get added to some big list you keep to make yourself feel like a man."

"You have it all wrong."

"Yes. I guess I did have it all wrong. I came here today wondering whether I would tell you that I . . ." Her voice broke and she gritted her teeth, fighting to regain control. "I was going to tell you that I was in love with you. I should have known better."

"It doesn't have to end like this," Christopher said in a low, pleading voice. "We can work this out. We can still be together. I never cared about that girl or any girl the way I care about you, Eesh."

"Now, see, if I really were a romantic, that's just the kind of thing that might move me," Aisha said. "But it won't."

She turned away and marched stiffly down the stairs, hurrying to get away before the sobs overtook her.

"'A therapist once told me that we're born alone and we die alone.

"'It's not true.

"'We all have an extended family, people whom we recognize as our own as soon as we see them. The people closest to me have always been marked by a peculiar difference in their makeup. They're the walking wounded, the ones to whom a psychological injury was done that they will never be able to define, the ones—'"

"Let's stop there, if you don't mind," Benjamin interrupted. He shifted on his bed, pulling a pillow from behind his back and tossing it aside.

"I thought you liked this book," Nina Geiger said. She was kicked back in his swivel chair, Doc Martens propped on the edge of his rolltop desk. She took a drink from a glass of water. Reading to Benjamin always made her thirsty.

Benjamin seemed uncharacteristically edgy. His concentration had been wavering almost since they started. It wasn't hard for Nina to guess why, and immediately she felt self-conscious. She set the paperback down on his desk. Obviously, things weren't going to be quite as smooth as she had hoped. On the ferry ride home from school that day she had, in a moment of giddy daring, blurted out her long-hidden feelings for him. He'd responded by asking her to the homecoming dance. A couple of hours had gone by like nothing had happened, but now he must have begun to realize what he had let himself in for.

"Yeah, yeah, James Lee Burke is great; I'm just not up for anything great," Benjamin said. "I'm not up for anything I have to pay attention to. I'm . . . distracted, I guess."

"Oh."

"It's not your fault," he snapped. "I'm probably just hungry."

"It *isn't* my fault?"

"No. Well, partly. Maybe. I mean, you kind of surprised me back there on the ferry. A *good* surprise; don't get me wrong," he amended. He ran a hand through his hair and pushed the black Ray Bans up on his nose.

"You can back out if you want, Benjamin," Nina said, trying to sound nonchalant. "Feel free to bail on the whole homecoming idea." She might well have to kill him if he backed out now, the jerk, but by the same token if he was just agreeing to go out with her from some sense of pity, well, that was no good, either.

Benjamin stood up, towering over her. "I don't want to back out."

"You do, don't you?"

"No!" he nearly yelled. "No. I don't. The fact is, I'm looking forward to it. It's just unexpected. One minute we're, you know, like buds. We're Fred and Barney. Barney Rubble, not the dinosaur. Then suddenly I'm supposed to start thinking about you differently. *Very* differently. Have you told Claire?"

Nina sighed. So that was it. Claire. Her sister. What a surprise. "I haven't had time, Benjamin. You and I decided this only like two hours ago. And you know I don't talk to Claire unless it's absolutely necessary or I need her to pass the salt."

"You want to go for a walk?" he asked suddenly.

"Should I bring the book?"

"No, let's just walk, all right? It's stuffy in here."

"Sure," Nina said. She stood back and let him pass. Here in his own home he moved as well as a sighted person as long as things weren't relocated too much and people didn't stand in his way.

He led the way through the house to the front door. From upstairs came the sound of an outraged feminine squeal—Zoey's, of course—and a loud male laugh, presumably Lucas's.

They walked along South Street, through the tiny cobble-stone-and-brick town of North Harbor, to Leeward, the road that followed the concave western coastline of Chatham Island.

"You'd better let me take your arm, if you don't mind," Benjamin said. "I can't count steps very well on Leeward. There aren't enough cross streets."

Nina let him find her arm and they set off over the sand-blown road, past small hotels and bed-and-breakfasts, mostly boarded up now that the tourist season was over and the slow fall season was well under way. The ocean crashed with gentle insistence on the beach, depositing green-black wreaths of sea-weed and sending shorebirds skittering stiff-legged away from the surf. The sun was setting across the water behind the main-land city of Weymouth, blanking out the detail of the ten-story bank and insurance buildings, turning them into black building blocks piled before a red-and-orange backdrop.

"How's it look?"

"Nice sunset," Nina said.

"Yeah?"

"A lot of orange and some pink. The clouds look like they're burning at the edges, you know what I mean?"

"I remember," he said in a softer tone. "Nice image, though. Thanks."

They walked on in silence. Nina knew he liked long periods when he could just listen to all the sounds she barely noticed, and smell the salt and the pine and the mouthwatering smoke of barbecues from the homes set back off the road.

"Sorry I got all tense on you," he said after a while.

"I understand. I mean, you're a nice person and you know I've been going through some bad stuff in my own life. So, really, it was sweet of you to ask me to the dance and all. I mean, I know you don't feel, you know . . . You know, like *that*."

"Oh, shut up, Nina." He said it gently. "You don't know what I feel. I don't even know what I feel."

"Sure I do. You still have it bad for Claire. I don't understand why—I think you're too nice for her. I think my sister is so cold she can poop ice cubes when she wants to, but if you're all in love with her . . ." She shrugged, unable to go on. Two hours of quiet pleasure had turned to dust. But at the same time, there was a feeling of relief. She wouldn't have to worry about whether she could deal with it or whether the internal demons of memory would ruin it all.

Benjamin grinned. "Poop ice cubes?" He laughed gleefully. "Now *that's* an image."

"I have the actual photographs of her doing it. I'd show them to you, only you can't see." Nina noticed a shape approaching rapidly from the south. "Hey, it's Aisha."

Aisha rode up on her bike, her explosion of springy black curls planed and reshaped by the ocean breeze. At first she seemed reluctant to stop, but then she pulled over. "Hi, Nina, hi, Ben."

"What's up, Eesh?" Nina asked.

"Nothing. Nothing. Well, I better get going. Um, is Zoey home?"

"She was when we left," Benjamin said.

"Okay, bye," Aisha said quickly. She got her bike going and rode swiftly away.

"What's with her?" Nina wondered.

"Christopher lives down that road, doesn't he?"

"Aha. You're right. Possible trouble. She looked kind of spacey." Nina dug in her purse and found her pack of Lucky Strikes.

"Are you sucking on one of your unlit cigarettes?"

"No," Nina lied, sticking a cigarette in her mouth.

"I can smell it."

"Must be the ocean."

"Uh-huh. Look, Nina. Of course I've thought about you," Benjamin said, plowing back into their conversation with jarring suddenness.

Nina raised an eyebrow. "Thought about me? What does that mean?"

"I mean," he said in an exaggeratedly patient voice, "that I know you use a shampoo that smells like coconuts, and that you occasionally wear a perfume that smells like vanilla, and another that smells like melon. Which probably explains why I often get hungry when you're around.

"And, of course I know that sometimes you're silently cussing me out and giving me the finger because you're mad at me. I also know you are a basically cool person. Plenty of free-floating hostility, plenty of strangeness, but no meanness. I know that you have soft fingers, and that you have . . . well, never mind. The point is, it's not like I've never thought about you. In *that* way. I mean, you are a girl, and I am a guy, and we do spend a lot of time together."

Nina nodded, not trusting her voice to respond.

"Don't nod. How the hell am I supposed to know if you're nodding? All I'm trying to say is . . . I don't know what I'm trying to say. I want to be straight with you because whatever else you are, you're my friend, okay?"

"Uh-huh," Nina managed to mutter.

Benjamin stopped and turned toward her. He aimed his sunglasses at her, as always just a little off-target, but close enough to almost make her believe he could see her and that he was looking into her eyes. "I'm in love with Claire. It's fading, and maybe it will more over time. I don't know. I know I like you. A lot. And maybe that will change into something more. That's all I have to say. I don't want to b.s. you, Nina, or make promises. Except I'll make the promise that one way or the other, I'll always be your friend."

Nina took a deep, shaky breath. So he *was* still in love with Claire, which was no surprise at all.

On the other hand, Benjamin had admitted that the thought of Nina as an actual *female* had occurred to him once or twice. "I want you to know what you're getting into with me, Nina, that's all. And now, if *you* want to change *your* mind about this weekend, I'll understand."

Nina chewed on her lower lip. It would be about a million times easier just to stay home from the game on Friday, and a billion times easier to skip the homecoming dance on Saturday. Weymouth High was a fairly small school. And by now everyone there, from cheerleaders to jocks to brains to the glue-huffing morons in detention, knew that she had accused her uncle of molesting her. Everyone was busy nodding and saying things like, *Wow, all this time I thought she was a lezzie and now it turns out she was just screwed up about guys.* And showing up at homecoming with Benjamin, whom half the girls in school had their sights on, would be like pouring gasoline on the gossip fire.

A very large number of girls, including, possibly, Claire,

would be pissed. So at least there was something positive.

"Nah. I can't dump you, Benjamin," Nina said. "People would feel sorry for you, sitting home all alone."

Benjamin smiled. "So what are you going to wear?"

"Like you would know the difference?"

"I didn't mean clothing. I meant I like the vanilla stuff better."

"Ow, ow. That hurts." Zoey Passmore winced and tried to pull away.

"That's what you get for throwing things at me without warming up first," Lucas said, unimpressed by her complaints. "You've pulled your shoulder muscle. If you're going to heave a book at my head, you should at least warm up—you know, stretch. All that time going out with a jock and you learned nothing." He poured some more oil into his palms, rubbed them together, and went back to work kneading Zoey's bare shoulder.

Lucas was leaning against the mountain of pillows at the head of Zoey's bed. She sat cross-legged with her back to him, T-shirt off and the shoulder strap of her bra lowered.

"I didn't heave a *book* at your *head* in a *jealous rage*," Zoey corrected him in a drowsy, relaxed voice. "Oh, that's good; yeah, yeah, like that. I just *tossed* a *magazine* to you."

"A very big magazine. Very fast toss."

"Do that some more. It's your fault, anyway. You asked for it."

"I was just quoting from the magazine," Lucas said mildly. "I didn't make up the statistics. I was just pointing out that in the article they said the majority of people our age are having sex. I didn't necessarily mean anything by it."

Zoey twisted her head toward the good side, pried open one eye, and gave him a look. He broke into a smile. "Okay, maybe I had a small ulterior motive."

"Yeah, *maybe*," Zoey said dryly. "See, your mistake was you shouldn't have gone right from talking about that to talking about Louise Kronenberger."

"I was making a joke. I was just saying she probably accounted for a lot of that statistic all by herself. Joke. Ha ha."

"Ow, not quite that hard," Zoey said.

"You should put some ice on it," Lucas said.

Zoey twisted around again. "So should you."

"Oh, that's funny, Zoey."

"Anyway, if you like K-burger so much, you'll have the perfect opportunity to get to know her," Zoey said with poisoned sweetness. "You have the big ceremonial homecoming king and queen dance. Maybe you could bring a copy of that magazine article. You could whisper statistics in her ear."

Lucas sighed deeply. "This is why I didn't want to get into the whole homecoming thing. I'm getting swept up into the whole school-spirit-popular-people-who-saw-who-with-who-else thing."

"You're trying to change the subject," Zoey said.

Lucas suddenly pulled her onto her back and crouched over her, pinning her arms over her head. "No, *now* I'm changing the subject."

He lowered his face to hers and they kissed, a long, slow kiss that left them both breathless.

Suddenly there was a knock at the bedroom door. And before Zoey could think of how to respond, the door opened.

"Aisha!" Zoey gasped. She pushed Lucas off her and began a frantic search for her shirt. Lucas grabbed a pillow and rested it on his lap.

"Oh, God, I'm interrupting something, aren't I?" Aisha said.

"No, no," Zoey said shrilly, leaning over the side of the bed to rummage beneath it. She came up with the T-shirt, untwisted it, and pulled it on over her head. "Come in, Eesh," she said. "We were just, uh . . ." Zoey looked helplessly at Lucas.

"We were discussing, um, statistics," Lucas said, sending Zoey a disgruntled glare.

"I just broke up with Christopher," Aisha blurted.

Zoey shoved a tumble of wispy blond hair out of her eyes and looked at her friend more closely. Aisha's dark eyes were puffy and outlined in red. It was a startling realization—Aisha had been crying.

"What happened?" Zoey asked, pushing Lucas away to make room on the bed for Aisha to sit beside her.

"This sounds like girl stuff," Lucas said. "I think I'll just head on out." He climbed off the bed and started toward the door.

"I caught him with some girl in his room," Aisha said bleakly.

"A girl? In his room?" Zoey was stunned. But not so stunned that she didn't notice the way Lucas seemed to cringe at this news.

"Bye," Lucas said, slipping out and closing the door behind him. "I'll go home and try that ice idea."

"Well, were they just talking, or what?" Zoey asked, waving a distracted good-bye to Lucas. She put her arm around Aisha's shoulders.

"They were . . . they were, well, not quite like you and Lucas just were, but close."

"He was just giving me a shoulder rub," Zoey said, blushing a little.

"The girl said they were making out."

"The girl?"

"The girl from the mall."

"The girl from . . . *That* girl? The girl with the hair?"

"She was really pretty nice," Aisha said.

"Pretty nice? She was making out with your boyfriend, wasn't she?"

"She didn't know. Christopher told her he didn't—" She had to stop and fight back a sob. "He told her he didn't have a girlfriend." She ended on a fierce note, her eyes blazing. "And now he doesn't, the rotten, stinking slug."

"I'm really sorry, Eesh."

"I'm not," Aisha said bitterly. "I've just relearned my lesson. See, it's my fault. I always said if you get too into one guy, he'll always dump on you sooner or later. Guys. They're all pigs."

"They're mostly pigs," Zoey agreed reasonably.

"*All* of them," Aisha insisted. "They only want one thing. You'll find out someday. Not that I can say *I told you so*. Not anymore." She wiped away a tear that had trickled down her cheek.

Zoey glanced at the door to her bedroom. She should be telling Aisha that she was wrong. Some guys weren't like that. Some guys could be counted on no matter what.

TWO

NINA SAT ON THE LIVING room couch, legs stretched out along its length, a notebook open on her lap, a bag of Doritos, a bowl of salsa, and a root beer on the coffee table within easy reach. A stubby, unlit Lucky Strike hung from the corner of her mouth. She had to strain to see what she was writing in the notebook because the only light came from the muted television. She scooped up some salsa and popped the chip in her mouth. Then she wrote:

5. Pee is blue.

She took a swig from the sweating can of root beer. Who decided this? Why not green? Why not purple? Why blue?

"What's on?"

Nina jerked and bit her tongue. She glared up at her sister. "Jeez, Claire. You creep around here like Morticia."

"What do you want me to do? Ring a little bell so you'll

know I'm coming?" Claire sat down in the wing-backed easy chair. She was wearing a silk robe and had her hair wrapped in a damp towel.

"Actually, that's not a bad idea," Nina said. "Would you mind?"

"What's on?" Claire asked again. Then she wrinkled her nose. "Hot sauce? Right before you go to bed?"

"I'm not going right to bed. I have this homework to do first. I'm going to stay up and watch Dave."

"You'll be in a coma all day tomorrow," Claire observed. "Nothing unusual about that, though, I guess. What's the homework?"

"Modern Media," Nina said. "We're supposed to list some of the hidden messages beneath the surface of commercials." She laughed. "My kind of class—watch TV, get a grade. I was so right to go with this instead of a lit. elective. Those poor suckers are all reading Faulkner. I'm observing that pee is blue."

"Excuse me?"

"TV pee. It's blue. You know, baby diapers, old people diapers, the 'liquid' is always blue. Why blue? Why not green or red? These are the big questions I'm dealing with here. I feel I'm on the cutting edge of human knowledge."

"Red would look like blood," Claire pointed out. "Red pee?"

"You're right. That would be like, *Hey, use our Depend Undergarments and pee blood.*" Nina nodded approvingly. "Thanks for clearing that up. It's so helpful having an all-knowing senior right here in the house with me."

"I don't know if that's exactly what your teacher had in mind," Claire said. "Let me have a drink of your soda."

"Here." Nina leaned forward as far as she could, just barely able to hand the can to Claire.

"What else do you have?"

Nina held her notebook sideways to read by the flickering blue-gray light of the television. "Well, first of all, I noticed that anytime you have a married couple in a commercial, the woman is always smarter, younger, and better looking than the man."

"Now, see, *that's* a good observation," Claire said.

"Um, and, wait, I can't read . . . Oh, yeah. That ad for the company that makes bulletproof vests? They say, *Every year schmuh police officers are killed.*"

"Schmuh?"

"Exactly. Instead of saying a number, they just say *schmuh* and hope no one will notice."

"Okay."

"Seriously," Nina insisted.

"Okay."

"Then I noted that it's okay to show animated earwax exploding out of your ear, but you never see a laxative commercial where—"

"I get the idea," Claire interrupted quickly.

"Then I noticed that girls who have their period always wear white. Which led to the question of blue body fluids."

"You'll be Mr. Mifflin's star student," Claire said dryly. She stood up, bent at the waist, and began unwrapping the towel, letting her long damp hair hang down. She stood up quickly and began fluffing it dry with her fingers. "I'm getting my ends trimmed tomorrow at the mall, so I'll have the car." She made a wry face. "I was going to shop for a dress for the homecoming dance, but as of right now I don't exactly have a date."

"You still haven't brought Jake to his knees yet? Huh. I'm starting to have a better opinion of old *Joke*."

"I may just have to stay home with you," Claire said.

Nina started to answer but stopped herself. Sooner or later Claire would find out, and it wasn't like Nina was doing anything wrong. Still. It was sort of two major announcements in one—first, she had to make the big announcement that actually, surprising as it seemed, she *was* going to homecoming. This by itself would be an event as rare as a major earthquake. Second, there was the matter of *whom* she was going to the dance with.

"I said . . . I said I may just have to stay home with you,"

Claire repeated. She was eyeing Nina closely from beneath a questioning brow.

"Uh-huh," Nina said, pretending to be absorbed by her notebook.

"Don't *uh-huh* me, Nina. I know you. What are you not telling me?"

Nina shrugged.

"Spill."

"I don't have to tell you everything, Claire."

"Yes, but you're going to anyway, so since it's late and I have to go dry my hair, why not just cough it up now and get it over with?"

"Going to the dance," Nina mumbled under her breath, pretending to be absorbed by the TV screen.

Claire sighed. "What would that be if you were speaking English?"

Nina rolled her eyes. "I'm going to the stupid homecoming dance, all right? No big deal."

Claire stared at her. "Oh, no big deal. It's only about the first actual date of your life. The first dance. The first school function of any kind that you've ever willingly attended. Is this because of the whole thing with Uncle Mark? Are you, you know—"

"Am I becoming psychologically unhinged?"

"You were born psychologically unhinged," Claire said.

Nina fell silent. The mention of her uncle had cast a pall over her. This was how it would be from now on. Everyone, even Claire, would see everything she did in the light of terrible events that had happened a long time ago.

"Sorry," Claire said, downcast. "That was over the line." Then she smiled her rare, wintry Claire smile. "Not the part about you being psychologically unhinged. That's just a fact. But I won't bring up that creep's name again."

"Cool," Nina said.

"So. Who's the unfortunate guy?"

Nina took a deep breath. .

"I won't laugh, I promise. Even if he's the biggest dork in school. Even if it's some defenseless freshman. Or at least I'll only laugh a little."

"It's Benjamin," Nina said.

Claire froze. For a full minute she didn't say anything. "Oh."

"Look, *you're* not going out with him anymore," Nina said defensively.

"No, I'm not."

"This isn't going to, like, you know . . . is it?"

"I always knew you had a crush on him," Claire said a little sadly.

"We're just friends. I think."

"It's not any of my business," Claire said. Her lips were narrowed to the point of disappearing.

Nina gritted her teeth. This was actually more awkward than she had expected it to be, and she'd expected it to be pretty awkward. She squeezed the ends of her cigarette between her fingers and peeked up at her sister.

"Well, I have to go finish drying my hair," Claire said with sudden, determined brightness.

"Yeah. See you tomorrow morning."

"Uh-huh."

"Good night!" Nina yelled after her sister. If there was an answer, she didn't hear it.

Nina and Benjamin. *Nina* and Benjamin. Nina and *Benjamin*.

Her sister and her former boyfriend. Her very recently *former* boyfriend.

Claire finished running the hair dryer over the ends of her hair and hung the dryer back on its hook beside the medicine cabinet. She began combing while searching her face for any blemishes. As usual, she found none.

Of course Nina had a crush on Benjamin; Claire had known that for a long time. But lots of people had crushes on lots of other people. People didn't usually act on their crushes.

Especially Nina.

Claire turned off the bathroom light and climbed the stairs to her bedroom. It was on the top level of the house, the only room on the third floor. Her bed was neatly made, her clothing put away. The lighting was soft—shaded lamps with pink bulbs. On her desk was a box that kept track of the barometric pressure, wind speed, and temperature outside. On a wall she had a large, National Geographic map of Antarctica.

Attached to another wall was a steel ladder that led to a square hatch in the ceiling. She climbed the ladder, graceful from long experience, pushed open the hatch door, and emerged into the chill air of the widow's walk, a section of flat roof covered in weathered wood and surrounded by a waist-high railing.

It was Claire's place, even more than her room was. No one else ever came up here—not Nina, not Claire's friends. From here on a clear day or night, she could see all of North Harbor, Chatham Island's tiny village. She could see the few streetlights shining silver on cobblestoned streets, the occasional porch light piercing the dark shadow of the hill that rose from the southern edge of the town. She could look across the water to Weymouth, the mainland city four miles away that glittered bright and cold, moonlight on glass-walled buildings.

To the north, past the slow sweep of the lighthouse's beacon, and to the east, only empty ocean—a vast, dark force that gently massaged the rocks and beaches of Chatham Island and could, on occasion, attack the island as if it were trying to sink it once and for all.

The breeze was too cool, sneaking under and through her robe. It raised goose bumps and reminded her that the full, brutal Maine winter was not so far off.

Benjamin had never come up to the widow's walk, but he had asked her, from time to time, to describe for him what she saw from here. And in the process of telling him she had realized how few details she had ever really noticed. By the end of their relationship she had learned to see much more clearly.

Well, if Nina was ready to take the plunge into dating, then Benjamin would be a good person for her to be with. He was smart and patient and understanding. He knew what had happened between Nina and that bastard Uncle Mark. He had been there when Nina had finally, after so many years of shamed silence, leveled the accusation.

Yes, if Nina was going to start dating, then Benjamin was a good choice.

It just seemed a little strange. Claire and Benjamin had done everything together. Almost everything. Everything *but*. Now, he would be going out with her own sister. It was an unnerving thought.

Claire pulled the robe tighter around her. She wished she'd

at least worn some socks. Still, she was reluctant to leave her aerie just yet. In warmer weather she often slept up here. During storms she liked to huddle under her slicker and watch the lightning snap the surface of the water.

When she had broken up with Benjamin, he'd said something to her . . . something about her being isolated . . .

She went to the tall brick chimney that fronted one end of the widow's walk. She reached around to locate the loose brick and pried it out. Inside the cavity was her diary. She took it out, sat down, and began riffling back through the pages. She'd written down what Benjamin had said. Yes, there it was, as she remembered it.

"You're an isolated, lonely, superior person, Claire. You sit up there on your widow's walk and watch the clouds overhead and the little people down below. And they have to be below you, that's the important thing, because you can't tolerate an equal for long."

She smiled as she read it. Benjamin always did have a way with words.

Nina and Benjamin.

Claire pulled the pen from the spine of the diary.

• • •

Monday, 11:30 p.m. The wind is out of the southwest at about seven or eight knots. The temperature

She squinted to read the mercury on the thermometer nailed to the railing.

is 59 degrees.

No wonder she was cold.

Nina is going with Benjamin to homecoming.
As things stand right now, I don't have a date. I see very little chance that Jake will suddenly change his mind. I've done everything I can think of to get him to

To what? To love her? He already loved her. To want her? Oh, he wanted her badly enough. That wasn't the problem.

forgive me.
To stop blaming me for things that happened years ago.

That's what stood between them. All that stood between them. His guilt over loving the girl who had been responsible for his brother's death. And now that guilt was corroding his life. He had been drinking. Drinking at the wrong times and in the wrong circumstances. He had narrowly avoided missing his last football game.

I gave up Benjamin for Jake. I felt threatened by the way Benjamin kept trying to force the truth from me. But now the truth is out.

I love Jake. But how long can I stand his rejection?

The breeze carried the melancholy, muffled clang of some distant buoy. Far, far out to sea, the faint lights of ships traveled south along the horizon.

Sometimes I wish everything would just go back to the way it was before. Jake with Zoey. Me with Benjamin.

Only now, Zoey was with Lucas. Nina might be with Benjamin.

And Claire?

Claire was isolated, lonely, perhaps even superior, on her widow's walk.

BENJAMIN PASSMORE

The only real images I have of either Claire or Nina are from years ago, back before I lost my sight. I remember Claire's hair, which was long then, just like it is now. I remember that it was dark, maybe even black. And I ~~remeber~~ remember an expression she wore, even as an eleven-year-old, a cool, appraising look, like everyone around her had to prove themselves to her satisfaction, and she wasn't going to be easy to impress.

Nina's a year younger, and I remember her as less grown-up looking than Claire. She had braces, and a cocky look that was sort of a better-natured, more mocking version of Claire's.

But I've had no visual input to update either picture, so those old images persist when I deal with these two girls, although I've added many, many details—the plush softness of Claire's lips, the heavy silk of her hair, the smooth skin of her legs, ~~hte~~ the heat I could always feel long before I touched her, the way she smells somehow of moonlight and ocean breezes. I think I will always know the beat of her heart, the cool precision of her voice, her laughter, so infrequent that when it came, it always shocked me.

And yes, I know she's calculating and self-serving and even ruthless when she feels she has to be. I know she's impatient with anyone less gifted than herself, that she exploits the insecurities she brings out in other people.

But I also know that underneath it all, sometimes <u>way</u> underneath it all, Claire is a decent human being, striving to figure out what's right and to do it. I ~~now~~ know that if I were ever in trouble, tomorrow or ten years from now, I could count on Claire to help. Of course, she'd bitch about it a little first.

Nina? I have less of Nina. A very old image joined to new information that, brought together in my mind, still doesn't form a complete picture.

No one is faster with a deadly accurate slam. And no one is so careful never to really cause pain. She's bold and provocative and individualistic, but she's also shy and ~~and~~ awkward and insecure. I think of her as a person who can blush in terrible mortification or laugh defiantly. There's no one I'd rather just hang out with, listen to TV with, walk with.

But Nina as something more than a friend? I don't know. That concept hasn't taken hold for me. I know it's strange, but in a way I can't picture Nina as having a body. Legs, arms, shoulders, lips, breasts. I think of her

as an attitude, a sense of humor, a lightning-quick jab
that makes me laugh.

But as someone I might hold? ~~Sa~~ As someone I might
touch and kiss? I don't know that Nina.

Not yet.

THREE

THE CLOCK OVER THE CHALKBOARD jerked the final minute and the bell rang. Zoey all but ran for the exit, snatching up her books and banging her leg on the desk in her hurry. She was one of the first people into the hallway, though hundreds boiled out behind her and from all the doors lining both sides of the stuffy, overlit hall.

"I have no idea what that woman is trying to teach me," she muttered under her breath. A freshman guy paused to look at her curiously. "Don't ever take trig, that's my advice," she told him. "In fact, just drop out now."

The second and third periods of the day were her least favorite. First period was fine. Journalism. No problem. After lunch everything was fine, too, with American lit., history, and French. But second period was trigonometry and it was followed immediately by gym. She didn't understand trig—she would never, ever, if she lived a thousand years, understand trig. Her brother and Claire and Aisha all laughed at her for being a mathematical idiot. The three of them took calculus, the creeps.

As for gym, well, that had just been stupidity on her part. She, Claire, and Aisha had all brilliantly decided to put off the junior-year gym requirement and take more exciting electives. Now they were among the very few senior girls still forced to make fools of themselves throwing basketballs blindly toward a back-board that she, at least, never hit; bouncing from trampolines; and, in Coach Anders's latest annoying brainstorm, playing tennis. The tennis had to be played outside, which would be even less fun when the temperature dropped to minus five and the wind blew through at fifty miles per hour. To make matters worse, the only other senior girls taking gym were on their way to becoming phys-ed majors. These girls enjoyed bouncing tennis balls off Zoey's head while she flailed away clumsily with her racket.

"One more year of this place," she muttered.

Then four years of college.

She sighed and headed down the hall, down the stairs, and down the lower-floor hall, heading on unwilling feet toward the gym.

A hand shot out from a crush of kids and grabbed her arm. Lucas twirled her to face him and put his arms around her. "What, you can't even stop and say hi?"

"Hi. I didn't see you," Zoey said. She kissed him lightly, and he pulled them both to an unoccupied few inches of locker-lined wall. They kissed with more concentration, far away for a few moments from the echoing shouts and slamming metal locker doors all around them.

"Now I'm in a much better mood," Zoey said, leaning against him. "Your hair's wet."

"Just got out of gym. Were you in a bad mood?"

"I'm always in a bad mood after trig. I don't personally believe there should be classes where nothing can be explained in English and it all relies on numbers and signs. Besides, when in my life am I ever going to have to deal with cosines, tangents, or any of that stuff?"

"You might have to cosign a loan. Or is that getting off on a tangent?"

Zoey groaned and made a face. "That's the kind of thing I expect from Nina."

Lucas kissed her again. And again, trigonometry, gym, and pretty much the entire rest of the world ceased to exist.

"Is that more the kind of thing you expect from me?" Lucas asked huskily.

"Mmm."

"Let's bail. We'll sneak off, get your folks' car out of the garage, cruise down to Portland or even to Boston. Have fun. What can they do to me? I'm the newly elected homecoming king. I am all-powerful."

"Don't tempt me when I'm on the way to gym class," Zoey said.

"Oh, I think you look cute in your little shorts."

"When have you seen me in my gym outfit?"

"I'm in algebra for the mathematically impaired on the third floor then," he said. "Perfect view of the field. The guys especially like it when the girls stretch out—you know, bending over to grab your ankles and all that. I'm trying to figure out how to smuggle binoculars into class."

"It must be nice having a one-track mind. So few outside distractions."

Lucas laughed. "It beats paying attention to algebra."

"I better get going; Coach Anders makes you run laps if you're late. Bye, I'm off to shower with strangers."

"I'll trade you. I'll go shower with the girls, you can do my algebra."

"On top of trig? I'd rather have my hair pulled out, one hair at a time."

"Hi, Lucas." Pause. "Oh, and hi, Zoey."

"Hey, Louise," Lucas said with careful nonchalance.

"Hi, Louise," Zoey said. Louise Kronenberger was wearing bell-bottomed jeans with a tight, loose-knit sweater over no bra. Lucas's eyes were darting down to peer between the mesh.

"Hey, homecoming king," Louise said. "We need to get together and talk about Friday and Saturday."

"We do?" Lucas asked. He shot an alarmed glance toward Zoey.

"We have a couple of official duties," Louise said.

"I thought all we had to do was look surprised when they announce we won, and then dance."

The actual announcement of the homecoming queen and king would come at halftime in the game, but for the last two years the administration had always leaked the results early. The precaution was thanks to an earlier homecoming queen who hadn't expected to win and had showed up tripping on LSD. She had become terrified of the opposing team's mascot and run screaming from the field.

"We want to look good for the dance, right?" Louise said.

The warning bell rang. A collective groan went up from the masses and people began disappearing back into classrooms.

"I don't care how I look, Louise," Lucas said. "I'd wear a bag over my head if I thought I could get away with it."

"I have to get going," Zoey said.

"Me too," Lucas said.

"Which way are you going?" Louise asked Lucas.

"Uh, third floor."

"Me too." Louise grinned. "We can talk on the way. Bye,

Zoey." She took Lucas's arm and began towing him along. Lucas looked back over his shoulder and sent Zoey a helpless look.

Zoey made a face and silently mouthed a single descriptive word in reference to Louise Kronenberger.

Lucas grinned. But he still followed Louise up the stairs.

"My towel's all gross," Zoey complained, wrinkling her nose at the dank smell. It actually smelled even worse than the rest of the locker room. She threw the towel into her open gym locker on top of sneakers, deodorant, shampoo, and an uneaten Snickers bar that had been in there since the first day of school. "Will someone remind me to take it home and wash it? Now what am I going to do? I'm wet, but if I use that rag, I'll smell like dirty socks all day."

"Don't look at me," Aisha said, raising her arms to let her shirt settle down over her. "You can't borrow *my* towel. Hey, do you believe Christopher? That walking hormone. No apology, nothing. Just hands out the rackets and balls like he doesn't even know who I am."

One of Christopher's many jobs included working part-time as equipment manager for the gym department.

"I was not going to ask for your towel, Aisha," Zoey protested. "Gross. Borrowing someone else's used towel?" She looked around distractedly. The truth was, she'd have gladly borrowed Aisha's towel. She glanced at Claire, doing her makeup, but Claire was ignoring her helpless look. "What did you want Christopher to do?" she asked Aisha, feeling cranky. "He was working, and Coach was right there the whole time. Besides, Eesh, I thought you'd already forgotten Christopher existed. Damn, I cannot put clothes on over wet skin—they'll cling."

"Cling to what?" Claire muttered, concentrating on her eyeliner.

"I don't really care what Christopher does anymore," Aisha said. "I was just saying that on top of everything else, he was rude."

"I'm freezing here," Zoey said, "and all I get is clever remarks and indifference."

Claire began methodically pulling paper towels from the dispenser on the tiled wall beside the sinks. "Here." She handed the wad to Zoey and returned to leaning over the sink to put on blush.

Zoey began applying the paper towels to various parts of her body. They stuck, making her look sort of like a shingled roof. Aisha tilted her head at a critical angle and looked Zoey over. "I think you may have a look going there, Zo. Let's take a picture and send it to *Glamour*. I see it as a continuation of the 'waif look.'"

"Zoey *is* the waif look," Claire said. "Or would be if she could look just a little dumber. You need to work on the blank, uncomprehending stare, Zoey, if you're going to go for that true Cara Delevingne thing. You already have the body."

Zoey sent Aisha a conspiratorial smile. "It's terrible when the wheels of fashion turn against you full-figured gals, isn't it, Claire?" Zoey teased. "Your little snide remarks don't bother me, not anymore. The whole world now sees that small is beautiful. This is my hour. Juglessness rules. The unbuffered shall inherit the earth. Flat is powerful."

"You're covered in wet paper towels, oh powerful one," Claire pointed out.

"New from *The Limited*—the wet paper towel bodysuit," Zoey said. She began peeling them off and slipped into her clothes, grimacing at the residual clamminess.

"That's another thing about Christopher," Aisha said, back to fuming. "He once told me I had big feet. But have you seen his forehead? No, because he *has* no forehead."

"I saw K-berger and Lucas having a very close conversation up in the third-floor hallway," Claire said, not even bothering to conceal the sly look in her eyes. "They look like a good couple to be home-coming . . . whatevers. Now, K-berger, there's a girl who will never be able to pull off the waif look."

"Homecoming is stupid," Aisha said. She fluffed her hair

with both hands. It sprang out in a voluminous, curly mass that Zoey greatly admired. "What's it even mean? Homecoming?"

"That's what all the girls say who don't have a date," Claire said dryly. "And this year, I agree with you—homecoming *is* stupid."

Zoey's jaw dropped. "You don't have a date? No wonder you're being so snippy. I assumed it was just PMS."

"Don't pick on Claire because she doesn't have a date," Aisha grumbled. "Two out of the three girls standing here don't have a date for homecoming. In fact, Zoey, you seem to be in the minority. Although personally I'm glad. I hate football games and I hate dances. I'd rather stay home and watch . . . whatever's on Friday and Saturday night."

"*20/20* on Friday," Claire said. She finished her makeup, and Zoey took her place at the sink. "Barbara Walters. I think she's interviewing some politician. Huge fun. Maybe we could watch it together. But if you do stay home, Aisha, Christopher will laugh and think you couldn't get any other guy."

Aisha's eyes narrowed. "You know, you're right."

"How would he even know?" Zoey reasoned. She snatched Claire's blush. "He's not in school except to work. He would only go to the dance if you invited him, Aisha."

"Oh, he'll find out somehow," Aisha said through gritted teeth. "Claire's right. He'll think he's such hot stuff that without him all I can do is sit at home and watch *20/20*."

"*SNL's* on Saturday night," Claire added. "For whatever that's worth. Not much, usually."

"What are you going to do?" Zoey asked Aisha. "You don't have any guys on hold or anything."

"I can get a date," Aisha said defensively. "Hey. How about Benjamin?" She shot Claire a *so there* look.

Claire shook her head. "He's taking Nina."

"*Excuse me?*" Zoey said, her eyes wide. "Benjamin is taking Nina? My brother, Benjamin, is taking out Nina, one of my best friends, and I don't know about it?"

"Nina probably thinks you'll make a big deal out of it," Claire said. "And you know Benjamin. Not exactly Mister Gossip."

"I'm his only *sister*," Zoey nearly yelled.

"Nina just told me last night," Claire said. "You know how she is about guy stuff."

"Yeah, I do know." Zoey's face turned serious. "By the way, have they arrested that creep uncle of yours yet?"

"It's complicated." Claire sighed. "Maine laws, Minnesota laws. My dad has a lawyer working on it."

"Great. So Nina suddenly emerges from the nunnery and instantly steals the only remaining guy around," Aisha said. "Now what am I going to do for a date?"

"Maybe Nina will trade you straight across," Claire suggested.

"Benjamin for Christopher. Throw in some cash and I think she might consider it."

"Very funny," Aisha said. "But I don't need your pity. I'll probably have a date by the end of the day. One that will make Christopher eat his liver."

"Not that you care what he thinks," Zoey added.

FOUR

LUCAS DECIDED AGAINST LUNCH IN the cafeteria. The food was lousy and he didn't feel comfortable eating with Zoey. Zoey, Aisha, and Nina had made a long-standing ritual of having lunch together—no guys, no outsiders, with the occasional exception of Claire. Zoey had told him he was welcome, but when he was there the conversation tended to die out, and he'd gotten the message—lunchtime was girl time.

He left the campus and headed toward the nearby Burger King. He had a little money now from doing some work on his father's lobster boat. He'd been mucking out the bilges, which was about as nasty a job as you could find anywhere, and doing some painting, which wasn't so bad. His father might be a son of a bitch, but he paid a fair wage for the work. A Whopper and fries wouldn't set him back too much.

The Burger King was filled with other kids from school, competing for space with business-women from the nearby office buildings and guys from a road crew that was repaving a section of the street.

Lucas got into line behind a dozen other people. With luck he would just have time to get his food and eat it as he walked back to school.

"Is that you, Cabral? You punk." The voice was harsh and challenging. Lucas steeled himself and turned around.

Two guys. One, short with a receding chin, a weedy red mustache, a reddish buzz cut, and dead blue eyes. The other, much larger, sullen, a shaved head, his muscular arms covered in crude tattoos. Both wore black jeans and steel-studded leather boots.

"Snake," Lucas said to the smaller of the two. "Did they finally let you go or did you escape?"

Snake smiled the fanged smile that gave him his name. "I hit eighteen, man. Birthday. The magic number."

"I didn't know you could count that high, Snake."

"Don't bust my balls, asswipe," Snake said. He jerked a thumb at the big guy. "Jones gets pissed when guys bust my balls."

Lucas thought of a smart remark but the truth was, while Snake by himself was a gutless little weasel, as part of a group he would be bolder. And Jones was big enough to be a group all by himself. "You know, Snake, I'd love to talk over old times, but you know, we're not supposed to be dealing with each other. It'd be a parole violation for you to be seen talking to a lowlife like me."

"Screw that. My parole officer's some old witch. I don't take any crap off her."

"You want something from me, Snake? Because if not, I think I'll bail. I didn't know they let people like you in here."

"Back to school like a good little boy, Cabral? Studying hard?" Snake stepped closer. "Or is it just the stuff, man. Is that it? You have some nice little piece warming you up at night, dude? Maybe a cheerleader or something? Yeah, I need to get me some of that. I been inside a long time, man. Maybe I could just borrow yours for a few hours. What do you got, a blond? A redhead?" He nudged Jones and laughed. "She's a white girl at least, isn't she?"

Lucas's face froze. Suddenly he was out of the Burger King, far from Weymouth High, all the way back in a dark, loud, threatening place where the rules of normal behavior didn't apply. He moved closer to Snake, till his face was just inches from Snake's empty eyes.

"Don't get in my face, man. You'd better have more than this big dumb lump of crap backing you up before you get in my face."

To Lucas's surprise, Snake didn't back down. "I got all I

need backing me up, Cabral. Dudes you don't even want to think about."

"More of your white-power morons?"

Snake blinked. "Like I said. We got some soldiers you don't want to think about messing with."

"Go crawl back under your rock," Lucas said in disgust. He pushed past Snake and headed for the exit. He threw the door open violently and sucked in the clear, cool outside air. He realized his hands were trembling, and he stuck them deep in his jeans pockets. He took several more deep breaths, trying to calm the quivering feeling in his stomach that was half fury, half fear.

He had known and dealt with guys like Snake in the Youth Authority. He'd almost gotten used to their simpleminded crudeness, the twisted, festering racism that had been nurtured in homes filled with hatred and alcoholic brutality. But here on the outside, back in the world, with all that now part of the past, it was a shock to see them again.

He wasn't really afraid, he told himself. Skinheads rarely took on people who could defend themselves. And Lucas was wary enough to stay out of their way.

"Jesus," he muttered. "Six weeks ago I was listening to Snake whimpering in his sleep in the next bunk, and in three days I'm happy high school homecoming king." The contrast brought a wry smile to his lips.

He stretched to get the tension out of his neck and back, swung his arms to loosen the muscles that had tightened in preparation for sudden violence, and walked back to school. He would try to find Zoey, right away, even before sixth period when they would be in history together. If he could find her and hold her in his arms, she would drive the memories away.

"You're not eating that, are you?" Zoey looked at Nina in alarm. "That's tamale pie."

"I know it sucks, but I'm hungry," Nina said.

"It's beef, Nina. You don't eat dead cow or dead Pig."

Nina shrugged. "It didn't make any sense, really. I mean, I ate dead fish and dead chicken. Besides, I'm allowed to change my mind." She took a tentative bite of the greasy mass.

"I was thinking about going *totally* veg," Aisha said accusingly. "You were my inspiration, Nina."

"I'm a work in progress, kids. I change, I grow, I gain new insights. Deal with it. Besides, I'm hungry."

Zoey looked over her shoulder. Claire was still coming through the lunch line. She might or might not decide to sit with them. Claire could just as easily decide to go off and sit alone. "Work in progress," she muttered, giving Nina a skeptical look. "So I hear, from third parties." She glanced meaningfully over her shoulder in the direction of Claire.

Nina looked mystified. Then her expression cleared. "Oh. I was going to tell you; it's not some big secret or anything."

"You told your sister *before* you told me? Has there been some sudden outbreak of sisterly devotion at the Geiger household? *I'm* your first stop for new and fascinating gossip. Then *I* tell Aisha. That's the normal order of the universe."

Aisha nodded agreement. "We feel betrayed."

Nina sighed loudly. "Look, it's kind of embarrassing, okay? I didn't want you two going *aww, isn't it sweet, little Nina has a crush on Benjamin*."

Zoey smiled at Aisha. "It is sweet, though."

"Aww, look, she's blushing," Aisha said, pointing at Nina.

"Our little Nina is in love. You know, if things work out, she could someday be my sister-in-law."

"You'd be the aunt to her children."

"We'd have little family get-togethers and Nina and I would make fried chicken and coleslaw while the kids played out in the backyard and Lucas and Benjamin drank beer and belched."

Nina drummed her fingers on the table. "Are you two done?"

"All I can say is, watch out," Aisha advised. "Guys are basically pigs. Speaking of which. See that guy over there? The tall one? Do you think he'd like to take me to homecoming? I think he's better-looking than Christopher."

Claire had come up behind them. "Just because Christopher is a pig doesn't mean all guys are," she said. "And that guy you're looking at is a sophomore. He's just tall." She set down her tray and took the remaining seat.

"She's right, Eesh," Nina said. "You have to take a much broader sampling before you can say that all guys are pigs. Which is the only reason Claire keeps burning through guys at a rate of one every couple of months. Or, more recently, one in about a week."

Claire sent Nina a tolerantly poisonous look. "You know, it's really not fair, your taking cheap shots at me when you know that I can't fight back."

"So fight back."

"You're still in your official 'victim' status," Claire said. "I'm trying to be a supportive sister and all, but you make it so difficult."

Nina laughed. "You don't have to treat me like I'm fragile. It's the opposite. I mean, what happened, happened a long time ago. Now that it's out in the open I feel *less* pathetic, not more. I'm now ruining *his* life, like he tried to ruin mine, so, to be honest with you, I feel pretty good. Better than I have since then."

"Yeah, but I still can't pick on you for having had no love life," Claire said, shaking her head.

"We could pick on Aisha for always talking about how *she* was too smart to get caught up in some big romantic thing," Nina suggested.

"Go ahead, you're right," Aisha said, agreeing readily. "I didn't listen to my own advice, and I ended up falling for some guy who's a weasel. Go ahead, give me your best shot. I deserve it."

"It's no fun if you're asking for it," Nina grumbled.

"I have to admit one thing, though," Claire said. "You handled it really well, Aisha. No weeping or wailing. Boom, it's over, get on with life. There's been like this epidemic of relationships breaking up lately," she observed. "Zoey and Jake. Me and Benjamin. But Aisha's the cool one."

Aisha smiled a little lopsidedly. "It was never any big thing."

"It must have been something fairly major. I mean, you were always above the fray, very cool about guys, and then suddenly you were hanging out with Christopher every time you got the chance."

"We barely ever saw you," Nina added, grimacing around her tamale pie.

"Talking about him. Engaging in public displays of making out and all. Jeez," Claire said, "that time I ran into you two out behind the gym after school, it was one of those scenes that should have been labeled 'young love,' or at least 'young passion.' You looked about ready to start a family." She paused to stare at Nina. "You're eating tamale pie?"

Aisha's face had fallen. She stared down at her tray.

"Let's talk about something else," Zoey said, pointedly giving Claire a look.

Claire looked at Aisha, then winced and sent Zoey a confused *how was I supposed to know* look.

"I've decided to eat dead stuff again," Nina said, trying to start the conversation in a new direction.

"I have to—" Aisha stood up and pointed vaguely in the direction of the door. "Some studying."

"Okay," Zoey said gently. "We'll see you later, Eesh."

Aisha fumbled picking up her books, and a tear dropped onto the table. Then she raced toward the exit.

Claire sat back and rolled her eyes. "Great. Maybe I should go after her."

"And display some more of that sensitivity you're famous for?" Nina asked.

"It's not Claire's fault," Zoey said. "You know Aisha. She always has to be so in control of everything. She keeps everything inside. She can't blame us for believing she really *is* in control."

Jake McRoyan stared blankly at the Xeroxed sheet on the desk in front of him. He had already written his name at the top, but at the moment that was the only thing he recognized on the page.

Since when did Ms. Rafanelli throw a surprise quiz at them on a Tuesday? She did quizzes on Thursday, not Tuesday.

He had actually made a brief effort to scan the assigned reading over the weekend. He'd looked at a few chapters, and it hadn't looked all that bad, as books went. The title involved bells for some reason, but it had been a war story. He'd rented a video of the movie that had been made from the book, but when he'd started to watch it with Lars Ehrlich, they'd decided to drink a few beers and take regular Nintendo breaks, and with one thing or another they hadn't seen much of the movie, either.

1. *For Whom the Bell Tolls* is the story of an American volunteer who fights in which war?

(a) The American Civil War

(b) The War of 1812

(c) The Spanish Civil War

(d) The War of the Roses

Well, forget *d*. Who would have a war and call it "The War of the Roses"? But it could be any of the first three choices.

"*c*."

The whisper was barely audible, but it was real all the same.

Claire, who sat behind him. Claire, who of course had read the book. She was as bad as Zoey when it came to homework. He'd hooked up with two little do-bees when it came to homework.

"Number one is *c*," Claire said.

The back of Jake's neck burned. Was he that obvious? Could she tell just by looking at the back of his head that he was clueless?

It made him furious. Just a few days earlier, Claire had rescued him with some homework he'd fallen behind on. Like he was some pity case all of a sudden.

Of course, in American lit. he was. He was holding on to a bare *C-*, and if it dropped to a *D*, he would be automatically suspended from the football team until he brought the grade back up.

His pencil hovered over the test. This was pathetic; it was just a little multiple-choice quiz to make sure people had read the book. It wasn't exactly a major essay test. Yet he'd been about to answer *a* when Claire had spoken. He'd have been wrong, because Claire definitely wasn't.

She was using this to get back on his good side. Like she'd tried to use the fact that she got him sobered up in time to make the last game.

His pencil still hovered.

He clenched his free hand into an angry fist. Damn Claire, anyway.

"Number two is *d*," the whispered voice said.

Ms. Rafanelli looked up, a puzzled expression on her face. She scanned the room for a moment, then went back to reading her book.

He could either write down the answers Claire was giving him and keep, maybe even slightly improve his low *C*, or he could ignore her, take the *D*, and be suspended for the homecoming game. He was furious at her. She was putting him in a terrible position. He couldn't keep taking her help and then go on treating her the way he had. It was sick. It was like she was seducing him, only with her . . . her niceness.

Claire. Nice. Right.

"Three is *a*."

This time Ms. Rafanelli looked up sharply and her focus was narrower. She knew the section of the room where the subtle sound of cheating was coming from. She probably guessed it was him. Could probably tell from the way he just sat there, with his pencil frozen in midair, looking pissed off, that it was him.

Do it or don't do it, he ordered himself.

He would never accept her help again. That was his decision. After this, never again.

He wrote down the answers in quick succession.

4. Hemingway is considered—

Jake felt a sharp fingernail pressing into his back. He controlled his reaction, keeping his eyes down on his paper. Claire drew her fingernail over the flesh of his back, drawing a distinct 4, followed by the letter *c*. It sent chills through him. He could feel his resolve draining away with each contact.

The next six questions went the same way. He would have an *A* on the quiz. It might be enough to raise him to a solid *C* in the class. He would stay on the team.

The bell rang and he got up, feeling stiff and exhausted, as if he had just gone through some terrible ordeal. He didn't want to look at her, to let her see in his eyes the power her simple touch had over him.

He left quickly and headed directly down the hall toward his next class. But she was at his side.

"Don't bother to say thanks or anything," Claire said.

"I didn't ask for your help," Jake muttered without looking at her.

"Yeah, but you'll get a ninety on the test."

"Ninety?" He stopped and stared. A mistake. He would never be able to stay angry at her when he was looking into her eyes.

She smiled her half smile. "Rafanelli would never buy you getting a perfect score, Jake. I gave you the wrong answer for question five. And I gave myself the wrong answer for question seven. That way it won't look like we cheated."

He shook his head in frank admiration. "Sometimes you're just scary, Claire."

"Thanks, I guess."

"What do you want from me?"

She seemed to consider the question for a moment. "I want you to love me, Jake. I want you to forgive me for what happened two years ago."

Jake met her level, unwavering gaze. Love her? Of course he loved her. The mere touch of her finger on his back had electrified him, setting off reactions he couldn't control, desires he couldn't turn off. If he could only stop loving her, his life might go back to normal. He might not see her face every night in the dark as he lay in bed. The memory of her might not war constantly in his brain with the memory of his brother.

Love me, Jake. Forgive me, Jake.

"One out of two isn't bad," he said sadly.

FIVE

MRS. GRAY GAVE THE SHALLOW pan a shake. "Are you ready, Aisha?"

"Ready." Aisha had four prechilled bowls of vanilla ice cream waiting in the freezer.

"Okay, bring them out. Kalif, turn off the lights."

The lights went out. Mrs. Gray poured a long stream of kirschwasser into the pan, then tilted the pan so the bubbling liquid nearly spilled into the fire of the stove. In an instant the pan went up in a brilliant flash, then settled down into gentler blue tongues of flame.

From the table Mr. Gray applauded. Mrs. Gray quickly spooned the cherries jubilee over the ice cream and Aisha just as quickly shuttled the bowls to the table.

"Excellent," Aisha said enthusiastically, spooning up a bite. "You could open a restaurant and give Zoey's parents some competition."

Her mother smiled at the compliment. "Thanks, but a

bed-and-breakfast is work enough. I don't know how the Passmores do it, breakfast, lunch, and dinner every day. They must
live in that restaurant."

"Zoey says they just about do," Aisha said.

They were eating in the breakfast room, a part of the house
reserved for guests when the tourist season brought people to
the bed-and-breakfast. As fall advanced, though, there were
fewer guests and the Gray family gradually reclaimed more of
the huge building.

"Saw a red phalarope today," Aisha's father said.

Kalif rolled his eyes. Aisha smiled. Her little brother was at
the age where their father just embarrassed him.

"*Phalaropus fulicarius* in Latin," Mr. Gray said.

"What did it look like?" Aisha asked, mostly out of politeness, but at least partly from real interest.

"Well, it was in its winter plumage, gray and white. Has a
call like *Peek! Peek!*"

Kalif looked alarmed, and Aisha smothered a smile. The
spectacle of her bookish, conservative father suddenly exploding
in loud bird noises, something he did regularly, was so incongruous it was hard not to crack up. He was a librarian at the
Weymouth main public library, a place where he fit in perfectly,
unlike here in his own house with his younger, more energetic
wife and his compulsively athletic son.

Aisha was closest to him in temperament. They were both intellectual, reserved, not very emotional people. And to her own surprise, Aisha actually had started noticing the birds that lived on or passed by the island.

"Coffee, honey?" Mrs. Gray asked her husband.

"Just half a cup."

"I want some, too," Aisha said.

Her mother gave her a look. "Since when do you drink coffee?"

"I have a lot of homework to do," Aisha said.

Her mother brought the coffee to the table and poured for Aisha and her father. "What homework do you have?"

"Calc, biology, French, you name it."

Kalif cracked his knuckles loudly. "Pressure getting to you? Huh? Huh? Going to crack? Going to lose it?"

"Is all *your* homework done, Kalif?"

"I knew I shouldn't have said anything."

"I was going to see if you wanted to go out to the mall tomorrow after school," Mrs. Gray said. "Tomorrow's Wednesday; the homecoming dance is on Saturday."

Aisha shrugged. "I don't need to go to the mall," she said nonchalantly.

"Don't you want to get something new to wear? The only things you have for dances are getting a little tight on you."

"What with you getting fat," Kalif interjected.

"Don't press the girl if she doesn't want to spend money on a dress," Mr. Gray said mildly.

"She can't go looking shabby, Alan," Mrs. Gray said.

"Actually, I don't think I'm going at all," Aisha said.

"Uh-oh, trouble in the land of lo-o-ove," Kalif said gleefully.

"You're not going to homecoming?"

Aisha shrugged. "Maybe, maybe not. It's no big deal."

"Are you having a problem with Christopher?" her mother inquired, trying her best not to sound like she was prying.

She *was* prying, and Aisha didn't appreciate it. "He's not even in school," she said evasively. "Homecoming is for students."

"Yep. Trouble," Kalif opined. "I'm not surprised. Christopher was always way too cool for you."

"Kalif, finish going through puberty first, then start worrying about other people's lives," Aisha said. "Look, I'm just not all that into dances and stuff, anyway. I go to school to learn, right? Isn't that the idea?"

"She has you there, Carol," Mr. Gray said.

His wife was undeterred. "Yes, you go to learn, but I thought you were going to this dance with Christopher, that's all. I just need to know whether you're going to want a new dress; that's my only interest in the matter. Kalif, clear the table. It's your turn with dishes."

"So what'd he do, dump you?" Kalif asked.

"No, not that it's any of your scrotelike business, but I dumped him. Actually."

"Big mistake. He was way cool."

"He was a jerk," Aisha said hotly. "And if I wanted to go to the stupid dance, I could easily find a date. Plenty of guys have asked me out."

"Yeah, right. *Human* guys?"

"Kalif, that's enough," Mr. Gray said quietly.

Aisha noticed her mother looking at her with an expression very close to pity.

"It's no big deal," Aisha practically yelled.

"As long as you're okay," her mother said in her concerned voice.

"Look. I caught him with some other girl, all right? So he's a toad, all right? So he's out of my life, all right? So forget about him. *I* have." She took a last sip of her coffee. "Now, *I* have homework to do. You can all sit around and discuss my private life if you want, but I'm busy."

She turned with perfect control and began walking away. Her mother caught up to her at her bedroom door.

"Mother," Aisha said patiently. She only called her mother

mother when she was annoyed. "I don't need a little heart-to-heart talk, okay?"

Her mother held up her hands in a gesture of innocence. "Not me. I was just going to say if he was trying to pressure you into sleeping with him, you did the right thing, dumping him."

Aisha felt weary. "Of course he was pressuring me. Guys usually do, but I know how you feel about that and I know how I feel about that. It wasn't about sex. It was what I said—I walked in on him and this girl and then he lied to me about seventy-five times in less than five minutes."

"So you dumped him for being a two-timing liar?"

Aisha sighed. "Yes, Mother."

Her mother grabbed her and crushed her in a hug. "My girl," she said proudly. "Teach that boy a lesson."

"I thought you really liked Christopher."

"I do. Or I did. But if he's going to lie to you, then bye-bye."

"Bye-bye," Aisha repeated.

"There are other boys. Find someone else to go to the dance with."

"You mean so I can rub Christopher's nose in it."

"Of course. How do you think your father and I got together the first time? Your father was the guy I went out with just to get back at my old boyfriend."

"So, you been working on your romance novel lately?" Nina asked. She was lying on her back on the floor of Zoey's room, throwing a troll doll someone had given Zoey up in the air and trying to catch it. Unfortunately, Nina was no athlete and she kept banging the hard plastic doll against the sloped ceiling, making a loud noise and distracting Zoey from her homework.

"No. Not lately," Zoey muttered. She was sitting at the desk in her dormered window, trying to compose a story for her journalism class. It was supposed to be an account of a speech the president had given on tax reform. It had not been an exciting speech, and every time she tried to read the printed version of it, her mind wandered off. Writing a story about a speech you couldn't force yourself to actually read was a challenge.

Nina threw the troll into the air. It hit the slanted ceiling, took a bad bounce, and landed on Zoey's head.

"Nina!"

"Sorry."

"I have a stuffed bear you could throw. It's soft."

"So are you ever going to let me read any of your romance novel?"

Zoey shook her head definitely. "No. First of all, it's not a novel. It's just a first chapter rewritten about twenty times. Second of all, you would laugh."

"Maybe not."

Zoey put down her pencil and rubbed her forehead. "I can't even write *this* stupid story. I'm not exactly ready to start writing romance novels."

Nina sat up. "Maybe it's the subject matter. Maybe you have a good feel for romance and you aren't into politics."

"I don't know that I'm an expert on romance," Zoey said dryly. "Now, Claire would be an expert."

"Yeah, well, I'm a total amateur and I can't ask Claire," Nina said, her sentence trailing off into a low mutter.

Zoey looked at her. "What are you talking about, Nina?" Nina was seldom so indirect.

Her friend shrugged. "I was just saying I don't know very much about all that stuff. I mean, I've only ever kissed one guy—I mean, voluntarily—and then I practically gacked up a kidney."

"Oh. Are you worried about going out with Benjamin?"

"Worried? Not worried, really. Quivering in terror, sure. It's just that I'm not very experienced. I'm like a Muslim in a liquor store. I'm like a Republican trying to understand rap lyrics."

Zoey waited patiently. Nina followed what she called her three-part comic tautology rule—funny examples should come in threes.

"Hang on, I'm thinking," Nina said, wrinkling her brow. "Okay. I'm like a fashion model in a bookstore. Come on, that one's good."

"So, you're saying you feel lost, confused, intimidated?"

"Yes, yes, help me, please." She clasped her hands in supplication.

"What is it you want to know?" Zoey said, feeling a little uncomfortable. After all, Nina was going to be out with her brother.

"All the dating protocol. You know, do you hold hands? If you do hold hands, is it just like shaking-hands style, or interlocked fingers, and what if your hand gets sweaty, and how do you know when to stop?"

"Well, Nina, really it's kind of up to you. I mean, what do you feel comfortable doing?"

"I don't feel *comfortable* doing anything. Not to be gross, but when I like even think about kissing a guy or whatever . . . especially whatever . . . I get these flashes back to my uncle and all. It's not like I'm hallucinating or going schizo; it's just I start thinking about it and it makes me sick."

"It's not gross, Nina, it's just kind of sad," Zoey said gently. "I mean, the whole dating thing is weird enough without adding extra levels of weirdness."

"I thought maybe if I could get used to the idea ahead of

time, I could deal with it when it happens. Like when I have to go to my gynecologist, I spend a week ahead of time going, 'It's okay, she's a doctor, she's not going to hurt you, she's just a nice old lady with no sense of humor,' and so on. I even write out little scenarios. You know, like I'll write that I'll go in, lose it, and end up running out into the street wearing one of those paper dresses they give you. Then when I'm there, it's just unpleasant, as opposed to terrifying."

"Well, no one exactly enjoys being in those stirrups," Zoey admitted. "Believe me, whatever happens between you and Benjamin, it won't be *that* unpleasant." She shook her head. "I can't believe I'm talking about this."

"So, show me how to hold hands the right way," Nina said.

Zoey scooted down to the floor beside Nina, feeling thoroughly foolish. She sat facing the same direction as Nina, side by side. "Okay, say you're at a movie."

"You're at a movie."

"Are you going to be making jokes all the way through this?" Zoey asked.

"So, we're at a movie."

"Put your hand like it's on the armrest."

"Why?"

"Because if you want him to hold your hand, you don't want to have your hand in your lap, right?" Zoey explained. "I mean, make it easy for the guy. You want him to have to rummage around in your lap looking for your hand?"

"No, then I would definitely hurl," Nina said. "We'd be talking supersonic popcorn." She held her hand up on an imaginary armrest.

Zoey ran her fingers through her hair, fiddled with the neck of her shirt, wiped her hands on her shorts.

"What are you doing?"

"I'm being the guy," Zoey said. "They usually take a while to get their nerve up." She let her hand creep along the imaginary armrest, until her elbow was resting and the side of her hand was touching the side of Nina's hand.

"Is that it?" Nina demanded.

"This is just phase one. He wants to see if you'll yank your hand away."

"Will I?" Nina asked anxiously. "I mean, should I?"

"No, Nina. You keep up the contact. Then, after a while he gets up his nerve to make the big jump." She slid her hand over Nina's.

"What do I do?"

"I would do this." Zoey turned her hand palm up and interlaced her fingers with Nina's.

"Okay."

"That's it."

"Doesn't seem like much," Nina said, sounding a little disappointed.

"It will seem like a lot more when it's a guy," Zoey reassured her.

"Yeah, that's what worries me. But I guess I can handle this. As long as I don't have to kiss or anything."

"Good, because I'm not about to teach you that," Zoey said.

"Maybe if it was just a little kiss-on-the-cheek kind of thing. Like a Hollywood air kiss."

Zoey smiled at Nina, still holding her hand. "Don't worry so much. It's Benjamin. Which, by the way, has advantages. You don't have to worry about long, lingering looks deep into each other's eyes. Also, you can go the whole night with a piece of spinach stuck in your teeth without him ever noticing."

"Yeah."

"It will all be fine. You won't panic and you won't hurl."

"It's not like I don't feel all those romantic kind of things," Nina said in a dreamy, reflective voice. "I do. I mean, you know, all those things you feel about guys."

"Yes, I know those things," Zoey said dryly. She thought back to the first time she had kissed Lucas. And the most recent time. She sighed.

"Mmm. Um, Zoey?"

"Yes?"

"We're still holding hands. I mean, I like you and all, but . . ."

BENJAMIN

Good TV shows for a blind person are, first of all, talk shows. Obviously. They're mostly ~~conservation~~ conversation and not much reliance on visuals. Also, comedy of any kind except juggling.

Nature shows, documentaries, anything on the Discovery Channel, you can forget. Ten minutes at a time of the sounds of wind whistling across the savannah and then the narrator comes on and says, "The lion pride has moved off through the trees," followed by another ten minutes of wind sounds.

By the same token, there are people who are good for blind people and others ~~hwo~~ who aren't. What you want are people who talk, and when they talk they have something to say. Generally, girls are better at expressing themselves in words, and so I've tended to have more female friends than male.

Convenient, huh?

Take Lucas. I like him, but the guy doesn't have a lot to say most of the time. Jake is even worse. He could be in the room for an hour and I wouldn't know it unless he farted or cleared his throat or something. Whereas when my sister's around, she usually has something to say and she says it well. She'll make a good writer someday ~~because~~ because when you ask her to describe something, she can make it come alive.

Her friend Aisha is the exception to the rule about girls. Very internalized, which may be great for her, but makes her almost invisible to me at times.

Now, Nina, as my father would say in one of his flash-back-to-the-seventies moments, is a trip. Listening to Nina is almost like hearing a performance of some sort. She has fun with words. Her own, mine, anyone's. It's one of the reasons I love to have her read to me. She doesn't just read; she interprets. She sort of *acts* the book, although I don't think she's even aware of it.

Then there's Claire. Not a very talkative person, really. She only makes small talk to be polite. Claire keeps her secrets, and the biggest secret she keeps is her real self. Why I was ever interested in her to begin with, I ~~coulnd't~~ couldn't say. Maybe <u>because</u> she was so withdrawn. I couldn't look into her eyes, or read her expression, or interpret her body language. I could only listen to her words and from those few clues try to understand a girl

300

who did not want to be understood.

Later, though, there was touch. And not even Claire
can conceal the meaning of a racing pulse, a tremor, a
soft yielding, a sudden sharp intake of breath.

SIX

ON TUESDAY NIGHT CHRISTOPHER LEFT Passmores', the restaurant
owned by Zoey's parents, at eleven twenty-five, after sending out the last late order, changing the fat in the deep fryers,
stoning the grill, finishing up the dishwashing, prepping pan-
cake batter for the morning shift, sweeping and mopping the
kitchen, mopping out the walk-in, turning off the lights, and
locking the doors.

He rode his bike to his apartment, watched the Top Ten list
on *Letterman*, and fell asleep just before midnight, the remote
control still in his hand.

Three hours later, his alarm went off. He made a cup of
coffee, spooned up a bowl of Grape-Nuts, showered, dressed,
and was on his bike, heading toward the ferry landing by three
twenty-five A.M.

The bundled newspapers from Weymouth, Portland, and
Boston, and of course the *Wall Street Journal*, lay wrapped in
heavy plastic on the dock. It was still pitch-black out, and he

was the only person awake in North Harbor or any other part of Chatham Island. It was cold enough to make his breath steam, and his hands had grown numb during the brief bike trip. Tomorrow he would have to remember gloves. And when it got really cold in the hard winter months, well, he had no idea what he'd do. He'd probably have to buy an island car.

He divided the newspapers. The heavy *Boston Globe*s in his backpack, the other papers apportioned in the two saddlebags.

He rode the easy parts of the route first, following level, smoothly paved Lighthouse Road, throwing a rubber-banded *Portland Press-Herald* here, a *Weymouth Times* there. Claire and Nina's house, dark and silent, got all four. Mr. Geiger liked plenty to read on his morning ferry ride to work.

Gradually the load grew lighter, and Christopher took on the teeth-rattling cobblestoned streets and the steep slopes that circled the base of the hill.

The two-thirds point in his route was Aisha's home. It was up a backbreaking hill, winding to the top of the ridge. He always paused and rested after reaching it. He deposited their two newspapers and rested his bike against the fence.

He had never been in Aisha's room, but he thought he knew where it was from her casual descriptions. It was around the right and toward the back.

Feeling a little foolish, he walked through the garden across frosted pine needles that crunched like cornflakes and located her two windows. He was disappointed to see that there was no light from inside. He would have loved to have looked at her. He had this fantasy that someday she would start setting her alarm for this time of morning. She would welcome him through her window and into her warm bed. Then he would go on with his route and she would go back to sleep, both of them happy and satisfied.

"Not likely," he muttered under his breath.

He headed back to his bike and finished the outer reaches of his route, the long easy coast back down the hill, the big, extended circle going down along the eastern shore around Big Bite Pond, then back to his apartment on the western shore.

By five he was done. He parked his bike and fell into his bed facedown.

He slept until seven, got up, biked to an empty house on Coast Road where he was installing storm shutters, worked till nine, rode to the ferry landing, and caught the water taxi over to Weymouth. The water taxi was free to him for the season, in exchange for work he had done during the summer, scraping and repainting the boat. On the trip over he caught fifteen minutes' sleep hunched over on the bench.

He arrived at Weymouth High just before ten and immediately began organizing the sports equipment room, cleaning balls, replacing torn basketball nets, and running equipment out to the field for the boys' and girls' gym classes.

On good days, this was his easy job, affording him ten minutes of sleep here, fifteen minutes there, crashed out on a soft pile of gym mats between classes.

He was scheduled to cook that night, and at the end of the workday at school he would catch the next ferry or water taxi and start setting up the kitchen for his shift.

He usually had one or two evenings a week free, but this wasn't one of them.

Not counting the work he did around the apartment building in exchange for reduced rent, he averaged seventy-five hours a week of work, earning a total take-home income of about four hundred dollars a week. So far he had saved nearly three thousand dollars. By the end of next summer he would have the tuition, room, and board for his first year of college.

Then, with hard studying and a clean academic record, he could go for student loans and grants and even a scholarship. He would have to overcome a weak high school record to make it into a good college. Without anyone's help. Without relying on anyone but himself.

It was a hard life, and he was entitled, he felt, to a little comfort where and when he could get it. Something Aisha just didn't seem to understand. He wasn't trying to pressure Aisha into it because the truth was, someday, way down the road, he could see the two of them together. Married, maybe. It was possible.

But what was not possible was that monogamy would start now. Especially a celibate monogamy. The pursuit of his goals already denied him any kind of life, and that was all the self-denial he could take.

Right now, living this life, he felt he needed more than promises of someday, someday. . . .

Nina finished telling her story and looked as boldly as she could manage at the psychiatrist. Dr. Kendall nodded several times and looked at her thoughtfully.

"And what is being done now about your uncle?"

Nina shrugged. "My dad has his lawyer talking to a lawyer in Minnesota about talking to the prosecutor there. Legal stuff. My dad said we might not know anything definite for quite a while."

"And how does that make you feel?"

"Claire warned me you liked to ask that question."

Dr. Kendall smiled. "How is Claire? She's stopped coming."

"Well, you know Claire. Actually, you *do* know Claire. Nothing gets my sister down for long. She always copes. But then, who am I to tell you this, right?"

"Actually, that's pretty close to my own feelings about Claire. Considering the death of your mother and the events of the accident and all that followed . . ." She raised her eyebrows philosophically. "She's a very adaptive person."

"How about me? Will I be needing shock therapy? I hear it's kind of a fun high."

Dr. Kendall looked alarmed, then laughed uneasily. "No, I don't think electroconvulsive therapy is necessary, Nina. I think maybe just weekly sessions for a while."

"The truth is, I feel fine. I mean, actually, I feel better than I usually do. If anything, I've been kind of up, you know? People keep coming over to me all droopy-eyed, asking me how I'm doing, and half the time I forget what they're talking about. Then it's like, oh yeah, *that*. I was hoping to be able to tell them all I was getting shock therapy, then kind of give a little spaz." She demonstrated, jerking her neck to one side and twisting her mouth. "I guess I could still *tell* them I was getting the juice."

"Why would you want to do that?"

Nina smiled. "My *other* therapist is an expert in getting people to drop the pity routine. He's blind."

"The same boy your sister was seeing?"

"Benjamin, right. There aren't a lot of blind guys around in school, just him. When he went blind, he started making a thing of it, you know? Like in his room he has posters up on the walls, only half of them are upside down. When people come over for the first time, he'll talk about how proud he is of this great art print and it will be like a map of Poland or something. Some people are very slow to get the joke, or else they'll play along because they think he'll have a breakdown if they tell him the truth."

"I see. He makes a joke out of his blindness."

"Yeah, but it's *his* joke. No one can make fun of him because whatever they're going to say, Benjamin's already said it better and funnier." Nina smiled and for a moment almost forgot where she was. "He's basically the coolest human being I know. His parents pay me to read to him sometimes and he's just so . . . I don't know. He's just very, very cool."

"Is there some romantic interest here?"

Nina snapped back to reality. The word *romantic* surprised her. "We're going out on a date this weekend," she admitted.

"Do you feel comfortable going out on a date so soon after what's happened?"

Nina nodded. "With Benjamin, sure. It's not like he's going to try and drag me off to a Motel 6."

"He's someone you can trust."

"Yes," Nina said softly. "I trust Benjamin."

"And your sister?"

"No, I don't trust her at all," Nina said quickly, although

what the shrink meant was obvious.

"I meant to say is this a comfortable thing between you and Claire, that you're going out with her former boyfriend?"

"He told me he's still kind of in love with her," Nina admitted. "Of course, so are half the guys in school."

Dr. Kendall glanced at her watch. "Our hour is about up, Nina. I think we've had a very productive first session. I want to leave you with one thing to bear in mind—you may be a little vulnerable right now. Incest and molestation are not minor events. You won't be able to just put them behind you as easily as you'd like."

Nina nodded.

"In the meantime, go slow with this boy Benjamin, okay? Give yourself some time to adjust to normal relationships with members of the opposite sex."

"I've given myself sixteen years, so far," Nina said.

"Mmm. Don't be in a hurry. But have fun."

"Okay." Nina stood up and stretched up on her toes. She rarely sat still for this long. "So, before I go, just tell me one thing. When they do the shock treatment, do they stick something in your mouth so you don't bite your tongue off?"

SEVEN

ZOEY'S MOTHER HAD SPENT THE afternoon at the oral surgeon having a molar removed. She was high on codeine and not in a condition to work. Mrs. Toombs, who worked as a waitress, was in Lewiston visiting her son and her daughter-in-law. Christopher was cooking, which left Zoey to handle the restaurant for the night, waiting on any tables and tending the bar.

Her father had asked whether she could handle it so he could stay home with her mother. Zoey had said yes, she could handle it as long as she got bartender pay, which was higher than waiter pay.

To Zoey's annoyance, there was a strong early dinner rush that had her running like a rat in a maze from dining room to bar to kitchen and around again. But by eight it had calmed down considerably. In fact, there was just one table occupied and some regulars at the bar who wouldn't mind pouring their own drinks if Zoey wasn't handy.

She pushed open the kitchen door, tore the top slip off the ticket, and slapped it down on the stainless steel counter that separated her from Christopher.

"Ordering," she said.

"You got much more out there, Zo?" Christopher asked, reading the ticket. His hands began to move automatically, pulling a metal plate of fish from the reach-in, bending over to get a steak and tossing it casually onto the grill, checking to see if he had sufficient baked potatoes. "I'll give 'em two small lobsters, okay? All I have left are small."

"They won't mind that," Zoey said wearily. "This will probably be the last table unless we're just cursed. Thanks for coming out there and busing those tables. You didn't have to do that, although if you hadn't, I'd be dead by now."

"No prob."

Zoey slid up onto the counter, grateful for the opportunity to take the load off her feet for a moment. She picked at a run in her panty hose. "It's times like this I wished I smoked or drank or something. Some little ritual so I would know I was taking a break."

Christopher checked the steak, glanced at the fish, and began methodically garnishing the plates. "So, Zoey. What has Aisha told you?" He kept his eyes down on his work, trying to look uninterested.

Zoey shrugged. "She mentioned you were more or less broken up."

"More or less? She said more or less?"

"Actually, closer to *more*. But I don't think I should be talking to you about this. Aisha's my friend."

"And I'm not?" He smiled winningly.

"You're my friend, too," Zoey said quickly, wishing she could just avoid this. She was sure to end up pissing off either Christopher or Aisha. Or maybe both of them. "It's a girl thing."

"Yeah, well, you know, I'm crazy about Aisha. I wish we could work something out." He was back to concentrating on his work. He moved away to turn the steak and poke at the lobsters. "I mean, I don't want it to end like this. It wasn't my idea."

Zoey started to say something, then stopped herself. Then she said it anyway. "Wasn't there some other girl?"

He shrugged. "That didn't mean anything."

"Then why was she in your room if she didn't mean anything?" Zoey demanded in exasperation.

He shrugged again. "She was hot-looking."

"Well, then, I guess you were totally helpless. What could you do if she was hot-looking?"

"I never told Aisha it was a strict one-on-one thing," Christopher pointed out.

"You never told her it wasn't, either. You should have figured out she'd be hurt."

Christopher winced. "That's just about exactly what your boyfriend told me."

"Lucas?"

"Do you have another?"

"Lucas knew you were seeing this other girl?" Zoey asked.

Christopher made a face. "Oh. Suddenly I have the feeling I should have kept my mouth shut."

Lucas knew? And he hadn't told *her*? He'd let Aisha walk into that scene and be humiliated? In a flash she remembered the way Lucas had sort of done a double take the day Aisha had shown up on the verge of tears and mentioned another girl. Part of her was relieved. She'd wondered if Lucas was reacting out of some personal guilt.

"It was a guy thing," Christopher explained helpfully.

"I'd better go check on the dining room," Zoey said, hopping down from the counter.

"Great, now Lucas will be pissed at me, too."

"I won't tell him you told me," Zoey promised.

"Look, Zo, what I really wanted to ask was whether maybe you could talk to Aisha. You know, see if there's any way we can maybe get past this." He shook his head ruefully. "I miss her. I'd appreciate it if you'd tell her that for me. That's all, just tell her I miss her."

．．．

"Okay. Scenario one," Nina said. She was in her room, lying on her bed, feet propped on the wall, staring up at a poster of the Black Keys. Her laptop was playing a One Republic song, just loudly enough that no one would be able to hear her talking to herself.

"It's Saturday night, we're supposed to meet at the ferry, he decides not to show up. There I am, standing around with Zoey and Lucas and Jake and Eesh. And Claire, who laughs and says, 'What did you expect? Like Benjamin would want to go out with you?'"

Nina considered the scenario for a moment. Not so bad, really. A little humiliating, but she could get over it and the real pressure would be off.

"Okay. Something better. Scenario two. Um, we go to the dance, we walk in together, the music stops, everyone stops talking and stares at us. Then they start laughing."

The humiliation level would be much higher because it would involve a lot more people. And they would all be thinking *Oh, look, Nina's pretending to like guys. Isn't Benjamin sweet to play along with her?*

Still, as unpleasant as that was, it wasn't getting to what really scared her.

"Scenario three. And you'll like this one, Dan," she told the poster. "We go to the dance, and then we have to slow dance, he puts his arms around me, and boom, flashback time. All the feelings start and I panic. I run screaming from the room while waves of laughter mixed with pity pursue me. Yeah, that's more like it."

Unfortunately, it wasn't possible to completely dismiss the scenario. In the recesses of her mind, a male's touch, any male, meant only one thing. She'd been eleven years old when her uncle had begun two months of almost nightly abuse. Old enough to know what was going on. Old enough to form detailed, precise, lurid memories full of his touch and the sound of his voice. Memories of shame and self-loathing, of wishing she were dead, of wishing she were horribly disfigured so that he wouldn't want her anymore. Memories that haunted her sleep and came boiling up to the surface whenever she felt sexually threatened. And a threat could be something very innocuous. At those times she felt like some timid wild creature like a deer, easily startled, ready to run from anything in blind panic.

Once a guy, a perfectly nice guy, had tried to kiss her, and she'd nearly thrown up. It was one of the events that had people believing she was gay. Or else wondering if she really was as crazy as she sometimes pretended to be.

"Scenario four. The dreaded kiss. We've danced, we've joked around, we've done whatever, and now he wants to kiss me. Or else he really doesn't want to but he figures it's the polite thing to do after the date. He leans close, and it's suddenly like I'm back *there*."

The image alone was deeply disturbing. It was a strange, churning mix of conflicting feelings. Part of her wanted Benjamin to kiss her. Really, really wanted. But another part of her grew sick at the thought of a man's mouth pressed against her own. Of a man's hands on her body.

"Stop it!" Nina cried. She rolled over and off the bed. She went to the laptop and turned the music off. Then she sat down in a chair and leaned forward, keeping her head between her knees to fight off the wave of nausea.

This was how she would behave on Saturday night. She could feel it. She could see the moment as if it had already happened. It would be the end. Not even Benjamin was that tolerant or patient. No guy ever would be.

Zoey was out of the restaurant by ten, leaving it to Christopher to close up for the night. She left carrying the zippered plastic deposit bag with the night's receipts. There was a tiny bank branch on the circle, installed there by Mr. Geiger as a convenience for his fellow Chatham Islanders.

The cobblestoned streets were deserted and dark, even at this relatively early hour. The only nightlife the island had was in the two restaurants, her parents' and Topsider's, which was just closing as she passed by.

She trudged on bruised feet up Exchange, feeling the sense of safety that was one of the best things about living on an island. Over in Weymouth there might be the occasional holdup or rape, but even the densest criminals knew better than to try to operate on an island with three hundred residents and the only escape route by ferry.

She reached the garish, fluorescent automatic teller machine and the drop box. She fished out the key and slid the bank bag inside. Then she headed toward home, circumnavigating the circle.

Something caught her eye, a movement from the grassy center of the circle. She peered closely and, even in the mix of streetlight and starlight, could see that it was Jake.

"Hey, Zoey," he said, raising a languid hand. He sat slumped back on a bench.

Zoey smiled awkwardly. Since their breakup, she and Jake had steered clear of each other—as much as you could when you both had to take the same ferry twice a day and share three classes.

She wasn't sure if he was just being polite or if he expected her to stop by. She decided the polite and decent thing to do was cross into the circle.

"You're out late," he said. "Work?"

"Yeah. My mom had some work done on her teeth."

"Uh huh. How's biz?"

She shrugged. It was odd, talking to him without other people around. Once they would have been sitting here together, making out and planning what they were going to do the next day or the rest of their lives. "I did okay on tips." She jangled the money stuffed in her pockets, a wad of quarters and singles and a few fives. "What are you doing out here?"

"Not a damned thing," he said flatly.

"Taking it easy, huh?"

"Yep. I guess that's it. I guess I'm taking it easy."

Again she was at a loss for something to say. Jake seemed like he'd been drinking, or else he was just very tired. His eyes were sad, but the rest of his face was frozen in a blank expression. He was breathing heavily, as though the air was thick.

"That was a pretty strange scene last weekend, huh? You know, with Nina and all," Zoey finally said.

He dropped his head forward and jerked it up and down twice in a nod. "Yeah. Yeah."

"Well. I guess I'd better head on home." She forced a tinny laugh. "See if my mom's OD'd on painkillers yet. She hates going to the dentist."

Jake said nothing, just stared down at the sparse grass.

"Anyway. Bye." She turned and took two steps before stopping and turning back. "Jake, are you okay?"

"Okay?" He lifted his head. "I'm always okay, Zoey."

"It's just that you seem depressed."

"Now, why would I be depressed?" There was the telltale edge of sarcasm in his voice, but even that was tired.

Zoey felt a flash of anger. It wasn't like Jake to wallow in self-pity. Look how Nina was dealing with her problems. She wasn't turning into a drunk and feeling sorry for herself. Or Lucas. And his life wasn't exactly a day at Disney World.

But in hot pursuit of her anger came guilt. She had been the one to dump Jake. Then, in almost no time at all, his relationship with Claire had fallen apart. He'd been on a real roller coaster emotionally, and at least a part of that was her fault.

"Look, Jake, I'm sorry things worked out the way they did for you. You're the nicest guy on earth, and you deserve better."

"No. Wade was the nicest guy on earth," he said. Now the slur in his speech was obvious.

He was drunk. Again. If he kept this up, he was going to develop a problem. Maybe he already had. "Look, I know he was your brother and all, but he wasn't very nice, really. Wade was a bully. I used to hate the way he treated you."

Jake stared at her like she was talking gibberish. "He was tough, see? He was—" He hesitated, at a loss for words. "He always said I was a wuss."

"He was wrong, Jake. He was just giving you a hard time."

"He was *right*." Jake emphasized the point by stabbing his finger at her.

"Jake, have you been drinking? You never used to drink."

"I've discovered I have a talent for it," he said, grinning.

Again Zoey realized how out of place she felt. It was amazing that such a wall could grow up so quickly between two people who had been close. "Jake, if you ever want to just talk . . . I'm still your friend."

"Thanks, Zo," he said softly.

"You should head home. School tomorrow and all." She clasped her arms tightly around herself to show that she was cold. "Besides, you don't want to get pneumonia."

"I'll do that, Zoey," he said. "I'll head home in just a little while."

"Good night," she said.

He didn't answer.

EIGHT

MIDNIGHT

ZOEY WOKE FROM A FITFUL sleep. The Boston Bruins shirt she slept in had become twisted. She flopped around to straighten it out and by the time she was done, she was wide awake. She got up and went over to the dormered window where she had a built-in desk. On one wall of the dormer were yellow Post-it notes she used to tack up great quotes, things to think about on nights when she couldn't sleep.

Soul meets soul on lovers' lips. —Shelley

She'd found the quote and posted it, thinking of Lucas. But now she found she was remembering Jake, so sad sitting in the dark circle. She had kissed Jake many more times over the years than she had Lucas. She had never felt for Jake the sort of overwhelming feeling she had for Lucas, but she had loved him nevertheless. And it seemed wrong to now just dismiss him from her mind when he seemed to need help.

Jake had always had an overdeveloped sense of duty. He felt bound by some loyalty to his dead brother. And yet he had always been an emotional guy. When he fell in love, he fell hard. And now he was caught between being loyal to his brother and hopelessly in love with Claire, the girl he blamed for his brother's death.

But how could Zoey help him? How could anyone, really, when the battle was all between Jake and Jake?

12:45 A.M.

Nina got up to pee, cursing the Pepsi she'd drunk before going to bed. The floor was cold under her bare feet, and after getting back to her room, she hopped back into bed and tucked the blankets around her toes.

Then she remembered she'd been dreaming. Not one of the awful dreams about her uncle, fortunately. She'd been dreaming about Benjamin. In her dream he could see. She was reading to him, some long, boring book, and she'd looked up to see him smiling. His sunglasses were on his lap and his eyes were actually focusing on her. *Who are you?* he'd asked.

Nina wasn't sure how she felt about the dream. It was certainly an improvement over her usual dreams, but at the same time it was slightly disturbing in a way. Benjamin had been asking who she was, like he really didn't recognize her, but at the same time there had been this slight leer in his expression.

It wasn't at all like the way she remembered her uncle looking at her, not really. Still, it had made her feel strange. In the dream and now, remembering it.

The dream obviously had some great metaphorical meaning that she was just too sleepy to make sense of right now. Maybe she'd remember to tell Dr. Kendall next week. Shrinks loved dreams.

She fell back asleep, wondering if it was possible that people met in their dreams, sharing the same dream, or if that was just some dopey romantic idea she'd heard from Zoey.

1:04 A.M.

Jake opened one eye, glued nearly shut by sleep. For a moment, he thought he saw Claire right there in his room. Then he realized it was just a shadow cast on the sheer curtains by the moon. His mouth was parched from the alcohol working its way through his system. He decided to get up and get a drink of water but fell asleep before he could act on the urge.

1:10 A.M.

Lucas drifted through a shockingly explicit dream involving

Zoey, a starlit beach, and slow motion. Several times he moaned in his sleep. Finally the sound of his own voice woke him up. He groaned and tried to go immediately back to sleep, hoping to complete the dream. Instead he drifted into a completely uninteresting dream involving cows.

1:45 A.M.

Benjamin pushed the button on the clock and it spoke the time: "The time is one forty-five A.M." He had been awake, lying in his bed for an hour after waking up from a dream. It was one of the "seeing" dreams he'd had often back in the days after he first lost his sight. This time, in the dream, he'd been dreaming he was blind and when he woke, he was relieved to discover that he could see perfectly well.

Then he'd been on the ferry, on a brilliantly sunny day. Many of the people he knew were there: Zoey, Jake, Claire, Nina. And then in the dream he'd realized that it *was* only a dream. The people he was seeing were all as they'd been when he was much younger. A ten-year-old Zoey, a Jake who was still a boy, a Claire in knee socks.

And then a little girl with braces had come over and taken his hand. She had an unlit Lucky Strike dangling from her lip and was carrying some large, boring-looking book. Nina.

I was just dreaming about you, she said.

Benjamin lay back in his bed and tried to forget the visual images. They were meaningless, just part of a dream. The real world was darkness.

2:08 A.M.

Claire smiled in her sleep. She was dreaming of a huge storm, rolling right over the top of the widow's walk while she ate peanuts under her rain slicker.

3:00 A.M.

Christopher's alarm went off, and he woke feeling tired and demoralized. His three hours of sleep had been fitful. He shouldn't have asked Zoey to talk to Aisha. That was so high school. Aisha would think he was being a wimp. She'd think he was crawling back to her, looking for forgiveness. Only he wasn't in the wrong here. He wasn't. If anyone should apologize, it was probably Aisha, only he was too damned tired to think of why.

Well, let it go, he told himself. *Forget about it. Shouldn't have let the girl ruin your sleep.*

He sat up in bed and shook his head, trying to clear away the bad feelings. He had work to do, papers to deliver. Couldn't sleep now. Papers to deliver. Like to Aisha's house.

He got up and made a quick cup of coffee.

4:28 A.M.

Aisha drifted through a shockingly explicit dream involving Christopher, an open bedroom window, and slow motion. Several times she moaned in her sleep. Finally the sound of her own voice woke her up. She looked first at the window. No, it was securely locked.

Then she heard what sounded like footsteps on the frosty pine needles outside, a sound like cornflakes crunching. A moment later, a second sound like a bike on gravel. She went back to sleep, annoyed at her subconscious for concocting ridiculous scenarios involving a guy she had already forgotten.

4:50 A.M.

Nina had another dream. Someone was holding her hand. Or, more accurately, several some-ones. One minute it was Benjamin. Then it was her uncle. Then, oddly enough, Zoey. Then it was her shrink, who was attaching electrodes. Nina pulled her hand away and stuck it under her pillow.

Nina

Once, like years ago when I was only fourteen and hence not responsible for the sheer dorkiness of my actions, I tried to simulate what Benjamin "saw" of me. I got out my tape recorder app and taped myself chattering away in a sort of <u>Pretty Little Liars</u> kind of sophisticated conversation, very cool. No, way past cool.

Now, don't laugh too much, because we both know that you've pranced around in front of the mirror making pouting faces and sucking in your stomach and thrusting out your buffers with your hands on your hips, imagining what you look like to some guy. I just had to be more inventive.

Anyway, I played back the recording, while smelling my deodorant, my toothpaste, and my shampoo in a sort of approximation of the input Benjamin got off me.

Okay, maybe that is stranger than pouting in a mirror.

Anyway, I was able to conclude from this experiment that I was probably making a very good impression on Benjamin. Assuming Benjamin liked girls who sounded like Lucy Hale on speed and reeked of Crest Mint Gel.

I don't think at that point that I had really begun to have romantic thoughts about Benjamin. He and Claire were just moving into total couplehood then, and I still mostly thought of him as Zoey's mysterious big brother.

In fact, I wasn't sure I even liked him until one day when he and I were in the Passmores' living room, waiting for Zoey for some reason or other. I was kind of at a loss for anything to say because what I really wanted to say was <u>Hey, if you're blind, can you still pee standing up?</u> Which, even then, seemed like a fairly idiotic question. Anyway, what I ended up doing was blurting out the whole tape recorder and toothpaste story.

He laughed till I thought he was going to collapse a lung.

Then he said, "Thanks, kid. That was the funniest thing I've heard in weeks."

Not the dumbest thing, or the strangest thing, which is what Claire, or a lot of my friends, would have said. The funniest. He was actually grateful to me for making him laugh.

I've liked Benjamin ever since.

NINE

THURSDAY MORNING WAS A COLD one as Zoey, Nina, and Aisha huddled together on the deck of the ferry. Not Maine-winter cold, which would drive them all belowdecks to the heated comfort zone, but crisp and windy. The water was the color of lead, beneath a sky like the underside of a mattress that stretched from horizon to horizon in unbroken gloom.

Nina was sucking frantically on her unlit cigarette and chattering at a mile a minute. Aisha seemed lost in some private reflection, occasionally smiling dreamily, then scowling as if to compensate. Zoey felt gloomy and distracted, watching Jake hunched forward in one of the last benches, looking sick.

"I don't know," Nina said. "I mean, how do you decide these things? On the one hand, I want to look all right so that people won't think I'm Benjamin's pity date, like *What's he doing with skank-woman?* But I don't want to suddenly turn into you, Zoey; no offense, but you know what I mean. I can't do the J. Crew,

Miss Perfect Teen, could-be-a-cheerleader-if-I-really-wanted-to, shop at The Gap, honor society with oak leaf clusters, listen to bands where no one has a tattoo, practically-ready-for-VH1 thing." She sucked on her cigarette and glared at Aisha. "What are you grinning about?"

"Just buy a dress you like," Zoey suggested. "Benjamin's not a person who is hung up on fashion. He doesn't know what fashion is."

"A *dress*. Like you're saying it has to be a *dress?*" Nina asked anxiously.

"I'm not saying that, Nina, although I imagine you'll want to wear a dress. You know, it's not quite the prom, but it's like the number-two dance of the year as far as getting dressed up and all."

"Hey, babe." Lucas dropped into the bench behind them, leaned forward, and squeezed Zoey's shoulders.

"Where have you been?" Zoey asked. "And by the way, I have to talk to you about something. Later."

"That doesn't sound good."

"It's not something we should go into now," Zoey said quietly but significantly. "All I'm going to say is you have to think about whose side you're on when you're keeping secrets."

"You mean—" He jerked his head slightly toward Aisha.

"You know what I mean," Zoey said, nodding discreetly.

"That was a guy thing, Zoey. What was I supposed to do?"

"Can we do this later?" Zoey said.

"What?" Aisha asked, surfacing from her reverie.

"Nothing, Eesh," Zoey said quickly.

"Lucas, you're a guy," Nina said, twisting around in her seat. "You think a girl should be herself more, or do you like it when she gets into the whole show-me-off-to-all-your-guy-friends-so-they-can-see-that-you're-like-enough-of-a-stud-to-get-a-babe-to-go-out-with-you thing?"

Lucas stared at her silently for a minute. "Could you repeat the question?"

"Please don't ask her to do that," Zoey said.

"I don't understand," Lucas admitted.

"She's asking for advice on what to wear to the homecoming dance," Zoey translated.

"Clothing advice?" Lucas said, making a face.

"Fortunately, I don't have to worry about what to wear," Aisha muttered.

"You can come with Benjamin and me," Nina said, grinning. "If—"

"I know," Aisha interrupted. "If I'm real quiet, he won't even know I'm there."

"Don't be doing that, Aisha," Nina chided. "Don't jump in and steal my punch lines."

"GOD, I'M COLD," Zoey suddenly exploded. "Why didn't I wear a coat?"

"Come sit back here with me," Lucas suggested. "I'll warm you up."

"See, that's the other thing," Nina said. "What am I supposed to do, get some dress that shows major cleave and freeze them off?"

"I'm going to tell you what to do," Zoey said, rubbing her arms with her hands. "Go to the bookstore at the mall. Buy the latest *Seventeen* or *Teen Vogue* and get whatever outfit they have on the cover. Or else some other magazine."

"Popular Mechanics," Lucas suggested.

"It's the day after tomorrow," Nina said bleakly.

"I wish someone would break my leg between now and then," Lucas said, falling into the bad mood. "I have to play the dork, and not only that, I have to act like I'm really grateful for the honor."

"I didn't vote for you for homecoming king, by the way," Nina said. "I voted for you for queen."

"Thank you, Nina."

"Don't pretend you're not looking forward to it, Lucas," Zoey said, shivering. "I s-s-saw you with K-berger getting all blushy. You two doing your little slow d-d-dance around the room with the spot-light; you'll probably love it."

Lucas leaned forward and wrapped his arms around Zoey's shoulders. She gratefully accepted the warmth of his body. "It wasn't K-berger I was dreaming about all last night."

Aisha looked up sharply, alert again. "What dream?"

"I don't think we want to hear about Lucas's dream," Zoey said.

"It was a perfectly nice dream," Lucas protested. "You, me, a starlit night. Very romantic."

"Romantic?"

"That's right, romantic. I'd even say it was poetic. What's that word? Lyrical. It was lyrical. Warm, gentle breezes, swaying palm trees, soft music."

"I don't think dreams mean anything, do you?" Aisha asked.

"Sometimes," Nina said.

Zoey shivered again and tucked her chin down into the neck of her sweater. "I hope I was dressed warmly in this dream."

"Well, it *was* a warm night," Lucas said.

"That's what I figured," Zoey muttered. "Aisha? I have to ask you something I've never asked anyone before in my life."

"What?"

"Can I stick my hands in your coat pocket?"

• • •

Benjamin shared two classes each day with Claire, first and last period. Calculus in the morning, physics at the end of the day. In both classes they still sat near each other, a holdover from the days when they were a couple. They were the most difficult classes for Benjamin since they each involved endless notations on the chalkboard. Their calc teacher was very good about always explaining verbally what she was writing on the board, but the physics teacher, Mr. Aubrey, tended to mumble and become so involved in scribbling that for Benjamin the class was reduced to the sound of chalk on the board.

This was one of those times, and Benjamin wondered, for the twentieth time since the beginning of the school year, if he hadn't gone a step too far, trying to deal with a physics elective.

Thankfully, he had a superb memory, particularly for all things mathematical, and it was something he had learned to develop even further. All of North Harbor, much of downtown Weymouth, the mall, the school, the individual classrooms existed in his head as neat, precise diagrams measured in numbers of steps.

In addition, he cataloged other clues—the direction of the airflow from fans and heaters in various classrooms; the sound of a fluorescent light that buzzed in the cafeteria and told him whether he was close to the start of the lunch line; even the distinctive breathing of different classmates. For Benjamin, the entire world was a series of remembered clues, assembled into maps he used for navigation.

But keeping all the complexities of physics formulas hanging in his mind, moving them, correcting them, reconfiguring them, all in his mind, was a real challenge. Especially when the teacher was spacing out. It would mean a lot of extra effort, going through the Braille version of the textbook. Unfortunately, Nina wasn't a lot of help in reading math.

The bell rang and Benjamin sighed with relief. He waited for the rush of departing bodies to thin out. He thought he had more or less understood the lesson, but he wasn't sure. He didn't even need it to graduate. He'd only taken it because it was reputedly the hardest class on the curriculum and taking it would show that he wasn't letting anything scare him.

"Sometimes your ego gets out of control, Benny boy," he muttered under his breath.

"Did you say something?"

Claire. The voice, the smell of her hair. "Just mumbling," he said.

"Yeah, you and Mr. Aubrey both," Claire said. "Did you understand any of that?"

"I'll manage it somehow," he said sarcastically.

"That's not what I meant, Benjamin. I wasn't being condescending. I meant *I* didn't understand what he was saying."

"Try it without being able to see the damned board." Benjamin was frustrated and taking it out on Claire, he realized, which wasn't fair. But he wasn't in the mood to be fair.

"It doesn't help," Claire said, showing no sign that his attitude was annoying her. "He writes just like he talks. The man needs a full-time interpreter."

"Really?" Benjamin felt better, despite himself. It was a relief to think that everyone else wasn't blazing right through and only he was failing to keep up. "I'm thinking an extra history class would have been a better choice as an elective," he admitted.

"Physics isn't an elective for me," Claire said glumly. "I have to take it if I'm going to go for the kinds of classes I want in college. The hallway's pretty much clear, by the way."

"Thanks." He started to walk away—four steps along the row of desks, careful for the ones that had been pushed out of line, a right turn, seven steps to the door.

Claire was still beside him. "So."

"So . . . so I guess I'll see you on the ferry," he said.

"Yeah, well, look, since there's no one around right now and there will be on the ferry—"

"Let me guess. Nina."

"I'd almost forgotten your annoying habit of reading minds," Claire said. "Come on. I'll walk you, then you won't have to be counting all the way."

Benjamin felt her take his hand and place it on her arm. Her touch sent a wave of warmth through him. He fought to keep his features impassive.

"First of all," Claire said, "I know you know all this, but I feel like I have to mention it anyway—"

"You're concerned because Nina has just gone through this whole thing with her uncle."

"You know, you might at least let me finish saying something before you guess the end."

"Sorry."

"I am a little worried," Claire admitted.

"Isn't this big-sisterly concern a little unusual for you, Claire?"

"This doesn't fall into the usual sibling rivalry category, Benjamin. What happened to Nina is different." Claire's voice was serious. He could hear the fresh edge of outrage.

"I know."

"We're coming to the stairs," Claire said.

"I know. Four more steps," Benjamin said. He stopped at the top of the stairs. "Look, Claire, you're right, I do know all this, okay? I know you're just trying to be a good sister, for the first time in your life—"

"If I'd been a better sister earlier, maybe I could have done something to help her," Claire said. "I hope that son of a bitch goes to jail and dies there."

Benjamin smiled. "That will be our 'happy thought' for the day."

"Yeah. I hate to wish that on anyone, I guess, but he has it coming. Anyway. Look, Benjamin, all I'm saying is be aware of how much this means to Nina."

"I know, it's her first real date."

"It's more than that. I mean, you do realize she's in love with you, right?"

Benjamin laughed. "No, she just has a crush on me because I'm conveniently nonthreatening."

Claire took both his hands in hers. "No, Benjamin, it's more than that. She's had a crush on you for a long time. As in years. It was no big deal as long as you and I were together and she wasn't at all serious about getting involved with guys, but both of those things have changed."

Benjamin began to feel uneasy. Rartly because he didn't like hearing Claire dismiss their relationship almost casually. Maybe she had written it off, but he had not. But he was also uneasy because there was truth in what Claire was saying. Things *had* changed. For Nina as well as for Claire and him.

"So. What is it you're afraid I'll do?"

Claire hesitated. "Don't . . ." She took a deep breath. "Benjamin, you're a very easy person to fall for."

Benjamin's heart tripped at her words and the way she had said them, but he fell back on his usual ironic detachment. "Yeah, a blind guy is every girl's dream. No need to do makeup."

"You're frighteningly smart and perceptive, you listen to people when they talk, you're kind and generous, you have a wonderful sense of humor. You're confident. And I know you always suspect people are lying when they tell you this, but you are also very good-looking. Frankly, if you weren't blind, you'd probably be the most arrogant, full-of-himself, stuck-up jerk in this school." Her voice grew soft. "Believe me, Benjamin, you are very easy to fall in love with."

Benjamin wanted to say something, but for once he was at a loss. He wished Claire hadn't said that last part. They were alone in the hallway of the now nearly deserted school. She was so close he could feel the heat from her body. He so desperately wanted to put out a hand, find her smooth cheek, draw her full lips toward his.

But it was Nina they were talking about.

"I'm just saying, as corny as it sounds, don't break Nina's heart, Benjamin. Don't lead her on if you're not serious."

"It'll be okay, Claire," he said, unable to avoid the bitterness.

"I'm easy to fall *out* of love with, too."

He felt her cool fingers stroke the side of his face. "No, you aren't, Benjamin."

She turned away and ran down the steps. Benjamin listened to the sound recede and disappear.

TEN

CHRISTOPHER WAITED OUTSIDE THE SCHOOL for the final bell to ring. He kept out of sight across the street in a recessed doorway and hoped for a good opportunity.

Zoey and Lucas, Aisha and Nina emerged together, which was unfortunate.

But then Aisha and Nina went off in one direction and Zoey and Lucas headed down Mainsail toward the dock and the home-bound ferry. Almost perfect. It would have been nice if Lucas was out of the picture, but the important thing was that Aisha wasn't around. When he was sure Nina and Aisha were gone, he fell into step behind Zoey and Lucas.

The day, which had started out unusually brutal, had warmed up nicely, and the oppressive cloud cover had broken up a little, letting in rays of slanting afternoon sun. Christopher caught up with Zoey after a couple of blocks. She saw him and gave him a guarded but still friendly smile. He pretended to have just noticed her.

"Oh, hi, Zoey. Hey, Lucas. School's out, huh? I guess I lost track of time."

"Yeah, we busted outta that joint," Lucas said, doing a tough-guy gangster voice. "They couldn't hold us."

"Right." Christopher forced a laugh. "Cool. So, uh, heading on down to the ferry, huh?"

"More or less," Lucas said. "What's up with you?"

Christopher shrugged. "Oh, not much. I have a couple hours off. Killing time." He looked at Zoey, then looked away.

"My old man would love you, Christopher," Lucas said. "He thinks people should work twenty-four hours a day."

"Yeah." Again Christopher gave Zoey what he felt was a pretty obvious look.

"Um, Lucas, I think Christopher wants to talk to me about something," Zoey said.

"I'm not stopping him," Lucas said. Then he made eye contact with Zoey. "Oh, you mean like something private."

Zoey smiled and Christopher made a point of staring up at a building, like he was counting the floors.

"Fine. I can take a hint. I'll just . . . I'll just go down to the Green Mountain and get a cup of coffee." He started to walk away. "All by myself."

Christopher realized he hadn't exactly handled everything with the subtlety he'd hoped to pull off. "I was just wondering,

Zoey. You know, what we were talking about at work last night. You know."

"Aisha?"

"Yeah, that's it."

Zoey drew him out of the traffic on the sidewalk into the mouth of an alleyway. "I can't be the middleman—or middle-woman—between you two, Christopher," she said sternly. "But she did say she doesn't *hate* you. She's just very disappointed in you. She thought you were better than that, that you meant more to each other than that."

Christopher cringed. Guilt trip. That's what it was, a guilt trip Aisha was laying on him. And he had no reason to feel guilty. No reason.

On the other hand, Aisha had not left his thoughts as easily as he'd hoped. In fact, she kept reappearing frequently. Through the night. While he was trying to get work done. Very frequently. Not that he was ever going to buy into her whole one-on-one-only thing.

But he did miss her. And he wasn't starting to miss her any less.

And it was just barely possible that he really had hurt her feelings and her sense of pride when he'd gotten that Angela girl to come to his room.

"I can't give you advice, all right?" Zoey said. "But it

probably wouldn't kill you to say you're sorry."

"Sorry." He tried the word out experimentally.

"What do you think you're doing, boy?"

Christopher froze. He registered a look of shock on Zoey's face. He turned around.

The blow was staggering. He fell straight back, collided with Zoey, then hit the hard concrete of the alley. The second blow he saw coming, a steel-buckled boot that slammed into his stomach, knocking the wind out of him. He gasped for air.

He heard Zoey scream. He heard a harsh voice laughing and taunting him. *Black boy's got a white girl in the alley.* A blow to his kidneys. Searing pain. His vision all red.

"Get the girl," a voice said.

"Let her go," a second voice countered. "Let's take care of nappy here."

Christopher tried to wipe the blood out of his eyes and get a look at his tormentors, but there was yet another blow. He vomited.

A sound of running feet.

A girl's voice, sobbing. His head being lifted and pressed against softness. *I wish I could just pass out*, he thought. And then he did.

ELEVEN

"DOWN, TWENTY-ONE, FOURTEEN, HUP, HUP!"

Jake saw the center move the ball back between his legs to the quarterback. Jake lunged forward, knocking Tony DeSantos aside, and began to run downfield. He ran ten paces and cut sharply left, turning to see the ball flying through the air. A good, rifled pass, a little high but within easy reach. Jake reached.

The ball flew through his outstretched fingers and hit the dirt five yards away.

"Dammit, McRoyan!"

Jake heard the sound of his coach's voice on the sidelines, an angry whine like a hornet. The practice was not going well.

He headed back toward the line of scrimmage. The quarterback, a fellow senior named Fitzhugh, shook his head. "You want me to just walk down-field and hand it to you next time, McRoyan?"

"You overthrew." Jake pulled off his helmet to wipe the sweat from his brow.

"Bull. Try paying attention next time. I'm not throwing passes just for my own entertainment. I was thinking we'd try to actually win our home-coming game for the first time this century."

Jake put the helmet back on and entered the huddle.

"Okay, third and four," Fitzhugh said. "Let's see if we can run against our own defense. Second chance, big Jake. Get us a first down and we'll all forget that last play."

"Eat me, Fitz," Jake said.

"Break!"

They formed up on the line, facing their fellow teammates, a defense that was known to be weaker than the threat they'd be facing the next night. The team from Bangor was reputed to have several players over two hundred and fifty pounds.

"Down, twenty-one, hup, hup, hup!"

Jake dropped back, spun, ran to meet Fitzhugh, grabbed the ball from his outstretched hand. His foot caught on something. He took two staggering steps, trying to regain his balance, then the express train hit him.

When the laughing defensive lineman finally let him up, he was face to face with the coach. "You want to explain to me what that move was, McRoyan?"

"I tripped."

"No kidding. You tripped. Swell. Are you in this practice, McRoyan?"

"Y'sir, Coach," Jake muttered.

"Because I don't think your mind is on football, son. You got your mind on something else? You got your mind on some girl, or what? Because this is a game for people who only have their minds on football. Am I clear on this?"

"Y'sir, Coach."

"We are going to win that game tomorrow night, because I am not going to spend the rest of the season taking crap off every butthole with an opinion in this town, do you read me? Do you *all* read me, loud and clear?"

"Yes, sir," a chorus of masculine voices rang out.

The coach softened just a bit. "Well, they say *bad practice, good game*. By those lights we'll have one hell of a game tomorrow night, because this is one sorry practice. All right, give me some laps and hit the showers."

Jake trotted around the field five times and headed for the locker room, feeling sour and tired. He ignored the good-natured and not-so-good-natured jibes from teammates, showered, and dressed quickly.

Lars Ehrlich fell into step beside him as he made his way across the gym floor and outside into the cool evening. An ambulance was blaring past at high speed in front of the school, red lights flashing crazily off the windows of the buildings.

"You want to bust my ass, too, Lars?" Jake asked without much interest.

Lars shrugged. "Nah. But you did suck out there."

"Yeah, well, you can eat me, too."

"You're hung over, man, that's the problem."

"You know something, Lars, I don't remember when it was you became my mother."

Lars laughed. "I don't give a rat's ass what you do, man. I'm just thinking about the game. We can't win without you."

"Probably can't win *with* me," Jake said. But the mention of the team did strike home. Lars was right. He was part of a team, not just one guy. He couldn't let the team down. Even Fitz, who was a certified jerk. "You heard Coach. Bad practice, good game. We'll do all right."

"Well, maybe tonight would not be a good night to be boozing. Not that I'm your mom."

Jake gave him a good-natured shove. "I'll be a real Boy Scout."

"Here." Lars held out his hand, palm down.

"What's that?"

"Just take it," Lars insisted.

Jake held out his hand and a small glass vial dropped into

his palm. "Lars, what is this?"

"It's just a little blow, man. No biggie. Do a couple lines before first half, then a couple more for the second half. Instant concentration. You can owe me for it."

"Coke?"

"Oh, don't go all virginal on me, dude. You were sweating like a pig out there. You're out of shape and you're not focusing and I don't want us to lose this game just because you're all screwed up over Claire Geiger."

Jake bristled. "I don't need this crap, Lars."

A police car raced past, apparently following the ambulance toward downtown.

"Okay, then flush it down the toilet. Whatever. But you know, a lot of alumni come back for homecoming, and in case it slipped your mind, the assistant coach from BU is probably going to be at the game. He might take notice of a couple of real hotshot players from his old alma mater. I know your folks are well-off, but my dad's been unemployed for a year, dude. Some athletic scholarship money would help. You hear what I'm saying?"

Jake nodded. "I hear."

"Cool. Later, man."

"Yeah, later."

TWELVE

"YOU KNOW WHAT, AISHA? MAYBE you should ask Jake to take you to homecoming," Nina suggested. "I mean, he's not taking Claire . . ."

Aisha shook her head. "Nina, you just love to cause trouble, don't you?"

Nina grinned over the top of her Orange Julius. "I like life to be entertaining."

Aisha looked around her at the mostly empty mall food court. She wasn't about to take up Nina's mischievous suggestion, but it was a reminder that if she wanted to go to homecoming, she had almost no time left to find a date. There was a guy in her calculus class she'd thought about, but when the moment had come to approach him, she'd put it off.

Maybe it was some lingering hope that things would work out with Christopher at the last moment. A hope based on the fact that Zoey said he was asking about her. He wouldn't be asking if he weren't still interested.

"Well, I'm basically done," Nina said, tossing her paper cup toward the trash bin.

"With your drink, or with shopping?"

"Both. I've made a final, irrevocable decision. I'm just going to wear the same dress I wore when Benjamin and I went down to that concert in Portland."

Aisha rolled her eyes. "In other words, we've just wasted all the time we spent here."

"I bought this," Nina said, holding up a *Rolling Stone* magazine. *"And"*—she fished in a bag and produced a pair of very dark shades—"I got these. Now Benjamin and I will be sort of making a joint fashion statement."

Aisha smiled. "And I got a three-pack of all-cotton underwear. So, I guess this shopping trip was a major success."

Nina started to say something, but Aisha held up her hand. "Shh. Listen."

"To what?"

"The P.A.—shh."

"Oh my God. They're paging *you*," Nina said. "Unless there's another Aisha Gray."

Aisha felt a shiver of fear. It had to be an emergency. She had never heard anyone be paged in the mall before. Her mom had been hurt! Or her dad had had a heart attack! She jumped up. "Where do I go? Where am I supposed to go?"

"Um, um, the um, the information place! That round thing where they give out strollers."

Aisha took off at a near run. Kalif, it could be her brother. Her heart was pounding.

"Eesh, it could be nothing," Nina said hopefully. "Maybe you dropped your wallet and they found it or something."

Aisha spotted the information kiosk and broke into a run. "I'm Aisha Gray, I'm Aisha Gray."

The old woman behind the counter stared at her in annoyance. "Yes, there's a telephone call for you." She punched a button and handed the receiver to Aisha.

"Who is this?"

"Aisha?" Zoey's voice, strained and edgy.

"Zoey? What's the matter? Is it my mom?"

"Listen, Aisha, it's Christopher."

Aisha's heart thumped and seemed about ready to stop beating. "Oh my God."

"He's hurt, Aisha." Aisha heard the sob in Zoey's voice and almost dropped the receiver. "We're at County Hospital."

"Is he okay?"

"I don't know yet." A long silence. "There was a lot of blood. I don't know."

· · ·

Nina slammed on the brakes, and her father's seventy-thousand-dollar Mercedes came to a stop with the front grille just millimeters from the car in front of her.

Aisha was out of the car before it had completely stopped, leaving the door open behind her, running to the big glass doors that opened electronically. She dashed into the crowded emergency room, a cacophony of crying children, Oprah's theme song on the TV, computer printer chatter, and repeated chime tones over the p.a.

She spotted Zoey. Lucas was just beyond her, but what held Aisha's gaze was the drying bloody stain smeared across the front of Zoey's sweater.

"Is he okay? Is he okay?"

Zoey ran to meet her, nodding vigorously and saying, "He's going to be fine, the doctor just came out and said he's going to be fine." Then Zoey was hugging her and Aisha felt like she might faint.

"They said it looked worse than it was. There was all this blood, but he just broke a couple of ribs and he's all swollen and bruised, but he's okay."

Aisha realized she was weeping, letting her tears moisten

Zoey's hair. "God. What happened? Was he riding his bike?"

Aisha could feel Zoey take a deep, steadying breath. "It wasn't an accident."

Aisha backed away to look at Zoey. "What do you mean? What was it?"

"Some guys beat him up. I think there were three of them." Zoey looked away. "Three white guys."

"Well . . . what . . . I mean, what, why did they beat him up?"

"They—they were skinheads or something."

Aisha felt a cold calm settle over her, blanking out her worry. "You mean they beat him up because he's black?"

"I think so," Zoey said. "We were talking, just the two of us. Lucas was down the street. I think they thought we were together. A black guy and a white girl."

Aisha nodded slowly. "I see."

"There wasn't any warning or anything. It all happened so fast. One second we were talking, then Christopher was on the ground and these guys were kicking him, calling him . . . you know."

Two uniformed policemen stepped out of a room, looking bored. They stopped and surveyed the four of them. "You two are new," the older of the two cops said, indicating Aisha and Nina. "Did either of you witness the incident?"

"No," Nina said. "We were at the mall."

The policeman nodded. "Well, anyone thinks of anything, give us a call. You may be contacted by detectives."

"Are you going to be able to catch the guys?" Zoey asked.

"There's no way to be sure. We don't have a lot of evidence yet. The victim says he never got a clear look at the guys who jumped him. And all you've been able to tell us is that they were white, young skinhead types. But we'll probably catch them sooner or later. These types of perpetrators aren't usually real smart. Sooner or later we'll get them."

Aisha was barely listening after the first few words. She had gone to the door of Christopher's room and was hesitating, her hand on the doorknob. She might be the last person Christopher wanted to see right now.

But then again, he had no one else to look after him.

She opened the door and stifled a gasp. Christopher was lying flat on his back. White bandages were wrapped around his chest, around his left leg and both arms. His head was bandaged, too, and those bandages were stained with seeping blood. There was a needle stuck into his arm at the elbow, attached by a long plastic tube to a clear pouch that hung overhead.

She moved closer and saw that his face was a mass of swelling. His left eye was swollen completely shut and the lid bristled with stitches. There were more stitches above his lips and just around the bottom of his ear.

When he spoke, his voice was a hoarse whisper, barely intelligible. "I look like hell, don't I?"

Aisha shook her head and fought unsuccessfully to hold back the tears. She sought a place where she could touch him, make some sort of physical contact, and found an undamaged patch on his shoulder.

"Does it hurt a lot?"

"Mmm. They were . . . stoned on all kinds of stuff. Doesn't hurt. Later, yeah."

"The doctor told Zoey you're going to be all right."

"Until . . . the bill," he said, trying feebly to laugh.

"Oh, God, Christopher."

"I'm fine, Eesh . . . cry. Don't cry."

"I'm sorry, I can't help it."

"Look, nurse will . . . kick you out, so I need you to . . ."

Aisha leaned closer so he wouldn't have to strain as much to make himself heard. He smelled of antiseptic and Vaseline. "Anything. I'll do anything."

"Make sure . . . Mr. Passmore knows . . . can't work tonight. Also, school . . . tell Coach. And the papers . . . Oh, damn . . ."

Aisha almost laughed. Typical Christopher. She'd been expecting something personal, and what he was worried about was his work. "I could deliver your papers," she said.

"No—"

"Sure I can. Do you have some kind of a list somewhere? In your apartment?"

"Late."

"I know. I'll just sleep through some classes."

He tried to nod, but the effort obviously hurt.

"Don't move. And don't worry, I'll take care of everything for you. And when they let you go, you can come stay at my house. We have plenty of rooms and they're all vacant, no customers. You could have your own Jacuzzi and silk sheets and all."

His eyelids drifted down. "That . . . last shot . . . made me kind of sleepy."

"Go ahead and sleep. Sleep as much as you can." She stroked his shoulder tentatively.

"Aisha?"

"Yes, I'm still here."

"Sorry."

"It's not your fault you're in here," Aisha blazed.

"No." He tried his fractured smile again. "Sorry. You know."

"Go to sleep," she whispered.

THIRTEEN

BY THE TIME THEY LEFT the hospital, it was after eight o'clock. They walked in a group down toward the ferry landing, unable to think of anything else to do, even though it was more than an hour's wait for the next ferry.

Zoey tried to make conversation with Aisha, but she had withdrawn into herself, silent, barely making eye contact with her friends. Nina, as always when she was in a serious situation, had very little to say.

Lucas was nearly as distant as Aisha, sullen, almost seething.

Zoey led the way to the Green Mountain, a coffee shop where the smell of fresh-roasted coffee and homemade cookies filled the air. They found a small table. Zoey had tea. Lucas and Nina had coffee. Aisha just sat.

"You should have something," Zoey suggested.

"No thanks."

"It might make you feel better."

"I don't want to feel better," Aisha erupted suddenly, the

first sign of emotion since she had emerged from Christopher's room.

"He's going to be fine," Zoey said. "He's in great shape; you always said so, remember?"

"Just leave me be, Zoey," Aisha said bitterly.

Zoey felt annoyed. More than annoyed, she had quite quickly become very angry. Christopher's blood still caked the front of her sweater and now she wore Lucas's jacket to cover the mess. "Aisha, Christopher is my friend, too. He's our friend."

"He didn't get beaten up for being your friend," Aisha snapped. "He got beaten up for being black."

"What's that supposed to mean?" Zoey said sharply.

"It means what it means. All right? It means what it means."

"It wasn't *my* fault he got hurt, dammit."

"It's all your faults. All of you." Aisha's voice was rising to a furious shout. "You were standing right there, but oh, no, you can't give any kind of description. But I'll bet if they were black guys, you'd have remembered. Damn right you would."

"You think I would protect those creeps?" Zoey shouted. She had never been so angry. It was like a volcano erupting inside her.

"The only reason this happened was because he was with you. Because he was with a white girl."

"You asked me to talk to him!"

"Why didn't you try and tell those bastards he was your friend; did you even try that?"

"Screw you, Aisha. You weren't there. All right?"

"Yeah, and you were, and your white boy-friend and a lot of other white people and all of you did nothing because it was just one more black kid getting what he deserved."

"Shut up! Shut up! You're so full of crap, Aisha—you know that's a lie!"

Lucas put a hand forcefully on Zoey's shoulder and pulled her back into her chair. She hadn't even realized that she had lunged forward. She was trembling. She felt nauseous. She felt like screaming at the top of her lungs and breaking things.

Aisha shoved her chair back with a loud scrape and started to leave. Nina stood in her way.

"Chill, Eesh," Nina said.

"Both of you," Lucas said. "Sit down, Aisha."

Zoey realized the room had fallen silent. All eyes were surreptitiously watching them. The manager of the place had stepped from behind the counter, like he was gearing up for trouble.

"Come on, Aisha," Lucas said in a calm voice.

Aisha hesitated, looking mad enough to start throwing punches, but at last she sat down.

"Look, you're both just upset," Lucas said. "It's normal. It's what happens when you're this close to violence. Believe me, I've seen more violence probably than either of you. You're just reacting."

"Come on," Nina added. "You two aren't mad at each other. You're mad at the guys who hurt Christopher."

Zoey forced herself to take several deep breaths. Her shoulder muscles were painfully knotted. Her hands were shaking.

"If I could, I'd kill them," Aisha snarled.

"I wish I had seen them," Zoey said, a tear running down her cheek. "I'm sorry. I was just scared and it happened so fast and I was screaming and trying to get help."

Aisha nodded grudgingly. "It's not your fault."

"I didn't know what to do," Zoey said bleakly. "I was really scared."

"I have to get some air," Aisha said. She stood up again. "I'll see you guys on the ferry."

Zoey started to protest, but she felt too weary to argue any more.

"I better go keep an eye on her," Lucas said. "Those guys may still be out there looking for trouble."

"Those guys?" Nina asked. "Do you know who they are?"

"No. No, I just meant guys like that. Guys like those may still be out on the streets."

He went after Aisha. Zoey let her head sink down onto the

table. She had the feeling she had missed something important, but the truth was, she was just too tired to care.

Lucas kissed Zoey good night at her front door. Neither of them was up for much more just then. He took the path behind her house up to his own home, skirting below the overhanging deck that was his home's only adornment. His father had added it because it gave a good view of the harbor, and more specifically of the lobster boat that was his livelihood.

Lucas had missed dinner, not that either of his parents cared one way or the other. His mother was in the kitchen, washing dishes. His father was already up in his room, getting ready to go to bed. Mr. Cabral kept very early hours, always heading down to the boat before dawn.

"You want something to eat, Lucas?" his mother asked.

She was a faded, worn woman, going through the motions of life, cooking, cleaning, attending church, sewing little doilies that decorated the backs and arms of all the clean but shabby furniture.

When he was a little boy, Lucas had tried to engage her, cheer her up, make her laugh. She had been uninterested, showing no more pleasure in his good behavior than she showed grief at his later petty criminality. She barely existed, Lucas knew. She wasn't really a person at all, just a subset of her husband.

In this house it was his father, Roy Cabral, who was the only power.

"I'm not hungry," Lucas said.

"It's in the refrigerator if you want some later. Pot roast."

"Okay, Mom."

"How was school?"

Lucas smiled. "School was fine." There was no point in telling her that what happened after school had not been so fine. This was hardly a liberal household. Neither of his parents would much care if a black guy minding his own damned business got the crap beaten out of him. After all, they didn't subscribe to any of the papers Christopher delivered.

Lucas went upstairs to his spare, functional room and flopped back on the bed. He shut his eyes, and inevitably the images were of Christopher lying delirious on the ground, and of Zoey cradling his bloody head.

Snake's work, he knew. And his pal Jones, and some other guy Lucas hadn't recognized. Typical skinhead treatment—three guys against one. Even that was bold for them. Normally they'd have wanted the balance even more in their favor. Probably they were drunk or high on crack.

He had nearly screwed up and blurted the truth to Zoey, which would have been a disaster. If she knew he could identify the perpetrators by name, Zoey would insist he tell the cops.

He wasn't going to do that. If he ended up testifying in court, there was every possibility that Snake and his skinhead friends would try to retaliate. Lucas wasn't worried for himself. He still had the self-preserving alertness that had served him well in the Youth Authority. But Zoey was another matter.

What the skins had done to Christopher was sickening, the product of marginal humans with below-borderline IQs and families so screwed up they made his home life look like a Hallmark commercial. But Lucas wasn't going to turn Christopher's problem into Zoey's problem.

FOURTEEN

AISHA RARELY DROVE HER PARENTS' island car, and she had never before driven it around at three o'clock in the morning. Fortunately, the ancient AMC Pacer had a decent muffler, unlike most other island cars. It had no front or rear bumpers, and the left window was a sheet of plastic held on by duct tape, but it did have a muffler, so the noise as she crept along dark streets toward the dock was minimal.

No one wasted money on a car useful only for driving to and from the ferry to carry groceries. *Real* cars were kept on the mainland in parking garages. In fact, it was almost a mark of pride among Chatham Islanders, whatever their social status, to be able to brag about having the worst, most rusted out, battered piece of junk on the island.

Aisha pulled the car to a stop announced by loudly squealing brakes. She yanked on the door release and slammed the door with her shoulder. It opened just enough for her to be able to squeeze out by using tricks a contortionist would have envied.

The dock was empty, lit by two globes casting lugubrious bluish light over the pilings. The first ferry of the day would not arrive for almost four hours. Even the early fishermen and lobstermen wouldn't be up for another hour and a half.

It was chilly enough to turn her breath to steam, but there was no wind. The water sloshed wearily against the pilings. A sleepy gull looked her over and dismissed her.

Aisha saw the plastic-wrapped papers, four piles sitting on the siding, glistening with frost. She grabbed the two smallest bundles and dragged them back to the car. Then she went back for the remaining papers. It was unbelievable to think that Christopher delivered all these papers by bike, pedaling all this weight up the long slope to her house.

No wonder he had such a nice, hard little butt. Not that she cared. Or maybe she did. Her feelings were a mess right now. The fact that he had been hurt did not automatically resolve all the problems they had. It would be naive to think that he would suddenly be willing to accept her terms for their relationship.

Aisha heard a sound, a squeaky door closing, and looked around. At first she could see nothing, then she saw a figure approaching from the direction of Passmores', a figure wreathed in steam.

Zoey arrived carrying two Styrofoam cups of coffee, waitress-style, both in one hand. Her other hand held a pastry box.

"What the hell are you doing here, Zoey?" Aisha demanded, not sure whether she was annoyed or amused.

"Same as you. I'm going to help deliver Christopher's papers. I've been waiting over in the restaurant. Here. It's fresh. I hope cream is okay."

She handed Aisha one of the coffees.

"Zoey, you don't have to do this, all right?"

"Eesh, what are you going to do? Crawl in and out of that broken car door at every stop? It would take you a week. You drive, I'll throw."

"I can handle it. Christopher is *my* boyfriend. At least he was."

"Look, Aisha, I know you want someone to be mad at over this, and since we don't have the guys who did it, you're being mad at me. That's fine, you can be mad at me if you want. I'm not leaving."

Aisha reluctantly took the coffee. She took a sip. "What's in the box?"

"Danish. One cherry, one apple. Cherry's mine. Shouldn't we put rubber bands around these papers or something?"

Aisha produced a big box of narrow plastic bags. She had found them when she went through Christopher's apartment, looking for his delivery list. "I'm not really mad at you, Zoey." She sat her coffee on the hood of the car, rolled a *Weymouth*

Times and stuffed it into a bag. "I'm just mad, period. For some stupid reason I thought this kind of b.s. was something I left behind in Boston."

"You told me about your school bus getting turned over down there," Zoey said. She began to roll *Portland Press-Heralds*.

"That was just the most dramatic moment," Aisha said. "People think racists are only in the old South and that's not true. Try being black and moving into most parts of South Boston. You'll think you were in Alabama." She shrugged. "I just thought things might not be that way here in Maine."

"They aren't that way here," Zoey said. "Not with most people, or even very many people."

Aisha smiled grimly. "Sure they are, Zoey. They're that way everywhere. I don't mean you or Nina or Claire, but still, lots of people. And see, I've had it so easy here on this island that it's like I forgot what the real world was like. It's like I was becoming white, forgetting who I really am. Today . . . yesterday, I guess, now. Anyway, it was wake-up time."

Zoey looked sad. "I guess there are creeps everywhere."

"Yeah, well, I had managed to convince myself that wasn't true. But the fact is wherever I go, and whatever I do or become or accomplish, there are a certain number of white people who will never see anything but a nigger. That's the fact, Zo. A fact for me and a fact for Christopher."

"Well, the facts suck, then."

"I'm not thrilled about them, either."

They worked in silence for several minutes, until all the papers were bagged.

"Sometimes things do get better," Zoey said hopefully. "I mean, we don't burn witches anymore or have slaves or put people in prison for owing money."

Aisha smiled. Zoey was nothing if not an optimist. She had unchallengeable faith in the future. She thought the future would be like *Star Trek*—black and white, even humans and nonhumans getting along and solving all their problems with a few adjustments to the warp engines.

Aisha had learned to be more cautious. She believed in what she saw and experienced, and a fair amount of that had been bad. Not all, but enough. Faith that the world would someday be perfect just seemed naive, especially when Christopher was lying in a hospital in a far-from-perfect world.

"I know you feel bad about what happened to Christopher," Aisha said. "And I was wrong to blame you just because you're white. I take that back. But it's not all as simple as you think it is. See, I'm as smart as you are, Zoey, maybe smarter in some subjects. I guess I'm more or less as pretty as you are. I can work as hard as you do, I can deal with people as well as you do, I even come from a family that's not much different from yours.

And what you think is *Hey, Aisha and I are friends, we're mostly the same, what's the big problem?*"

"We are mostly the same," Zoey said earnestly. "You and I are more alike than I'm like Claire, for example. We're more alike than you and Nina."

"Only we're not. No one will ever call you a nigger, Zoey, or tell you to get out of town and go back to the ghetto where you belong. And no one is ever going to refuse you a chance or a job or whatever because you're the wrong shade. Cops aren't going to pull you over because you look suspicious driving a nice car, or . . . or treat you like you must be a shoplifter every time you walk through a department store. That's a big difference between you and me, Zo. It's not your fault, I know you're not racist, but just the same it's hard for me not to resent it sometimes when it's like the whole damned world is ready to open up to the lovely, lily-white Ms. Zoey Passmore but just waiting for the right time to try and step on the lovely, ebony Ms. Aisha Gray."

Zoey nodded silently. There were tears in her eyes. "I do know all that, Aisha. Really. I just don't know what I can do about all those things."

"Neither do I," Aisha admitted. "Wait for the human race to grow up, I guess, like I could live that long."

"In the meantime, I still want to be your friend."

Aisha sighed. She took Zoey's hand and squeezed it. "Okay, Zoey. Friends. But only if you let me have the cherry Danish. I don't like apple."

"I feel like it's the least I can do."

"Come on, white girl. I'll drive, you throw."

Nina

I was always fascinated by other people's love lives. When Zoey kissed some guy, or Claire did, that didn't set off any of the alarms inside me. It wasn't about me, so it was safe. When guys were interested in me, and yes, there were a few, that was different. The first time a male had shown any interest in me it had turned out pretty badly. The memory of those events intruded anytime a guy so much as smiled at me. It was like once, when I was little, I found a worm in a peach. Half a worm, actually.

I will pause a moment while you grasp the fill meaning of that fact.

For a long time after that I would not eat peaches. But it didn't bother me if someone else ate peaches. In fact, it sort of fascinated me, because underneath it all I had the normal amount of interest in peaches. I mean, I knew the difference between a good-looking peach and a skanky peach. And there were plenty of times when I'd get a sort of internal quiver, a little warmth, a little urge to have a peach, but the memory of the worm kept getting in the way.

Am I being too metaphorical?

Anyway. I'd ask Zoey what it was like when she'd make

out with Jake, and the one time she kissed Tad Crowley at a party, and later with Lucas. And Zoey being Zoey, her version of events involved words like "wonderful" and "exciting" and "amazing." Even "transcendent" once. Words that don't really convey much hard information.

So, like a dolt, I asked Claire and caught her in a rare helpful mood. She only rolled her eyes once, and made no more than half a dozen smart-ass remarks at my expense. Then she explained making out with a guy you really like.

She said the entire rest of the world just ceases to exist. You don't see, you don't hear, you don't breathe, you don't think, you don't remember.

Then you stop, and the world comes rushing back in. And that's no fun, so you start up again.

It was the exact opposite of what I felt. For me the very thought of kissing a boy was nauseating, a swirl of guilt and self-hatred and fear. I didn't see any way that my feelings would ever become like Claire's and Zoey's and Aisha's feelings.

And yet, I had hope.

Actually, I have started eating peaches again.

FIFTEEN

BENJAMIN WOKE TO MOZART'S SYMPHONY Number Forty, having programmed his playlist the night before. The music carried through on the speakers in his bathroom, clearly audible as he showered, shaved, deodorized, and combed his hair.

"Why," he asked his invisible reflection in the bathroom mirror, "would a girl who likes the Black Keys and the Strokes want to go out with a guy who likes Mozart?"

"Why?" he asked, sticking a toothbrush in his mouth, "wou a gir who ever even goes ou choose e?"

He quickly finished brushing, then answered his own question. "I'll tell you why, Bat Boy—because you're safe. You're nonthreatening. Story of your life, man."

He located and put on underwear, a shirt, hopefully white if his mother had put it in the right part of his closet, a pair of pants, definitely denim, and a pullover. Color unknown, but once described by Zoey as "something that would go with anything." Good enough.

A jacket. It would be cold at the game tonight. The leather jacket. He didn't mind being non-threatening, but a little macho wouldn't hurt. Would it?

Jeez, this was going to be so different from going out with Claire. Claire wasn't exactly a tender, easily bruised flower. It would take a baseball bat to bruise Claire.

Nina was different. Not that she wasn't tough in her own way, but there was this big, unhealed wound on her soul. She was vulnerable. This was a big thing for her, going out with him. Probably Claire had been exaggerating in saying that Nina was in love with him, that was too much, but she *was* sort of putting herself on the line in a way that Claire never did.

"I guess she has a right to start off with someone safe," Benjamin said thoughtfully. "Although . . . I *am* wearing leather. I don't know what color leather it is, but it's manly just the same." He laughed and headed out to the hallway.

"Zoey! You ready?" he yelled upstairs.

Zoey came clattering down the stairs. "Here I am. Ready?"

"Ready."

"Bye, Mom!" Zoey yelled.

"Bye, you two," their mother called from the kitchen.

Outside the air was brisk, but Benjamin felt direct sunlight on his face. It was clear, or at least not completely cloudy. They set off at a walk, Benjamin keeping the count of his steps almost unconsciously as he swung his cane from side to side in a narrow arc.

"I cannot wake up," Zoey complained.

"That's what you get for going out in the middle of the night."

"Sorry, did I wake you up?"

"Nah. I hear everything, you know that. What did you do, go deliver Christopher's papers?"

"Aisha and I, yeah. Thank God it's Friday."

"Mmm. Big night tonight." Benjamin smiled. "How is Lucas doing with the homecoming king deal?"

Zoey laughed. "You'd never guess that being popular and well liked could piss someone off so much."

His sister shifted into her ever-so-casual voice. "So, tonight I guess you're taking Nina to the game."

"Uh-huh. You know how I love listening to football. The crowd murmurs, the crowd starts yelling, there's the sound of a loud crunch from the field, the crowd sighs heavily. Almost as fun as tennis. Thock, thock, thock, thock, crowd groans, then one of the players starts yelling, That was in; what are you, blind?'"

"Maybe Nina can describe the game to you," Zoey said, still in her overly casual voice.

"Well, we'll probably be busy making love under the seats,"

Benjamin said. Zoey was being subtle, which wasn't her greatest talent.

"Very funny."

"That was where you were heading, wasn't it? A few well-chosen words about not doing anything to upset Nina; after all, she's in a sort of vulnerable condition right now? Claire already gave me that line. Jeez, what do you people think I am? The ruthless despoiler of virgins?"

"Of course not," Zoey said. Now she sounded embarrassed. "It's just she's my friend, and you're my brother, and I want it all to work out so there aren't any major conflicts."

"Look, she's going out with me precisely because I'm safe. I mean, come on. I grope in slow motion. I can't kiss anyone without directions from ground control to guide me in. We'll do the thing tonight, we'll do the dance tomorrow night, she'll probably decide it was dull and get on with her life."

"Is that what you think? That you're just a sort of tryout for her?"

"Training wheels. That's my role in life. For someone like Nina, I'm a safe place to start. For someone like Claire, I'm more a curiosity, a unique experience so that someday she can say *Oh, yes, I've had them all. Why, I even had a blind guy once.*"

"I don't believe I'm hearing self-pity from you."

Benjamin stopped and did a sort of double take.

"Damn. You're right. Slap me if I do that again."

They resumed their progress. Benjamin was still disturbed that he had given vent to what sounded a lot like bitterness. That was the wrong attitude. Yes, he'd gotten dumped. But in the same week Claire had dumped him, Zoey had dumped Jake. These things happened to everyone. Especially lately.

"Anyway, I'm just saying that underneath Nina's abrasive and occasionally weird exterior there is a very sweet girl, so don't be fooled."

"Uh-huh. Got it. By the way, what little advice did you give her about me, Mom?"

Zoey laughed. "I told her that underneath your abrasive and occasionally weird exterior there was an abrasive and occasionally weird interior, so she shouldn't be fooled by your nice guy act."

SIXTEEN

LUCAS STOOD ON THE GRASS at the far end of the field and watched the early part of the homecoming game with a sense of impending doom. Not just because the Weymouth team was being beaten by the team from Bangor. Frankly, he didn't really care who won. Inasmuch as he was at all interested in football, it was an abstract interest, not tied to any one team.

But as each play went by, the moment drew nearer.

He had already seen the suit—a white tuxedo. Each of the five candidates for homecoming king had been supplied with a white tuxedo, rented for the occasion and currently hanging in the boys' locker room. They'd be a little chorus line of Barry Manilows.

He was standing behind the opposing team's goalpost, idly wondering why Jake was playing such lousy ball. He was probably burned over the white tuxedos, too, since he also was one of the nominees. Tad Crowley, a third candidate, was standing nearby, smoking marijuana and admiring the distant legs of the cheerleaders.

It was a cool, almost cold night. Thermoses were in heavy use in bleachers packed with students, parents, alumni, and those other members of the local population who lacked meaningful lives.

At halftime Lucas, Tad, Jake, and the other two male candidates were due to march out onto the football field wearing the white tuxedos. They would be joined by the five female candidates. The big announcement of the king and queen, already known to everyone in the school, would be made by the principal.

The moment when his name was read out over the p.a. would be the most embarrassing moment of his life. Worse than the strip search when he'd entered the Youth Authority.

Zoey and the female candidates were already in the girls' locker room doing their hair and whatever else it was girls did to get ready.

On the field, Jake went out for a pass. The ball sailed through his fingers.

"I think we're getting our butts kicked," Lucas remarked.

Tad sucked in smoke, and in an I'm-holding-my-breath voice said, "You think Maddie's a real redhead?"

The gun popped, ending the first half, and the team, muddy and dispirited, began to trot across the field in their direction, aiming for the locker room to be berated by their coach.

Lucas cursed. With a sigh, he headed toward the gym. Tad put the joint out on the bottom of his shoe and fell into step beside him.

"Do I look high?" Tad asked.

"Red, unfocused eyes, idiot grin? No, no one would ever guess."

The vanguard of the team passed by across the grass at a jog, slinging their helmets and muttering.

Jake separated himself from them and slowed to fall in with Lucas and Tad. Jake and Lucas had been bitter enemies back before Jake had discovered the truth about the night his brother was killed. And even afterward, there was the fact that Lucas had, by some interpretations, stolen Zoey away from Jake. Recently the two of them had managed to remain polite, but not exactly close to each other.

Jake was muddy and sweating. He looked distracted.

"What's up, big Jake?" Tad asked.

"We're down twenty-seven to seven," Jake said grimly. "Haven't you been watching the game? Or did you just decide you couldn't stand it anymore?"

"I was watching the cheerleaders," Tad admitted.

"They might be the ones playing in the next half," Jake said. "I suck tonight."

"I doubt it's all your fault," Lucas said mildly.

Jake pointed angrily at his teammates, now a dozen yards away. "Tell them that. They're putting the whole thing on me."

"It's this damned dress-up monkey show," Lucas said. "Get that over with and you'll be set for the next half."

"Pathetic," Jake said. It was clear he was referring to himself.

Lucas didn't know how to respond, so he kept quiet.

After the darkness they had traversed from the football field, the fluorescence through the back door of the locker room was blinding.

Jake went straight to the showers, ignoring his dirty, depressed teammates and their occasional sullen barbs. Lucas sighed and picked up the plastic-sheathed tuxedo, shaking his head in disgust.

"By the way, I will have to kill the first person who gives me any crap about this," he said in a conversational tone.

He undressed down to his underwear and pulled on the slick, cold tuxedo pants. "Oh, man," he complained. "These things are about two sizes too big around the waist."

"That's so K-burger can fit in there with you tomorrow

night at the dance," one of the football players said. He got a high five for his wit.

"Let's not get into tomorrow night," Lucas said. "One disaster at a time. Besides, this is it for the tux. Tomorrow night I think I'll dress myself."

Jake had toweled off and opened his locker. Lucas saw him look around quickly, then bend over, sticking his head and one hand into the locker. There followed a sharp snorting sound. Then another. Jake emerged, wiping his nose.

"I must have a cold," he told Lucas.

"Yeah, it's going around," Lucas said, playing along with Jake's lie. It wasn't any of his business if Jake was doing coke. It was amazing, given what he knew about Jake, but it wasn't Lucas's problem.

It was also ironic, Lucas realized. He was the one who had just been released from jail, and he was going to walk out on the field perfectly straight, flanked by one guy who was stoned and another guy who was high.

"This younger generation," he said to himself. "What's the world coming to?"

Zoey and the other four girls had to take off their high heels and walk barefoot across the gym floor. Upon reaching the door to the outside, they used each other as supports while they put the heels back on. Then they waited for the white convertibles that were to pick them up and sweep them in semiregal splendor around the football field.

"So where are the guys?" Louise Kronenberger asked. "I can't believe we have to wait for them."

"Yeah, *you* never keep guys waiting," Kay Appleton said, with a wink at Zoey. "Any guys."

"Was that a subtly snide remark?" Louise asked.

Not all that subtle, Zoey thought. "We're going to freeze to death out there. Bare shoulders and a plunging neckline in October? Maybe in Florida."

"Maybe Lucas can warm you up on the way out there," Louise suggested. "He looks like a guy who could warm someone up."

Zoey seethed, but was determined not to show it. Louise was one of those girls who enjoyed making other girls feel insecure. Probably she had a really bad self-image and had to try to compensate, Zoey told herself.

Psychobabble could be such a comfort sometimes.

"He does know how to dance, doesn't he?" Louise asked. "I mean slow dance. You know, where to put his hands on the girl's body, how to move around?"

"I wouldn't know," Zoey said through chattering teeth.

"It seems to me they used to give the girls little fur things to wear over their shoulders," Kay said.

"Not politically correct. Fur is dead," Zoey explained. "And I guess flannel just wouldn't work with the image."

The door opened and Jake was the first one out, snapping his fingers, bobbing his head and looking like he was ready to go. "Ladies, ladies, and more ladies," he said. "You all look beautiful. Even you, Zoey; no hard feelings, you always did look great, Lucas is a lucky guy. Marie, Amelia, Kay, you're hot. Louise, as always."

"You're in a good mood," Kay said dryly. "Twenty-seven to seven. Just think how happy you'd be if it was fifty-seven to seven."

"We'll be back in the second half," Jake said. "Don't worry, no problem, big Jake has the situation totally under control. I've just been dogging it so that the last-minute comeback will be even more amazing."

Lucas and the rest of the guys came out, most looking content enough. Lucas was scowling.

"Somehow I feel you got me into this," Lucas accused Zoey.

"Wasn't me," Zoey said.

"It was Aisha," Lucas said darkly. "She denies it, but this is all her fault. She should at least be here to see what she's done."

"She's in the stands with Nina and Claire and Benjamin," Zoey said. She smiled and fluttered her eyelashes. "I asked her to take some pictures. Who knows when I'll see you dressed up again?"

"Any word on Christopher?"

Zoey's face fell. "She said he was much better, but she wasn't able to spend much time with him. He was still dopey."

Lucas gave her a significant look and then directed his gaze at Jake. "He's not the only one."

Zoey stared at Jake. He was flirting happily with Louise as though he didn't have a care in the world, laughing at her jokes as well as his own.

The white convertibles pulled up in a long procession. Zoey had been scheduled to drive out to the field with Tad Crowley. She pulled Kay aside. "Do you mind if we switch and I drive out with Jake? He's being a little weird."

"What are you doing?" Lucas asked suspiciously.

"Jake doesn't use drugs," Zoey explained under her breath. "I just want to see if he's all right."

"Zoey, trust me. I spent two years living with every kind of druggie known to man. The boy's buzzed."

Zoey began to argue, but it was time to get going. She climbed into the car, arranging herself precariously on the top of the backseat with her feet resting on the leather cushions.

Jake hopped in beside her, still grinning and tossing lines at Louise, Lucas, and everyone else within hearing.

The car took off, adding a stiff breeze to Zoey's chill. Her arms were goose bumps. Her teeth were literally chattering. "It's f-freezing out here," she said.

Jake shrugged. "It's not bad. You cold? Here, you want my jacket? I can still loan you my jacket, right, without Lucas getting all bent and thinking I'm like trying to get you back? Although you do look good in that dress, I have to admit. Showing leg through the slit, with the heels. And the cleave and all."

"Jake," Zoey said through her shivering, "I don't *have* any cleavage. You're mistaking me for Claire. And as for this dress—"

"Claire's not so hot," Jake said in his new, rapid-fire way. "She thinks she is. I mean, a lot of people, especially guys, think she is. But she's not. I'm not saying anything bad about her or anything, but underneath it all she's just a cold, selfish person. She doesn't care. She thinks she can get away with anything and like everyone is just supposed to go *Oh, it's all right, it's Claire, so we just have to forgive and forget.* See, because it's Claire and everyone thinks she's this . . . this, I don't know."

"Jake? Are you . . . all right?"

"To tell you the truth, Zo, I'm great. I know I sucked in the first half, but I'm stoked for the big comeback. Stoked."

"Stoked on what?" Zoey asked.

Jake cracked his knuckles and slapped his hands together.

"Get this little thing over with and boom. Back in the game. I'm so good I could even catch Fitz's lousy passes. You watch. Is Claire here, even?"

"Yes. She's with Nina and Eesh and Benjamin."

"I know, everyone thinks I lost it first half, but don't give up on me yet. Hundred-yard game, and almost all of it in the second half. Cool. Count on it."

Zoey turned and looked back at the car behind them. They were just coming under the brilliant stadium lights, and cheers were going up from the onlookers. A pothole sent her lurching and she grabbed Jake's shoulder for support. Glancing back again, she caught a cool, dubious look from Lucas.

Suddenly Jake stared at her, hard, some idea lighting up his eyes.

"What?" she asked him.

He smiled. "You know something? This is what we'll remember when we get old."

"Is it?" She smiled. "I guess it's one of the things we'll remember."

He nodded. "Yeah. I always figured homecoming would be you and me. Prom the same thing. You and me, Zoey. You and me and I'd gain a hundred yards or more and be the big hero. It's okay, though. Things change. Onward and upward, right?"

• • •

"And hee-e-e-ere they come," Nina announced. She laughed and nudged Aisha. "Zoey must be freezing her cheechees off." For the benefit of Benjamin, who was on her right side, she elaborated. "Picture five white convertibles coming across the field. A guy and a girl in each, along with the drivers who, judging by the little red hats, are all Shriners. Our proud male candidates are in ill-fitting, Las Vegas white tuxedos with powder-blue cummerbunds. Girls in powder-blue gowns, long, glittering, slit up one leg and down the chest. Very Miss America. Jake is waving like he's running for senator. Lucas looks like he may make a run for it at any moment. Zoey is turning a deeper shade of blue than her dress."

Nina was delighted to hear Benjamin laugh. The stands were crowded and they had been forced close together. Her leg was actually touching his, and she was finding she enjoyed the contact. In fact, she was feeling almost giddy. If Claire hadn't been sitting just beyond Aisha, Nina might even have gone all the way and tried to hold his hand. Or not. But in this environment, with everyone bundled up in the great outdoors, everything seemed safe.

"We're having a minor problem," Nina said. "The car exhausts are steaming so much it's like someone turned on a smoke machine. Steaming cars, steaming breath, steaming cups of coffee all around in the stands, the stadium lights turning everyone gray, and here's Mr. Hardcastle to make the big announcement."

"The announcement everyone already knows," Benjamin observed. "I like this. It sort of crystallizes the whole school experience—a series of surreal, semimystical rituals that no one understands, that very few people care about, and that always involve elements of embarrassment and discomfort."

"These are supposed to be the best years of our lives," Aisha said.

"God, I hope not," Nina heard Claire mutter.

"At least you guys are all seniors," Nina said. "It will be over for you soon. I'll still be trapped here in bizzaro world for an extra year."

"You're all looking at it the wrong way," Benjamin said. "High school never goes away. Stupid teachers become stupid professors become stupid bosses. One set of inexplicable rules and regulations gets traded for another set. Cramped, stuffy classrooms become cramped, stuffy offices. Face it. There's no escape."

"I'll be killing myself now," Nina said.

"You're being awfully philosophical tonight," Claire said.

"I may have eaten too many Jolly Ranchers," Benjamin said with a sly grin. "Sugar depression."

On the field, Mr. Hardcastle was using the word *tradition* for the tenth time in three minutes. He began introducing alumni from the stands. A guy who had graduated in 1959 and now owned a string of oil and lube shops. An old woman who had graduated some time during the Jurassic period and was now the style editor for the newspaper.

"Too bad Christopher had to miss all this magnificence," Nina said.

Aisha smiled. "I guess being in the hospital isn't all bad."

"When's he going to bust out of there?"

"He's getting out Sunday, although he won't exactly be doing cartwheels for a while."

"Damn," Nina said. "And I know how he loves cartwheels. I can help you guys do his papers tonight. Claire will help, too. Isn't that right, Claire?"

Claire nodded glumly.

"I'll drive," Benjamin offered.

"Oh, here we go. The big moment," Nina said.

The band began a staccato drumroll that rose and fell on the breeze, sometimes sounding like nothing more than a flag snapping in the wind.

"The first runner-up for Weymouth High School home-coming queen is . . ."

"That's it, drag it out, Hardcastle," Nina said.

". . . Zoey Passmore!"

"Hey, she came in second. Cool," Benjamin said. "Any more coffee?"

Nina unscrewed the thermos bottle. "Yeah, if it turns out *Penthouse* magazine has nude pictures of K-burger, then Zoey will take over the official duties, whatever they may be."

"Is Jake jumpy or is it just my imagination?" Aisha asked.

"The first runner-up for Weymouth High School homecoming king is . . ."

"Just in case they also have nude photos of Lucas."

". . . Tad Crowley!"

Nina noticed that Claire actually looked disappointed Jake hadn't won the number-two slot. Nina rolled her eyes. Amazing. Claire was acting like it mattered. "Could this be any more bogus? We all know who the winners are; the only suspense was over the runners-up."

"And the new homecoming king is . . ."

The drumroll swelled.

"Lucas Cabral!" Nina yelled out. "But I'm just guessing."

Mr. Hardcastle's face fell as the sound of Nina's shout carried down to the grandstand. But he went ahead as though nothing had happened. ". . . Lucas Cabral."

"I heard that name somewhere before," Nina said.

Benjamin nudged her in the side. "Together on the next one."

Nina grinned and elbowed Aisha. There was a tittering sound from the people close by. Obviously a number of people had the same idea.

"And the new Weymouth High School homecoming queen is . . ."

"LOUISE KRONENBERGER!" a hundred voices yelled. "BUT WE'RE JUST GUESSING."

SEVENTEEN

AFTER THE HALFTIME CEREMONY WAS over and Jake was back in his pads and jersey, he went into a toilet stall to do a few more lines. His conscience was now only a whisper in the back of his brain as he tapped the powder out in the crease of a folded piece of pasteboard and used a rolled-up dollar bill as a straw. The initial buzz had begun to wear off and he wanted to hit the field at absolute maximum velocity.

As the team trotted back out to the field he made a race of it, challenging his teammates to catch him and signaling that he was back. Back in a major way.

The very first play was a pass. Fitz had overthrown, as usual, but Jake leapt, got two fingers on the ball, brought it tumbling down, and caught it as he fell for a first down.

A roar went up from the crowd, and an answering roar went through him. This was more like it. He was back in control. He could barely wait for the next play.

In the third quarter the Weymouth team brought the score

to within ten points. By the end of the game they were within a point.

They had still lost, but the humiliating first half had been wiped away. And back in the locker room after the game, the mood was more upbeat than it had been at halftime.

"What the hell," Lars Ehrlich said, "we nearly won and they had linemen big enough to be in the NFL. Did you see that number thirty-two? The guy's a truck."

"This is true," someone else agreed. "Nobody ever expected us to win."

"If you'd played the first half like you played the second half, McRoyan, we *would* have won." Fitz was not ever one to accept a loss gracefully. Normally, neither was Jake. But this was about more than just winning. His own personal honor had been at stake. If he hadn't gotten his act together at the end, the whole school, hell, the whole town, would have pointed to him as the one who blew it. Now at least some self-respect had been salvaged.

Still, Jake was feeling desperately weary, despite the stinging hot shower. More tired than he remembered ever feeling. Too tired to want to go out and celebrate the near-upset with the guys, though a semi-official party had been organized. It was a party for football players and cheerleaders and it would mean rehashing the game half the night.

Only a small amount of the coke was left in his locker, but it ought to be enough to buy him another hour of energy, enough to get to the ferry and home. He went to his locker and slid the vial into the pocket of his jeans.

Then he felt something strange. A circle of silence had formed around him. He looked up guiltily and saw his coach, wearing the grim expression that had silenced the locker room.

"Hey, Coach," he said warily.

"McRoyan, we have a little problem."

Jake shrugged. "I know, I blew the first half."

"Yes, you did, but that's not our only problem. The Bangor coach thinks you had an amazing recovery during half time."

Now the room was dead silent. Jake closed his locker door, a deafening noise.

"Must have been the pep talk you gave us," Jake said.

The coach tilted his head and focused sharply. "The Bangor coach wonders if maybe it wasn't more than a pep talk. He's made a formal request that you be given a drug test."

Jake felt his stomach lurch. He glanced at Lars, but Lars was looking down at the floor. Jake forced a heavy laugh. "He's nuts, Coach. You know I'm not into that stuff."

"Look, Jake," the coach said, kindly for him, "here's the deal: I can't force you to take the test—"

"I have nothing to hide," Jake protested wildly.

"Now, listen to me. Listen to me closely. Are you listening?"

Jake nodded. He could feel the hard knot of the vial in his pocket. His heart was thudding like a sledgehammer in his chest.

"If you agree to take a urine test and it comes up negative, okay. If it comes up positive for any controlled substance, you're off the team permanently. Do you follow me so far?"

"Yes, sir," Jake murmured.

"However, you can refuse to take the test, in which case I will have to suspend you from the team until you agree to take a test. Are you getting this? If you test positive now, you're gone. If you refuse the test, hey, maybe next week you have a change of heart. You take the test, you pass, you're back on the team. Is that clear?"

It was clear. His coach was telling him to refuse. Refuse until the drug was out of his system. But it would mean admitting his guilt. No one would have the slightest doubt as to why he had refused.

"I think drug tests are bull," Fitz said, unexpectedly coming to Jake's defense. "They ought to be unconstitutional."

"The school board doesn't give a rat's ass about the Constitution," the coach said. "This is *their* policy, although personally I'll tell you right now any athlete who thinks he's going to improve his performance over the long run with drugs is just a fool. Make your choice, McRoyan."

Jake raised his head and tried to look his coach in the eye. But he found himself staring off over the heads of everyone around him. His face burned. His hands felt clammy. His pulse was racing, though whether it was from anxiety or the lingering effects of the cocaine, he couldn't tell.

"I don't think I'll take the test, Coach."

The coach nodded grimly. "I kind of thought that might be your decision. You're suspended for a week. If you can pass a test then, I'll put you back on the team."

"Yes, sir," Jake said.

"Everyone gets one free mistake in my book. But don't pull this again, McRoyan. Whatever the damned school board policy, *my* policy is I don't have druggies on my team."

Jake left the gym with the burning feeling of eyes following him. He dodged around the moving mass of people heading out toward the parking lot, some in high spirits, others rehashing the game, parents trying to be cool with their kids, and their kids wishing the parents would just go home so they could take off to the dozen or more parties already under way.

One or two yells followed him, derisive remarks from some, a more encouraging cry from someone else, but he didn't acknowledge anyone. He pushed on through, trying to get as far away from them all as quickly as he could.

He had lost the game. That was the fact. And he had been suspended for suspicion of drug use. If he didn't clear the next drug test, this would go on his permanent record, and no college, not even the humble Maine schools he'd applied to as safeties, would be interested in a known druggie athlete.

He fished in his pocket for the vial of cocaine and blindly threw it into the bushes.

He ran toward the dock, realizing even as he ran that he had no good choices. His parents would probably take the water taxi back to the island. His friends—and Claire—would all be on the ferry. He couldn't avoid them all.

He needed time to think. He needed to disappear somewhere for a while, wait for the water taxi's last run, after his parents were safely gone.

Suddenly, down the street, came a loud group of kids, a mix of seniors and juniors. Some he knew fairly well, like Tad Crowley. Others he knew only by sight.

"Hey, yo, big Jake!" Tad yelled. "What's up, man?"

Jake shrugged. "Not much."

"You want to party? My mom's out with her boyfriend and we have . . . *obtained* . . . a keg."

Tad was obviously pretty well lit already, Jake realized. They weren't exactly in the same circle, and if Tad weren't feeling unnaturally expansive, he never would have invited Jake over. Still, it was a place to hang for a while. And a couple of brews would take the edge off.

Tad Crowley's home was an apartment in an old, four-story brick building right in the quaint Portside section of Weymouth. Jake was able to lean out of the window and see the ferry landing. Perfect. Easy, downhill walking distance to the water taxi.

Inside, the lights were low and the stereo was cranked up on some old Grateful Dead. Jake found the keg resting in the kitchen sink on a pile of slushy ice. Louise Kronenberger was bent at the waist, her lips wrapped around the tap, swallowing while a handful of other people stood around counting, "Fifteen, sixteen, seventeen . . ."

At twenty Louise broke away and came up for air, gasping and giggling and looking flushed. Tad Crowley started to take her place, but then he noticed Jake. "Hey, your turn, man; you've got to need it more than me, running around all night and all."

Jake squatted and took the tap in his mouth. He pressed the lever and the cool beer began to flow while the crowd began a count. At twenty-nine he came up for air, feeling bleary and giddy.

That was better. Much better. He sat down heavily on a couch and sighed in relief. This music wasn't his favorite kind of stuff usually, but it sounded cool right now. Laid back, and that's what he needed. He needed to relax.

He began rubbing at a sore spot on his thigh where one of the Bangor linemen had nailed him hard with his helmet.

"You hurt yourself?" Louise sat beside him. Close beside him. She was wearing a skirt that rode up as she squirmed to make herself comfortable.

"Just a bruise," Jake said. The thick sound of his voice was funny. He smiled broadly.

"Caught a buzz yet?"

"Either that or my mouth just stopped working," he said.

"We wouldn't want that," Louise said. "So. Jake McRoyan partying with all us lowlifes. Aren't the Virgin Islanders having a private party tonight?" She laughed appreciatively at her own joke.

Jake stared at her legs. When she moved, he could see a flash of her white panties.

"I'm thirsty again," he said.

"Me too. What a coincidence."

"Too bad I can't walk," he joked.

Louise stood up. She swayed as she reached for his hand and pretended to be hauling him to his feet.

"Uh-oh, Louise found herself some new meat," a laughing voice said from somewhere.

Jake stood up, spread his arms to gain his balance, and followed Louise to the kitchen.

"What did I do last time?" Louise wondered, wrinkling her brow with concentration. "Twenty. This time, twenty-one. You count, okay?"

Jake kept count as well as he could, but he repeated fifteen twice, which brought Louise up sputtering in hysterics. "You're lucky you have a really, really great body," she said. "'Cause you can't count worth a damn."

Jake bent to the tap. This time neither of them kept count. Jake drank till his lungs burned from lack of air. When he stood up, the world was reeling.

"Now . . .'m buzz," he said. "'S go siddown."

He took a wobbly step back toward the living room, but somehow he didn't reach the couch. Instead, he realized, he'd come to be lying on his back on an unmade bed. Louise was beside him. She was undoing the buttons on his shirt, her fingers fumbling.

"'ts goin' on?" he asked.

Louise didn't answer. She finished opening his shirt and began running her hands and lips over his chest. Her fingers felt like ice, but her mouth was hot on his.

Jake squinted, trying to focus. The coke had worn off completely, leaving a weariness that had been deepened by the beer.

He felt barely awake, in some halfway state between consciousness and nothingness. "Claire?" he asked.

"Yeah, it's Claire," a girl's voice said, laughing.

Jake nodded, closing his eyes. "Love you."

EIGHTEEN

"IT'S KIND OF EERIE BEING out this late, or early, or whatever it is," Nina said. "I'll bet the four of us are the only people awake on this entire island."

"Actually, I think *you're* the only one really awake," Aisha grumbled.

"That's because I'm a creature of the night," Nina said. Aisha pulled the car into a U-turn to pull away from the front of Nina's house and head toward the dock. A light rain was falling, making the streets glisten and blanking out what little moonlight filtered down through the clouds. Zoey was breathing heavily in the backseat. Not exactly snoring, but the stage just before snoring. She was lying against Lucas, who had never been entirely awake to begin with. "You got a stereo, Aisha?"

Aisha pointed at the dashboard. "It gets only one station. Country."

"Pass," Nina said.

Zoey woke up with a snort. "I'm awake, I'm awake."

"We know you are," Aisha said, grinning at Nina.

Zoey rubbed her eyes. "I do hope Christopher gets better soon. I don't know how he does this every night. He's like the Energizer Bunny."

"Was Benjamin awake when you left?" Nina asked Zoey.

"Are you going to be like this?" Zoey asked grumpily. "I mean, if you and Benjamin are going to be seeing each other, then you have to leave me out of it."

"I was just curious," Nina said with a nonchalant shrug. She dug out a cigarette and popped it into the corner of her mouth.

"You know, if you're going to *not* smoke something, Nina, why don't you *not* smoke cigars?" Aisha suggested. "Then you could look really weird."

Nina puffed contentedly.

"So. Not that I'm getting into this," Zoey began, "but how did everything seem with Benjamin tonight?"

"Not that you're getting into it, it was no biggie. I mean, it was like all of us together doing something. We've all done stuff together lots of times."

"I guess tomorrow night's the big test, huh?" Aisha said. "Dancing, holding hands, screaming little bits of conversation at each other over the music." She wiggled her eyebrows meaningfully. "The big *K*."

Nina sat up. "The big kitty? The big kelp? The big karma?"

Aisha tucked her thumb into her fist, making a little mouth, and kissed it noisily.

"I'm not thinking about that," Nina said. "I'm only going to deal with things as they come up. Scratch that," she added hastily as Aisha and Zoey began to giggle. "You guys know what I mean."

"Are we there yet?" Lucas asked, coming out of his stupor.

"You know, I could do this myself," Aisha said. "If you guys are going to bitch the whole time."

"Island solidarity," Lucas muttered.

The car pulled into the brightly lit zone of the ferry landing. The plastic-wrapped newspapers lay waiting. Nearby lay a large bundle of rags. Nina wondered why anyone would pile a bunch of rags on the dock, but then her eye was drawn by a slight movement.

"Hey, hey!" she cried. "That's a person."

Aisha braked and the four of them piled out, approaching the inanimate figure cautiously.

"It's Jake," Zoey said, putting her hand over her heart. She knelt beside him and tried to wake him by grabbing his hand. "He's ice-cold."

"He must have hopped the water taxi when it came to drop off the papers," Lucas said. "I'm guessing Jake may have been having a little too much fun." He nudged him fairly hard in the side with his boot. "Come on, Jake. Party's over."

Jake stirred and blinked. He squinted to focus. "Wha—?"

"You're on the dock," Zoey said.

"And he's in deep flop if he shows up back at his house and his dad sees him like this," Nina said. "I can't believe *Joke* is this messed up. Just because we lost the dumb game?"

"It's not about the game," Zoey said. "Come on, Jake, we have to get you out of here."

"Zoey?" he said thickly.

"Yes, Jake. Come on. Try and stand up. Lucas, give me a hand."

Lucas looked doubtful, but came and took one of Jake's arms, draped it over his shoulders, and tried to get him up. Jake lay limp at first, but finally staggered up. He wobbled for a moment, then stumbled to the dock railing. He leaned over and began vomiting into the water below.

Zoey went over and stroked his head, murmuring soft encouragements.

Lucas wasn't amused. "Should we just leave him here to sleep it off?"

Jake finished and stepped back from the railing. Zoey used her scarf to wipe his mouth.

"What are you all looking at?" Jake demanded belligerently.

"Jake, no one is looking at you," Zoey insisted.

"Leave me alone, you . . ." He searched for the right word. "All of you," he finished with a bearlike sweep of his arms.

Nina realized that Zoey was crying silently, biting her thumb.

"Let's take him to my house," Nina said suddenly, surprising herself. "My dad sleeps like a corpse. We can stash him in our guest room."

"I don't know how your sister would feel about that," Aisha said.

"He's sort of her boyfriend," Nina said. "Used to be sort of her boyfriend. Whatever."

"Good idea," Lucas agreed quickly. He looked pointedly at Zoey. "He's *Claire's* boyfriend."

"Come on, Jake, get in the car," Zoey said. She took his arm, a frail figure beside him, and led him away.

"Look, Lucas," Nina told him in a low voice, "it doesn't mean anything."

"Really," Aisha agreed. "They *were* together for a long time. You can't expect her not to try and help him out when he's this screwed up."

"You're the only one, Zo," Jake said as Zoey tried to push him into the backseat. "Everyone else . . . Screw 'em."

"Watch your head. That's right. Easy."

"Don't take me home, okay? Wade . . . he'll laugh 'cause I . . . 'cause I think . . ."

Nina felt a chill. She saw the hard expression on Lucas's face soften a little and he turned to her.

"Sort of the downside of true love, huh, Nina?" he said. "You still sure you want to start playing this game?"

Claire woke to the sound of car doors closing. There was no nocturnal traffic on Chatham Island normally, and she was sleeping with her windows open, just her head sticking out from under the goose-down comforter.

She wrapped the comforter around herself and went to her window. In the front yard Lucas and Zoey were manhandling a big, shambling figure between them. Nina and Aisha ran ahead to open the front door. Claire glanced at her clock. It was almost four in the morning.

She heard the sound of heavy steps on the stairs and loud whispers. Claire waited. Finally, after ten minutes, there was the sound of footsteps retreating. The car drove off.

Claire dropped the comforter back on her bed and put on warm sweats and a bathrobe. She went down to the lower floor, retrieved several items from the bathroom she shared with Nina, and found Jake snoring in the rear guest bedroom.

They had pulled covers on over his clothes, stuffed a pillow under his head, taken off his shoes, and closed the blinds so that he would sleep through the dawn.

Claire set vitamin pills, aspirin, and a pitcher of tap water on the nightstand. Then she sat on the bed beside him and lifted his head. "Come on, Jake, just wake up for two seconds."

His eyes opened without focusing. "Thirsty," he croaked.

"Yeah, I thought you might be." It had been a long time since she'd been drunk, but she remembered what it felt like. She put the pitcher of water to his lips and he drank greedily. Then she poured three vitamin B pills and two aspirins into her palm. "Open up."

She tossed the pills in his mouth and gave him the pitcher again. "That will help. A little, anyway. If you need to throw up, use this wastebasket. All you have to do is roll over."

"Claire?"

"Yes, Jake."

"Claire?"

"Yes, Jake, it's me."

". . . kicked me off the team."

Claire bit her lip. He'd been kicked off the team? Was that real, or some drunken hallucination? "Don't think about it now. Just lie back and close your eyes." She pressed him back against the pillows.

In a moment he was unconscious again. Claire sat in the

small rocking chair at the foot of the bed and closed her eyes.

"I don't seem to have a very good effect on the guys I hook up with, do I?" she asked the darkness. "First Lucas. He ended up spending two years in Youth Authority. And now Jake."

"What am I supposed to do about you?" she whispered. "I can't change what happened. I can't bring Wade back to life."

If Jake were a different person, he would be able to get past this loyalty to his brother. While Wade was alive, he had relentlessly belittled and harassed Jake, making him the object of every joke, feeding his own ego at the expense of his adoring little brother. And now, it was as if even in death, Wade was finding a way to make Jake miserable.

But Jake wasn't interested in the truth about Wade. Wade was his big brother, period. He would probably never allow himself to see any further than that. And Claire, whatever else she might be, was the person responsible, in Jake's mind, for Wade's death.

In the same position, *she* would find a way to resolve the conflict. She was not a person who believed in absolutes, and she refused to be trapped by them.

But Jake was a different person. There were no shades of gray for Jake: it was all black and white, right and wrong. To love her was to betray Wade. She could not coexist in his mind alongside the memory of Wade, and the more Jake tried, the more he destroyed himself.

Claire sighed. Wade could not be made to go away. Which meant that in the end there was only one solution.

She felt something crawling down her cheek and touched it with her finger. She was surprised to discover that it was a tear.

Zoey led Lucas up the dark stairs to her room. Lucas's father was up and on his way to work each day before dawn, like all the professional fishermen and lobstermen on the island. Lucas didn't want to run into him and face the possibility of having to explain why he was out.

Zoey closed the door behind them and flipped on the light. It had seemed like a perfectly normal thing, to invite Lucas to sleep over for a few hours. But now, with him in her bedroom, both moving quietly like a pair of burglars, it began to seem a little more dubious.

Lucas yawned. "I'm beat. What a bizarre night. Dragging Jake up the stairs, driving around like vampires on the prowl throwing papers." He sat down on Zoey's bed and unlaced his boots.

Zoey fidgeted nervously, not quite sure how to proceed. Normally, she would change into her favorite Boston Bruins jersey and crawl under the covers.

"Urn, I'll hit the bathroom," she said, snatching up her

nightshirt. She brushed her teeth and combed her hair and changed into the thin cotton shirt. It came most of the way down to her knees, so it wasn't exactly provocative. Still, it was what she *slept* in. Not what she wore when she had guests over.

She went back to the room and found the lights turned off, for which she was grateful. Maybe Lucas had already fallen asleep. That would be best.

She slid beneath the covers and had the shocking and completely unfamiliar experience of touching a bare leg with her foot. She nearly yelped out loud. But that was being silly. They were practically adults. It wasn't like they couldn't sleep in the same location without it being some big thing. Zoey repeated the phrase in her mind—yes, that's all it was, sleeping in the same location.

She rolled onto her side, facing away from him. "Good night," she whispered.

"Don't I get a good-night kiss?"

"Sure." She twisted her head toward him, intending to accept a light peck on the lips. Instead his arm went around her and he drew her against him. His kiss left her gasping.

"Lucas," she said.

"Yes?"

"We are *not* doing that."

Long silence. His face was inches away in the darkness. His

arms were around her. She could hear his breath coming fast.

"Um . . . Why not?"

Zoey shrugged, feeling uncertain. "I just haven't decided that's something I want to do. At least not yet."

"How about if I've decided that it's something I *do* want to do?"

"It's one of those things that kind of has to be unanimous," Zoey said. "Come on, you know I only let you come up here because of your dad. You know I wasn't planning on having sex."

"No?"

"No."

"Okay. Excuse me for just a minute," Lucas said with deliberate politeness. He rolled away and in the darkness Zoey could hear him screaming into his pillow in frustration. It went on for longer than she would have expected. Finally he surfaced again.

"Did that help?" Zoey asked tentatively.

"No. It didn't. Look, Zoey, I don't know how it is for girls, but for guys this whole thing is sort of important. In the way that air is sort of important if you want to breathe."

"Well, it is with girls, too, but—"

"See? That's the problem. With girls there's a *but*. With guys there's no *but* anything. It's like, if someone said to me right now, you can have sex with Zoey, but we have to cut off your hand, I'd probably say, okay, what the hell, a hook will look cool."

"That's kind of flattering in a way," Zoey said, trying to defuse the level of tension. "Insane, but flattering."

"Insane, exactly. That's what it makes me, insane."

Zoey sat up in the bed, drawing her knees up and encircling them with her arms. "Lucas, look, I think I understand how you feel, but it *has* to be different for girls. First of all, guys don't get pregnant, have kids, and end up on welfare. Second of all, girls have a greater risk of getting AIDS and all the other popular sexually transmitted diseases. And third, the problem with you guys is that sex is *all* you think about, whereas females, being a little higher on the evolutionary scale, also think about things like commitment and love and all."

"But I do love you," Lucas said, sounding almost desperate.

"Let me ask you a question. Do you even have a condom with you?"

"A condom? Do I have one?"

"I thought so. See, you love me, but you're willing to take the risk I could get pregnant or catch something."

"So, you're saying if I get some condoms . . . ?"

"No, I'm saying when *I* decide *I'm* ready, you'll be the very first person to know."

Lucas lay silent in the dark. Whether he was seething in

anger or nodding in agreement, she couldn't be sure.

"I'll be the first person to know," he repeated. "Not Jake?"

Zoey sighed. "Lucas, I was just trying to help him out because he was in bad shape. Would you like me if I were the kind of person who just walked away?"

"I think I'm going to have to scream into my pillow some more."

"You're not the only one," Zoey said softly. "You know, I do love you, too."

"Yeah, right."

"Go to sleep."

"Hmm. Can I tell everyone we slept together? I mean, we are, technically."

"Go to sleep."

"Good-night kiss?"

"Sleep."

She heard him scream into his pillow once more, and a few minutes later they were both asleep.

BENJAMIN

Love is a fairly useless word. It is imprecise. It isn't specific.

You love your mom, you love your country, you love ice cream, you love the girl you love. I love you like a brother, I love the smell of napalm in the morning, you're gonna love this one, I ~~elve~~ love what you do for me Toyota, gotta love it. Same word, different meanings.

Even romantic love has all sorts of different levels. I mean, Romeo had a different thing going with Juliet than Mr. and Mrs. Macbeth had together. Although, who knows? Maybe if Romeo ~~smf~~ and Juliet had survived, gotten married, grown old, they too might have ended up murdering their houseguests and chatting with witches.

My point is, there are four women who are important in my life. My mom, whom I love. Your basic filial love. My sister, Zoey, whom I also love. This would be your brotherly love.

Then there's Claire, whom I love. Romantic love. The boy-girl thing, with sort of a self-destructive, why-am-I-doing-this? sort of edge mixed in. Love as a form of protracted conflict.

Then there's Nina. I love Nina in kind of the same way I love Zoey. Like a sister.

Except she's not my sister, which means that all the while I've ~~beeeen~~ been aware that possibilities existed beyond the very definite limitations of brotherly love. Aware of the possibilities, but determined not to think about them and screw up a really good friendship.

And there's something a little disturbing about the idea of a person migrating from the "love-you-like-a-sister" category over into the much more intense "can't-wait-to-kiss-you-again" category. It's no different than one day saying "Man, I love ice cream" and the next day saying, "No, I mean I really love ice cream. I want to have Ben and Jerry's baby."

It still seems like something that ought to be illegal, or at least frowned upon.

NINETEEN

THEY CAUGHT THE SEVEN-FORTY FERRY from the island and rode across choppy seas, under a high, full moon, toward the glittering mainland and, Nina thought melodramatically, *destiny*.

"You look . . ." Benjamin said, letting the question hang.

"Fetching," Nina supplied. "It's complimentary, but not over the top."

Benjamin smiled. "And I particularly like that . . . um, that—"

"Dress."

"And the color, why it's . . . it's . . ."

"Depressing," Nina said. "It's black."

"Still, it goes nicely with your eyes—"

"Which are gray."

"Yes, I know that," Benjamin said smoothly. "I was asking how many. Two, right?"

"Arranged so that there's one on either side of my nose," Nina said. "I read in *Seventeen* that's the fashionable arrangement for eyes this season."

"And me? How do I look?" he asked, giving a little turn on the steel deck.

As usual, he looked good, having a wardrobe that consisted almost entirely of subtle, muted colors that worked well in almost any combination. "Well, I don't want to make you self-conscious," Nina said, "but the green plaid doesn't really go all that well with the yellow stripes. Or the paisley."

"Damn. I've made another fashion faux pas. Imagine my embarrassment."

They both laughed and Nina realized she was feeling almost relaxed, as if this night didn't represent a major change in her life. As if there weren't a dozen horrible scenarios floating around in the back of her mind, ranging from slightly embarrassing to move-to-another-state embarrassment.

Benjamin fell quiet for a moment and Nina didn't interrupt. He was listening to the sound of the engines, the intermittent crash of waves against the hull, and the murmur of other conversations. She listened with him, and searched his familiar face for a sign that he had magically changed in the way he felt about her. Was he being nicer? Gentler? More considerate? Probably not, she concluded. Benjamin was just being himself, neither more, nor less.

"I like the way you do that," he said.

"Do what?"

"The way you know when I want to listen, and you wait very patiently."

"Sure," Nina said, feeling awkward. She began looking in her purse for her cigarettes.

"So. Aren't we all supposed to be surprised that Claire and Jake are going to this dance together?"

Claire. Nina had wondered how long they'd be able to go without her name coming up. She looked across the deck and spotted them, Jake and Claire, leaning back together by the stern railing, close but not touching. And not really talking very much, either. "I think Jake owed her big time for last night," Nina said. "And I guess she really wanted to go to this dance."

"She does have a way of getting what she wants," Benjamin observed.

"That's what you like about her, isn't it?" Nina asked.

Benjamin smiled and gave the uncanny impression that he was looking at her from behind his sunglasses, trying to read her expression. "How about if we make a deal right up front here. How about if we don't talk about Claire?"

"What'll we talk about instead?"

"Hmmm. Infomercials. Favorite cheeses. What to bring to a desert island. And the meaning of life."

"Okay. Sounds cool. But we'd better start with the easy one first."

"Meaning of life," Benjamin said, nodding.

"Let's have it down by the time we dock."

The ferry came into Weymouth and the seven of them disembarked, part of a sparse crowd. It was difficult for islanders to do much nighttime partying on the mainland, since the last ferry returning to the islands left at nine. Late-night functions like dances meant taking the more expensive water taxi home.

Aisha felt a little strange, walking through the streets with her friends. Tonight she was the only one not part of a couple. Even Nina had a date, and she and Benjamin were talking away, occasionally laughing out loud. It was nice to see Nina having a good time that involved a member of the opposite sex, but it did drive home to Aisha the fact that she was the odd person in a group of seven.

Although, come to think of it, she felt happier than Claire and Jake looked.

Official visiting hours at the hospital were over, but the feeling had been that they should give it a try just the same. The truth was, if they hadn't planned to go and see Christopher, Aisha would have just stayed home.

Aisha had discovered a door on an earlier visit that bypassed the heavily monitored emergency room, and she led them inside. The brightly lit hospital corridors were mostly empty, and they made their way quickly, suppressing giggles and making morbid jokes, like a group of party crashers with very bad taste in parties.

Aisha knocked at the door to Christopher's room and, on hearing a muffled response, they went in. She was relieved to see that Christopher was sitting up, looking relatively normal again. The swelling had gone down sufficiently to allow him to see out of both eyes. He was flipping through the channels on the TV.

"Hey, what is this?" he asked. "You didn't all have to play dress-up just to come visit me."

Aisha gave him a little kiss. "We're on our way to the homecoming dance."

Christopher cocked an eyebrow suspiciously. "And who's your date?"

"We're all sharing," Zoey piped up. "Actually, I'm sharing Lucas two ways, with Louise Kronenberger and with Aisha." She sent Lucas an exaggeratedly suspicious look.

"Still on the good painkillers?" Lucas asked.

"No, and I've noticed something—TV is much better when you're delirious. Thank God I'm getting out tomorrow. I'd lose my mind if I had to spend any more time in here. I even lost my roommate." He indicated the vacant bed across the room.

"Lost?" Nina asked.

"Not as in dead," Christopher said. "As in gone home."

"Tomorrow we'll have you all set up," Aisha promised. "The Governor's Room. Jacuzzi, big four-poster bed, antiques, and my mom, who wants to try out a bunch of recipes on a helpless guinea pig."

"I get to move in next," Jake said, speaking for the first time.

"Yeah, well, you guys have all been very cool," Christopher said, suddenly serious. "Delivering my papers and all. Zoey's dad covering for me at the restaurant. Mr. Geiger I know has covered most of my bill here in the hospital."

"Liberal white guilt," Nina said with a shrug. "Besides, the old man's rich."

"Of course he did say he wants the papers up on the front porch from now on," Claire said. "Not halfway across the yard."

Christopher smiled crookedly. "I'm just saying everyone's been very cool in this. Especially certain people." He put his arm around Aisha's waist.

"Island solidarity," Benjamin said. "When we're not busy stabbing each other in the back, we try and help each other out."

"Hey, you guys better get going," Christopher said. "I know Lucas has vital duties as homecoming king."

"Please don't use that phrase," Lucas pleaded. "Whenever I hear it, I get a headache."

"Go on, before the nurse busts you all," Christopher said. He took Aisha's face in his hands and gave her a kiss on the lips. "That's the best I can do until those stitches come out," he apologized.

"That was plenty good," Aisha said with feeling. The others had started to leave discreetly. "We'll have to work together on the period of rehabilitation."

"I'll see you, babe."

She kissed him on the head and opened the door to the hallway. The others were bunched together, making *aww, wasn't that sweet* faces.

"Hey, Lucas," Christopher called out. "Can you come here a minute?"

Lucas looked surprised. He went back into the room.

Lucas was inside for several minutes. When he came out, he looked distracted and grim. But he quickly plastered on a smile. "Come on, let's get out of this place."

"What was that all about?" Zoey asked.

Lucas shrugged. "Oh, he just, uh . . . he said he wanted me to, you know, keep an eye out for Aisha. Manly protective stuff."

Aisha laughed as though she believed him, but she could see that Zoey's eyes were clouded with doubt. And Lucas sounded less than convincing.

But an orderly turned down the hallway, forcing them into a panicky, giggling race for the exit, and the moment for voicing suspicions was past.

TWENTY

THE MULTIPURPOSE ROOM WAS A sea of bodies in motion, bouncing, spinning, hair tossing, arms and legs that seemed to belong to more than one body. The lights were low and filtered through pink and red crepe paper, deepening shadows and making bare skin glow unnaturally, as though everyone in the room had just come from a tanning bed.

The band onstage was one everyone had seen before, and most had danced to before. They played an eclectic mix, one minute hard rocking, then veering off into sanitized, school-board-approved rap.

"So," Nina said, surveying the scene. "This is a school dance."

"Haven't you been to one or two dances?" Benjamin asked her, speaking loudly over the music.

"Maybe for a total of ten minutes," Nina said. "Hey. Where are you guys going?"

All the island contingent had arrived together, but Claire

and Jake had already wandered off in one direction, and now Zoey and Lucas and Aisha were sidling away.

"Lucas has to go find out when the big presentation is!" Zoey yelled in her ear. "Eesh and I are just going to hit the girls' room."

"Wait, I'll go with you," Nina said, leaving Benjamin's side.

Zoey shook her head. "Nina, stop worrying; you'll be fine. Don't think of it as a date. You're just hanging out with Benjamin."

"There's a band and I'm wearing a dress," Nina protested. "That's not hanging out."

"Bye, Nina," Zoey said with a wink.

Nina watched her disappear and then went back to Benjamin. One or two kids on the dance floor were sending looks in their direction. But it had not been the full stop-and-stare she'd feared.

"How's it look?" Benjamin asked.

"Like teen night in hell," Nina said bleakly.

"Cool," Benjamin said with a smile.

"People are looking at me."

"Admiringly?"

"No, more like *What's the deal? Why is Nina here? She never comes to dances.*"

"Since when do you care if people look at you?"

"Since I know what they're wondering is, Does she have a date? Benjamin? No way, Benjamin wouldn't go out with Nina. Besides, she doesn't even like guys, does she?" Nina was beginning to feel the first trickle of panic. People were staring, more and more now. Each of them analyzing the situation. Each of them remembering what they'd heard about Nina's uncle. Hundreds of amateur psychiatrists working up their analysis of her while they danced and rubbed their bodies together.

Nina swallowed hard. She felt something touch her arm, then slide down to her hand. Benjamin's fingers wrapped around the fist Nina had formed.

"Come on, Nina," Benjamin said. "This is the moment when you either go forward or back."

"I know what they're all thinking."

"Ten minutes from now they'll have forgotten all about you."

"It's like I'm trying to be someone else. That's always a mistake. Be yourself, right? And I'm trying to be some other person."

"No, it's like you're trying to be yourself without a lot of old fear getting in the way, Nina. Hey. Did you bring your shades?"

For a moment Nina was confused. Shades? Then she remembered. With her free hand she opened her purse and looked inside. "Uh-huh."

"So?"

Nina hesitated. Her stomach felt like it was turning. She was sure she must be blushing brightly; she could feel the heat in her face. And she was definitely avoiding eye contact with everyone. She could walk away now, go back and catch the ferry home. Benjamin would find someone to spend the rest of the evening with.

She would be alone and safe. She could remain the same person she'd always been, not have to break new ground and suddenly try to emerge from the years of shame and secrets.

There was a sudden break in the music. With a loud twang the lead guitarist had broken a string. Relative quiet descended as the music faded out.

"I'm guessing we have everyone's attention now," Benjamin said dryly.

It was true. Without the distraction of the music there wasn't much for people to do but stare, subtly or openly, at what seemed like the impossible spectacle of Nina Geiger and Benjamin Passmore holding hands.

Nina took a deep breath. "Okay," she muttered under her breath, "now that I have everyone's attention." She reached into her bag and pulled out a Lucky Strike and stuck it in the corner of her mouth. Her hands were shaking so badly she almost couldn't do it. Then she retrieved the sunglasses, the Ray Bans identical to the ones Benjamin wore, snapped them open, and put them on.

Finally, with a supreme effort, she unclenched her fist. Her fingers, clammy and sweaty, intertwined with Benjamin's.

The music started up again. The crowd started dancing.

"Are we still being stared at?" Benjamin asked.

"A little less," Nina admitted. Her teeth were chattering as if she were cold.

"Well, we are officially on a date then, I guess."

"So, I guess we'd better dance," Nina said, trying not to sound like she was telling the dentist to go ahead and drill.

Benjamin laughed. "You think it's been scary so far. Wait till you're around me when I'm dancing."

Lucas danced a little with Zoey, and danced once or twice with Aisha, and drank some punch. But it was hard to get into the party atmosphere. Christopher had pretty well killed any remaining chance that he might enjoy this evening.

Christopher had called him back into his hospital room to ask whether Lucas could get him a gun.

A *gun*. Like Lucas was a gangster or something. He'd told Christopher to forget it. First of all, he'd been busted for drunk driving leading to a fatality, not for holding up 7-Elevens. Second of all, he hadn't even been guilty of the drunk driving.

Third of all, getting a gun so he could go looking for the guys who beat him up was dangerous and stupid beyond imagination.

But Christopher had sounded determined. It was a matter of getting his respect back, he said. Most of the serious screwups Lucas had known in YA were there over one type of respect or another. Respect was a popular word among violent losers. He'd told Christopher that, but Christopher wasn't thinking clearly.

Lucas wondered how good his reasoning would be under similar circumstances. Probably about the same as Christopher's, he had to admit.

It was going to force a grim choice on him. He could either stand back while Christopher tried to handle things on his own. Or he could drop the dime on Snake, and maybe have to face the consequences.

After a while one of the girls from the homecoming committee came and found him. Perfect. He was really in the mood for some more b.s.

"I have to go get ready for this dumb-ass ceremony dance thing," Lucas told Zoey, leaning to put his lips to her ear.

"Good luck," Zoey said. "Aisha and I will spend the time picking up guys."

Lucas gave her a dirty look and Zoey grinned back angelically.

He went back to the room behind the bandstand, where the music was reduced by cinder-block walls to a dull, throbbing noise like a bad headache. Half a dozen girls and guys from the organizing committee, the principal, and two teacher-chaperons were there, milling around importantly, along with Louise Kronenberger, looking flushed and happy.

She tossed her voluminous brown mane and looked him slowly up and down. "Finally, our big moment," she said.

"Yeah," Lucas said unenthusiastically.

"They already explained to me, we wait till Hardcastle's given his speech and put everyone to sleep. Then the band starts up, slow dance, out we go, take a little bow, and dance around the floor."

"I can't slow dance worth a damn," Lucas said.

"I tried to tell you we should practice."

"Zoey wouldn't have been real happy about that idea."

"Zoey," Louise said impishly, as if the name were a joke. "Zoey doesn't have to worry about *you*, does she?"

"No, she doesn't," Lucas said.

"I know, I know. My reputation precedes me. But really, Lucas, at least ten percent of my reputation is exaggerated." She laughed gaily at the joke. "Seriously, just hold on to me and I'll get you through it." She gave him a look from beneath half-closed lids.

There was a flurry of activity as Mr. Hardcastle and the student who was to introduce him left the room, followed by the two teachers and the rest of the committee members.

They were alone. Louise moved closer, smiling at the way he sidled away. "Like my dress?" she asked.

"What there is of it," Lucas said, keeping his eyes firmly on her face and away from the cleavage on display.

"Boy, Zoey does have you whipped," Louise said.

"We island kids have very low libidos," Lucas joked, still backing away. "Toxic ferry fumes or something."

"I wouldn't say that," Louise said dryly. "Jake's an islander."

Lucas knew instinctively that he did not, under any circumstances, want to ask Louise what she was talking about. Unfortunately, that didn't stop her.

"Yeah, we had a very nice little party last night," she said, laughing all the while. "Although I have to admit, I think he may have thought I was someone else."

Lucas sighed. Perfect. What was it with people that they were constantly dumping their secrets on him? Zoey had already given him hell for knowing that Christopher was being unfaithful to Aisha. Then there had been Christopher's brilliant gun idea.

Now K-burger had just announced that she had seduced Jake. Wonderful. Who was he going to piss off by keeping *this* secret? He knew who he'd piss off by telling.

"Look, I didn't hear that, okay?" Lucas said.

Louise shrugged. "I'm sorry, I like guys. And guys like me. Usually, at least, when they don't have some girl's leash around their . . . necks."

"I love Zoey," Lucas said, feeling virtuous. It was a damned shame Zoey wasn't there to witness his stellar performance.

"Yeah, but Zoey's hanging on to the big *V*, isn't she? I don't know why. I mean, Lucas, you could have any girl in this school. Zoey ought to realize that."

"It's none of your business," Lucas said coldly.

Louise laughed. "In other words, I'm right about Zoey."

The door to the room opened and one of the committee girls said, "Okay, it's time. As soon as you hear the applause die down after Mr. Hardcastle gets done speaking."

"That shouldn't take long," Lucas said.

"I can't believe you're enough of a wimp to let Zoey control you, Lucas. I had this image of you as being more . . . I don't know. Tougher. I thought you were something special."

"Let's just get this over with," Lucas said. Louise wasn't the first person tonight to have a confused image of him.

"Okay. But while we're dancing close, and you have your arms around me, keep in mind that there are girls in the world beside Zoey the Pure."

TWENTY-ONE

"I GUESS THIS IS THE big moment," Nina said. She was standing by the refreshments table with Benjamin. They were still warm and flushed from dancing, though the lengthy speech by Mr. Hardcastle, having something vaguely to do with why Weymouth High was such a truly swell school, had given them a chance to cool off a little.

"Spotlight up," Nina announced. "And here's our happy couple."

"'Symbols of all that's right with Weymouth High,'" Benjamin quoted sardonically from the principal's speech. "Aren't you glad you came? You'd have missed all this magnificence."

"I am glad I came," Nina said. She looked at him, and reminded herself for the hundredth time that he was her date. Her actual date. And better than that, he was a guy she liked more than she'd thought possible. "I'm very glad."

"You're not going all sincere on me, are you?"

Nina smiled. "I would never do that to you, Benjamin."

The band began to play, a slow, almost mournful tune. "Oh, this is nice. Lucas is trying to hold her at arm's length, and Louise is trying to squeeze her big buffers right up into his face."

"Gee, if I'd known that, *I* would have tried to be homecoming king," Benjamin said.

Nina punched him in the arm, and he groaned. It was a proprietary action, Nina realized, like she was jealous that he would think about another girl, but it had happened naturally, without her even thinking about it. And Benjamin had acted like it was perfectly normal.

"You know, I *never* look at other girls," Benjamin said self-mockingly.

"Now I'm definitely glad I came. Zoey is standing a few feet away from them, doing this smile she does when she's really on slow boil."

Zoey was standing with Aisha, watching Lucas move Louise around the floor with the minute attention of a cat watching a mouse.

"Should have been you," Aisha said comfortingly. "Homecoming queen, I mean."

"That's not what I care about," Zoey said. "Although it would be nice to win something, *some*time. It's just why couldn't it have been Amelia or Kay or Marie who won?"

"Or for that matter, it could have been Jake or Tad or someone else who won for king."

"That would have been okay, too," Zoey agreed.

"Basically, anyone but the combination of Lucas and Louise," Aisha said.

"Basically."

"You shouldn't be worried just because she has bigger boobs than you do, Zoey. You put way too much on that. That's really *not* all that guys think about. Besides, you know Lucas loves you."

"It's not her boobs I'm worried about," Zoey said. "Give me some credit. It's just that, well . . . you know what everyone says about Louise."

"You mean 'Lay Down Louise'? 'Easy Louisie'? I may have heard certain ugly rumors," Aisha said.

Zoey shrugged and looked away in embarrassment. "Lucas has sort of been wanting to, you know . . . And I've been saying no. Or at least, not yet."

"Look, Zoey, you can't get into just competing—"

Her words were cut off as the song ended and the audience applauded more or less enthusiastically for the end of the big ceremonial dance.

Lucas smiled grimly and nearly pushed Louise away. Zoey found that extremely gratifying.

"I guess there won't be any little princes and princesses, from the look of it!" Aisha yelled to Zoey, clapping with the rest of them.

Lucas came straight over, smiling now as if the burden of the world had just been lifted from his shoulders. "It's over, it's over. I've done my little thing for school spirit. Jeez, I can't slow dance worth spit."

"You looked good," Aisha said, making a gagging sound.

"No, don't start with me, Aisha." Lucas shook his finger at her. "I still think you're the one who started this by nominating me."

The music stayed slow, and couples were drifting around the floor again, locked in embraces. "Come on, Lucas," Zoey said. "If you can dance like a dork with Louise, you can dance like a dork with me."

"I'll just go and drink punch with the pathetic, dateless people," Aisha said good-naturedly.

Lucas took Zoey in his arms. She laid her head on his shoulder. It felt very, very good to be close to him like this. Seeing him with another girl had driven that feeling home to her.

She looked across the room and saw Jake standing stiffly beside Claire, staring into blank space.

It was funny the way emotional bonds were forged, seeming stronger than any steel at the time, and then were broken, leaving two people who had shared almost everything feeling like strangers.

Today she had her arms around Lucas. Once it would have been Jake. Today she would swear that nothing could ever drive her from Lucas. But once she had felt just that same way about Jake.

There were so many ways for things to go wrong, it seemed. And so few chances that they would all go right. She was glad when Lucas slowly turned her away so that she could no longer see Jake and be reminded that even the things that felt so perfect, like the feel of being weightless in Lucas's arms, could someday end.

Then she saw Nina standing with Benjamin. They were holding hands, looking uncomfortable, maybe a little giddy, but holding hands. Sort of the way Zoey had taught Nina.

Zoey smiled. Things didn't always turn out badly.

Benjamin could feel the pulse in Nina's wrist. Her heart was racing. Fear or excitement or both. But then, his own pulse was speeding, too. Nina's nervousness must be catching.

"I have to go to the place," Nina said.

"The *place*? You mean, what, the supermarket?"

"Very cute. The ladies' room. I was trying to be delicate."

"As long as you wash your hands afterward."

"You want me to park you somewhere?" Nina suggested. "Aisha's over by the food."

"Cool." Benjamin took her arm and fell in step with her. Here, in an environment this unstructured, he was genuinely blind. You couldn't use step-counting to get around a big crowded room filled with rowdy kids. "So, Aisha with the food. Is she fat or anything? You know, so I don't make some insensitive remark?"

"Yes," Nina said. "Aisha must be, oh, two, two hundred fifty pounds. Somewhere in there. Maybe three hundred."

Benjamin laughed. Obviously Nina was lying. But then, he had set her up. He knew perfectly well what Aisha looked like, having had her described several times over the years. Of course, Nina knew that, too.

Even as nervous and preoccupied and scared as she was, Nina was still right there, always sharp and on top of things. There were times when they could have almost been some old-time comedy team who had worked together for so many years, they'd become two halves of the same brain.

But something was happening. Something different. She wasn't plain old Nina to him right now. The way she smelled, the sound of her voice, the softness of her hand on his, the silkiness of her hair brushing against his cheek when she leaned close to talk to him. It was making his heart race.

"Hey, Ben." Aisha's voice.

Nina moved away. "I'll be right back unless the line is really long."

"What's up, Aisha?" he asked, immediately missing the warmth of Nina's hand.

Silence. She had probably shrugged. Then, "Oh, sorry. Not much."

"Too bad Christopher couldn't be here, huh?"

Now she was nodding.

"Well, soon, right? You think you two will get back together after he gets out of the hospital?" He felt uncomfortable making small talk about someone else's relationship, but it was either that or stand there like a redwood.

"I haven't really thought about it," Aisha said. "I mean, I don't know that this has really changed anything basic. But I know I don't feel like this is the time to be pushing the issue. You know?"

"Sure. Wait till he's healthy. Then bust him."

"Mostly it was miscommunication," she said, sounding thoughtful. "I mean, we barely knew each other as people before we got involved. I didn't know how he felt about certain things."

Benjamin nodded sagely. "It's good to get to know someone first, I guess."

"Yeah, well, you people of the male persuasion don't usually want to wait around for friendship to develop first," Aisha said darkly. "You guys seem to think the order should be sex first. Everything else second."

"Guys. We're such pigs," Benjamin said. "So, you want to have sex?"

"Very funny," Aisha said tolerantly. "Are you having a good time with Nina?"

"I always have a good time with Nina."

"Yeah, but this is a different kind of good time, isn't it?"

Benjamin squirmed a little uncomfortably. "Not really."

"You were holding hands."

"Uh-huh."

"And you were dancing."

"We're at a dance. What are we supposed to do? Juggle chain saws?"

"You two look good together," Aisha said. "Sort of like if Christian Slater and Winona Ryder were going out. Cool, but not phony."

Benjamin was ashamed to feel gratified by that comment. "Look, we're just friends at a dance together. Don't make a big thing out of it. We've been friends for a long time."

"You never held her hand before. I mean, you and I are friends, right? We're at a dance together, right? You and I are not holding hands."

Benjamin sighed irritably. "Is there any punch or cookies or anything left?"

"You know, you're blushing."

"No I'm not."

"All I'm saying is, Nina is a *hand-holding* type of friend. She's a *dance-with* type of friend. This is all new. She didn't use to be in either of those categories."

"Things change," Benjamin admitted.

"Don't get pissed off about it. Jeez, Benjamin, this is the way it should be. It's what I was just saying. First you're friends, then the other things. Very mature."

Were there those other things? Benjamin wondered. But then, hadn't he wanted to hold her hand? He clenched and unclenched his hand unconsciously. Yes. He had enjoyed holding her hand.

And dancing? Yes, he'd liked that, too.

And there was no one whose company he enjoyed more.

Still, that didn't make it anything more than friendship, really. Did it?

"Friendship," he muttered aloud, momentarily forgetting about Aisha. How did you know when friendship had become something more? How would he know if and when he crossed that line in his feelings for Nina?

"What did you say?" Aisha asked.

He shook his head. "Nothing. I was just mumbling."

"Hey, Nina," Aisha said.

Nina said something, but a group of girls nearby had burst out into a prolonged explosion of giggling.

"What?" he yelled.

She put her mouth close to his ear. He could smell her shampoo, her perfume. Her. Nina's breath tickled his ear. He realized his heart was beating fast again. And then he realized he desperately wanted her to stay just as near as she was.

His reaction almost made him laugh. So. Maybe the line had already been crossed without his noticing it.

"I said, I'm back," Nina said.

"I'm glad," he said.

It's time, Claire told herself heavily. Time to do what she had come here tonight to do.

"Come on, Jake," she said softly, taking his hand.

"We've already danced a couple times," Jake said stiffly.

"I know. I want to dance this dance."

Jake sighed. "Well, I owe you, don't I?" he said sarcastically. "How can I say no?"

"One last dance, Jake. The very last."

She drew him with her onto the floor. For a big guy he danced well, with more grace than would be expected of a football player. Claire enjoyed the hard, washboard feel of his stomach and chest, the ridged muscles of his back, even though they were tense, as they had been all night.

He was fighting his feeling for her. She could see it in his eyes, and hear it in the strain of his voice.

"Jake, Jake," she said wearily. "We have not been a lucky couple, have we?"

He shrugged his answer.

"It's enough to make me believe in fate. And I guess there's no fighting fate, is there?"

Again he didn't answer.

"For the record, Jake, I think you are an amazing, decent, sweet guy. One of a kind. I'm sorry about all the conflict I've caused in your life, and the pain."

He met her gaze for almost the first time that night. He looked troubled.

"But this is it," Claire said. "This has to be the end. It's either me or Wade. One of us had to lose and . . ." She took at deep breath. ". . . he's already lost all he could."

"Claire—"

"No, don't, all right?" she said harshly. "This is hard enough. I really do care for you, and I know you care for me, so don't make me any sadder by saying it. There's just too much history between us. And to tell you the truth, I'm not a person who can go around for long feeling guilty. I'm sorry about what happened two years ago. I'm sorry you can't deal with this without trying to destroy yourself. But you can't. Which leaves only one solution."

His arms tightened around her, holding her close. She pressed her cheek against his shoulder and blotted her tears on his shirt.

He took her face with his hand and forced her to look at him. He kissed her for a long, still moment.

Then she took another deep breath. She let the emotion run out of her, turning her thoughts away. She thought of her widow's walk. She thought of how much she liked to be up there, watching the lightning illuminate the darkness, watching snow drift down to settle on the little town below.

She had always been able to do what she had to. And now she pulled away, leaving the warmth of Jake's arms. She turned and, with dry eyes, walked away.

Nina had been feeling increasingly uncomfortable since the band had eased into all slow songs. She hadn't danced slow with Benjamin yet. And now the entire room, at least all the people who had dates, seemed to have settled into slow-motion making out, barely acknowledging the music anymore, oblivious to the looks of others around them.

Nina set down the glass of soda.

"Are you ready for me to step on your feet some more?" Benjamin asked.

"Um, how about if we go outside for a minute. I think it's stuffy in here. No air. Don't you want to?"

"Sure. Lead on."

She led him around the perimeter of the dance floor, noticing again the way whispers seemed to follow them. She was painfully aware of the discomfort she felt, as all the feelings she'd not yet learned to bury rose to the surface.

She reached the door and pushed open the bar. A blast of chill air slapped her. Outside, more couples were making out along the wall. A group of guys and girls was walking slowly around the building, drinking from beers concealed in their coat pockets, moving to stay out of range of the chaperons. In the nearby parking lot a half-dozen guys seemed to be egging each other on to a fight. A teacher was running to intervene.

"Full moon," Nina said, automatically describing the things Benjamin couldn't see.

"A faint smell of pot, beer, and car exhaust," Benjamin said with a smile.

"I wouldn't be surprised," Nina said. She rubbed her arms with her hands, trying to stay warm.

"Are you okay?" Benjamin asked.

Nina sighed. "Yeah. I'm okay."

"That wasn't very convincing."

"I guess it wasn't," she acknowledged. "I guess I'm just not used to all this."

"What aren't you used to? The bad music? The cheap vodka someone dumped in the punch?"

"Ahh," Nina groaned, covering her face with her hands. "I'm such a dweeb. Why do you even want to go out with me? God. I'm pathetic. My hands are sweating and my heart's going like a scared rabbit's, and I feel like I'm ready to hurl."

Benjamin laughed. "Don't do *that*. Or at least, aim away from me."

"You don't understand, Benjamin."

"I'm making you sick?"

"It's not really very funny," Nina said, feeling defeated and depressed. Here it was at last—the moment when she ruined everything. The final scenario.

"I never thought I'd hear you saying something wasn't funny," Benjamin said.

"It's pathetic, how about that? *I'm* pathetic."

"No, you're not. I like you a lot, Nina. And I have very good taste. I would never like someone who was pathetic. What is this about?"

Nina groaned again in frustration and anger. "It's about the way I felt inside when you asked me to slow dance just now. I know it's dumb. I know it's *you*, not . . . someone else. And I know it's *now*, not five years ago. And I'm sixteen, not a little kid anymore. But these feelings . . ."

Benjamin waited patiently for her to go on, but she couldn't. She was choking from the lump in her throat. Tears had begun to fall down her cheeks. She was ruining it, as she'd known she would. Benjamin would be sweet and understanding, but it would still be the end.

The end, after all the time she had wanted for this night to come.

"Nina, we don't have to slow dance. We don't have to kiss or anything like that."

Nina laughed bitterly. "Yeah, I'll bet kissing me would be the top thing on your list right now. Right behind getting the hell out of here and away from me."

"At the risk of making you feel even more panicky, Nina, I do want to kiss you. I've wanted to kiss you all night. All night I've felt like, jeez, I really am blind not to have realized—" He shrugged and sucked in a deep breath. "It's just that there you were, all the time, and I never realized it."

Nina bit her knuckle till she could taste blood. He was saying the things she'd hoped for years to hear him say. But at the same time she felt like running away, running all the way back to the ferry and hiding in her room. Her stomach was in knots. It wouldn't work. It never would.

"But, you know, we really can just go back inside and hang out," Benjamin said.

"Yeah," Nina managed. "Okay."

She moved to where he could take her arm. Out here in a dirt field with no landmarks to navigate by, he was almost helpless. She led him back to the door and pulled it open. Music and warmth came billowing out.

Nina stopped. A panicky, giddy, reckless feeling had taken hold of her. She let the door handle go and swung around. She darted her face forward, eyes closed, and quickly kissed Benjamin's mouth.

Only he moved and she missed his mouth.

A slow smile spread across Benjamin's face. "Feel better? Now that you've kissed my nose?"

A terrible, ghastly embarrassment flooded Nina's brain. She had kissed him on the nose. The big moment of her entire life and she had kissed him on the nose. This was not part of any scenario.

But another part of her could not help but acknowledge that it *was* funny.

"I've always really liked your nose," she said. Then she broke up in giggles.

"How about we try again? This time I'll stay still."

Nina's giggles died away. She took a deep breath, and then another. His hand had touched her bare shoulder and from there traveled to her cheek.

He was very close now, and she knew that soon the memories would rise to destroy this fragile moment.

She closed her eyes, trembling.

She felt a softness on her lips.

She felt the warmth of his breath. The muscles in his back and shoulders as her arm went around him. The luxurious, glowing heat that spread through her, banishing the chill of the Maine night.

Nina kissed him back.

And she did not hurl.

FIND OUT WHAT HAPPENS NEXT!

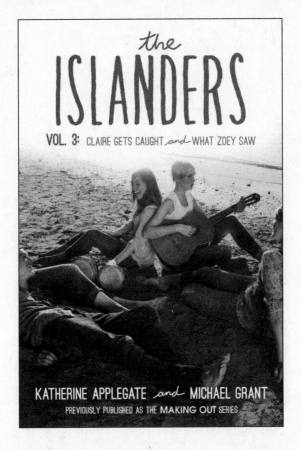

the
ISLANDERS

VOL. 3: CLAIRE GETS CAUGHT *and* WHAT ZOEY SAW

KATHERINE APPLEGATE *and* MICHAEL GRANT

PREVIOUSLY PUBLISHED AS THE **MAKING OUT** SERIES

ONE

THE WAVES WERE MORE GRAY than blue, and when Lucas stood up on his board, his longish blond hair was the only splash of color in a tableau of sea and sky that could almost have been a black-and-white photograph.

Zoey Passmore pulled the cowl neck of her sweater up over her chin and ears and slid her hands up inside the sleeves. The beach sand had lost all of the warmth from the sun that had shone so encouragingly earlier in the day, and she kept to the blanket. She'd collected driftwood from the beach and fallen limbs from the pine trees behind her and piled them with ex-Girl Scout expertise in a nice little pyramid. But she didn't want to light the fire until Lucas was with her for fear she'd burn up all her stash of fuel before he finally got tired of surfing.

Lucas fell from the board, diving into the water headfirst and surfacing moments later to shake the water from his hair like a dog. He grinned and held up a single finger, indicating one more wave.

1

She watched him reclaim his board and paddle back out, black rubber tight on his legs and butt, his feet bare and probably frozen by now. But she couldn't begrudge him the opportunity. There were rarely surfable waves on Chatham Island. This was a fluke, the result of a major storm far out over the Atlantic. It had brought them just the skirts of its clouds and enough of a surge to send Lucas scrambling to wax his old board and squeeze himself into a wet suit he'd clearly outgrown.

He caught a wave and had a good, long ride, bringing the board within a few feet of the narrow beach before he tumbled.

But he kept his word and emerged from the surf, lifting his board free of the foam that surged to within a couple of yards of Zoey's feet.

"Quick, light the fire!" he yelled. "I'm numb."

Zoey smiled. His hair was wet and tousled, his body outlined in perfect detail by the tight wet suit. She felt a definite twinge. He looked incredible. Too incredible for Zoey's own good. She fished in her bag for the matches, but without taking her eyes from him.

She tore her eyes away and found the matches. He planted his surfboard upright in the sand and flopped onto the blanket beside her, smelling of salt and laughing in sheer delight.

"Damn, I'd forgotten how much I loved that." He pulled the zipper halfway down his chest and inhaled deeply. "If only

I'd been able to breathe. I guess I'll have to break down and buy a new suit."

Zoey struck a match, but it was instantly blown out by the wind. *Don't say it,* she warned herself. *Don't say it.*

Then she said it anyway. "I think that suit looks pretty good on you." Her voice wobbled a little and she concentrated on lighting a second match, cupping it in her hands. She touched the flame to the dried grass kindling. It crackled loudly and caught fire.

Lucas rolled toward her and without warning stuck his hands under her sweater, pressing them to her bare stomach.

Zoey squealed and tried to push him away, but he held on. "Get those icicles off me!"

"I can't wait for the fire," he said. "I need warmth now. My hands are numb."

"I warned you it was freezing out there. You're the one who said 'Don't worry, I'll be plenty warm in my wet suit.'"

Lucas slid his hands around her back and drew her against him. Then he rolled onto his back, still holding her tight. "My lips are numb, too."

Zoey lowered her mouth to his and kissed his cold lips. She closed her eyes and kissed him again, more deeply, a vision of him rising from the surf still firmly fixed in her mind. Within seconds his lips were as warm as her own. She kissed his cheeks

3

and pressed her hands to them. She kissed his eyelids and his neck.

"Now are you warm?" Zoey asked.

"Mmm. Now even other parts of me are warm," he said.

"Don't be crude."

"I meant my feet."

"Sure you did," Zoey said. She gave him a light peck on the lips and rolled off him. "Are you hungry?"

"That depends. Is there anything *else* on the menu? I mean besides food. You know, maybe something for some *other* form of hunger?"

"We have hot dogs and we have s'mores. That's what's on the menu."

Lucas sighed. "Okay, then I guess I'm hungry." There was no mistaking the pouting tone in his voice.

"Lucas, I thought we were going to give that topic a rest," Zoey said testily.

Lucas sat up and wrapped his arms around his knees. "I'm sorry. But you know, one thing kind of leads to another. We make out, we touch each other, first thing you know, I'm thinking about the next step. It's like . . . like saying hey, we'll get all dressed up, we'll drive to a fancy restaurant, we'll sit down and order this great meal, only, surprise, we're not going to eat anything."

Zoey was silent for a moment while the fire snapped and spread a glow around them. "You're using a food example.

You must be hungry."

"I'm starving," he admitted ruefully.

"Look, Lucas, if every time we make out you're going to say I'm leading you toward sex, then what am I supposed to do?" She held up her hand quickly. "Scratch that question. My point is, I really, really like kissing you. Really, really. But I'm not going to be able to enjoy it if you keep saying step one has to lead to step two has to lead to step three when I'm not ready for step three. You know?"

Lucas shrugged and looked away. Then he looked back at her, dissatisfied but not angry. "So if I want one and two, I have to shut up about three."

Zoey sighed heavily. It wasn't like she never considered step three. They weren't all that different, not really, she and Lucas. Except that it was more complicated for her than for him. It must be nice to be a guy and have everything be so simple and straightforward—just be led around by your hormones and never have to think about consequences. "Lucas, don't you want this to be a choice I can make for myself, one way or the other, and that I can feel good about?"

He absorbed that for a moment and winced. "Yeah, yeah," he said, making no attempt at sincerity.

Zoey smiled and hugged him. "We can still do some more of steps one and two."

"Okay. But first, we eat."

Zoey said good-bye to Lucas as night fell over Chatham Island and the tiny village of North Harbor. He went off toward his home, tired from the surf and, Zoey was sure, still a bit disgruntled and unsatisfied. She herself was feeling edgy, as she often did after making out with Lucas. She'd intended to go straight home and finish the journalism class assignment that was hanging over her head, but she didn't feel like concentrating. She was full of pent-up energy. She waved her arms back and forth at her sides, realizing how strange it would look to anyone who might be out on the streets and saw her.

She decided to stop by Nina's house. Zoey hadn't talked to her since the night before at the homecoming dance. Normally Nina could be counted on to drop by on just about any day of the week, especially a weekend day. But so far the day had been Nina-less.

Zoey walked the length of Center Street, crossing to walk through the parklike center of the circle. An island car, muffler blasting, front bumper held on by string, came rattling by and Zoey waved. Mrs. Gray, Aisha's mother. There were few of the island's three hundred permanent residents Zoey didn't recognize.

She reached Lighthouse Road, the northern edge of the island where cobblestones, low picket fences, and neatly tended gardens ran into sharp-edged, slick-wet rocks and sudden explosions of ocean spray. She went in through the gate of the Geiger house and instinctively looked up at the widow's walk, a railed deck atop the third story of the old house. Sure enough, there was Claire Geiger, Nina's sister. She was wearing a bright yellow rain slicker. Her long, voluptuous black hair streamed out from under an incongruous yellow rain hat.

"Damn," Zoey said under her breath. She herself was still wearing just a sweater, no coat.

Claire peered down, leaning casually on the rickety-looking railing. "Hey, Zoey."

"Hi, Claire. It's going to rain, huh?" Zoey yelled up at her, craning her neck.

"Zoey, we are completely blanketed with nimbostratus."

"Uh-huh," Zoey said.

"Rain clouds. Nimbostratus. But forget these." She waved a hand dismissively. "This is nothing. What's great is that there's a monster Canadian cold front rolling down toward upstate New York and Vermont."

"Yeah, that's cool, all right," Zoey said dryly. If Claire hadn't had the good luck to be very beautiful and endowed with a natural elegance that emerged even from beneath a rain slicker, she would have spent her life as a nerd. Yet because she was the person she was, her fascination with weather, her natural solitude, her distant reserve all added to a sense that she was

7

a unique individual, not to be judged by anyone's standards but her own. Whatever *those* might be.

"Snow," Claire said, her eyes glowing as if she were announcing the advent of universal world peace. "There's a serious possibility of major snow in Vermont. Say, around . . . Killington? And next weekend is a three-day weekend?"

Zoey clicked. "Ski trip? Are you thinking ski trip?"

Claire smiled her infrequent smile. "Very likely. I'll let you know."

"Excellent," Zoey said enthusiastically. She and Claire didn't share much (except for some ex-boyfriends), but they did both like to ski. And even though the school year was less than two months old, Zoey had been feeling hemmed in lately. A road trip would be just the thing.

She had no idea whether Lucas would like the idea. He'd never mentioned skiing. But snowboarding was very similar to surfing.

And yet, it brought up the question of spending a weekend with Lucas away from family.

"Where would we stay?" Zoey yelled up.

"My dad knows a guy with a condo there. This early in the year he won't have rented it," Claire said. She smiled knowingly. "Don't worry, I'm sure there will be plenty of beds for whatever arrangement you want."